Bet...

Georgie Ha... ...oftly and

'A splendid debut, fas... ...and well-written.' *Iain Pears*

'A promising debut, a traditional whodunit in a contemporary setting which directs our suspicions to several possible culprits. Georgie Hale creates a fast-paced story with dramatic denouement.' *Manchester Evening News*

'The cracking debut novel from Georgie Hale . . . A splendid read, full of the unexpected.' *Huddersfield Examiner*

'A well-told, intelligent story which never flags and makes one look forward to her next.' *Birmingham Post*

'A promising debut. The plot is moved along briskly and there are enough plausible suspects to keep you guessing until the guilty party is revealed.' *Sunday Telegraph*

'This novel is as compelling as Georgie Hale's first . . . she maintains the suspense right to the end with lots of twists along the way.' *Coventry Evening Telegraph*

By the same author

Tread Softly
Without Consent

About the author

Goergie Hale has spent most of her life in Coventry, although many of her family live on the Isles of Scilly. She studied at Liverpool University before working first as a social worker, then at the University of Warwick. She has a strong interest in the criminal justice system. She is married, with two grown-up daughters. Visit her web site, www.georgiehale.com, to find out more about Georgie Hale and her novels.

GEORGIE HALE

Better than Death

NEW ENGLISH LIBRARY
Hodder & Stoughton

Copyright © 2003 by Georgie Hale

First published in Great Britain in 2003 by Hodder and Stoughton
A division of Hodder Headline
First published in paperback in Great Britain in 2003 by Hodder and Stoughton
A New English Library paperback

The right of Georgie Hale to be identified as the Author
of the Work has been asserted by her in accordance with the
Copyright, Designs and Patents Act 1988.

1 3 5 7 9 10 8 6 4 2

A CIP catalogue record for this title is
available from the British Library

ISBN 0 340 81834 4

Typeset in Plantin Light by Palimpsest Book Production Limited,
Polmont, Stirlingshire
Printed and bound in Great Britain by
Mackays of Chatham Ltd, Chatham, Kent

Hodder and Stoughton
A division of Hodder Headline
338 Euston Road
London NW1 3BH

For Clive.
With all my love. Forever.

PROLOGUE

And in those days shall men seek death, and shall not find it; and shall deserve to die, and death shall flee from them.

Revelation, 9: 6

I

When he heard the news, Matthew Cosgrave was in the garden; making the most of one of those cold, clear autumn mornings that can almost convince one that winter will never come. Gardening had become something of a passion for him in the five years since Daisy's death; tending his plants, making them grow. He bent to bed in the last of the winter pansies he'd grown from seed, only half-listening to the drone of the midday news drifting from the open kitchen window.

It was towards the end of the bulletin that the newscaster's singsong voice announced, 'Police believe that the body recovered from the water . . .'

Matthew was later to wonder how it was that he could have so entirely failed to register the rest of the item. But it was those first words that had hijacked his attention.

Recovered from the water . . .

He was momentarily overcome by memory, the image so strong that it almost winded him. The small body, face down, the thin organza of her party frock billowing around her like a broken sail. The spreading tendrils of blonde hair, streaked green with pond weed. The pale, curled hands bobbing on the surface like tiny water lilies.

Recovered from the water . . .

'Matthew!'

Elizabeth's voice brought Matthew back with a start. He stared down at the pansies, disorientated. Then, straightening slowly, he composed himself, pursing his dry lips into the semblance of a whistle as he turned towards his wife, frightened that she might read his thoughts.

'Matthew, did you hear that?'

Elizabeth Cosgrave stood in the kitchen doorway, a streak of flour across one cheek, the halo of her hair golden as the sun caught it, the apron that she had tied around her waist emphasising the neat swell of her stomach. Her expression, the tone of her voice, silenced Matthew's whistle before it started. Her hand was at her throat, working the fine gold chain of her necklace as if it were a rosary.

'On the radio,' she whispered. 'It's Spike. He's dead.'

The following morning, the *Daily Telegraph* carried a short report of the death of James Vardon, senior lecturer in mathematics at Imperial College, London, who had gone missing while swimming near his parents' home in Cornwall, and whose body had been recovered several miles down the coast some eighteen hours later. Dr Vardon, the article continued, was the only son of retired High Court judge Sir Hubert Vardon. Matthew reread the brief, impersonal account. He had imagined that seeing the news in black and white, reading Spike's name in print, might make things real. But still he couldn't quite believe that his best friend was dead.

'I wish you didn't have to go.' Elizabeth was crumbling an uneaten slice of toast between her fingers.

Matthew put down the newspaper and regarded her with concern. Neither of them had managed any sleep the previous night and she was sheet white, exhaustion coupling with the morning sickness that had dogged her pregnancy. He reached across the table and touched her cheek.

'If there was any way I could get out of it . . .'

The meeting, at a hotel near Heathrow, had been arranged for weeks: Dan Chambers, the chief executive of the American parent company was in the UK for one day only, fitting in a whistle-stop tour of the European subsidiaries on his way to Japan. It wasn't open to negotiation.

Matthew sighed. 'I'll be back this evening, love.'

'Go. I'll be OK.' Elizabeth rubbed a brisk hand across her eyes as Matthew got reluctantly to his feet. 'Really, I'm fine.'

'I'll try not to be too late.' Matthew bent down to kiss her.

She gripped his hand for a second 'Drive carefully.' Then, forcing a smile, she added, 'Hope the meeting goes well.'

The roads were already snarled with traffic as Matthew drove out of Leamington Spa. He found himself handling the car less impatiently than normal, taking fewer risks than he might otherwise have done. He had recognised the strength of Elizabeth's grip, understood her panicky concern for his welfare. It had been the same after Daisy's death, and not just for Elizabeth; he remembered all too well himself that sense of the abrupt removal of all life's certainties, the realisation that those certainties had never, in reality, existed. For a long while, it had been hard for either of them to control the sudden surges of terror; the fear that nothing, nobody, was safe any more. It had only been in the last few months, since the confirmation of her pregnancy, that Elizabeth had truly seemed to relax again. And now this . . .

Matthew turned on the radio, flicking quickly from the news programme to Radio Three, trying to allow the calming strains of Mozart to clear his mind, help him concentrate on the meeting ahead as he negotiated his way into the hectic traffic on the M40.

'Life goes on,' he said to himself out loud.

Life had to go on.

The meeting was a struggle. Several times, Matthew lost concentration, coming to with a start to find the other board members looking at him quizzically. Pulling himself together, he managed to deliver his report, grateful that he'd prepared the figures so thoroughly the previous week.

If Dan Chambers picked up on Matthew's distraction, he chose not to comment on it. Matthew's hand was grasped as warmly as ever at the end of the meeting, and he found himself the recipient of the man's habitual, impeccable American smile as he was thanked for his input.

Frank Masterton, Matthew's managing director, was either more astute or less discreet.

'Everything all right, Matthew? Elizabeth keeping well?' he enquired.

The atmosphere had lightened as soon as the chief executive had taken his leave, and the board members were dividing into small knots as pre-lunch drinks were served.

Barely waiting for Matthew's neutral reply, Masterton went on, 'Just wondered. You don't quite seem to be firing on all cylinders today. Not a criticism, you understand. The presentation was fine, as always. Absolutely fine.'

It was a criticism, of course. The man was a workaholic, and expected nothing less of his staff. Matthew felt compelled to offer some sort of an explanation.

'We had some bad news yesterday. An old university friend of mine – he died.'

'Same age as you?' Masterton shook his head. 'No age at all, forty-five. Heart, was it?'

In the high-powered world they both inhabited, heart attacks were the commonest cause of death.

'No. He . . . drowned.' Matthew swallowed hard, the word catching in his throat like a sharp stone.

'*Drowned?*' The other man's eyebrows shot up. He looked as if he might be about to say something else. Matthew was relieved when instead he opted for silence. After a moment, he put his hand on Matthew's shoulder. 'Hard on you both.'

Unable to think of a suitable response, Matthew said nothing.

Masterton glanced at his watch. 'Lunch, I think.' He strode towards the dining room, turning as he got to the door. 'Oh, and, Matthew, double-check those Italian flash forecasts when you get back to the office, would you? See if you can make them look a bit more attractive before Montelli gets to see them.'

Lunch, more business meeting than social occasion, was protracted. Matthew would have preferred a quick motorway sandwich on the way back to Leamington, but that wasn't the way Masterton operated. It was rare to get the entire board together in one place, and the managing director wasn't one to waste such an opportunity. It was almost four o'clock by the time they got back to their various cars. The journey back would be a nightmare, Matthew thought sourly as he left a message on the phone at home to say that he wouldn't be back until seven at the earliest, then rang the office and left instructions with Dorothy, his secretary, to arrange for the breakdowns he would need to be faxed over from Milan ahead of his return.

The drive from London to Leamington was always boring. At that time of the afternoon it was, as Matthew had predicted, not only boring but painfully slow. It gave him time to think. It wasn't more than five minutes into the journey that his mind had switched off from work and returned to Spike. How could Spike Vardon, one-time captain of Blackport University swimming team – Spike, who knew the Cornish coastline around his parents' home in a way he had never come to understand the intricacies of the London Underground system that he'd used for half his life – how could Spike have drowned, and on what should have been one of the happiest days of his life?

With a great swoop of sadness, Matthew recalled his friend's round, boyish face suffused with a grin of sheer excitement the night he had turned up on the doorstep, uninvited, with the news that he was to be engaged. Could it really only be a fortnight since that last meeting?

Matthew and Elizabeth had been stunned and delighted in about equal measure by the news. Spike, in their minds, had developed into the archetypal bachelor over the years: absent-minded, bookish and completely disorganised. That chaos theory had become his chosen field of research at the university was a standing joke. Such domesticity as he'd required had been satisfied by his frequent weekend visits to Leamington.

Or so they'd thought.

Spike's words had tumbled over themselves like so many boisterous puppies as he'd described Jane, the amazing girl he'd been introduced to at the choral society and who had, just seven weeks after their initial meeting, agreed to become his wife. Matthew had never seen his friend so buoyant. Spike had enthused about how much they would have in common with his new fiancée – how she was a Blackport graduate, the same as Spike and Matthew, and a primary school teacher, as Elizabeth had been. They would be able to spend weekends together, the four of them. Go on holiday. Even, Spike had added blushingly, maybe bring up their children together. It had made Mathew realise just how much Spike must secretly have wanted a family of his own.

The hopes and plans he'd confided that night – all wasted.

The almost stationary snake of tail-lights ahead of Matthew blurred as he remembered how happy Spike had been. He banged his fist against the dashboard, suddenly furious at the sheer randomness of fate. It just didn't make sense.

None of it made any bloody sense at all.

It was well after six o'clock when Matthew reached Leamington. By the time he drew into Langton Industrials, the executive car park was all but deserted. Frank Masterton's schedule had taken him off to Frankfurt after the Heathrow meeting; while the cat was away, the mice tended to get off work a little earlier than was normally expected of them. Nodding to the security guard at the porter's lodge, Matthew made his way up to his office on the first floor.

His secretary, efficient as ever, had left the required faxes on his desk together with his post, which had been divided into the neat piles that accorded with her personal filing system: those letters needing immediate attention at the front, followed by a less urgent 'pending' pile and lastly those that were for information only. Matthew riffled through the 'immediates', stuffing a couple of memos into his briefcase along with the faxes, then turned his attention to the small stack of papers on the side table to which was attached a Post-it sticker with the legend 'personal' in Dorothy's round, neat hand. It comprised a reminder for Matthew's professional subs, and a badly written letter from a local student requesting sponsorship for a gap-year expedition to Peru. Matthew, after a brief glance, consigned it to the bin before turning his attention to the remaining item, a paper-clipped sheaf of A4, at the front of which was a heavily embossed card bearing the crest of Blackport University.

Matthew felt his throat constrict as he scanned the invitation to Blackport's centenary reunion weekend. He remembered Spike all those years before, when they were still students themselves, calculating that by the time the university was a hundred years old, they would all be forty-six. The very notion of middle age had seemed ludicrous at the time. A whole crowd of them, somewhat the worse for beer, had vowed to meet up at whatever celebration the university put on. Spike had been on the phone as soon as the reunion had been advertised in the graduates' magazine a few months previously. They'd planned the trip with relish, laying odds on who else from their year would be there, trying to guess the career path of this student or that, how they would look, whether they would even recognise each other after almost twenty-five years. Somehow, the invitation brought home to Matthew in a way that nothing else had that his friend was really dead.

Carefully, he placed the papers face down on the desk, his hand shaking slightly, knowing that he could not bear to go back to Blackport alone.

It was only then that he noticed another, smaller sheet of paper, caught up with the reunion documents by the paper clip. It was without interest that he pulled it free, turned it over and unfolded it. There was no sense of dread, no seismic shift of needle on paper to warn him of what was to come. A couple of lines, typewritten and unsigned. A child's simple rhyme: 'One, two, three, four, five / Once I caught a fish alive . . . Spike Vardon. Gone to meet his maker.'

Matthew was about to screw it up. It must be some sick bastard's idea of a joke. But as his eyes travelled to the bottom of the page, he felt his throat constricting again. Not in sorrow this time, but in shock.

Beneath the rhyme was printed in block capitals: 'REMEMBER DONNA O'MARA?'

It wasn't a joke, Matthew realised instantly.

It was a threat.

2

The inquest into Spike Vardon's drowning recorded a verdict of accidental death.

Spike and his new fiancée had spent the last day of his life in Cornwall with his parents. The four of them had gone out for lunch to celebrate the engagement. The wine waiter at the restaurant confirmed that a bottle of champagne and two bottles of claret had been consumed; much of it, the waiter had noted, by Spike himself. In the afternoon, Spike had gone for a walk with his fiancée, who had later rejoined his parents at their house. Spike had apparently decided to take a swim in Polperron Cove, the nearest beach. A farmer working in the fields above had seen him strip off and head for the water, but, having registered the sight, had taken no further notice. Spike had swum there since he was a boy, the farmer told the court, so there was nothing remarkable in it. He'd been too far away to detect anything unusual in Spike's demeanour, he'd added.

When Spike hadn't returned by teatime, the family had gone to look for him. They had found the neat pile of his clothes on the sand, already wet from the incoming tide. His body had been washed up the following morning near Falmouth, several miles up the coast. There were no suspicious circumstances. The newspaper report of the proceedings carried the Truro coroner's warning as to the consequences of swimming whilst under the influence of alcohol.

$\star$ $\star$ $\star$

Matthew went over the reported details of the inquest again
and again on the long drive down to Boslowan Major, the
Cornish village where Spike had spent his childhood and
where his funeral was to take place. Would the verdict have
been different, he asked himself, had he taken the letter he'd
received to the police? He glanced across at Elizabeth, who
was asleep in the passenger seat, then ran an irritable hand
across his face and told himself not to be so fanciful. What
possible bearing could an apparent reference to an incident
that had occurred – or, more to the point, had *not* occurred
– some twenty-five years previously, have had on the inquest
into Spike Vardon's death?

In the intervening period since the letter had arrived,
Matthew had attempted, and to a large extent managed, to put
it into some sort of logical perspective; the more so because
there had been no further communications. The envelope had
been destroyed before Matthew had been able to check it –
cleared away with the rest of the day's refuse by the cleaners
– but he would have laid odds on a Blackport postmark. The
letter was quite obviously the work of some crank with a
long memory, prompted by the newspaper reports of Spike's
death. And as for it being sent to Matthew . . . well, anyone
could have got hold of his office address through the register
at Companies House, he told himself. The pressures of work,
together with his own refusal to speculate on a problem that
he was unlikely ever to resolve, had all but put the matter out
of his head.

The enforced mental inactivity of the journey to Cornwall
now brought it back with a nagging insistence that Matthew
found impossible to ignore. Why would anyone want to
go to the bother of looking up his address? Why would
anyone want to send him the ridiculous bloody letter at
all?

His mind veered infuriatingly towards other questions,

ones that until now he had steadfastly refused to allow himself to consider. Accidental death had been the verdict. That as a student Spike had been the strongest swimmer in the entire university, that the drowning had occurred in a calm sea, on a sunny, windless afternoon, that there was a horrible finality in the way that untidy, disorganised Spike had neatly folded his clothes before swimming off for the last time – they were observations that no one investigating Spike's death seemed to have taken the time to make.

With conscious effort, Matthew relaxed his grip on the steering wheel. He hadn't even been at the bloody inquest. How was he to know what had actually been said? Spike's death was simply one of those inexplicable accidents that happened from time to time. It could have been cramp. Or a freak current. The coroner would have heard all the evidence before coming to his conclusion. Accidental death. The same verdict that had been recorded for Daisy.

Accidental.

Then, as now, it seemed to Matthew such an entirely inadequate word to describe a tragedy of such magnitude. An accident. A bit of a slip-up. Better luck next time, the verdict seemed to say.

It was more than twenty-five years since Matthew had visited Boslowan Major. He'd maintained a mental picture not just of the place, but of the journey down there. He was surprised at how much had changed. He noted the wind turbines that marched across Bodmin Moor, the proliferation of heritage centres and amusement parks along the way. The journey from Leamington took less than four hours in the Jaguar. Twenty-five years earlier, it had taken him more than four-teen hours from Blackport in his clapped-out Mini; it had seemed like the other end of the earth. The trip had involved the tortuous negotiation of town after town along the way.

Matthew could still remember some of the mantra of the south-western end of the trip: Bath, Shepton Mallet, Exeter, Launceston, Indian Queens, Redruth, Camborne . . . At the time, the names had had a faintly exotic ring to his northern ear. Even when, years later, he and Elizabeth had lived in Somerset, it had still seemed like a different country.

The village of Boslowan Major itself had grown beyond recognition. An ugly development of holiday homes had sprung like a rash over the downs where he and Spike had meandered their unsteady way back from the Smuggler's Rest that first long vacation, putting the world to rights as only a couple of pleasantly drunk students could do. Even the pub had been altered. A brightly painted extension housed a children's soft-play area. A banner strung across its roof advertised early-bird meals to those eating before seven in the evening.

It took Matthew some time to realise he was lost. He took several wrong turnings and drove for miles down a rutted lane before discovering that it was a private entrance to a farm.

'How much further?' Elizabeth, now awake, was clutching the map that Matthew had declined to look at.

He glanced across at her again. The peace that sleep had brought to her face had vanished, and she was chewing nervously on her lower lip.

'Nearly there.'

Unwilling to admit that in fact he had no idea where they were, Matthew cricked his neck as he attempted to read the map sideways, then swore softly as he realised they had been driving in an almost complete circle. Slamming the car into reverse, he executed a clumsy three-point turn and headed back to the centre of the village. Elizabeth, tense and silent, stared out of the window, locked in her thoughts.

They stopped at the pub for directions. While Elizabeth

took herself off to the ladies, Matthew went into the men's lavatory to freshen up.

It was with some surprise that he realised how important it was to him that he should look his best. He stared at his reflection in the speckled mirror. It was a strong face; the jaw determined, the lines around the mouth beginning to settle, even at mid-forties, into hardness. He looked what he was: Matthew Cosgrave, manager of men; admired by the board of Langton Industrials on to which he had recently been promoted; disliked, feared even, by the workforce he was clear-sightedly and ruthlessly beginning to rationalise. A cold fish – that was one of the politer ways he'd heard himself described by the union leaders.

He wondered what they would think of him if they knew that, while still at university, he and four of his fellow students had stood trial for the gang rape of Donna O'Mara.

'Pull yourself together, for Christ's sake,' he muttered as he splashed water onto his face. 'We were innocent.' He gazed into the cold grey eyes in the mirror as if seeking reassurance. 'The courts found us innocent.'

Finally, Matthew located the picture-postcard church. The car park was filled with an incongruous variety of vehicles. Matthew took the last remaining space, manoeuvring his Jaguar alongside a battered, mud-splashed Land Rover. Elizabeth was fiddling in her handbag, applying lipstick, combing her hair; more, Matthew recognised, as a delaying tactic than through vanity. He reached across and took her hand and they both sat quite still for a moment, staring out of the windscreen.

A compost heap towered beyond the low wall of the car park. Flies buzzed lazily around a rotting heap of last month's floral tributes.

Sic transit gloria mundi – the words sprang into Matthew's mind. Spike's passion for classics had been a close second only to his love of mathematics; he'd been much given to such quotations. His voice was so real that Matthew actually turned his head.

'I suppose we'd better go in.' It was Elizabeth sitting next to him, of course.

'Yes.' With a squeeze, Matthew released his grip and got quickly out of the car. It was the first time either of them had been inside a church since the day of Daisy's funeral.

They made their way through the lurching ranks of head-stones. Twenty or so people, as motley a collection as their vehicles, were standing outside the church as if making the most of the wintry sunshine before they were swallowed into the church's gloomy interior. Matthew and Elizabeth stood together, several yards short of the rest, like newcomers in a playground. Close family friends only, the unwelcoming announcement in the *Telegraph* had decreed. It would have precluded those of Spike's students or colleagues who might have wished to attend. Matthew recognised none of the other mourners.

'Do you think we should go inside?' he murmured to Elizabeth, who had her eyes shut, her face turned to the sun. He glanced at his watch. 'They're running late.' With a facetiousness that he despised even before the words left his mouth, he added, 'Typical Spike. He always was a hopeless time-keeper.'

Elizabeth didn't respond.

The other mourners, as if by some silent cue, were stubbing out cigarettes, straightening ties and beginning to shuffle their way through the side door into the church.

'He's here.' A woman in a dusty, oversized black coat and a knotted headscarf nodded towards the hedge that bounded the churchyard as she trudged up the path from her vantage point beside the lich-gate.

Above the hedge, Matthew saw the cortège approaching. He ran his finger around the inside of the collar that suddenly felt a size too small for him. Reaching for Elizabeth's hand, he moved slowly towards the church, standing aside to allow her to enter first. She chose a pew at the back, as he had known she would; even after five years, it was still too painfully soon since they had been centre stage themselves for her to do anything else. Matthew didn't look at her. Now that they were inside the church, he didn't dare. He knelt on the unyielding hassock, eyes closed in pretence of prayer.

There was a scuffling behind them, and the west doors were pulled open. The organ, which had been playing inconsequentially, marking time, wheezed into silence. Matthew pulled himself up from his knees. He heard Elizabeth breathe in sharply, and wondered if she might be crying. The congregation stood, a couple of heads craning discreetly to gain the first glimpse of the procession as it entered.

The priest passed in a rustle of vestments. '"I am the resurrection and the light" . . .' His gaze was fixed in the middle distance. He sounded slightly bored.

Spike's parents walked behind the coffin, ramrod stiff, not of a generation to give vent to their emotions. They both seemed much smaller than Matthew remembered them. Alice Vardon's hands, clenched by her sides, were trembling uncontrollably.

Matthew's attention moved to the slight figure walking alone behind the Vardons. Jane Davenport was not in the least as he had visualised her. Given Spike's rapturous description, he had imagined someone far more seductive; had even worried, briefly, that Spike might have been taken in by the lure of what in their younger days they might have referred to as 'a bit of crumpet'. His concern, he realised, could not have been more misplaced. Whatever had attracted Spike to Jane Davenport, it had not been her looks; the girl who followed Spike's coffin was uncompromisingly plain. She looked almost impossibly young, her hair pulled back into a severe ponytail, her ghost-white face devoid of makeup. Her bent head, her thin hands clasped in front of her, gave her the air of a postulant nun, but for the heavy band of diamonds and emeralds on the ring finger of her left hand.

The service was conducted with all the usual platitudes. The congregation struggled with a couple of hymns. The vicar referred to Spike as 'James' and gave a lengthy sermon. He talked of the brilliant mind, the academic career cut so tragically short. He referred to the dutiful son, the caring fiancé. He made Spike sound ordinary, dull. He told them they should not mourn Spike's death, but give thanks for his life. The vicar at Daisy's funeral had made some similarly fatuous remark. Matthew felt an almost overwhelming urge to hit him.

Towards the end of the service, an anthem was sung. The organ crept up a stealthy phrase of notes, unfamiliar to Matthew. He glanced down at the order of service as the choir intoned, '*Agnus Dei, qui tollis peccata* . . .'

Missa brevis; Benjamin Britten. Matthew wondered who had chosen the piece; Britten had never been one of Spike's favourites.

The choir took up the strident, discordant refrain. '*Dona nobis pacem.*'

The words rebounded from the cold stone walls, filling Matthew's head.

Dona . . . *Dona* . . . Donna . . .

Sweat was pouring down his face. The heavy pillars seemed to be closing in on him, crushing him

'Matthew.'

He started. Elizabeth's voice was a whisper, but it had brought him back to his senses as surely as if she had slapped his face.

'Matthew?'

The choir had finished. The vicar was intoning, '. . . thanks be to God, which giveth us the victory through our Lord Jesus Christ . . .'

Matthew breathed in deeply, almost gagging as the mingled scents of chrysanthemums, candle wax and ancient wood filled his nostrils. 'I'm OK,' he murmured, clutching the pew in front of him, concentrating on the white ridges of his knuckles as the vicar led the funeral party back up the aisle and out of the church. 'I'm OK,' he repeated, trying to rid himself of the ridiculous notion that Spike Vardon had been trying to make contact with him from beyond the grave.

3

The tea that followed Spike's funeral was held at the family home. When Matthew had been young, it had been the house of his dreams: large, rambling and with a casual elegance that spoke of generations of money. He had made it his goal to own something similar one day. Twenty-five years on, the place, like the Vardons themselves, seemed diminished. Matthew's tutored eye told him that the roses that lined the long driveway were badly in need of pruning. Weeds flourished amongst the once-immaculate herbaceous border. One of the stone lions that guarded the steps leading up to the house had a chip to its front paw, he noticed as he parked nearby. He glanced at the gleaming bodywork of his brand-new Jaguar and felt the briefest surge of malice.

The gathering was an inevitably awkward affair. Matthew and Elizabeth nodded at strangers and they nodded gravely back, in the manner required of such occasions.

'We needn't stay long,' Matthew murmured. Left to himself, he wouldn't have gone back to the house at all. It had been Elizabeth who had reminded him how much they had needed people around them after Daisy's funeral.

She seemed to have relaxed, once they were away from the church. Or maybe it was that her concern for Matthew had overtaken her own emotions; it had taken him all of the slow journey behind the cortège to convince her that he was fine; that the faintness he'd experienced in church was probably down to no more than their lack of lunch.

'We ought to socialise,' Elizabeth whispered now. She moved determinedly away from his side. Matthew watched her circulate from one knot of Spike's elderly relatives to another, introducing herself, shaking hands, offering condolences; going through the motions, but so gracefully that only he could recognise the strain behind her attentive expression.

Knowing he should follow suit, he instead helped himself to the sparse buffet, guiltily acknowledging to himself how hungry he was. He accepted a glass of the dry sherry that appeared to be the only available alcohol and drank it quickly. He took another, glancing, as he did so, at the Vardons. They were deep in conversation with a small group of their guests, as if at a cocktail party; conducting themselves with typically upper-class sang-froid. 'Breeding', Matthew's mother would have called it. He downed the sherry. Sooner or later, he would have to speak to them. He wondered what he would say, after so many years.

'Hello. You must be Matthew.'

The voice behind him almost made him jump out of his skin. He turned to find Spike's fiancée gazing up at him uncertainly.

'Jane.' Hastily, he put down the empty sherry glass and held out his hand. 'Spike told us so much about you.' He tried and failed to think of something to say that didn't sound utterly banal. 'I'm so sorry.'

'Thank you.'

There was an awkward pause, broken as Elizabeth rejoined them, introduced herself and gave Jane a brief, unselfconscious hug.

'Spike talked so often about you both that I feel I know you.' Jane gave a tight smile as she glanced around at the room. 'Apart from his parents, I haven't met any of these people before.'

'Dear God, this must be so difficult for you,' Elizabeth said quietly.

Jane nodded, then said with a brittle laugh, 'Well, funerals are never the easiest of occasions, are they? What with the sherry and the cucumber sandwiches.' She flushed, abruptly dropping the unconvincing attempt at nonchalance. 'Oh God, that was so tactless. Spike told me—' She broke off, looking quickly from Elizabeth to Matthew as if unsure whether she should continue. 'You . . . you lost your little girl, didn't you?'

Matthew cleared his throat uncomfortably as Elizabeth's eyes filled abruptly with tears.

The arrival of Spike's father was almost a relief.

'Matthew.' The hand that Hubert Vardon held out was wrinkled and liver-spotted, but his grip was firm. 'I hadn't expected you to come.' His tone was as astringently cultured as it had always been. The smile he bestowed barely touched his lips; his eyes, behind their faint rheumy film, were icy.

He's an old man, Matthew told himself. He's just lost his only son, for God's sake. But none the less, his hand clenched involuntarily as the other man released it. Vardon was still trying to antagonise him; still treating him as if he were something that Spike had trodden in and brought unwittingly into the house to contaminate it, even after all these years. Matthew could hear the harshness of his own voice as he replied aloud, 'My wife and I were Spike's closest friends. Of course we came.'

For the first time in many years, he was aware of the vestiges of his northern accent.

The ensuing silence was on the point of lengthening into embarrassment when Jane touched Hubert Vardon's arm and said gently, 'I think the vicar's getting ready to go.'

'Yes.' Vardon nodded. His face seemed suddenly to sag, as if he were only then recalling why they were all together.

'I must thank him.' He inclined his head towards Elizabeth. 'Please excuse me.' He went to move off, then turned. 'I'm glad to see that you appear to have made something of yourself, Matthew. I can't say that I anticipated it.'

Matthew was relieved to get back to the car. Cocooned in its luxurious interior, hearing the muted, reassuringly expensive engine purr to his command as he put his key in the ignition, he thanked God that the hideous afternoon was over. He looked back at the chipped stone lion as it retreated in his rear-view mirror. Jane Davenport was standing at the top of the steps, alone. She raised her hand in an embarrassed half-wave. Matthew knew that he should respond in some way. The girl could scarcely be held responsible for Vardon's crass behaviour – she barely knew him, for God's sake. But all Matthew wanted to do at that moment was to get as far away from the place as possible. Putting his foot on the accelerator, he turned the car sharply at the end of the drive, and Jane disappeared.

'God, I can't believe the rudeness of that vile old man!' Inside the house, two hot pink spots on Elizabeth's cheeks had been the only sign of her fury. Now they were alone, she gave full vent to it.

'I was never Hubert Vardon's favourite person,' Matthew replied curtly.

'Because of what happened when you were at university? But that's bloody ridiculous!'

It had been almost a decade after the trial that Matthew and Elizabeth had met, but Matthew had been careful from the start to conceal none of it from her, even though he'd been terrified that the sordid nature of the case would frighten her off. It hadn't. He found himself touched now, as he had been then, by her unswerving, unquestioning loyalty as she went on indignantly, 'Quite apart from the fact that you were innocent, why should the wretched man imagine you were any more responsible for what happened than Spike? Or any of the others?'

Matthew raised his shoulders slightly. 'It was my birthday bash, I suppose. I was the only reason we were out that night. Or why we were quite so plastered, at least.' He tried unsuccessfully to keep the bitterness from his voice as he added, 'Vardon always made it clear he thought I rather lowered the tone. Grammar school boy, and all that.'

'So a quarter of a century later, he's still blaming you because you had the wrong school tie?' Elizabeth snorted. 'The frightening thing is that the bigoted old bastard ended up a High Court judge! No wonder there's precious little respect for the judiciary these days.'

Matthew shot her a wry sideways smile. 'You sound like your mother.'

'It's true though.' Elizabeth wasn't so easily thrown off her stride. 'That a supposedly rational adult could behave like that towards you, simply because you had the misfortune to get caught up with some blackmailing little tart who claimed—'

Matthew shivered involuntarily. 'Let's just forget it, shall we?' His voice was sharper than he'd intended.

'OK.' Elizabeth shrugged, a touch huffily. 'I'm just angry at the way he treated you, that's all.'

For a second, Matthew was tempted to tell her about the letter. But only for a second. He knew that Elizabeth would only fret and blow it out of all proportion – Spike's death had been shock enough for her to bear, especially in her condition. The first months of the pregnancy hadn't been easy for her, at nearly forty. He glanced across at her, thinking that she looked hardly older than when they had first met, even after everything they'd been through together. He felt a sudden surge of gratitude, mingled with an almost overwhelming sense of responsibility. How could he even consider burdening her with his worries, at a time like this?

Placing a reassuring hand upon the small bump of her stomach, he smiled. 'Forget Hubert Vardon, my darling. Forget everything. We've got our whole future ahead of us, and that's all that matters, isn't it?'

He knew he was speaking the words as much to himself as he was to Elizabeth.

4

It was Elizabeth who talked Matthew into attending the reunion weekend at Blackport University. He needed a break from the office, she told him, and it would be a waste of time for the two of them to go off on holiday somewhere, when she still spent most mornings with her head down the loo. There were bound to be other people there whom he knew. It would do him good to reminisce, catch up with everyone's news. She didn't mentioned Spike by name, but Matthew knew what she meant.

The reunion was to take place on the second weekend in December. Elizabeth arranged to spend a few days with her mother in Hampshire, and could be heard on the phone making plans for her sister to join her down there. It seemed to Matthew that the whole thing had been decided for him.

He wasn't at all sure he wanted to go. Part of him dreaded being there without Spike, after they'd planned the trip together, and he said as much. There were other doubts he didn't share. Although he had received no further letters, instinct told him to keep away from Blackport and the inevitable memories of the trial that it was bound to resurrect. But, on the other hand, he had to admit to himself that he was anxious to see if the other lads, with whom he and Spike had stood accused, would turn up. He found himself wondering if Toby Gresham-Palmer, Ben Fellows and Pete Preston had also received letters. It was that thought that eventually tipped the balance. Despite his misgivings, Matthew agreed to go.

★　　★　　★

The weekend was scheduled to commence with a service of dedication on the Friday evening.

Matthew had arranged meetings in Manchester at one of the firm's subsidiary companies for the Friday afternoon. That way, he reasoned, if the reunion proved to be a mistake at least he wouldn't have an entirely wasted journey. The meetings, inevitably, ran on longer than intended, which meant Matthew caught the worst of the rush-hour traffic, so that it was well past six by the time he reached the outskirts of Blackport.

At first, he barely recognised the place. A new stretch of motorway linked the town with the M6. A rebuilding programme had transformed the site of the old steelworks into a sprawling development of suburban dolls' houses. The grim dockland approach to the town centre had been replaced by an incomprehensible system of ring roads that took him over and under and round the few remaining landmarks of his student days.

Matthew was hopelessly late for the dedication service by the time he finally reached the university. He drove round looking for somewhere to park, not too concerned that he'd missed the service; pomp and ceremony had always struck him as a bit of a waste of time.

The campus was scarcely more recognisable than the rest of the town. A multistorey car park had replaced the old porter's lodge. The university, Matthew estimated, as he drove past the largely unfamiliar buildings, must have doubled in size since his time there. It had gobbled up much of the housing that had surrounded it. A space-age construction whose floodlit front façade announced it as the Centre for Micro-Biological Research had replaced the crumbling Victorian terraces that had stood behind the students' union. New science labs covered the site of the disused church that had doubled up, in Matthew's time, as a lecture theatre. The halls of residence had also mushroomed, several high-rise towers supplementing the mock-Georgian blocks that he remembered.

The students had evidently already gone home for Christmas; the makes of cars that flanked the broad streets on both sides suggested older, wealthier inhabitants. The gathering alumni had clearly done pretty well for themselves – a powerful statement that education paid, Matthew thought wryly as he negotiated a three-point turn and made his way back to the multistorey, where he managed to squeeze the Jaguar into a space clearly designed for something smaller, before setting off again on foot.

'I'm afraid the service is almost over, sir.' The porter standing guard at the bottom of the steps of the assembly hall clearly recognised a well-cut overcoat when he saw one; his tone was a good deal more apologetic than that of his predecessor when Matthew and Spike had rolled up outside this same building, hung over and several minutes late for their graduation almost twenty-five years earlier. On that occasion, it had been only Spike's charm that had gained them admission.

'That's OK.' Matthew smiled, more at the memory than at the man. He was obscurely heartened to see that the assembly hall, at least, appeared unchanged.

'The dinner's in the students' union.' The porter winked. 'You could always get over there a bit early,' he suggested. 'Get yourself a pint in before the rush.'

'Good idea. Thanks.'

Matthew strolled back towards the union, drawing his coat around him against the cold. The evening was clear and starry, and his breath wreathed out in front of him, bringing to mind the smoke from the poisonous French cigarettes he and Spike had favoured at the time. His misgivings were beginning to disappear along with the tensions of the day. It was as if the intervening years had been stripped away and he was a carefree student again. He felt suddenly glad he'd decided to come.

He paused outside the sports complex. It had been massively extended since his time, but the building housing the swimming pool, newly constructed the year before he had started at the university, appeared unchanged. He caught a whiff of chlorine in the steady plume of steam being pumped up from the extractor fans. Closing his eyes, he breathed in deeply and transported himself back to the first time he'd entered the placc; the first time he'd met Spike.

Matthew had found it harder than he'd anticipated to fit in, that first week at university. He'd quickly come to realise that living at home, which had been presented as a necessary way to cut down on expenses, was not such a good idea as his parents had made out; being forced to leave parties at ten thirty, in order to catch the last bus back out to Warrington, had not been the best way to make friends, he had soon discovered. Especially girlfriends. The sexual revolution of the sixties had yet to reach Warrington by the mid-seventies, and Matthew, the product of a boys' grammar school, had had little experience of women – a deficit that he had been determined to rectify as speedily as possible. It had been in pursuit of this aim that he'd decided to join the university swimming club. He'd always been good at swimming, had achieved a county cap to prove it by the time he was fifteen; it had seemed the obvious place to start.

He'd turned up to the first practice in a lather of anticipation, his eighteen-year-old imagination feverish at the prospect of big-breasted Amazons in wet Lycra, only to discover that training was on a strictly single-sex basis.

Matthew crossed the road and peered in through the frosted glass. Beyond the streaming condensation that insulated the swimmers from the outside world, he could hear the slap

of the water, the voices echoing and bouncing off the tiled
walls. He smiled to himself, recalling his disappointment
that first evening as he'd walked self-consciously out of the
changing room in the new trunks he'd brought specially for
the occasion, only to realise the pool was full of men.

He'd noticed Toby Gresham-Palmer first, although he
hadn't known Toby's name at the time. None of the lads
who were to become his flatmates had been familiar to him,
that first evening. Toby had been making a point of standing
on the high diving board, flexing his muscles; he'd always
taken care to be noticed first, conceited prat that he was.
Matthew grinned to himself in reminiscence. The coach had
soon sorted Toby out, bellowing to him to get down and stop
poncing about.

They'd been divided into two heats, part relay, part time-
trial. Two lengths freestyle; the first in each heat guaranteed
a place in the big competition coming up the following week.
There had been a lot of horseplay, a lot of goose-stepping
behind the coach's back, but beneath it, Matthew had sensed
that every one of them had wanted to make the team as much
as he did.

He'd swum in the first heat. He could still remember his
pleasure as he touched the side of the pool first, comfortably
beating Toby into second place. The second heat had been
won by Pete Preston, an athletic-looking Phys. Ed. student.
Before the race, Pete had been messing about as much as
anyone; once in the pool, it had been a different story. He'd
powered through the water, utterly focused, taking a good ten
seconds out of Matthew's time. As soon as the race was over,
he'd been laughing and joking again, barely out of breath. Ben
Fellows, beaming modestly as he'd touched the side, had won
the third heat, his mop of fiery curls unvanquished by their
soaking.

There had been a swim-off to decide who would be the

fourth member of the team, and who would be reserve. The lardy-looking runner-up of Ben's heat wasn't in the same league; even before it started, the race had been between Toby and the skinny lad who had come second in Pete's heat. Matthew shook his head, remembering that first impression of the boy who was to become his closest friend. Spike had appeared to swim the heat well inside himself; as if he hadn't cared whether he won or not. He'd seemed simply to be enjoying himself, a characteristic that was to drive the coach insane for the whole time Spike was in the team.

Toby had been desperate to win; being reserve had never been part of his game plan. Matthew could still see him, face red with effort as he'd broken the water to gasp for breath. Toby had managed to stay neck and neck with Spike for the first length, but at the turn, he'd begun to lose it. His earlier preening had seen to it that everyone was cheering for the opposition. Matthew remembered feeling almost sorry for him. As if to spite them all, Toby had put in a final burst with about ten metres to go. Spike had glanced across at him as he drew level. He must have recognised the desperation in Toby's face. There had never been any doubt in Matthew's mind that he had slowed up deliberately, although Spike would never have it when they talked about it later. Toby had touched the edge a split second ahead, punching the air in triumph. Spike, the best swimmer out of them all, had started off in the team as reserve.

He'd been the sweetest-natured man that Matthew had ever met.

And he was dead.

'Can I help you, sir?'

Matthew started convulsively.

The security guard shone a torch into his face and repeated the question.

'No. I was just . . .' Matthew had no idea how long he had

been standing outside the sports complex, lost in memory. No wonder the man was regarding him with such undisguised suspicion. 'Just going back over old times. I'm here for the reunion.'

The guard's expression cleared. 'Changed a bit since your day, I expect,' he grinned.

'Yes, indeed.' Matthew rubbed his hands together, suddenly aware of how cold he was. 'Still, better get over to the union and see just how much all my old pals have changed as well, I suppose,' he joked.

Checking in for the dinner proved an elaborate business. The system was sufficiently complicated to make Matthew suspect that it had been designed by one of the academics; it was several minutes before he managed to marry up the number on his ticket with the table plan to which he was directed. Seventy-eight, the last two digits on the ticket, related to his year of graduation, he finally realised. Several of the names on his table were familiar. He was delighted to see that he had been seated next to Pete Preston. At least one of the old crowd had made it.

Matthew was well down his second pint, and beginning to feel quite mellow, by the time the union started to fill up. From his vantage point close to the table plan, he scanned the faces of those who were coming through the doors, rubbing their hands against the cold as they headed for the bar. Some were older than he; many more a great deal younger. Matthew's attention was caught by a strikingly beautiful girl with waist-length auburn hair. Catching his eye, she smiled at him, and for a moment he felt his pulse flutter as if he were back at one of the union hops. Then the girl looked away from him, her face lighting up as she was joined by a tall, equally striking man with dark, curling hair, at least fifteen years Matthew's junior. Matthew smiled to himself ruefully.

Who did he think he was trying to kid? He turned his attention to what his fellow guests were wearing. Some had ignored the 'lounge suit' directive on the invitation and had opted for casual clothes. A few even appeared to have resurrected their student jeans and sweatshirts. Most, though, were smartly dressed. Matthew felt vindicated in his choice of the new charcoal-grey suit that he'd had made as a present to himself to celebrate his latest promotion, and which Elizabeth had deemed too formal. It looked as expensive as it was. Glancing round, he was glad he'd stuck to his guns. He'd made a success of his career. Why shouldn't his clothes say so?

The bar was getting more crowded. People were beginning to mill round the notice board, bellowing and shrieking as they recognised familiar names. Matthew had to stand up in order to see anything at all. A fat, elderly man waved to him and began to make his way across. Matthew did a quick mental run-through of his old lecturers; the face was vaguely familiar, but he couldn't quite place it. He was discomforted when the man, having fought his way through the crush, introduced himself as a contemporary from the Economics department.

Conversation quickly petered out, once they had exchanged information on where they lived and what they were doing.

'Better make a move, I suppose,' the man murmured, nodding towards the bottleneck that was forming in the double doors that led from the bar.

'Guess so.' Matthew glanced at his watch. He hoped the stilted exchange wasn't a foretaste of the rest of the event, but suspected it might well be. Where did one start, after so many years? He surveyed his companion's sparse grey hair as he followed him towards the refectory. Had he looked as staid and middle-aged to the red-haired girl as this man did to him?

It seemed to take an age for people to get themselves sorted out. It was clear that few of Matthew's fellow diners had looked at the table plan. Some were milling around just inside the room; others, laughing and pulling wry faces of apology, exacerbated the jam by attempting to swim against the tide and get back into the bar to consult the notice board. The crush made Matthew irritable, his natural dislike of poor organisation compounded by the thunderous rumbling of his stomach. It was amazing, he thought, that a group of people whose very presence presupposed they were university graduates could be so dozy. He caught his tight-lipped reflection in one of the refectory's long, uncurtained windows. It could have been his dad muttering the words. Glancing across at the red-haired girl, who was laughing up at her partner as they fought their way towards a table of boisterously chattering youngsters, Matthew told himself firmly to chill out.

Finally, he inched his way to his designated table. He was the first to do so. As he waited for the rest of the party to arrive, he studied the refectory, surprised that it appeared to have changed so little. Surreptitiously, he rolled back the edge of the tablecloth to reveal familiar green Formica.

'Good God, I do believe these are the same tables as when we were here!' A tall man, sharp-suited and with thick, immaculately styled black hair, peered at the Formica, then pulled out the chair on Matthew's right and sat down. 'Jonathan Freeman,' he said, holding out his hand.

'Matthew Cosgrave.' Matthew realised why the name had struck him as familiar when he'd read it on the table plan; he recognised the man as the presenter of a television current affairs programme. He glanced at Freeman's dazzling shirt and heavy gold cufflinks, aware that Freeman was similarly pricing him, and felt even more vindicated in his choice of suit.

The table began to fill. Matthew recognised the florid, beefy man who took a seat opposite as another contemporary. He'd been a prop in the rugby team; Tim somebody. The man grinned in mutual recognition, and raised his pint. The matronly woman sitting next to him was also vaguely familiar, but Matthew couldn't place her. He was amazed when she introduced herself as Sonia Beesley, one-time disc jockey on the university radio station. Twenty-five years earlier, she'd been reed thin and had favoured platform shoes and an improbably orange mop of Afro curls. She was now, Matthew discovered, deputy head of a comprehensive school in Birmingham.

The only other person of whom Matthew had any recollection was the shabby, bespectacled man on Sonia's right, whom Matthew remembered as being on the same Maths course as Spike. He had barely changed at all. Matthew wondered whether he should mention's Spike's death, but the man, after a vague, unfocused smile, pushed his glasses up the bridge of his nose and concentrated on the menu.

The tables had been pushed together in sets of four, forming squares that seated sixteen, four on each side. The two places to Matthew's left remained empty. Matthew leant across Pete Preston's place and picked up the name card next to it. 'Linda Preston', the neat italic read. Matthew wondered if it could be the same Linda that Pete had been dating in the final year: a pretty blonde from the women's swimming team who had been studying History. She had sat in the spectators' gallery every day of the trial, he remembered.

'We seem to be a chair short.' A tanned woman with glossy chestnut hair and a low-cut scarlet cocktail dress was sitting on the other side of the empty places. Matthew had noticed her in the bar. From a distance, he'd estimated her age as late twenties; closer-to, he guessed her tight, wrinkle-free skin and improbably round breasts had more to do with her bank balance than her age. She must be another of his contemporaries, although he didn't recognise the face.

She might look like a walking advertisement for plastic

surgery, but she was none the less striking. She had the air of a woman who was used to being admired, and it appeared Jonathan Freeman was only too willing to oblige. He leant across Matthew, took her hand and purred, 'Remind me.'

'Sylvia Johnson.' The woman had a slight American accent. She seemed altogether too exotic to be a Blackport graduate. 'Sylvia Guttenberg, these days.'

'Sylvia?' Freeman stared at her in amazement. '*Sylvia?* Good God! I'd never have recognised you. You look *fabulous!*'

The woman flashed him a wry smile. 'I'll take that as a compliment, shall I? Long time no see, Jonathan. Not in the flesh, anyhow. I've caught you on the box, though. Always knew you'd make it.'

Freeman gave a modest laugh and smoothed his hair. 'And what are you up to these days? Still writing?'

'Sure am. I'm a big name in the States, I'll have you know,' she said with mock severity, then smiled to display sharp white teeth. 'I guess it's a tad dumbed down from the stuff I used to do. Erotic horror, my editor calls it.'

'Sounds fascinating. Tell me more.'

'Vampires, ripped bodices, you get the picture.' Sylvia shrugged tanned shoulders. 'Literature it ain't.'

Freeman chuckled. 'Nothing wrong with ripped bodices.' He let his eyes stray meaningfully over her cleavage.

Sylvia raised a well-plucked eyebrow. 'It pays the bills.'

'So I see.' Freeman shook his head admiringly. 'You live in the States, I take it from your accent?'

'Is it that obvious?' Sylvia looked gratified. 'I tried the starving-in-a-garret routine for a few years after I left this place. Took a couple of hundred rejection slips to make me realise maybe I wasn't going to be the next Virginia Woolf, after all. So I took myself off to California to be a nanny. Only meant to stay there the year. Ended up marrying the kids' father.' The words were accompanied by a smug half-smile.

'Lucky man. He doesn't mind you being so far from home?'

'My God! *Arnold*?' Sylvia threw back her head and gave the kind of laugh that Matthew could imagine her practising in front of a mirror. 'He's history.'

'California's a long way to come for a reunion.' There was by now an unmistakably predatory gleam in Freeman's eye. 'I hope it proves worth the effort.'

'Well now, Jonathan, so do I.' She gazed at him appraisingly as she ran a scarlet-tipped nail around the rim of her glass, then added with a sly grin, 'Anyhow, the trip's tax-deductible. I'm hoping I might pick up some material while I'm over here.'

'We'll have to see what we can do to make the trip worthwhile then, won't we?' Freeman smiled broadly.

'What did you study while you were here, Sylvia?' Matthew was tiring of the flirtation that was being conducted across him. He held out his hand. 'Matthew Cosgrave, by the way.'

'Hi.' Sylvia turned to him with a dazzling, automatic smile. Then she examined his face more closely, her head on one side. 'Matthew Cosgrave,' she repeated. 'Say, aren't you one of the boys in that rape case? Wow! I've never met with a real live rapist before!'

'You haven't met one now.'

Sylvia's eyes widened at the sharpness of Matthew's tone. She laid her hand on her cleavage and attempted to look contrite. 'Forgive me. I was on the student paper with Jonathan. I covered the whole trial. When you're used to getting nothing more exciting than the athletics championships, or some kid getting fined for smoking dope, a case like that makes an impact.' She leant towards Matthew and whispered confidentially, 'Do you know, I even used it as the start point for one of my novels, *The Curse of the Virgin*. I guess I should thank you boys. That book paid for my first divorce.'

'Really?' Matthew didn't return her smile.

Sylvia shrugged. 'The trial just kinda stuck with me, I guess.'

'What a very ghoulish girl you are,' Freeman drawled. 'You must get your publicity people to send me a copy of the book. Maybe I could . . .'

The rest of his sentence was lost amidst a sudden scraping of chairs at the table behind. Matthew turned to see a slight, harassed-looking woman trying to negotiate a wheelchair between the cramped tables.

'Matthew?' The woman's face relaxed into a beam of recognition that took ten years from her. Leaning awkwardly over the wheelchair, she held out both her hands to him.

'Linda!' Matthew jumped to his feet. 'Here, let me help you.' His gaze moved from her to the occupant of the wheelchair. He prayed his face didn't register his shock as he said in a voice made loud by embarrassment, 'Pete! Good to see you, mate!'

5

Matthew tried not to stare. He tried to focus on Pete Preston's face, rather than the slack torso, the wasted legs, the awkward angle of the feet strapped to the footplates. The face itself was shocking enough; an old man's face, lined with pain.

Pete met his gaze. 'You're looking well, Matthew,' he said with a smile that held no trace of irony.

Matthew squeezed round the wheelchair. Taking over from Linda, he busied himself in steering it to the table.

'Thanks,' Pete said, when he had been manoeuvred into position. 'I can usually manage on my own, but this place is a bloody obstacle course.'

Matthew smiled and nodded, his brain frantically readjusting to the stark contrast between his remembered image of muscular, athletic Phys. Ed. student Pete Preston and the hunched, broken figure sitting beside him. How should he handle the situation? Ignore it? Ask Pete what was wrong with him? He wished fervently that Elizabeth were there with him; she would have found the right words.

Conversation was postponed by the arrival of the waitress. Wine glasses were filled, orders taken for the first course; an uninspiring choice between cream of tomato soup, prawn cocktail or grapefruit. Matthew chose soup, on the basis that it was the most filling, and requested some more bread. The waitress looked dubious and said she would see what she could do.

'Not lost your appetite, I see,' Linda observed with a smile.

Matthew patted his stomach, grateful for the banality of the remark. 'Afraid not.' There was a pause. He took a sip of his wine, a cheap red, acidic and too cold. Should he ask how they were? But it was all too bloody obvious how they were. He took another, bigger, sip. 'So where are you living, these days?'

'Near Birmingham,' Linda replied. 'Chelmsley Wood.'

Pete was struggling to free his napkin, which was caught in the spokes of the wheelchair. Linda appeared not to have noticed.

'Really?' Matthew wondered whether he should offer to help. 'I was there only the other week, visiting one of our suppliers.' He had thought it a depressing place, grey and without character. 'We're practically neighbours, in that case,' he went on quickly. 'We live in Leamington.'

Pete frowned. 'I'd got in my head you'd gone down south, somewhere.'

'We used to be in Somerset.'

'We?' Linda smiled enquiringly.

'Elizabeth. My wife.' Matthew was eager to grasp the conversational straw. 'We've been married nearly . . . well, it's nearly fifteen years now. Incredible, isn't it? It doesn't seem five minutes since we were all swapping addresses and promising to keep in touch on graduation day, does it?' He knew that he was babbling. 'She was at Exeter. Trained to be a teacher, as a matter of fact.'

'Where does she work?' Pete enquired. 'A colleague of mine used to teach over Leamington way.'

'She's . . . she's given it up now.' Matthew didn't want to have to explain that after Daisy's death, Elizabeth had no longer been able to bear the constant contact with other people's children.

He was relieved when, rather than pursuing the subject, Linda pulled a face and said, 'I don't blame her.'

'And how about you?' Pete had won the battle with the napkin. Turning clumsily in his wheelchair to study Matthew properly, he asked, 'What are you doing with yourself these days?' He glanced at Matthew's suit. 'Something a bit more lucrative than teaching, by the look of things.'

'I'm an accountant.' Matthew didn't elaborate. 'You?'

Pete shrugged. 'Still enriching the minds of the young and impressionable. Not Phys. Ed., obviously.' It was his first reference to his disability. 'Just the Geography, these days.'

'That must be interesting,' Matthew replied, not knowing what else to say.

'Hmm . . . Well, I guess "interesting" covers a sufficient multitude of sins.' Pete's grin transformed him into something closer to the man Matthew remembered. He looked around. 'I hoped there might be a few more of the old faces here tonight. I thought Spike Vardon might have had the decency to turn up, at least. It was his bloody idea, after all. Do you remember? We'd all been at that swimming club do—'

'I remember,' Matthew cut across him.

So they didn't know about Spike. Which meant that Pete hadn't had a letter.

Matthew's relief was tempered by the realisation that he was going to have to break the news to them.

'Oh, bloody hell,' Pete said slowly, when, as briefly as he could, Matthew had told them what had happened.

'Poor Spike,' Linda whispered, her eyes filling with tears.

'But *drowning* . . .' Pete shook his head in disbelief. 'Christ, who'd have imagined it?'

'Gee, that's terrible.' Sylvia Guttenberg had been listening in on the conversation. 'How'd it happen, Matthew?'

'An accident.'

Sylvia frowned. 'That was some bad luck for a guy who

could swim like a fish. I used to cover some of the tournaments. Spike was captain, wasn't he?'

'The inquest brought in a verdict of accidental death,' Matthew said coldly. 'You're not going to get any material for your next novel there, I'm afraid.'

Linda glanced at him in surprise, but the arrival of the waitress with the starters prevented further conversation. Matthew attacked his soup. It was lukewarm and from a tin, but he was grateful for the diversion.

Pete's head was bent forward over his bowl. The wheelchair was slightly too far away from the table, and each time he took up a laborious spoonful of soup, a few drops dribbled into his lap before he could get the spoon to his lips. Linda murmured something to him, but he shook his head.

Matthew wondered if he had imagined the hint of impatience in the gesture. He averted his eyes from the spreading orange stain on Pete's napkin.

Across the table, Sylvia Guttenberg prodded her prawn cocktail with a disdainful fork, pushed the plate away, and lit up a cigarette. A couple of others around the table looked disapprovingly at her, but no one commented. She had abandoned the house wine after one sip, and was now well into the bottle of claret she had ordered in its stead.

To Matthew's right, Jonathan Freeman picked up his glass, sipped fastidiously and wrinkled his nose. Sylvia raised an eyebrow and gestured towards the bottle of claret. It was like watching the elaborate courting ritual of two exotic birds.

'Excuse me,' Freeman murmured, and stretched his arm across Matthew as she reached for the bottle and leant forward.

'Would it be easier if Sylvia and I swapped seats?' Matthew pushed back his chair and stood up.

Pete glanced up at him without comment before going back to his soup.

Matthew turned to Linda and asked about her work. She taught in the History department at the same school as Pete, she told him; it made it more convenient with the transport, she added unselfconsciously. Matthew listened solicitously, anxious to make amends for the alacrity with which he had switched places, embarrassed that he found Pete's disability so hard to handle.

'I took a few years out when the kids were small. I went back to teaching after the accident,' she said.

Matthew wondered if she was going to offer any details, but she didn't. Instead, she showed him a photograph of their four children. Matthew got the impression that money was tight. He suppressed the unworthy thought that Pete's education at boarding school hadn't got him far.

'Do you have a family?' Linda asked, as she put the photograph back in her bag.

'No.' Matthew was aware that the response sounded abrupt to the point of rudeness. 'Elizabeth's . . . we're expecting a baby. Next May.' He prayed no one would make a crack about why it had taken them so long, but Linda, looking genuinely pleased, said only, 'Congratulations! You must be very excited.'

'You'll find out what real work is then, mate!' Pete observed.

It seemed dishonest, somehow, not to mention Daisy, but he'd cast enough of a pall over the evening by telling them of Spike's death. Matthew pushed his soup bowl away from him and, by way of changing the subject, said, 'Frightening, isn't it, when you look round? Where have the last twenty-five years gone?'

For the next few minutes, the conversation meandered inconsequentially as they attempted to identify people on other tables, put names to faces. The waitress reappeared and removed the remains of the first course.

'You'll have to come over and see us one weekend,' Linda

said as plates of pallid turkey were placed in front of them.
'In fact, we're thinking of having a party some time over
Christmas.' She rummaged in her bag and produced a pen
and some paper. 'Put your address down, and I'll send you
an invite.'

Matthew scribbled it down, half an ear on the conversation
that Sylvia Guttenberg, on Linda's other side, seemed determined to strike up with Pete. He heard the words 'trial'
and 'rape'.

Linda heard them too; Matthew felt her stiffen. She turned
to Sylvia and said in a high, brittle voice, 'I don't think we
need to bring any of that up here, do you?'

'Yeah, yeah.' Sylvia waved an unsteady hand. The bottle
of claret stood all but empty by her glass. 'But isn't it *weird*? I
mean, come on! Talk about nature mirroring art.' Her slightly
unfocused gaze wavered from Linda's face to Matthew's. 'It's
exactly the way I wrote it.'

'I'm afraid I don't have the faintest idea what you're talking
about,' Linda replied, icily enough for the other conversations
around the table to peter out.

Sylvia leant forward, her elbows on the table, the neckline
of her dress gaping to expose the matching scarlet lace of her
bra. 'In my novel. All these guys getting picked off by the
woman they'd . . .'

A piece of turkey lodged in Matthew's throat. He coughed
violently.

Sylvia didn't appear to notice. 'C'mon, it's some coincidence, isn't it? Spike's dead, Pete's . . .' she glanced at
the wheelchair then whispered loudly, 'well, you know . . .
crippled. Don't you think it's kinda—'

'I think it's time we changed the subject,' Linda said crisply.
'And I think it's time you stopped drinking.'

Sylvia pulled a face at her then, turning to Matthew, waved
her fingers and intoned in a ghostly voice, '*The Curse of the*

Virgin.' She giggled. 'Better watch your step, my friend.
Could be your turn next.'

'I need the lavatory.' Pete jerked his wheelchair back from
the table, banging into the chairs at the table behind.

'Let me help.' Matthew leapt up.

'I'm OK.' Pete's voice was angry. 'I can still just about
manage to take a piss on my own, thanks.'

Clumsily, he began to steer himself between the forest of
chairs. Linda, who had half-risen, sat down again and studied
her glass.

'An overactive imagination. The penalty for being a nov-
elist, one imagines.' Freeman draped a casual arm around
Sylvia's shoulder. 'If you cast your mind back to the trial,
my sweet, I don't think you'll recall too many virgins. My
recollection is of some grubby little scrubber with—'

Linda's cheeks were burning. Matthew, his patience snapping, said in a loud voice, 'For Christ's sake drop it, the pair
of you.'

A number of people at adjacent tables turned to stare. Sylvia
raised an eloquent eyebrow, shrugged, and poured the last of
the wine into Freeman's glass. There was an awkward silence.
Then Sonia Beesley said brightly from the other side of the
table, 'How do you find teaching in Chelmsley Wood, Linda?
I couldn't help overhearing . . .'

Conversation started up again around the table. After
a while, Pete reappeared, heralded by a further clatter of
scraping chairs as people made way for him. Matthew cursed
the organisers for not putting them all at a table nearer
the door.

Rubbery Christmas pudding was served and cleared, largely
untouched. At the top table, the university's vice chancellor,
a small, pink man with half-moon spectacles, was shuffling
through an ominously bulky sheaf of papers.

'Great,' Freeman commented, following Matthew's eye.

'Looks like we're here for the duration. I interviewed the pompous bastard once. Far too fond of the sound of his own voice.'

Pots and kettles sprang to Matthew's mind, but he curbed the urge to say so.

Getting unsteadily to her feet, Sylvia giggled, 'In that case, I think I need the little girls' room.'

'I wonder if Ben knows about Spike,' Linda said, as soon as Sylvia had embarked on her erratic journey towards the door. It was as if there had been an unspoken agreement that the subject wouldn't be raised again in her presence.

Matthew shook his head. 'I don't know. I never heard from him after the— after Blackport. Did you?'

'We were never that close,' Pete said. He didn't seem keen to pursue any subject that might lead back to the trial. 'So you're still in accountancy?' he asked with what Matthew suspected was rather less than genuine interest. 'Did you go into practice, or do you work in—'

'You knew Ben had gone into the priesthood?' Sonia Beesley chipped in from across the table.

'Ben?' Linda's mouth dropped open. 'A *priest*?'

'That's what I thought, when I first found out!' Sonia's eyes were dancing with suppressed laughter. 'I taught for a while at a Catholic school – oh, it must have been fifteen years or so ago. Ben – Father Benedict, I should say – came once to take assembly. We were both about as gob-smacked as each other, when we recognised one another.'

'Good God! I've heard it all now.' Matthew shook his head in amazement.

'How was he?' Linda asked, her eyes widening with curiosity.

'Just the same. Only wearing a cassock.' Sonia grinned. 'I must say, I was rather tempted to remind him of some of the things you lot in the swimming club used to get up to together. My tutor group would have been quite impressed.'

The grin vanished as she flushed suddenly. 'I mean drinking, and so on.'

There was a moment's awkward pause before Linda said, 'I hope someone's let him know about Spike.'

'I expect Spike's parents would have written,' Matthew said.

A friend of the family, Ben Fellows had known Spike longer than any of them; the two had come up to Blackport from the same school. Matthew shook his head again in disbelief as he tried and failed to square the memory of the stocky, carrot-haired Irishman, fond of his Guinness, with the image of Ben as a priest. He couldn't even recall the other man ever going to church. He wondered if the Vardons had kept in touch with Ben over the years, and tried to remember if Spike had ever mentioned his name. Surely he'd have said, if he'd known Ben had entered the priesthood? Yet another subject, Matthew realised sadly, that he would never now be able to discuss with his friend.

All those things he'd never said, questions he'd never asked, because he'd imagined they had all the time in the world. How could he, of all people, have been so stupid?

'Anyone heard anything of Toby?' Linda's query broke into his thoughts. 'I'd have expected him to be a household name by now.'

'Not as much as he'd have expected himself to be,' Sonia Beesley grinned, raising a ripple of reminiscent laughter around the table.

'Toby Gresham-Palmer?' Jonathan Freeman's expression was one of amused contempt. 'I had a letter from him, a few years back. He'd got hold of my agent's address somehow. I think he was hoping I could pull a few strings, get some work put his way.' He gave a self-deprecating smile, not quite convincing. 'Happens all the time, when you're in television.'

If he'd expected someone to follow up on the comment, he

was disappointed; Sonia was more interested in talking about Toby. 'So he did go on the stage, then?' she asked curiously. Matthew remembered that she and Toby had been an item briefly during their final year.

Freeman shrugged dismissively. 'He'd done a bit of work in rep, from what I can remember of his c.v. A few walk-on parts on the box – *Casualty*, *The Bill*, that sort of stuff.' The corners of his mouth twitched as he added, 'He'd done some modelling too. Knitting patterns, mainly.'

'*Knitting* patterns?' Linda hooted.

'What a wanker.' There was no humour in Pete's voice. Matthew glanced at him in surprise, wondering if Toby and Linda could have been an item at some stage too. It was a possibility, he supposed; it had certainly been Toby's stated ambition to work his way through the entire female population of the university.

'Well, I'm off for a bit of air,' Freeman murmured, as the vice chancellor rapped his coffee spoon against his glass in an unsuccessful attempt to gain his audience's attention. Matthew suspected that that was the last any of them would see of Freeman or Sylvia Guttenberg that evening.

The vice chancellor's speech lasted for thirty-four minutes and twenty-nine seconds. Matthew timed it. As he had suspected, the main aim of the event was to tap up the assembled alumni for contributions to the university's building fund, and the speech covered every major project that had taken place over the past decade – in every mind-numbing detail. As the man finally sat down, Matthew stifled a yawn.

'You look like I feel,' Pete grinned, his humour evidently restored. He jerked his head towards the bar. 'Fancy a nightcap?'

'Sounds like an excellent idea to me.' Matthew was on his feet in an instant.

A lot of people had beaten them to it, by the time they'd negotiated the wheelchair back into the bar, so that the only table still unoccupied was stuck out of the way in a corner. Matthew was dismayed to notice that Sylvia Guttenberg and Jonathan Freeman were sitting nearby, but they were engaged in a sufficiently intimate conversation for them to be unaware of anyone else in the room; Matthew was only surprised that they weren't already in one or the other's bed. He asked what Pete and Linda wanted to drink, and made his way across to the bar, ordering a double Highland Park and downing it while Pete's pint was being pulled; it had been that sort of an evening. He ordered another, picked up the three glasses, then stopped. He thought he recognised the slight figure standing in front of the notice board by the door, her back to him. He hesitated, then wove his way across the crowded room towards her, wondering if he could be mistaken.

Whatever would Spike's fiancée be doing there?

If anything, Jane Davenport looked even younger than she had on the day of Spike's funeral. Unlike most of the other women present, she had made no concession to the occasion: her hair was pulled back into the same unforgiving ponytail, her white blouse, knee-length navy skirt and flat shoes plain to the point of dowdiness.

'Matthew!' The smile transformed her face.

'Jane! What a very pleasant surprise! I . . . can I . . . get you a drink?' Matthew gestured to the ones he was already carrying. He was still recovering from his sense of dislocation at seeing her there; he'd entirely forgotten Spike's mention that she was a Blackport graduate too. He looked around to see if she was with anyone, but she appeared to be on her own. 'Which table were you on? It was such a crush in there . . .'

'I didn't actually go in, when it came to it. I . . . I wasn't sure I could face . . .' Jane coloured slightly, then straightened her shoulders and gave Matthew a determined smile. 'Sorry. I sound like a total wimp, don't I? How was the meal?'

Matthew pulled a face. 'Well, let's just say you didn't miss much. But how good to see you again! You must come over and meet Linda and Pete Preston. I've just been telling them all about you.' Embarrassment was making him overhearty. He remembered the way he had driven off, the day of Spike's funeral. 'We're over there, in the corner. Let me introduce you, and then I'll get you that drink.'

Once the initial awkwardness had passed, Jane proved to be surprisingly easy company. Within minutes Matthew, Pete and Linda were talking about Spike quite naturally; Jane eager to hear every detail of their memories. There was a lot of laughter.

'Spike told me you met through the choral society,' Matthew said, after Pete had recounted the time Spike, absent-minded even then, had turned up in tracksuit and trainers, damp towel under one arm, for what he'd imagined to be a rehearsal of the university choir only to discover that his tenor solo was to be performed in front of an audience of dinner-suited local dignitaries.

'Yes.' Jane's face was suddenly wistful. 'We were doing Britten's *Missa brevis*.'

Which was why it had been sung at Spike's funeral. Matthew was taken aback by the strength of his relief. Not that he had seriously believed Spike had been speaking to him from beyond the grave. He grimaced to himself in embarrassment at the stupidity of the notion. He wasn't usually given to such flights of superstitious nonsense.

The mention of the funeral seemed to bring them all back to the present. Linda made a determined effort to keep the conversation going, but it wasn't many minutes before Pete stretched awkwardly and yawned, 'Sorry to be a party-pooper, but I think I'm off to my pit fairly shortly.'

Linda looked at her watch. 'God, is that the time?' She pulled a face, then laughed. 'That's what having a houseful of kids does for you, Matthew. You find you can't take the late nights any more. Just you wait!' She got to her feet. 'It's been so nice to meet you, Jane,' she said warmly. 'I do hope we can see each other again sometime.'

Jane smiled up at her. 'I'd like that.'

'There's always the disco tomorrow night.' The words were hardly out of Matthew's mouth before he realised what a crass suggestion it was. Why the hell would Pete want to go to a disco?

'We're off in the morning, I'm afraid.' It was Linda who came to his rescue. 'We thought it was a bit too much to expect Pete's mum to oversee the tribe for two nights on the trot.'

Matthew stood up. 'Can I give you a lift anywhere?' he asked, to cover his embarrassment.

Linda looked surprised. 'You're not staying on campus, then?'

'No.' The idea of a cramped single room and a bathroom at the end of the corridor hadn't appealed to Matthew. He felt suddenly guilty at the thought of the luxury awaiting him at the Grand. He didn't elaborate.

'Enjoy the dancing!' Pete threw over his shoulder, as he pointed the wheelchair towards the door.

'Poor man,' Jane said when the couple had made their goodbyes, her gaze following Pete as he wheeled himself between the steadily emptying tables. 'Was he always like that?'

'No, not at all. He was a real athlete when I knew him.' Matthew raised a hand, as they left the bar, but neither of them looked back. 'It must be bloody terrible for him.'

'What happened?'

Matthew admitted he had no idea. 'It isn't really the kind

of question you can ask, is it?' He glanced at his own watch. 'Do you fancy one for the road?'

Jane was looking pensive when he returned with an orange juice for her, another whisky for himself.

'Thanks for introducing me to Pete and Linda,' she said as he put her drink down in front of her. She paused, then: 'I don't know whether this makes any sense to you, but I think the only reason I came up this weekend was because I hoped some of Spike's friends might be here. There wasn't . . .' She stared into the glass. 'There wasn't time for me to be truly part of his life. There are so many things about him I'll never know now.' She looked up. 'It makes it so much harder to bear, if you know what I mean.'

'Yes.' Matthew realised the single monosyllable was horribly inadequate.

Jane said in a quiet voice, 'I'm sorry. Of course you know what I mean.' She hesitated, searching Matthew's face as if wondering whether she should continue. 'I can't imagine what it must be like to lose a child.'

Matthew drained his whisky, half-choking as the acrid liquid hit the back of his throat. He took a deep breath, forced a smile. 'It was a long time ago.'

'Does that make any difference?'

'No.' Matthew wished he could tell her that it did. 'I should be going.' He looked at his empty glass. 'I'd better call a cab.'

'You could always stay here, if you like.'

For an instant, he misunderstood the quiet words and stared into Jane's still face, more shocked than he could have believed possible. Christ, it was only a matter of weeks since Spike's funeral, and here she was suggesting . . .

'I'm sure there would be plenty of spare rooms on campus, if you want one,' she said.

'No, I'll be fine. Really.' Matthew sprang to his feet, hot

with embarrassment at the rebuff he had so nearly uttered. 'Anyway, I think I'm OK to drive. It isn't far to the hotel.'

She nodded, almost absently.

'I . . .' he held out his hand. 'Perhaps we could meet up somewhere tomorrow. If you're not too . . .'

'That would be nice.' The words were automatic. Matthew wondered if he had offended her in some way. Was it conceivable that she had been trying to make a pass at him after all?

Suddenly, she gripped the hand that he still had extended to her. Her eyes were full of tears as she looked into his face. 'I don't believe Spike's death was an accident, Matthew,' she said.

6

Matthew's brief periods of sleep that night were punctuated by vivid, distressing dreams. By five, he was wide awake, staring at the luminous digital clock on the radio alarm by the side of the bed, all hope of further sleep abandoned. At six, he got up, poured himself an orange juice from the mini-bar, and flicked on the television. He gazed at the screen, trying to push from his mind the images of the nightmare that had jerked him back to wakefulness. Spike and Daisy, holding hands as they laughed and beckoned him. Daisy had been trying to say something. Bubbles had come from her mouth; her long golden hair had floated about her shoulders like seaweed. Spike had had no eyes. A small fish had darted in and out of his empty eye sockets.

Matthew massaged his own eyes and made himself a cup of strong, black coffee. It was just a dream; engendered, no doubt, by his conversation with Jane the previous evening. It had been cut tantalisingly short by the arrival of Sylvia Guttenberg, Freeman in tow and apparently in no hurry to leave, the more so when Matthew had reluctantly introduced Jane as Spike's fiancée. The last thing Matthew had wanted was for Sylvia to get involved in any further speculation about Spike's death. He had found himself babbling as he steered the conversation round to Freeman's television career, a topic still in full flow when the barman had finally called time. Whatever it was Jane wanted to say had been left hanging in the air, unsaid.

Matthew had agreed to meet up with her later that morning. He found he was dreading the meeting. He wondered if he ought to tell her about the anonymous letter. But of all of them, Spike had been the most upset by the trial. It had been the one subject, in all the years since they'd left Blackport, that Matthew had never discussed with him, as if there had been some unspoken vow of silence between the two of them. He knew instinctively that Spike would not have told Jane about it.

He was suddenly, achingly, desperate to be home. He'd decided the previous evening to cut short his stay; he could do without a tour of the campus, and the thought of the evening disco filled him with dread. He'd drive back after lunch. Maybe he and Elizabeth could go out for dinner somewhere, just the two of them. He picked up the phone and dialled home, before remembering that Elizabeth wasn't due back herself from her mother's until the following day. He let the recorded message run through to the end, just to hear her voice, then replaced the receiver feeling more alone than ever. He tried her mobile, but it was switched off. Matthew smiled ruefully. Elizabeth remained stubbornly unconvinced of the virtues of mobile phones; he doubted she'd have consented to possessing one at all if he hadn't insisted on buying it for when she was in the car on her own.

He took a long bath, telling himself that he should be enjoying the rare luxury of a Saturday morning with nothing to do. Wrapping himself in the plush towelling robe he found hanging behind the bathroom door, he lay on top of the bed for a while and tried to concentrate on the television.

It was still not much after seven when he went down to breakfast, and the restaurant was deserted except for a group of Japanese businessmen sitting at a large round table by the breakfast bar. Matthew nodded to them as he went up to select a cereal, and they all nodded politely back before returning to their rapid, impenetrable conversation.

Matthew worked his way systematically from one end of the lavish buffet to the other, telling himself that at least it passed the time. With his newspaper turned to the crossword puzzle and propped against his pot of coffee, he contrived to make breakfast last for over an hour, as around him the restaurant began to fill to the point where he realised he should relinquish his table. Putting his pen back in his pocket, he wiped his mouth on his napkin, wandered back to his room and packed his overnight bag with unnecessary care.

By the time he checked out, it was still only just after eight thirty. As he waited to settle his bill at reception, he browsed through the leaflets on display, wondering how to kill the remaining couple of hours until he was due to see Jane Davenport. They had arranged to meet in the coffee shop of Anderton's, one of the big department stores in the town where, Matthew hoped, they would be less likely to be interrupted than on campus. The last thing he wanted was to risk the ghoulish Sylvia Guttenberg flapping her ears again.

He toyed with the idea of making the journey out to Warrington, to revisit his childhood, but decided he couldn't face fighting his way through the city centre traffic. Not that Warrington had ever held much interest, he admitted to himself, even when his parents had been alive. He hadn't been able to move into the Blackport flat quick enough. He recalled his father's inability to comprehend the sheer extravagance of paying rent when there had been a perfectly good bed lying empty at home.

'The new dockland development might interest you, sir.' The receptionist cut through the memory as she returned with his credit card receipt.

Matthew realised that he was holding a leaflet promoting Blackport's commercial revival.

'There are some very smart new offices going up,' the receptionist went on, clearly under the impression that Matthew was in Blackport on business. 'A lot of investment's coming into the area.'

Matthew was impressed by the girl's enterprise. Langton Industrials could do with a few more like her.

'Thanks,' he smiled. It was as good a way as any to pass a couple of hours, he supposed.

He took the receptionist's advice and walked. It was a cold day, but sunny, and he enjoyed the exercise; his head still felt woolly from the previous night's whiskies. He passed the entrance to the campus, feeling mildly guilty as he spotted a straggling crocodile heading towards the new arts centre on the first of the campus tours. He walked the mile or so across town, noting the few landmarks that he remembered: Blackport Central police station, the town hall. He turned away from the new ring road and struck off into Heckton Fields, the grimy network of crumbling Georgian squares and terraces that had once housed Blackport's captains of commerce. The buildings were of a roughly comparable age to those in the centre of Leamington Spa, Matthew realised. But whereas Leamington had managed to retain its Regency elegance, Heckton Fields was simply old. A shabby, dispirited atmosphere still permeated the area. In Matthew's day, it had housed a mix of students, street girls and those elderly freeholders who lacked the means or energy to move out. Tracts of it were largely unchanged, apart from the proliferation of kebab houses and Asian restaurants. Other streets had been flattened and replaced by blocks of narrow mock-Victorian town houses, outside which were parked the types of car that suggested the area might be on the up.

Not only the buildings, but many of the street names were different, and Matthew quickly became lost. He stopped to get his bearings, deciding that he would take the next right turn in the hope it would lead him towards the docks. Confusingly, the ring road was ahead of him again. He traversed it by means of a series of dank, litter-strewn underpasses, menacing even in daylight. Blinking in the pale winter light as he emerged, he experienced a sudden jolt of recognition. He was in Allenby Terrace; standing opposite number twelve, the building that had housed the flat he'd shared with Spike, Pete, Toby Gresham-Palmer and Ben Fellows.

The street appeared, as yet, to have escaped the urban planners, although it looked as if demolition was on the cards; already in an advanced state of decay in those days, the big, three-storey houses were now derelict, covered in graffiti. Another few months, and Matthew might have missed the chance to see it again. He gazed up at the boarded windows of number twelve and was all but overcome by a powerful wave of nostalgia. How delighted he had been to swap the suffocating neatness of his parents' council house in respect-able, working-class Warrington for the cheerful, dilapidated squalor of the flat – how relieved to be independent at last. It had been that same heady, self-centred sense of freedom that had led him to scorn the family party that his mother had planned for his twenty-first in favour of a night on the tiles with his flatmates, during which he had sunk a drink for each of his twenty-one years. A night of which, as a consequence, he had only the very haziest recollection. A night that was to lead to all five of them standing trial for a rape they hadn't committed.

Although never questioning his innocence, Matthew's parents had never forgiven him. They had been suspicious of his need to further himself, to turn his back on the steady shop-floor job his father could have secured for him. The trial had realised all their prejudices. For their only son to have spurned his own family, to have intoxicated him-self into oblivion in the company of a bunch of students, had been as shameful in their eyes as the alleged crime itself.

Involuntarily, Matthew shivered. This was a mistake, he told himself. The past was a place better not revisited.

Turning his back on Allenby Terrace, he briskly retraced his steps through the echoing underpasses and headed towards the shops. He'd barely given the annual dilemma of Elizabeth's Christmas present a thought, he reminded himself. Maybe an hour in Blackport's high street would solve it for him.

Although it was still before ten o'clock, the stores were already too busy for comfortable shopping. The term was an oxymoron in itself, in Matthew's opinion. In the first jewellery shop that he tried, he was ignored completely; in the second, pounced upon with such alacrity that any half-formed ideas he had been harbouring escaped him immediately. He turned into a small arcade and spotted a dress shop, its name, Alla Moda Boutique, stencilled discreetly in gold across its elegantly arranged window. Matthew wandered in, more because its obvious exclusivity ensured that it was quieter than its neighbours than because he expected to gain inspiration there. He glanced at the spare, tasteful display of merchandise, his mind a blank; he didn't even know what size Elizabeth was, now that she was pregnant. He was about to leave when his eye was caught by a scarf draped artfully across a simple black sheath dress. The scarf was patterned in shades of ochre and bronze shot through with a discreetly shimmering gold that reminded him of Elizabeth's hair.

Hesitantly, Matthew fingered its seductive, velvety softness. Sensing her prey, an elegant, stick-thin woman in her fifties bore down on him. Matthew asked the price. The woman's response, which was to extol the quality of the fabric, the originality of the design, told him that it must be exorbitant. He was right. For a full minute, the frugality instilled in Matthew by his parents warred with his desire to buy Elizabeth a Christmas present that would knock her off her feet.

Bearing his gift-wrapped package, and feeling more pleased with himself than he had all morning, Matthew headed for Anderton's. Once inside the stifling entrance lobby, he consulted the store directory, then fought his way through the overpoweringly perfumed cosmetics department towards the lift, his eardrums assaulted by the tinny jingle of piped Christmas carols, his pleasure at his recent purchase quickly vanquished by irritability as he was bumped and barged by the purchases of his fellow shoppers. And although Matthew didn't care to admit it, by apprehension at the prospect of his forthcoming meeting with Jane Davenport.

The lift was an age coming, and was as packed as everything else in the store. Matthew bundled in, to find himself wedged beside a pushchair and its wailing cargo. The young woman in charge of it looked exhausted. She was weighed down with bulging plastic carriers. More bags spilt from the rack beneath the pushchair. She had a couple of older children with her: a boy of three or four, who was struggling vigorously to free himself of his mother's firm grip on his podgy wrist, and a girl of about six, who stood patiently rocking the handle of the pushchair in a vain attempt to pacify the baby inside.

The girl had the same pinched wheyface as her mother. Her clothes were shabby, her long pale hair lifeless and grubby. She caught Matthew's eye, her clear blue gaze at odds with the pervading air of poverty that hung around her. Matthew swallowed and looked away, overcome by the child's resemblance to Daisy.

They all got out of the lift at the third floor. Matthew was disconcerted to realise that the coffee shop was on the same level as Santa's grotto. A jostle of small children, some noisy with impatience, some struck dumb with wide-eyed anticipation, queued with their parents outside the scarlet-curtained entrance. The mêlée was being overseen by a plump, harassed-looking assistant, dressed unbecomingly as a pixie. Shelves of toys flanked the beleaguered adults on all sides – overpriced suggestions to their children of what might be demanded of Santa. Head down, Matthew tried not to remember other Christmases as he made his way to the coffee shop.

Jane was not there. It was some minutes before the appointed time of their meeting, but Matthew had neither energy nor inclination to do anything other than find a table and wait for her. The coffee shop was on a mezzanine level overlooking the shopping area below. He chose a seat near the steps, so that he could see Jane's approach, ordered a coffee and the mince pie, which he was advised was on special offer with it, and settled down to wait.

'More coffee, sir?' The waitress hovered at his elbow with a full pot. Matthew nodded, realising that he had consumed both drink and mince pie whilst lost in thought. He glanced down at the milling shoppers below, trying to pick Jane out in the crush. His eye was caught by the shabby woman with whom he had shared the lift. She and her children had not joined the queue for Santa's grotto; at five pounds per child, Matthew could well imagine why. From his vantage point, he observed the family, feeling obscurely uneasy. They were standing beside a shelf of toy cars. The baby in the pushchair was now asleep, its head lolling sideways. The little boy, on all fours, was running a model tractor along the floor, oblivious to the forest of adult legs surrounding him. The girl was standing very still, curiously alert, her eyes not on the toys, but on the other shoppers. As Matthew looked on, the mother glanced around, reached out, and slipped one of the cars down next to her sleeping baby before moving quickly on with the pushchair, leaving her daughter to prise the tractor from the grip of the now-bawling toddler.

Matthew's attention was, by this time, fully engaged. He watched the girl yank her brother towards the rack of Barbie dolls by which their mother was already standing. Matthew suspected that the routine was not new to her. Again, the woman darted furtively forward, and he saw a gaudily dressed plastic doll disappear into the pushchair's hood. He also saw two burly security guards approaching rapidly from the far side of the floor.

Matthew found himself praying that the little girl would see the men too, and warn her mother, but the child was facing the other way, warily eyeing the overweight pixie in charge of the queue for Santa's grotto. With the inevitability of a film viewed many times, Matthew watched the men bear down on the unsuspecting family group. The woman froze as she felt the hand on her shoulder. Matthew caught the split second of weary resignation before she whirled round and shoved one of the men away from her. She was screaming at him, creating enough of a commotion to attract the attention of everyone in the vicinity. Swearing profusely, she bellowed her innocence to the watching crowd.

Matthew saw the little girl's hand dart into the pushchair to remove the Barbie doll. The second security guard saw her too. As she tried clumsily to replace it on the rack, the man grabbed her arm. The child's face was white, but it was not her fear that tore at Matthew. It was the brief glance of naked longing that she shot at the doll before she too began struggling and shouting. The baby, disturbed by all the noise, let out a piercing wail. The little boy began to kick savagely at the guard.

Before Matthew knew what he was doing, he was down the steps, elbowing his way through the eager crowd of on-lookers, randomly scrabbling banknotes from his wallet, his eyes almost blinded by tears. He heard his own voice, urgent and incoherent, as he thrust the notes at the guards.

'I'll pay for any loss,' he heard himself shouting in a madman's voice. 'Please, let them go. Please.' He seized the guard's wrist, forcing him to release the girl who, with one desperate glance at her mother, grabbed her brother's hand and bolted. The crowd, many of them sufficiently acquainted with poverty to sympathise, parted and closed around the two children as if they had never been.

'Just piss off, pal, and let us do our job.' The security guard shook himself free of Matthew's grasp and glanced resignedly at the wall of bodies between him and his prey.

The other, younger guard was less stoical. 'You bloody do-gooders make me sick,' he snarled. He tightened his grip on the woman's arm. 'Thieves cost this shop thousands every year. And that means higher prices for everyone.' He sounded as if he had learned the words by heart. He jerked his head towards his audience. Emboldened by an answering murmur of assent, with his free hand he jabbed Matthew in the chest. 'Now that might not matter to you, mate, with your fancy suit, but the rest of us—'

'I'm sorry.' Matthew cleared his throat. 'I shouldn't have . . .' Asking himself why on earth he had allowed himself to become involved in the tawdry spectacle, he turned away, all but stumbling over the doll that the child had attempted to replace. It was dressed as a princess, its skirt a confection of net and sequins, a silver-coloured tiara in its hair. He bent down to retrieve it and, before he had time to think, held it out to the woman, together with a twenty-pound note. 'Your little girl . . .' He attempted to moderate his tone, but his voice was still unsteady. He searched the woman's face, looking for some sign of understanding. 'It's none of my business, I know. But I saw how much she wanted . . .'

The woman's fingers folded around the note. The doll fell

back to the floor between them. She glanced at the expectant
on-lookers as if trying to gauge where their sympathies lay,
then shouted, 'I saw you staring at her in the lift.' She tried to
shake herself free, then glared at her captor's colleague who
was standing, with the air of one who had seen it all before,
waiting for the drama to burn itself out. 'It's perverts like him
you should be going after, instead of—'

'OK, love. Save it for the coppers.' The older guard took
the handles of the pushchair. 'I'd make yourself scarce, pal,
if you don't want to be sharing a cell with her,' he threw at
Matthew over his shoulder as the woman was escorted, still
protesting, towards the manager's office.

The spectacle over, the crowd began to drift off. A young
couple steered their daughter away from where Matthew was
standing. The father turned back to give him a long stare.

For the second time, Matthew picked up the doll. Carefully,
he smoothed its yellow nylon curls and straightened its flimsy
plastic tiara.

'Are you all right, Matthew?'

He spun round, as guilty as if he had been about to steal
the thing himself, at the sound of Jane Davenport's voice.

'Yes. I'm fine. I . . .' He bundled the doll back on to
the shelf.

Jane touched his arm in the briefest of contacts. 'Shall we
go and get a coffee?'

Matthew's coat was still draped over the back of his chair
where he had left it. It wasn't until he had ordered another
pot of coffee from a waitress whose suspicious expression told
him that she had witnessed the incident below, that he realised
that the carrier bag containing Elizabeth's Christmas present
was missing. As discreetly as he could, he scanned the area
around the table. He'd caused too much of a commotion in the
store already to make a fuss.

'Is there a problem?' The 'sir' that the waitress added as she returned with a tray had a distinct ring of insincerity to it.

'No, everything's quite all right, thank you,' Matthew replied briskly. He would just have to put the damned scarf down to experience and start again with Elizabeth's Christmas present. Served him right for meddling in things that didn't concern him.

'She drowned, didn't she? Your little girl?' Jane said when she had poured them each a coffee.

Matthew was disconcerted that a near-stranger had so accurately read the situation. 'Yes.' He cleared his throat. To his acute embarrassment, he felt tears prickle behind his eyes. What kind of fool must she think him?

'What happened?'

'To Daisy?' Even saying his daughter's name made Matthew's heart contract.

'Not if you don't want to talk about it, of course,' Jane said quickly.

Matthew glanced across at her. He didn't; he never spoke of Daisy's death, not even, these days, to Elizabeth. But somehow it seemed churlish to say as much, when Jane had so recently had her own grief to bear.

'It was her sixth birthday.' Matthew swallowed, trying to rid himself of the constriction in his throat. 'She'd been off school for a couple of weeks. Chickenpox.' He gave a tight smile. 'Full of beans but still infectious.'

He could see her – Daisy, grinning and gap-toothed as she'd hurled herself onto their bed at some ridiculously early hour that last morning, bouncing up and down to wake them up, her face blotched with calamine lotion where she'd painted the last of her spots with the old makeup brush her mother had found for her.

'Elizabeth had taken time off to look after her.' He dragged his mind's eye from the sweet, dappled face. 'But she had to go in that morning. Elizabeth, that is. It was her class assembly. She'd gone back to teaching – just part time – when Daisy started at pre-school. We were living in Somerset. A little village near Glastonbury – Swaddlington.' Matthew glanced up. 'Elizabeth went for a school a few miles away, rather than the one in the village. She thought it was better to let Daisy stand on her own feet. You teach, don't you?' he asked. He knew he was stalling, still unsure how far he could get. 'Spike mentioned . . .'

Jane nodded silently.

Matthew took a deep breath. 'Anyway, I said I'd work from home that day. It was hot, so we were out in the garden. We'd bought an old farmhouse. Lots of land. Daisy had had a new bike for her birthday . . .' She flooded into his head again – golden hair streaming out behind her, brown legs, already lengthening away from toddler chubbiness, pumping the pedals as she circuited the lawn. *'Look at me, Daddy, look . . .'* He could hear her high, excited laugh.

'I'm sorry, Matthew. I didn't mean to pry.' Jane's words dragged Matthew back to the overheated restaurant. Across the Tannoy, a syrupy mid-Atlantic voice was singing. '"Away in a manger . . ."'

Daisy's favourite carol.

'No. It's OK. It's just—'

'It was insensitive of me to—'

'No, really. I'm fine.' Matthew prodded some stray crumbs from his mince pie around his plate. He was surprised to realise that he was finding it oddly comforting to talk to someone who hadn't known Daisy, who wouldn't be infected by his pain. Maybe that was how counselling worked, he thought inconsequentially.

'We were going to have a picnic when Elizabeth got back,' he continued. 'We'd had to postpone Daisy's party, because of the chickenpox, but we wanted to make the day as special for her as we could. She'd brought all her dolls out into the summerhouse. We decorated the trees with bunches of balloons.'

He could see them, pink and yellow, Daisy's favourite colours. Shiny and bright, bouncing in the evening breeze as the ambulance men had trudged up the lawn, bearing his daughter's body on a stretcher.

'Anyway . . .' he cleared his throat again. 'We got everything ready. Elizabeth was due home about one. Then she rang to say one of the children had fallen over in the playground and banged his head, and that she was going to have to run him down to the hospital. Daisy was desperately impatient to get started – she'd had her bike, but we'd persuaded her not to open the rest of her presents until Elizabeth was home. When things got delayed, she got a bit . . .' he shrugged, seeking a word that wouldn't come across as a criticism, '. . . a bit . . . silly.'

'Of course she did.' Jane's face was full of compassion. 'It's hard to wait for anything when you're six, isn't it?'

Matthew nodded, grateful that she seemed to understand. 'I knew Spike had bought her a book. Charles Kingsley's *Water-Babies*.' He glanced up at Jane. 'Spike was devoted to Daisy.'

'Yes.' Her voice was soft. 'Yes, I gathered that.'

'Spike had told her the tale of *The Water-Babies* the last time he'd come to stay. She always insisted that he did her bedtime story when he was with us.' He closed his eyes, remembering her small hand in Spike's great paw as the two of them made their way up the stairs together. 'The story absolutely enchanted her. Spike rang a couple of weeks later to say he'd found the perfect birthday present for her – a beautifully illustrated old copy of *The Water-Babies*. He'd picked it up in an antiquarian bookshop somewhere. God knows how much it must have cost him.'

'Not that Spike would have bothered about that,' Jane smiled.

'No.' Matthew felt himself flush. He remembered guiltily how foolish he had thought Spike at the time to give such an obviously valuable book to such a young child, when a paperback would have done just as well. 'I thought that if I let Daisy open his present before lunch, we could have a quiet time reading it together until Elizabeth got home.' He recalled Daisy's expression as she had torn the wrapping; the way she had run her fingers over the embossed leather cover as if instinctively recognising its worth. 'She was enthralled,' he said. 'I really think the book delighted her even more than her new bike. We read it right through to the end together. As soon as we'd finished, she wanted to go back to the beginning. I could see that she was getting drowsy. After a while, she nodded off.'

Matthew could feel the weight of her head against his shoulder as they sat together on the bench beneath the willow tree. He could see her small hand, curled into a fist as she slipped her thumb into her mouth – a habit that had been beginning to embarrass her, but to which she had still resorted as sleep overtook her. He could smell the sticky warm scent of her: baby shampoo and wax crayon and the chocolate that, as a birthday treat, she had been allowed to eat for breakfast. Why couldn't he have stayed there on the bench? Savoured that precious time, instead of easing her weight cautiously away from his shoulder and leaving her there, alone, as he tiptoed back into the house?

'I had some phone calls to make to the office. I was away longer than I had intended. When I came back . . .' He could feel the colour draining from his face, feel his chest begin to close up as though he himself were drowning. He looked down at his plate, struggling to regain his composure. '. . . she wasn't there.'

His voice came out much louder than he had intended. He could hear the edge of hysteria in it. A woman at the next table glanced across, then quickly away again.

'Our land backed on to the grounds of a hotel, Swaddlington Hall. It had been a big country house. It was one of the reasons we bought the place. There was a big trout lake. I mean really big. Lots of ducks and moorhens. The rural idyll.' He gave a tight smile. 'Daisy loved it there.'

'I'm sorry.' He felt Jane's fingers on his hand. They were cool and soothing. Like nurse's fingers, Matthew thought irrelevantly.

'No.' He looked up, attempting to inject some sort of normality back into his voice. 'No, it's all right.'

As if anything could be all right ever again. He had left his daughter unattended. Neglected her safety to discuss business. Talked through the new German contract with the sales director while his little girl woke up to find herself alone. Disputed projected figures while she wandered off, book in hand, through the paddock to the lake.

To look for the Water-Babies.

How many Deutschmarks had his daughter's life saved the company? It was a question he would ask himself every day for the rest of his life, along with the other, more terrible questions. How long had it taken Daisy to drown? Had she felt pain? Had she, in her terror, called out to him to help her? The police had said that she would have been unconscious as she went into the water, that she had hit her head on the landing slip as she lost her balance and fell. A quick and painless death, they'd told him. But how could they be sure?

'The gate into the paddock was always kept locked. Always,' he whispered.

'I shouldn't have asked.' Jane's fingers were still on his hand. She increased their pressure briefly before she withdrew them.

Matthew gave an awkward cough, then laughed shakily. 'The coffee's gone cold.' Suddenly businesslike, he beckoned the waitress, ordered another pot. He hadn't arranged to meet Spike's fiancée here today so that he could use her as the bereavement counsellor he'd spurned at the time of Daisy's death. He barely knew the woman.

'So tell me,' he said briskly when the fresh coffee had arrived, 'what exactly did you mean last night when you said you didn't believe Spike's death was an accident?'

7

Jane's coffee remained untouched as she recounted the events of what was to be the last day of Spike's life. She described the early morning drive down to Cornwall, the celebratory bottle of champagne with Spike's parents, the long lunch that they had organised at Hubert Vardon's golf club, the afternoon walk to visit the church where she and Spike were to be married.

It sounded as if the Vardons had been calling most of the shots that day, Matthew thought sourly. But nothing that Jane had so far told him had even begun to answer his question.

'How did Spike seem?' he prompted.

Jane didn't meet his gaze. 'I'd sensed when we first set off from London that there was something wrong.'

'Wrong? In what way?'

'He was a bit . . . distant. I'd gathered that he didn't get on all that well with his father, so at first I assumed he was just a bit nervous about introducing me.' Jane gave a short laugh. 'I was pretty nervous myself.'

Matthew could imagine.

'Lunch didn't go as badly as I'd feared it might.' Jane frowned. 'Well, apart from Spike having far too much to drink. The Vardons were actually very pleasant – they seemed genuinely pleased for us.' A small smile. 'They said they'd given up on Spike ever marrying. Hubert Vardon was keen to start making arrangements for the wedding, which is why we walked over to the church after lunch. After a while, they went back to the house. Spike's mother was feeling tired. I get the impression she isn't all that well.'

'And Spike?'

'We kept on walking.'

'And he seemed OK? Apart from having had a lot of wine?'

'It's . . . it's hard to explain.' Jane turned the spoon in the sugar bowl, watching the small brown crystals regroup each time she dented the smooth surface, like footsteps in wet sand.

'Try.' Matthew fought his growing sense of impatience. She'd heard him out, he told himself. He shouldn't try to rush her. But still, it was only with effort that he didn't take the spoon away from her. Why couldn't she just come out with whatever was on her mind?

It was a long time before Jane said slowly, 'He was very quiet – I mean edgy quiet, not . . .' she shrugged. 'When I asked him if he was all right, he practically bit my head off. It wasn't like him at all. He was always so easy-going.' She glanced up and gave Matthew the ghost of a smile. 'I was beginning to wonder if he was going off the whole thing. His father had come on so strong about the arrangements for the ceremony, and you know how much he hated being organised by anyone.'

'So what happened?' Matthew was still unclear where the conversation was leading them. 'Did you have a row?' The question sounded abrupt, even to his own ears. He could see that he'd hit a nerve.

'Sort of.' Jane's eyes filled with tears. She stared at Matthew in silence for a moment then said, 'I let it go for a while – I knew he'd drunk too much. I thought the fresh air would sort him out. But he just got worse. It was as if he'd completely shut off from me. I was starting to lose my own temper. In the end I said if he didn't tell me just what the hell was the matter with him, I was going straight back to London. That was when he became . . . agitated.'

'Agitated?' Matthew repeated, alarmed by the caution with which Jane had selected the word.

'He said he hadn't been honest with me. He said there was something he needed to tell me before we got married. Something he'd done, before he met me. He was babbling – incoherent, almost. It was hard to make out what he was saying.'

Something Spike had *done*?

'None of us is what we seem.'

'What?' Matthew felt his mouth go dry. Motionless, he waited for Jane to continue; wondered what might be coming next.

'It's what Spike said. "None of us is what we seem."' She stared at the pattern she'd made in the sugar. 'He started to laugh then. But there was something not right. Something . . .' she searched for the right words, '. . . bitter. Savage, almost. He was frightening me, and I said so. That seemed to bring him back a bit. He apologised, said it was just the wine talking. He said he'd go for a swim, clear his head. I tried to get him to come back to the house with me, but he said he'd be better off on his own until he'd sobered up.'

She looked up and said flatly, 'The Vardons were napping when I got back. I didn't want to disturb them, so I took a book out into the garden. I must have dozed myself. It was nearly six when I woke up and went back inside. Alice Vardon had set the table for tea. She thought Spike and I were still out together.' She pressed the spoon down into the sugar then folded her hands, the top one clutching the other so tightly that her knuckles stood out white. 'Hubert and I went out to look for him. We found his clothes on the beach. His body was picked up the following morning, five miles down the coast.' She looked up, her face stricken. 'Why didn't I make him come back with me, Matthew? Why did I let him go off alone?'

Matthew had absolutely no idea how to answer her. His brain was still circling those first words, trying to make some sense of them. What was it that Spike had thought so vital to tell her before the wedding?

What else *could* it be?

'I should have said all this at the inquest, shouldn't I?' Jane was searching his face.

'Well . . . I don't know . . .' Matthew tried to marshal his thoughts. 'I can't really see that it would have made any difference to the verdict.'

'It wasn't an accident,' Jane cut across him. 'I'm sure of it. Spike killed himself. There's something else the coroner doesn't know. Something I found.' The words came out in a rush. She put her hand to her mouth as if trying, too late, to prevent their escape.

'Something you found?' Matthew echoed, his thoughts racing.

'I went back to London after Spike's body had been recovered. Everyone wanted me to stay down in Cornwall, but I just wanted to be . . .' She shook her head. 'I . . . I went to Spike's study. At the university.' She shrugged slightly. 'I suppose I thought I'd feel closer to him there. You know, amongst his things . . .' Her voice cracked. She drank her cold coffee, her hand trembling as she replaced the cup carefully on its saucer. After a moment, she said, 'There was a letter.'

Matthew felt his heart sink. 'Did you notice the postmark?' he asked carefully.

'Postmark?' Jane looked confused.

He realised he'd jumped the gun. 'Sorry. I just wondered if . . .'

'The letter was propped up in front of his computer. Spike

must have typed it out before we set off for Cornwall.' Her hand went to her throat. 'He must have had the whole thing planned, mustn't he? Before we even . . .'

'What did it say?'

'It was written in Latin. "*Prima est haec ultio, quod se Iudice nemo nocens absolvitur.*"' Jane glanced at Matthew, as though expecting him to understand the meaning of the words. 'It's from Juvenal's *Satires*. I looked it up. It translates as "This is the first of punishments, that no guilty man is acquitted if judged by himself."'

The words hung in the air between them. There was a moment of complete silence.

'There wasn't a . . . ?' Matthew swallowed, checked himself. 'It didn't say anything else?'

'There was something written underneath.' Jane's face was troubled. 'Printed. "Remember . . ." and then some other words.' She shook her head. 'But they'd been so heavily crossed out they were impossible to read. The paper had been scored right through.'

'Where is it now?' Matthew tried to steady his voice. 'Can I see it?'

Jane looked away. It was a moment before she said in a low voice, 'I burned it.' Her head came up and she stared at Matthew, her mouth trembling. 'I shouldn't have, should I? What right had I to destroy it? Spike couldn't even have known that I'd be the one to find it. His father would have understood Latin, wouldn't he? Maybe Spike intended—' She picked up her cup, realised it was empty and put it down again. 'I've been over it and over it in my head. I don't know what to do.'

Matthew's brain was reeling. OK, so Spike would have found the reference to Donna O'Mara upsetting; he'd been pretty upset himself. But suicide? Was it really possible that the reference to the trial could have had such a devastating effect on him? Matthew recalled how Spike would shy away from the subject, clam up if ever it were mentioned. He shuddered. That Spike could have taken his own life was difficult enough to contemplate. That he might have done so as the result of something that had happened a quarter of a century earlier . . . It was utterly unbelievable. Yet it was the only explanation that made any sort of sense.

'Do you think Spike could have blamed himself in any way for what happened to Daisy?'

Jane's words took Matthew so completely by surprise that he could do no more than stare at her.

'It's just that when you told me he'd bought her that book, and said that she'd been leaning into the water . . .' Jane paused, then went on earnestly, 'Spike had been talking about Daisy while we were in the church, saying how much she would have loved to be a bridesmaid. And I wondered if maybe—'

'*Daisy?*' Until a second ago, Matthew's head had been filled with Donna O'Mara, the trial, memories sordid enough for him to have been considering the possibility that they could have driven his friend to suicide. The sudden, dislocating mention of his little girl's name seemed an obscenity. An insult to her memory. Matthew could feel his face reddening. 'That's rubbish' he said sharply. 'Absolute rubbish,'

Jane looked down at the table, her own face flooding with colour. 'I didn't mean to distress you.' She paused, waiting for a response that didn't come. She straightened up. Matthew could hear the beginnings of resentment in her voice as she said, 'Maybe I shouldn't have told you any of this.'

'Maybe you shouldn't.' Matthew regretted the hurtfulness of his words even as he spoke them, the more so when he caught Jane's expression. 'I'm sorry,' he said stiffly. 'That was unforgivably rude.'

She shook her head. 'It doesn't matter. I shouldn't have

come.' She got quickly to her feet. 'It isn't as if it makes any difference now, is it? It doesn't make Spike any less dead.' The pretence at cynicism didn't suit her, and it didn't last. Tears were suddenly coursing down her cheeks as she added in a low voice, 'It doesn't make me any less of a useless cow that he wasn't able to talk to me, instead of walking out into the sea.'

She looked very young as she struggled to button her jacket, her hands trembling.

'Sit down.' Matthew reached out. The heavy stones of her engagement ring bit into his palm as he took her hand. She was his best friend's fiancée, for God's sake. She'd turned to him for help. And he might as well have slapped her in the face, for all the good he'd been to her. 'Listen to me, Jane.' He hesitated, wondering if he would live to regret what he was about to say. 'I think I may know what Spike was talking about. There was something that happened. When we were all very young.'

As briefly and unemotionally as he could, Matthew told Jane about the trial. For a long time after he had fallen silent, she sat absolutely still, staring down into her cup as if expecting to find an answer there.

'So it was true, what Sylvia Guttenberg told me,' she said at last.

'What?'

Jane looked up. 'I bumped into her on campus this morning. She was trying to tell me about some book she's written.'

'Oh, Jesus.' Matthew ran his hand through his hair. Why the hell hadn't he told her about the trial straight away? He might have guessed Sylvia Guttenberg would be only too pleased to fill her in at the first opportunity. 'Listen to me, Jane,' he said urgently, 'I don't know what that stupid woman's said to you, but—'

'"No guilty man" . . .' Jane held his gaze. 'You're right. It wasn't anything to do with Daisy, was it?'

'We were innocent!' He grasped her hand, desperate to make her believe him. 'For God's sake, you knew Spike! Do you imagine for one moment that he could have done something like that? That any of us could?'

'So why would he have written that note?'

It was the obvious question, of course, but one that Matthew had no intention of answering. He'd said far too much already; God knew what he'd be unleashing if he told her that Spike hadn't typed the letter at all.

'You didn't tell Sylvia about it, did you?' he demanded.

'I thought she must still be drunk. What she was saying seemed so completely ludicrous that I . . .' Jane shook her head and gave a small, bitter laugh. 'I said I didn't believe a word of it. I told her to go and sleep it off. God, what an idiot I must have looked!'

'I'm sorry.' Matthew didn't know what else to say. He looked down at the small hand he was still clasping in his own. 'Truly sorry.'

'Don't be,' Jane said wearily. She withdrew her hand. 'At least it makes some sort of sense, now.'

'We did nothing wrong, Jane. You do believe that?'

She searched his face, then said quietly, 'Of course I do. I might not have known Spike for long, but I know he wasn't capable of hurting anyone, let alone . . .' her voice tailed off.

'I just wish to God I'd told you sooner, instead of you having to hear it from that bloody woman,' Matthew said angrily.

'Does Elizabeth know?'

'About the trial? Yes, of course. I told her when we first—' Matthew broke off. He was just making things worse, he realised.

'Then you must have trusted her more than Spike trusted me.' Jane bent to pick up her shopping bags. Matthew could see that she was struggling not to cry again.

'It was a long time ago,' Matthew floundered. 'He probably just thought—'

'Maybe.' She closed her eyes briefly, then opened them again. 'Thank you, Matthew.' The effort that went into her smile was painful to watch. 'This can't have been easy for you.'

'What will you do?' Matthew tried not to think of all that remained untold. 'About the note?'

'I don't know.' Jane looked down. 'Nothing, I think. What good would it do? It would devastate his parents.'

Matthew nodded. Surely it was better, kinder, for all of them, to keep things as they were?

'I'd better go.' Jane got to her feet.

'Maybe we could meet up again sometime,' Matthew said on impulse.

'Who knows?' Jane held out her hand and shook his in a gesture that seemed oddly formal after the intimacies of the last hour, then picked up her bags and walked quickly away.

Matthew watched her until she was swallowed up amongst the shoppers. He didn't know why he had suggested that they meet again. He didn't know why he'd told her about the trial. He didn't even know whether he'd made things better or worse by doing so; maybe if he'd kept quiet, she'd have gone on believing Sylvia Guttenberg was no more than a harmless, befuddled drunk.

Most of all, he didn't know what had possessed Spike to take his life.

So many things seemed unclear to Matthew as he summoned the waitress, paid the bill, and made his way out of the store. The only thing that seemed absolutely clear to him was that he must find out exactly what had happened in that flat in Allenby Terrace all those years ago, and why someone had chosen to resurrect it almost a quarter of a century after the event.

8

Blackport Municipal Library had moved since Matthew's day. He remembered it, from his infrequent visits, as a draughty, echoing building, its red-brick frontage a lasting memorial to the eccentricities of Victorian architecture. Or not so lasting, it transpired. The site where it had stood had become a multiplex cinema. Matthew had to retrace his steps almost as far as Heckton Fields to locate its replacement, a brightly coloured box of a building that looked as if it could be made of Lego.

The information desk was all but obscured by its display of posters. Advertisements for adult learning courses, poetry competitions, a gay rights forum, jostled with each other for attention. The desk was manned by a nervous-looking boy who, judging by the number of times he disappeared into the back office for advice, was new to the job. Matthew had read every poster by the time he reached the front of the queue. He asked the boy for access to back issues of the *Echo*. The boy blinked and muttered something unintelligible before disappearing again, to be replaced by an older man who invited Matthew to follow him up to the 'local studies' department. Matthew was led briskly past racks of CDs and shelves stacked high with pamphlets, and at similar speed through a computer centre banked with flickering screens. A spiral staircase took them up to the first floor and through a language centre, where hunched figures sat at desks, staring intently into space, headphones clamped to their ears. The library appeared to be equipped with everything other than books, as far as Matthew could see. He remarked as much to his guide, and evidently hit a nerve; reading was a dying art, the man responded with disconcerting passion, one that should be kept alive at all costs. Matthew was regretting what had been a harmless observation as finally they reached the local studies desk. He was relieved when the librarian was forced from his hobbyhorse by the necessity of finding the relevant material.

The man produced several reels of film from one of a bank of filing cabinets behind the desk, showed Matthew to a machine the size of a large television and demonstrated how to thread the film and turn the handle.

'Doing some research, are we?' The librarian evidently felt he had found a soul mate; he seemed in no hurry to go. 'This little lot should keep you going for a while.'

'Yes.' Matthew said curtly. 'I'd better get started.'

There was more material than he had anticipated; each large reel carried a month's back issues. He started with July. He fiddled with the focus and began to scan the pages, amazed at how parochial the paper seemed: the whole of the front page for the first of the month was taken up with reports of Blackport carnival, together with a large, grainy photograph of the carnival queen. There was no hint of national news at all.

Despite the triviality of the material, Matthew was soon absorbed. A detached house in Oultonshaw, an affluent area on the outskirts of the town, could be bought for twenty thousand in 1978, he learnt from the property supplement. A trainee accountant's job was on offer at an annual salary of three thousand two hundred. A businessman's lunch at the Manor Hotel would have set him back sixty-five pence; a seven-night break on the Isle of Wight fifty-five pounds. The Plaza was showing *Saturday Night Fever*. It seemed such a short while to Matthew since they'd all been at the university, yet the *Echo* read like an historical archive.

Fascinated, he wound the reel on until he got to the weekend's television schedule, unfamiliarly scanty with just three channels: *Play of the Week* on BBC Two, *That's Life* on One. He scanned the photographs, smiling at the long hair, the kipper ties. Another lifetime.

He could easily have spent the entire day on the seductive nostalgia trip. But it wasn't the reason for his visit, he reminded himself. The information he sought was spread over five months; five reels of film. He'd already spent the best part of half an hour on one day. Forcing himself back to the matter in hand, he turned the film at dizzying speed until he reached 18 July 1978; three days after his twenty-first birthday.

The banner headline took up most of the front page, and even after twenty-five years, it hit Matthew like a slap in the face. 'STUDENTS QUIZZED ON RAPE OF LOCAL GIRL.'

Sweat was already breaking out on Matthew's palms as he began to read the report beneath.

Police confirmed today that five students from Blackport University were being held at Blackport Central police station, following the alleged gang rape of a seventeen-year-old local girl. The five men were said to be helping police with their enquiries. Detective Sergeant David Shenfield of Blackport CID refused to confirm reports that one of the suspects is the son of a leading barrister. 'Following the introduction of the Sexual Offences Amendment Act two years ago, I am prevented by law from making any comment which might lead to the identification of any of the suspects in this case,' DS Shenfield told *Echo* crime correspondent Sydney Barker.

Shenfield. The name brought the man's image flooding back
to Matthew as he read the few brief lines. He recalled the
shock of being wrenched back from a solid thirty-six hours'
sleep to the worst hangover of his life, to find his field of
vision completely filled by the solid, beefy face a few inches
from his own; so close that he had been able to smell the
nicotine, see each close-cropped, bristling hair on the other
man's head. Matthew had been so far from coherent thought
that at first the looming apparition was simply part of his
jumble of alcohol-induced dreams. As he had come to and
struggled out of bed, it had even crossed his mind that this
was some kind of prank set up by the others to round off
the celebrations. There had been several other policemen
in the bedroom; Matthew had half-expected the uniformed
WPC by the door to start stripping off. But it hadn't taken
him long, even in his befuddled state, to realise that this was
no prank.

Shenfield had been a big, powerfully built man. His presence had seemed to fill the interview room at the police
station; not just by his physical size, but by the way he'd stared
Matthew out, had sat chain-smoking and saying nothing,
while with growing horror Matthew discovered what was
happening; that he – that all five of them – had been accused
of rape. Shenfield had just sat there as one officer after
another asked the same questions while Matthew babbled his
innocence. The man had given absolutely no clue to what was
going on in that big bullet head. He'd used no violence, had
not made the slightest threat of violence, yet he'd frightened
the hell out of Matthew to the point that he'd almost wished
he'd had something to confess. In his whole life he'd never
so much as nicked a sweet from the local newsagent's, had
regarded the police, in so far as he'd thought about them at
all, as a vague, reassuring presence from whom one might
seek directions, or the time. Yet in that police station he'd felt

he had crossed some invisible line – he on one side, the forces of law and order on the other. He'd already been branded a criminal.

Matthew shut his eyes now, remembering. 'Helping police with their enquiries.' The harmless phrase failed even to begin to express how utterly helpless he'd been made to feel in the face of such overwhelming injustice. Quickly, he turned the handle on the viewing machine, telling himself his queasiness was induced by the jerky movement of the film.

Subsequent issues of the *Echo* reported the suspects' release without charge, then, in bolder print, their arrests the following week. In reporting the event, the newspaper had come as near as it dared to getting round the anonymity law.

University authorities refused to confirm that James Vardon, son of leading barrister Hubert Vardon, QC, is a third-year student in the Department of Mathematics. Mr Vardon senior is believed to have visited the five accused while they were being held in police custody.'

The *Echo* had been sailing pretty close to the wind, and Vardon, Matthew recalled, had sent a strongly-worded letter to the editor threatening legal action.

No further insinuations had appeared.

Matthew had to search harder for reports of the sequence of remands that led up to the crown court trial. Thankfully, they had all been granted bail at the first hearing. Hubert Vardon's efficiently professional arrival on the scene the day they were first arrested had seemed like the coming of the cavalry, and the team of solicitors and barristers he'd gathered together had been more than a match for the police prosecutor. Matthew had suspected at the time that it was only Shenfield's dogged persistence that had prevented the case from being thrown out at the magistrates' court for lack of evidence.

Reeling quickly through August, September and October, Matthew came at last to November, and the reports of the trial itself.

It had hung over them all, a Sword of Damocles, throughout the summer. Had graduation not taken place the week before Matthew's fateful birthday, he doubted that any of them would have turned up to receive their degrees for fear of attracting further publicity. 'Innocent until proven guilty' might be a tenet of the British legal system, but it hadn't felt that way in the summer of '78.

Worried sick, they had gone their separate ways, returning to Blackport only for the many interim hearings. Matthew had been desperate to make contact with the others, with Spike in particular, but Hubert Vardon had advised against it, and as he had been their only life-raft in the troubled waters into which they had been so abruptly pitched, none of them had been inclined to ignore him. They had done nothing wrong. But, as Matthew's father had never missed an opportunity of observing, the prisons were full of people who had done nothing wrong.

'BLACKPORT GIRL RELIVES NIGHT OF TERROR', trumpeted the headline. Matthew recalled the sensation of utter helplessness as the five of them had sat in the dock and had been forced to listen to the prosecutor presenting the jury with a pack of lies so outrageous that Matthew had been hard put not to jump up and proclaim their innocence. But Hubert Vardon had decreed no interruptions. His advice before the trial had been simple and compelling. They were to show no antagonism. They were to answer questions politely, but without giving more information than necessary. They were not to deviate from their original version of events, however much the prosecutor tried to tie them in knots. Above all, they were not to allow themselves to be provoked.

Matthew scanned the article, every detail of the trial

flooding back to him as if it were yesterday. The court-room, smaller than he'd expected, stifling hot and packed to capacity. The barristers, leaning across each other, chatting and laughing as if it were some social gathering rather than the event that might alter the rest of his life. His father's closed expression, his mother's clamped lips as they'd sat, bolt upright and rigid with embarrassment, in the public gallery. The sudden change in atmosphere as the clerk had called for everyone to rise and the judge swept in. The endless rigmarole of swearing in the jury, the barristers fussing over this juror and that, trying to get the most favourable balance, when all he'd wanted to do was to get on with it. He closed his eyes, and was back there that first day in the dock with Spike, Pete, Toby and Ben Fellows. He felt again the dryness of his mouth as his turn came to identify himself and enter his plea of not guilty. He experienced afresh the horrible awareness of the jurors' hostile eyes boring into him as the prosecution case was opened.

The police prosecutor could have been Shenfield's twin: a heavy, florid man who looked as if he might have been more at home in a rugby league strip than a wig and gown. His accent had been discernibly local and therefore instantly plausible to the jury. Matthew had listened, appalled, as quickly, expertly, the man set out his stall. It had been clear from the outset that the prosecution had decided on an 'us against them' approach. Despite the *Echo*'s alacrity to claim Donna O'Mara as a local girl, it had transpired that she had in fact come over from a village in southern Ireland to spend the summer with relatives in the town; a tenuous link with Blackport, but sufficient for the prosecutor to make much of the town/gown issue. He'd portrayed Donna O'Mara as innocence personified: a convent schoolgirl, naïve to the ways of a big town, a visitor to Blackport, a guest, experiencing what should have been a happy and enjoyable visit to one of the town's night clubs. His description of Matthew and the others as 'university-educated' was made to sound a censure. They were cast as outsiders; sophisticated, predatory. A bunch of overprivileged louts who felt they were above the law.

Matthew had glanced at his friends sitting beside him in the dock, heads bowed, and had wondered if the man could be talking about the same people.

The prosecutor's assertion had been that they, 'this group of arrogant, drunken young men' – Matthew could recall the exact phrase – had deliberately plied the girl with vodka when she became separated from her cousins, and had then offered her a lift home in their taxi with the predetermined intention of seducing her. And when she resisted their overtures, had brutally raped her. One of the jurors, a middle-aged woman, had swivelled her head to stare at the dock, her eyes filled with disgust.

Witness after witness had been brought to the stand to testify to the defendants' presence in the club, to the amount of alcohol consumed, to seeing a group of rowdy youths, the defendants, getting into the taxi with a young girl. Cross-examination had been scant. None of that particular evidence was in dispute, apparently. The defence lawyers had barely bothered to get to their feet that first day. Matthew had begun to wonder if they might have put too much trust in Hubert Vardon's judgement.

The main prosecution evidence had rested with Donna O'Mara herself. Matthew had been stunned when she came to the stand. The giggling girl Toby Gresham-Palmer had been chatting up in the club that night had borne no resemblance at all to the plain, mousy-haired creature who'd stood before them, tears already welling up behind heavy-rimmed, unflattering glasses. Hubert Vardon had warned them that the prosecution would advise her to make herself appear as vulnerable as the defence team would seek to portray her as provocative. At the time, Matthew had been shocked at the man's cynicism; he'd made the whole process sound like some sort of a game. But when Donna O'Mara had taken the stand, he'd realised just how right Vardon had been.

Matthew's face tightened as he recalled the way O'Mara had given her evidence. He'd forgotten the extent of his anger, the sheer injustice of having to sit without comment while she'd lied and lied. Eyes downcast, mouth trembling, she'd spoken in such a low voice that that several times the judge had had to ask her to repeat herself. It had been quite a performance. With frequent pauses for sips of water, she had recounted how she'd met the accused in the club. Blushing, she'd agreed with the prosecutor's suggestion that she'd been flattered by the men's attention. Falteringly, she'd admitted her foolishness in accepting the offer of a lift. But at home, she'd said, the village taxi was often shared by those returning from the local hop. She hadn't seen the harm in agreeing to go up with the lads for a coffee while they rang her aunty to come and collect her. Matthew's lip curled unconsciously as he recalled the way she'd played up to the jury. Even the judge had seemed on her side at that point, asking if she needed a break, advising her to take her time. Christ, what an actress. That brave little smile as she'd said she was all right, then went on to describe how Toby had sat down on the sofa beside her and kissed her. That quick, blushing little glance at the foreman of the jury as she'd admitted she'd quite enjoyed it at first. That had been a clever touch. It had made her more plausible, more vulnerable than ever. The foreman had leant forward, nodding his head slightly in response, Matthew recalled; the sympathy had been coming off the whole bloody jury in waves.

Then, guided gently by the prosecutor, O'Mara had gone in for the kill. The faint titter of understanding laughter from the public gallery had quickly faded as, her voice pitched even lower, she'd recounted how Toby had tried to put his hand inside her clothes, how he'd become angry when she'd protested, how she'd struggled and tried to push him away, pleaded that she was a virgin. She'd told how Toby had slapped her, called her a tart, a prick-teaser, how he'd forced his hand between her legs. The court had been in absolute silence as she'd described how, suddenly, they'd all come at her, like a pack of wild animals, dragging her from the sofa, holding her down as they stripped her and, each in turn, raped her. A single tear had rolled down her cheek as she shook her head and whispered that no, she hadn't struggled. She'd been too terrified for that. She'd just lain there until they'd finished with her.

Matthew had momentarily felt as ashamed as if the lies she'd been telling had been the truth. The prosecution had schooled her well, Vardon had remarked coolly as the court adjourned until the following day. Matthew remembered the surge of pure panic that had overcome him. She was going to win. She'd almost managed to convince *him*, for God's sake; the jury had been eating out of her hand. He'd said as much to Vardon as they'd walked from the courtroom. Vardon had stared at him coldly and told him to pull himself together. Matthew could still recall the contempt on the older man's face. It was the first time he'd realised just how much Hubert Vardon disliked him.

The following day, the cross-examination had begun, and everything had changed. During the course of the morning, Donna O'Mara's testimony had been expertly, clinically, taken apart. It had been like watching a combine harvester run over a fieldmouse. Toby's barrister had opened. Within minutes a very different picture had begun to emerge from that of the shy, innocent convent girl the prosecution had portrayed. O'Mara was questioned about her sexual experience, about her past relationships, about the boy from her home village who would tell of her voracious sexual appetite. It had been clear that the boy's willingness to testify had caught her on the hop. Her cheeks had been burning as she'd cast a nervous glance up into the public gallery at what Matthew had presumed to be members of her family before denying any involvement with him.

The barrister had moved on. A photograph that Pete had taken outside the night club was produced; Spike and Ben waving bottles of lager, grinning wildly at the camera and pointing to Matthew, who was slumped over some railings, shirt open to the waist, hair awry, apparently in the act of vomiting. Behind them, Toby was also looking at Matthew, his nose wrinkled in disgust. And next to Toby, the Donna O'Mara the court hadn't until then been shown. Barely recognisable in her tight skirt, platform shoes and garish makeup, her arms draped around Toby's neck, a smudge of her scarlet lipstick clearly visible on his cheek. Matthew had caught a couple of the younger male jurors smirking at each other with raised eyebrows as copies of the photograph were distributed amongst them by the usher. O'Mara had barely glanced at her copy before agreeing in a low voice that yes, the young woman in the picture was she. The barrister had insisted she repeated the identification so that everyone could hear her.

Next, she had been asked why she hadn't rung her aunt from the club, why she hadn't simply continued on in the taxi when the boys were dropped off. It had been put to her that she'd gone into the flat with the full intention of having sex with Toby. That, having done so – with considerable enthusiasm, his client would maintain – she had panicked and made up the rape claim rather than explain to her aunt where she had been and what she had been doing. Her tearful denials had been brushed aside. Why had she accepted money from Toby for a taxi home after the alleged offence? Why had she returned to her aunt's house, rather than go straight to the police? Slipped in through a window instead of raising the alarm? Washed her underwear and taken a bath, thus destroying any possible forensic evidence? Mentioned nothing of the rape until her aunt quizzed her the following morning about her late return? Most damning of all, why had she delayed reporting the alleged attack to the police for a further twelve hours? A refusal, the barrister had been at pains to make clear to the jury, to which the defence team would return later.

Systematically, each part of her evidence had been discredited. Why, if the defendants had acted like a pack of wild animals as she claimed, did she have no injuries? No bruising? Did she honestly expect the jury to believe her claim that she was so terrified she had put up no resistance? Wasn't the claim, like the rest of her testimony, no more than a malicious fabrication?

By the end of the second day, Donna O'Mara's credibility had been effectively destroyed. And she still faced cross-examination from four further barristers. Matthew's mother had allowed herself a small glass of sherry after tea that evening.

The following day, the other lawyers had had little more to do by way of cross-examination than clear up odd points on behalf of their individual clients. More crocodile tears had been shed by O'Mara, but it had been clear that the tide had turned. The prosecutor had seemed to have accepted what Matthew and the others had known all along: that the case against them was a joke. No attempt had been made at re-examination, no further witnesses called. It had been time to open the case for the defence. And if Donna O'Mara hadn't already regretted her decision to make false accusations, she'd soon been about to do so.

Spike's barrister, an old family friend, had opened. He'd

taken the jury through a brief résumé of the agreed facts and had made what Matthew had considered a surprisingly low-key attack on Donna O'Mara's reliability as a witness. But of course the man had known that he still held his trump card up his sleeve.

Spike had been called to the stand. Matthew could remember him as clearly as if it were yesterday, barely recognisable in suit and tie, his hair tamed into a short back and sides. He'd seemed almost a stranger. He'd clearly taken his father's advice to heart; his answers had been terse – monosyllabic when he could get away with it – as the evidence was recapped. It had not been until towards the end of his testimony that the defence's *coup de grâce* had been delivered, and the reason for O'Mara's delay in going to the police became clear. Spike had told the court how, in the night club, there had been some banter about the fact that his father was a well-known barrister. Donna O'Mara had been present at the time, he'd confirmed. He had also confirmed that on the afternoon following the alleged attack, she had turned up at the flat to say that unless he gave her money, she intended to go to the tabloids with a story of drunken student orgies that his father wouldn't want to read. The idea had struck Spike as so ludicrous that he'd laughed in her face and thrown her out. A couple of hours later, Donna O'Mara had gone to the police with her tale of gang rape. And the following day, the *Blackport Echo* carried the report linking the case with 'the son of a leading barrister'. Matthew had stared at Spike in amazement. Why hadn't he told any of them about the blackmail attempt? But glancing at his co-defendants, he'd seen the wisdom of Vardon's refusal to let them communicate with each other; the expression of astonishment on each of their faces had told its own story. No one would be coming back at Spike suggesting it was something they'd cooked up between them.

The trial had continued for another three days, but it had seemed little more than a formality. Donna O'Mara had been shown up as the conniving blackmailer she was. In the end, the jury had taken less than an hour to find each of the defendants not guilty. The following month, Matthew had read that Donna O'Mara had been arrested for perjury. He'd started work in Birmingham a few weeks later. He never had found out whether she'd been sent to prison; at the time, all he had wanted to do was put the whole sorry business behind him and move on. And for twenty-five years, that was exactly what he'd done.

It hadn't taken the *Echo* long to change its allegiances. 'GIRL LIED IN BLACKMAIL ATTEMPT ON BLACK-PORT STUDENTS', the final headline read.

As Matthew looked down at the report of the verdict, everything suddenly seemed blindingly obvious. She was at it again. She could easily have seen the announcement of Spike's engagement; it had appeared in both the *Telegraph* and the *Times*. What better time to stir up the muddy waters of the past? What if she'd decided to have one more attempt at blackmail? The anonymity law had changed again since the days of the trial; there would be nothing to stop her from having Spike's name, all their names, plastered across the front of one of the tabloids. Matthew grimaced at the thought of the havoc such publicity could wreak; he could imagine Frank Masterton's reaction, for one. Had she demanded money from Spike, threatened to break the story ahead of his impending wedding? Was that what had driven him to kill himself?

Another idea hit Matthew. If Donna O'Mara had seen the engagement announcement, she could also have seen the reports of Spike's death. Had that panicked her? Was that the reason there had been no further letters? Had Spike's suicide let the rest of them off the hook? Matthew was ashamed at how relieved he felt at the possibility.

'I'm sorry, sir, but we're about to close.'

The librarian's hushed voice brought Matthew back to the present with a start.

'That's . . . that's OK,' he said. He glanced once more at the *Echo*'s final headline. 'I'm finished here anyway.'

Once more, the man was irritatingly chatty as he lead Matthew through the deserted reference section and down the stairs. Matthew, his attention elsewhere, had to keep dragging his attention back to what the man was saying.

'Are you another writer?' the man asked as they reached the foyer. 'I meant to tell your colleague this morning about our readers' group. But she'd gone before I got the chance to ask her.' He pushed his glasses up the bridge of his nose. 'We could offer only expenses, I'm afraid, but—'

'I'm sorry?'

'We meet every fourth Saturday. Two till four. If you ever felt like—'

'What colleague?'

'Oh.' The man looked crestfallen. 'Sorry. I thought you were together. Writers are like hens' teeth round this neck of the woods, and I was hoping—'

'What colleague?'

'We had a lady in earlier.' The librarian flushed, clearly alarmed by the sharpness of Matthew's repeated question. 'She was looking at the same back issues, so I just assumed you were . . .'

Matthew made a conscious effort to moderate his tone. 'What was she like?' He forced a laugh. 'I'm just on a nostalgia trip, myself. Big reunion at the university this weekend. She was probably a fellow student.'

'Oh, I wouldn't have thought so.' The man looked doubtful. 'She said she was researching a novel. An American lady. The readers' group would have found her fascinating,' he added wistfully.

*   *   *

Matthew strode back towards the Grand, his pace quickened by anger as he scythed his way through the swell of late-afternoon shoppers. Christ, as if the situation wasn't complicated enough, without Sylvia Guttenberg deciding to write a sequel to *The Curse of the* bloody *Virgin*, or whatever the damned book was called. And stirring up God alone knew what in the process.

He was still feeling angry when he reached the Grand. He hesitated at the bottom of the wide stone steps, wondering whether to go back onto campus and try to locate Sylvia Guttenberg; have it out with her. But with no idea where she might be, it could take him hours. Matthew massaged the bridge of his nose, the force of his anger already beginning to evaporate. It had started to rain, icy needles that penetrated the thickness of his overcoat and numbed his face. Did he really need the trudge back to the university on what would, in all probability, turn out to be a wild-goose chase in any event? Staring at close-printed text all afternoon had left him with the makings of a storming headache. And he still had the drive to Leamington ahead of him, he reminded himself.

Turning his back on the teeming street, Matthew made his way up the steps and pushed open the swing door on the seductive warmth of the hotel.

He had left his bag in reception. It was while he was waiting for it to be fetched that it occurred to him that the prospect of a room on campus was likely to be even less appealing to a wealthy Californian than it had been to him. A query to the receptionist proved him right. On impulse, Matthew asked the girl to call Sylvia Guttenberg's room to say he was down in the lobby. The answer came back almost immediately that he should go on up.

Matthew took the lift up to the third floor. He glanced at himself in the mirrored wall, automatically smoothing his damp hair and brushing the clinging drops of rain from his coat. His thawing cheeks were fiery red in the sudden warmth. He stepped out into the hushed, discreetly lit corridor, taking a moment to gather his thoughts before scanning the numbers on the closed doors until he found the one the receptionist had given him. He paused, then rapped sharply.

Sylvia opened the door almost immediately. She was wearing one of the hotel's plush towelling robes, her hair slicked wetly against her skull, small rivulets of water tracking down over her collarbone into the deep V of her cleavage. Her skin looked warm and pink.

'Hi.' She gave Matthew a slow smile as she stood aside to let him in. 'I was just taking a shower.'

Matthew felt his anger return full force. The bloody woman was trying to seduce him. It was obvious that below the robe, she was naked. He walked briskly into the room, his eyes averted.

'Drink?'

'No thanks.'

'Why, Matthew, I do believe you're blushing!' Sylvia arranged herself in one of the easy chairs.

'This isn't a social visit.' Matthew remained standing. 'Would you mind telling me what you were doing at the library this afternoon?'

'Any reason why I should?' There was mockery in Sylvia's voice. She crossed her legs, the robe falling open to reveal her thighs.

Matthew looked away. A pair of heavy gold cufflinks very similar to those Jonathan Freeman had been wearing the previous evening lay on the dressing table amongst the clutter of Sylvia's cosmetics, he noticed.

She followed his gaze. 'You always were such a stuffed shirt, Matthew.' She gave a throaty laugh. 'That rape stuff gave you guys some street cred, if you did but realise it. You should try playing it up a bit. Makes a girl intrigued.'

'I do hope you're not attempting to rake up some sort of scandal about Spike's death.' It sounded ridiculously pompous.

'Is there any?'

Matthew was wishing he'd never embarked on the confrontation. He was making himself look a fool. And far from getting the bloody woman to back off, he was merely sharpening her interest.

Sylvia lit up a cigarette and regarded Matthew through a plume of smoke. As if reading his mind, she went on, 'Because if there isn't, I don't see why you're getting so hot under the collar, my friend.'

'I simply don't want Spike's fiancée being made more distressed than she already is,' he said stiffly.

'Ah. Plain Jane.' Sylvia took a long drag on her cigarette. 'I'm not so sure I'd trust that one, if I were you. What's the saying? Still waters run deep? But your chivalry does you credit, Matthew.' Smoke curled around Sylvia's sharp white teeth as she laughed suddenly. 'Unless you've been paddling there already, you bad boy.'

'Don't be so bloody disgusting.' Matthew had never been able to comprehend how a man could strike a woman, but in that moment there was nothing he wanted to do more.

'Oh, lighten up, for God's sake.' Sylvia was still smirking. 'A good screw would probably do you both the world of good.'

'When I want advice from a . . . a tart like you, I'll ask for it.' Matthew clenched his fist against the almost overwhelming urge to slap her. 'In the meantime, I should warn you there are libel laws against—'

'Oh, please! Spare me the litigation.' Sylvia yawned, stubbed out the cigarette and got to her feet. 'Get real, Matthew. I write fiction. Make-believe. Remember? Any resemblance to real life is purely unintentional.' She walked over to the dressing table and picked up a card. 'My phone number. Just in case there's ever anything you feel you'd like to share with me.' She held it out to him, then, when he made no move to take it, shrugged and slipped it into his pocket, her fingers lingering teasingly against him until he pulled away from her.

Matthew strode from the room, not bothering to close the door behind him.

'In the meantime, by all means feel free to go to the police, the press, anyone you fancy. As my agent always says, no publicity's bad publicity.' Sylvia's laughter followed him down the corridor. 'Have a nice day.'

Matthew was back on the motorway within half an hour, having broken every speed limit to get there. He couldn't put Blackport behind him fast enough.

9

It was late by the time Matthew got back to Leamington. The motorway had been busy, driving rain and an elaborate contraflow system north of Birmingham adding to the congestion. Matthew was hungry, tired and depressed at the thought of the empty house that awaited him. More than anything, he longed for Elizabeth's company. He felt an unfamiliar sense of loneliness at the thought of opening the front door to silence, darkness. He was accustomed to his own company; his job saw to that. Trains, planes, solitary hotel rooms were part of his way of life. But he was seldom physically on his own anywhere – surrounded by strangers, maybe, but not alone. He wondered if Elizabeth felt lonely when he was away. He'd never given the matter much thought he realised as, finally, he swung the Jaguar into the drive and pulled up in front of the house.

Reluctant to go inside, Matthew sat for a moment surveying the place that had been his and Elizabeth's home for the past five years. It was an impressive building, double-fronted, with generous bow windows flanking the large Georgian-style portico. It looked important, more established than might be expected of a new house; its Cotswold stone already beginning to mellow. It had settled into its surrounding acre and a half as if it had always been there. He and Elizabeth had chosen it, when they had first moved up to the Midlands after Daisy's death, for no better reason than that it was so entirely different from the rambling, haphazard farmhouse they'd been so desperate to leave. No paddock for a pony. No lake. No memories. An empty canvas. But none the less it was a house to be proud of, Matthew thought as he glanced up at the blank eyes of the seven bedrooms, their graceful sash windows artfully designed to belie modern double glazing. Solid. Substantial. A far cry from the council house in Warrington. Or the dilapidated Blackport flat.

Matthew's momentary satisfaction was swept away by the thought of Allenby Terrace and all that it entailed. He was overcome by his desire to talk to Elizabeth, to discuss with her all that had happened in the past weeks: the letter, his meeting with Jane, his jumble of fears and suspicions about Spike's death. He'd kept quiet for too long already, was beginning to feel that his silence, however well-intentioned, was in some obscure way a betrayal of Elizabeth's trust. It was time for them to talk. Once made, the decision was like the lifting of a huge weight. Without even taking his bag from the boot of the car, Matthew unlocked the front door and went to the telephone.

There was no reply at Elizabeth's mother's. The mobile, predictably, was still switched off. Probably at the cinema together, Matthew guessed; Elizabeth had mentioned something about a film they wanted to see. He wandered into the living room feeling oddly deflated. The familiar furniture sprang into view as he switched on the overhead light; the cream brocade chairs that would have been a nightmare when Daisy was around, the pale carpet that would have been inconceivable. In the hearth, filled with dried flowers, stood the elegant porcelain vase that Matthew had brought back from a visit to Japan. Something else that would have to be changed before the new baby came along.

Everything was tidy, ordered, except for the Christmas cards that already crowded the marble mantelpiece. It was the first year since Daisy's death that Elizabeth had allowed

any card – Christmas, birthday, even anniversary – to be
displayed. This new pregnancy had signalled the beginning
of a new life for her; a fresh start. Matthew wondered if he
would feel the same way once the child was born. It wasn't
a question he asked himself often. The pregnancy had made
Elizabeth happier than he'd hoped ever to see her again and
that, for the time being, was enough.

He walked over to Elizabeth's chair and ran his finger over
the faint hollow of the cushion where her head had rested.
This is what it would be like if she were dead, he thought
suddenly, and was gripped by a fear so great it all but took
his breath away.

'This is ridiculous,' Matthew said to the empty room. She'd
be home tomorrow, for God's sake. What he needed was a
decent meal, a good bottle of wine and the undemanding
company of strangers. Flicking off the lights behind him, he
walked briskly back to the car and headed into Leamington.

The Lindens was a small, privately run hotel in the centre
of town; an exclusive converted Victorian villa with enough
character to make it more popular with many of Matthew's
overseas visitors than the larger modern places on the outskirts. He entertained there frequently, and was greeted with
friendly familiarity by the head waiter, who showed him to
a quiet alcove table in the corner and left him to mull
over the wine list at his leisure. Matthew began to feel the
tensions of the day dropping away from him. He ordered a
bottle of Châteauneuf-du-Pape and settled down to enjoy his
evening.

An excellent meal, the bottle of wine and a couple of com-
plimentary brandies later, Matthew was feeling comfortable,
sleepy and disinclined to move. His bag was still in the back
of the car, he remembered. It would be easier to stay the
night here than to call a cab, or risk the drive home after all

he'd drunk. The head waiter was only too willing to oblige; the Lindens was patronised mainly by businessmen, and was never full at weekends. Once in the room, Matthew showered quickly, flicked through the television channels until he found some late football, and lay down on the bed. He was asleep within seconds.

He got up early the next morning, feeling refreshed and cheerful at the prospect of Elizabeth's return. She would have Sunday lunch with her mother before coming back, he knew; the chief ritual of any weekend visit there. His mother-in-law was that unhappy combination of an excellent cook with no one but herself to cater for. She loved to have someone to feed, and Sunday lunch would be an elaborate, long-drawn-out affair. Matthew would have plenty of time to call in to the office for a couple of hours.

The thought pleased him. He was involved in some tricky negotiations concerning the Italian subsidiary, a sprawling, ramshackle components factory on the outskirts of Milan. The American parent company was keen to ditch it, and Langton Industrials had been trying to sell it off to one of their competitors for some time. Before he'd set off for Blackport, Matthew had had an indication from the prospective purchaser that the deal could be going pear-shaped. He needed to look at the figures again without the constant interruptions of a normal working day, see if there was any leeway he could offer to sweeten the sale. The subsidiary was an increasingly cumbersome and expensive irrelevance to the streamlined core business that the parent company was set on creating. Its sale had been Masterton's own baby until Dan Chambers had given Matthew responsibility for it. It was a test, and he knew it. With a price tag of some twenty million pounds, any failure on his part to pull the deal off would not look good.

* * *

The planned couple of hours turned, inevitably, into the greater part of the day; it wasn't until Matthew glanced up from his computer screen to find his office in near-darkness that he realised that it was after three o'clock. Elizabeth would be on her way home. The thought filled him with a warmth that even the seemingly intractable problems of the Italian deal couldn't diminish.

He called in at the supermarket on the way home, collecting bread, cheese and fruit for supper and selecting a big bunch of roses and freesias – Elizabeth's favourites. He'd light a fire, set the food out on a tray in the living room, put some relaxing music on the hi-fi. And when they'd eaten, he'd tell her all about what had happened in Blackport. He'd concentrated so hard on his work that he hadn't given the matter consideration all day, but as he loaded the shopping into the car he was once again filled with relief at the thought of sharing everything with Elizabeth, talking it through, listening to her views, which were always more subtle, more perceptive than his own. The tingle of anticipation he experienced at the prospect of seeing her again reminded him of when they had first met. It was a while since he'd felt like that, he realised.

He was surprised, on reaching the house, to see Elizabeth's car already in the drive, the lights blazing through the undrawn curtains of the living-room window. Lunch evidently hadn't been as elaborate as usual. Or maybe Elizabeth had decided to get home before dark; Matthew hadn't thought of that. He felt vaguely disappointed that he wasn't able to set up the homecoming as he'd planned it. He unloaded the car, his face set into a rueful, apologetic smile as he balanced the bouquet awkwardly on top of the shopping, slammed the boot and turned towards the front door. As he did so, the door flew open. The expression on Elizabeth's face stopped Matthew in his tracks. She was sobbing uncontrollably.

'What's happened?' His throat was suddenly almost too dry for speech.

Hair awry, eyes red with weeping, Elizabeth tore down the drive and threw herself into his arms, knocking the unheeded flowers to the ground.

'Where have you been?' she cried, beating her fists against his chest. 'Where the hell have you been for the last twenty-four hours, you bastard?'

'I rang the hotel yesterday morning. They said you'd checked out.' Elizabeth was already beginning to calm down as she sipped the glass of water Matthew had given her once he'd got her back into the house. 'I thought you'd decided to come home early so I rang here, but no one answered.'

'I did try to call you.' Matthew shook his head at her and smiled, trying to lighten the situation. 'Maybe if you'd just turn on your mobile every once in a while . . .'

'You're always saying that,' she retorted angrily. 'So why was yours switched off? I kept trying it all day.' Tears were welling in her eyes again. 'I was so worried about you, Matthew.'

'Oh, sweetheart.' Matthew pulled her head against his shoulder and stroked her hair until gradually her sobs subsided. He'd switched the mobile off when he'd gone into the library. He must have forgotten to turn the damned thing back on again, he realised.

'I didn't know where you were. I thought something terrible had happened to you. I thought . . .' Elizabeth bit her lip, trying to control the tears. 'I didn't know what to do. Mum didn't want me to drive back alone, but I wanted to come home. I hoped maybe you'd be here . . .'

'So when did you get back?'

'Late.' She shrugged, a small movement against his chest. 'Around midnight, I suppose.'

'You've been here all night?' They could only have missed each other by a few hours. Matthew bent and kissed the top of Elizabeth's head, cursing his decision to go to the Lindens. It seemed so self-indulgent now. Cowardly, almost. He imagined her coming into the silent house alone after her long drive, spending a sleepless night getting herself into more and more of a state while he slept soundly, full of wine and good food, a mere five miles away.

Briefly, he told her how he'd come back from Blackport early, had taken himself off for a hotel meal, had ended up staying the night and then gone straight from there to work. He could feel her gradually relaxing against him as he talked.

'I did try the office,' she murmured.

'The phone would have been switched through to Dorothy. I must have been so engrossed in what I was doing . . .' Matthew squeezed her shoulder. 'Oh, darling, I'm so sorry. I'd never have gone into the damned office this morning if I'd known you were here.' He shook his head, gesturing at the bag of groceries and the flowers lying on the coffee table where he'd dumped them and gave her a wry grin. 'I'd even planned a romantic homecoming supper for you.'

Elizabeth tested a smile of her own, then looked down at the soggy ball of her handkerchief. 'Wasn't too romantic as it turned out, was it?' She glanced up, almost shyly. 'I wasn't checking up on you, you know. It's just . . .'

'I know,' Matthew said gently.

'Sorry.' She pushed her hair back from her face, sniffed loudly and smiled again. 'Can we put it down to my hormones?'

'Hormones it is.' Matthew was cheered to see her more herself. 'Now why don't you put your feet up for a bit and I'll rustle up some supper? I don't suppose you've eaten much since you got back, and you've got to take care of yourself, you know.'

He fussed around her, making her comfortable, lighting a fire.

'Thanks, Matthew.' Elizabeth caught his hand and smiled up at him. 'Thanks for everything.'

He bent down and kissed the top of her head. 'Just keep your phone on in future. Promise?' He grinned. 'And before you say it, I promise I will too.'

She was dozing, when he came back in with the loaded tray. He put it down cautiously on the table, and stood gazing at her, feeling a flood of tenderness. Her head was on one side, her hand pressed against her face so that the skin, pink from the warmth of the fire, was plumped up over her cheekbone, brushing against the fair sweep of her closed lashes. The resemblance to Daisy, that last day Matthew had seen his daughter alive, was almost unbearable.

It was his ragged intake of breath that woke her.

'I'm not much company, am I?' The sleep had recovered her. Grinning, she pulled herself up in the chair and ran a hand through the wilderness of her blonde curls. 'God, I'm starving!' She set about the bread and cheese then, mouth full, said, 'So I take it the reunion wasn't a huge success, as you came back a day early?'

'Not really my scene,' Matthew said carefully. The ferocity of Elizabeth's panic had shaken him; had made him realise afresh the fragility of her new-found happiness.

'Many there you knew?'

'One or two.' Matthew hesitated, knowing that he wasn't going to tell her. He cut some bread and concentrated on buttering it before looking up forcing a smile. He felt an obscure sense of loss for the closeness they'd once shared as he added, 'No one special.'

Elizabeth nodded, helped herself to more cheese. Then a

huge grin broke over her face. 'Hey, guess what? I think I felt the baby move this morning.'

Matthew didn't have much time to consider the problem of Donna O'Mara during the following days; work provided him with more than enough to occupy his brain. The latest figures for the subsidiary company were not good, necessitating an unscheduled and wholly unsatisfactory trip to Italy. The potential buyer, Giovanni Montelli, the proprietor of a flourishing engineering business in Ancona, was quibbling about the price. The man was a shrewd operator, at pains to make it clear that the sale was at least as much in Langton Industrials' interests as it was in his own. Matthew was tempted to call his bluff. Something about Montelli's attitude made him suspect the man was keener on the deal than he was letting on; almost too keen. Back in his hotel room, Matthew pored over the figures, checking there was nothing he'd missed. He requested further stock checks with the manager at the plant, but they came back much as he had expected them. But Montelli was on to something, he was sure. He just couldn't put his finger on what. He stuck to the asking price. Montelli refused to budge. Several heated meetings in overpriced restaurants failed to produce a solution. Before he left, Matthew arranged a land valuation, wondering if that might throw something up. It would take time, he was told. Italy being Italy, that probably meant too much time.

He arrived back at Heathrow late the following Friday afternoon, delayed by the almost permanent fog at Milan airport, dyspeptic from too much garlic and red wine, and no nearer sorting the problem of the sale. To compound matters, the delayed flight meant that he'd missed Elizabeth's visit to the maternity hospital for her scan.

He called her as soon as he was off the plane. 'Darling, I'm so, so sorry,' he said, his hand pressed against his ear to shut out the Tannoyed chaos of the arrivals area. 'How did you get on?'

'Fine. Everything's fine.' Elizabeth's voice was deliberately cheerful. 'The right number of arms and legs and everything.'

'Oh God, I wish I could have been there for you. The bloody plane was late leaving Milan. Who in their right mind would chose to build an airport somewhere it's permanently bloody foggy . . . ?'

'Don't worry about it. How was the trip?'

'Complete bloody waste of time. Listen, I'd better go. You know what the M25's like on a Friday.'

'Dinner about seven? I'm trying out that new recipe from the *Sunday Telegraph*. The saladly thing. I thought something light, as you've been in Italy all week.'

'Great.' Matthew hesitated. 'Better say eightish, to be on the safe side. I'll just have to pop into the office on the way back. It shouldn't take long.'

He thought he heard a faint sigh on the other end of the phone, but Elizabeth's voice was bright as she said, 'OK. Hope the M25's not too horrendous.' Matthew was about to ring off when she added, 'Oh, by the way, Jane Davenport phoned.' She paused, as if expecting a response. 'I didn't realise she was at the reunion. I felt a bit daft when she started talking about it.'

'Didn't I say?' Matthew could feel himself colouring, as if he'd been caught out in some kind of guilty secret. 'Did she leave a message?'

'She's going to ring back over the weekend. Listen, you get off now. I'll see you later on.'

Matthew could visualise her, standing in the kitchen, the phone tucked under her chin as she prepared the dinner. He could hear the rhythmic sound of chopping over the faint babble of the radio. She would have thought about the meal with care; one of the thousands of small tokens with which she quietly cemented their relationship. Matthew was suddenly desperate to offer her something in return. 'I'd have been with you if I could this afternoon. You do know that, don't you?'

'Of course I do.' Her voice was warm, understanding. 'I told you, don't worry about it.'

He heard the urgency in his own voice as he said quickly, 'I love you, Elizabeth.'

An elderly woman turned from the luggage trolley she was pushing to smile at him.

Elizabeth's laughter was surprised. Pleased. 'I should jolly well hope you do!' she said.

10

Elizabeth took Matthew's hand as soon as he got in through the front door. Smiling, she led him into the dining room. She had set the table with care: candles, a linen tablecloth, cut glass.

'What's the occasion?' Matthew checked the number of places set, wondering if he'd forgotten a dinner party.

'Look.' Elizabeth's eyes were sparkling with excitement.

Against Matthew's glass was propped the scan photograph.

'Gosh.' He stared at it. He realised the reaction was hopelessly inadequate, but the fuzzy black-and-white image he held in his hand looked like nothing more than an indistinct jumble of blobs caught in the arc of some ghostly searchlight. Had Elizabeth been scanned with Daisy? He realised that he had no idea. He'd been working out in the Middle East a lot at the time; Elizabeth had spent most of the pregnancy with her mother. It hadn't been until Daisy was born, until the first time he'd held her in his arms, that he'd been smitten.

'Look.' Elizabeth took the photograph from him. 'There's the spine.' She ran her finger down the delicate trace of white dots. 'That's an arm. And that's the head. Can you see?'

Matthew sat down heavily. Now it had been pointed out, he could see the profile of a tiny, skeletal face, the eye socket stretched alien-like towards the back of the skull. His emotions were more difficult to untangle than the image in front of him, he realised as Elizabeth leant over him, talking excitedly of the strong heartbeat, the way the baby had wriggled away from the probe as if resenting the intrusion.

The baby.

It was there, inside her. Forming. Growing. Miraculous. Terrifying.

Daisy's usurper.

His child.

He was relieved when the telephone spared him from further comment.

'I'll get it.' Elizabeth brushed the top of his head with her lips. 'And if it's Frank Masterton, I'm going to tell him you're in the bath. This is our night.'

Matthew was still gazing at the scan photograph when she returned.

'That was Pete Preston's wife.' A slight frown was playing across Elizabeth's features. 'She's invited us to a party the Saturday before Christmas. She said she'd talked to you about it last weekend.'

'Did you say we'd go?' Matthew tried for casual, but it didn't sound convincing, even to his own ears. Why on earth hadn't he simply told Elizabeth who he'd met at the bloody reunion?

'I said I'd check with you and ring her back.' Elizabeth took the photograph from him and laid it carefully on the table. It was a moment before she looked up and met his eye. 'What happened?'

'What do you mean?' Matthew took a sip of water, more to avoid her gaze than because he was thirsty.

'First Jane Davenport, now the Prestons. You said you didn't see anyone you knew.'

'No, I didn't. I said—'

'Matthew.' Elizabeth put out her hand. 'Look, I know I've

been a bit wrapped up in the pregnancy, the last few weeks.'
She touched his cheek. 'It must have been horrible for you at
Blackport. You must have missed Spike terribly, and I hardly
even asked you how you'd got on. All I could do was give
you a hard time about where you'd been.'

'It was understandable,' Matthew smiled uncomfortably.
'You were just—'

'Don't ever feel you can't talk to me.' Elizabeth paused
then added quietly, 'I'd hate that.'

'Silly girl.' He brought her fingers to his lips and kissed
them.

What was there to say? Spike was dead. No amount of
talking could alter that. He'd never know what had driven
his friend to respond in the way he had, but in doing so he
seemed to have stopped Donna O'Mara and her poisonous
bloody letters. Why worry Elizabeth, when nothing had come
of them?

'So where's this amazing salad?' he grinned. 'I'm absolutely
starving.'

Chelmsley Wood was as unattractive as Matthew had remembered it. He made several wrong turns before finally drawing
up outside a row of semis in one of a drab network of identical
streets on a sixties housing estate that was well past whatever
prime it might have had. The houses were equally identical,
save for the concrete ramp taking up most of the meagre
garden in front of the Prestons' semi. The Jaguar looked
hopelessly out of place; Matthew found himself hoping it
would be safe.

He'd thought long and hard about accepting Linda's
invitation. A large part of him wanted to distance Elizabeth
from anything in any way connected to Blackport. But to
refuse might make her the more suspicious; several times
during the week she had attempted to steer the conversation

back to the reunion. In the end, he'd passed off his reluctance
to talk about it by telling her about Pete's disability, and his
own shock at the discovery. The explanation – which wasn't
a complete lie in any event – had seemed to satisfy her. It
had also made her adamant that they go to the party rather
than risk hurting Pete's feelings.

One of the Prestons' sons answered the door; a tall,
muscular teenager, sharply reminiscent of his father at the
same age. He greeted Matthew and Elizabeth easily and
showed them into the living room where a couple of dozen
people were already gathered. A mismatch of paper-chains,
tinsel and balloons festooned the ceiling. The room was
warm, and full of laughter.

'Matthew!' Pete propelled his way expertly towards them,
a grin of welcome on his face as he held out his hand. 'I'm
really glad you could make it. And you too, Elizabeth. Now,
what do you both fancy to drink?'

Elizabeth smiled. 'Something soft for me, please.'

'Of course! Congratulations! When's the baby due?'

'Middle of May.'

'Bad planning.' Pete shook his head, mock-severe. 'Right
at the beginning of the exam season, poor little blighter.'

Linda, bustling in from the kitchen with a plate of sausage
rolls to add to the already loaded table, rolled her eyes to
heaven. 'Once a teacher . . .' She put down the plate and
gave Elizabeth a hug. 'Lovely to meet you. Matthew's told
us all about you.'

Elizabeth laughed. 'That sounds ominous.'

Matthew began to relax. He could see that she and the
Prestons were going to get on.

Another of Pete's sons brought orange juice for Elizabeth,
a generous Scotch and soda for Matthew. They were introduced to the other guests, a chatty, gregarious mixture
of family, neighbours and colleagues from school. The

time passed more quickly and pleasantly than Matthew had expected. The room was too small for anyone to be left standing alone, and the introductions were followed up with easy conversation. Elizabeth was whisked away by Linda to talk to one of her colleagues, also pregnant. Matthew got into conversation with Pete's brother Steve who, it transpired, worked for one of Matthew's suppliers. They talked shop for a while, moaning companionably about share prices, the Euro, exchange rates, before moving on to the day's rugby union fixtures.

'Pete and I are going over to Leicester the day after Boxing Day to see the Barbarians play,' Steve said. 'Should be a good game.'

'It must be hard for him.' Matthew looked across to where Pete was sitting. 'I'm not sure I could go and watch, if I'd been as good as he was.'

Steve followed his gaze and shrugged. 'What's happened's happened. No point in him spending the rest of his life feeling sorry for himself, is there?' As if reading Matthew's thoughts, he added, 'If that sounds callous, it's Pete's philosophy, not mine. He's a pretty special guy, you know.'

'What did happen?' Matthew ventured, wondering if he should have asked as Steve's face clouded.

'Pete was out jogging.' Steve's expression hardened. 'Some bastard knocked him down. Didn't even have the guts to stop.'

'Christ.' Matthew swallowed the rest of his drink. 'Did you ever find out . . . ?'

Steve shook his head. 'Police said it was possible the driver didn't even realise it had happened. Not if it was a lorry.' He looked down. 'I don't buy that. I never have. He'd have had half Pete's leg plastered over his bumper, for a start. Sorry,' he grimaced, 'not much of a conversation for a party.'

'No, please. I'd like to know.'

'Pete's spinal cord was severed. That was six years ago. He'll never get any better than he is now.' Steve shrugged. 'The visibility was crap: pitch-dark, pouring with rain. Just bad luck, I guess. Linda used to warn Pete not to jog at night. Stupid bugger never did listen to anyone.' His face softened as he glanced across towards his brother. 'Still doesn't.'

Matthew shivered involuntarily. Suddenly the room seemed shabbier, less cheerful. Pete and Linda were putting a brave face on things, but the accident must have devastated the whole family. He tried to rid himself of the image of Pete lying mangled and broken on the wet tarmac and wondered fleetingly if it might have been better if his friend hadn't survived.

He saw that Pete was making his way across, and quickly changed the subject. The three of them discussed the Barbarians chances against the Tigers. After a while, Steve wandered off to get himself another drink.

Pete watched him go, then said in a low voice, 'Could we have a word, mate?'

'Sure.' Matthew felt the first flicker of anxiety as he looked down at the other man.

The smile had deserted Pete's face. 'Not here,' he said quietly. Raising his voice, he called across to Linda and Elizabeth, 'Matthew and I are just going out for a breath of air, OK?'

Matthew followed the wheelchair through the kitchen and the untidy lean-to behind it, and down another ramp into the small back garden. It was chilly, after the fug of the crowded living room, and the air was damp with the hint of drizzle.

As soon as they were away from the house, Pete said without preamble, 'I had a phone call from Jane Davenport last week. She was in a bit of a state.'

'How did she know where to get in touch with you?'

'Linda sent her an invite to the party.' Pete gave him an odd look. 'Why?'

'No reason. Sorry.' Matthew shook his head, quelling a ridiculously possessive stab of resentment. He'd been half-expecting her to ring him back all week – would have rung her, if he hadn't been so tied up with work. It seemed she'd contacted the Prestons instead.

'Listen.' Pete glanced back towards the house. 'Sylvia Guttenberg's been in touch with her, apparently. Rang her at school. She's been sniffing around about Spike's death.'

'Shit.' Matthew closed his eyes.

'Do you buy all this stuff about Spike committing suicide?'

Matthew paused. 'Did Jane tell you about the note he left?' he asked cautiously.

'She mentioned it. Look, Matthew, just where does she fit into all this? How much does she know?'

Something guarded in Pete's expression told Matthew the next question was unnecessary, but he asked it anyway. 'You've had one as well, haven't you?'

Pete scanned Matthew's face. 'And you? Fuck.' He glanced nervously towards the house, then hitching himself awkwardly to one side, produced a card from under the cushion of his wheelchair. 'This arrived at school. Linda hasn't seen it. I didn't want her to . . .'

'When?' Again, Matthew knew the question was redundant. It was a Christmas card; a robin on a snow-covered fence, a sprig of holly in its beak. Which meant it must have been sent recently. The nightmare wasn't over at all.

'Last week.' Pete breathed in hard. 'Blackport postmark.'

Matthew's hands were trembling as he opened the card.

The usual banal greeting; a couple of lines from a carol: 'All poor men and humble / All lame men who stumble . . .'

And beneath, in block capitals, the words Matthew dreaded: 'REMEMBER DONNA O'MARA?'

11

A muffled bellow of laughter drifted down from the house, serving only to emphasise the silence between Matthew and Pete.

'We're going to have to go to the police,' Matthew said, suddenly decisive.

'The police?' Pete sounded appalled.

'I don't want any of this dragged up any more than you do,' Matthew snapped. 'But what option do we have? I thought Spike's death had frightened her off. But now she's started up again.'

'She?'

'Donna O'Mara.' Matthew stared at Pete in amazement. 'Who else?'

'Not the police.' Pete shook his head vehemently. His hands plucked nervously at the arm of the wheelchair. 'Listen, I've been thinking. What if Sylvia Guttenberg sent the card? It arrived about the time she'd been pumping Jane. What if it was her idea of a sick joke?'

'Sylvia Guttenberg? Why the hell would she want to do a thing like that?'

'Jane said there was something Spike had crossed out. A name. How long do you think it would have taken that meddlesome bitch to work out what, in view of her rabid interest in the trial? In fact . . .' Pete broke off, his face clearing as if the idea had only just occurred to him, 'what if she sent all of them?'

'That's absolute crap!' Matthew said incredulously. 'I don't like the woman any more than you do, but to suggest—'

'No, listen,' Pete cut across him. 'Why would anyone else dredge up the trial after so long?'

'How about Donna O'Mara?' Matthew couldn't believe what he was hearing. 'For God's sake, Pete—'

'Why would she?'

'Blackmail?' Matthew gave a derisive laugh. 'It wouldn't be the first time, would it?'

'So why hasn't she asked for any money?'

It was a good question. 'How the hell should I know? Maybe she—'

'What if Sylvia Guttenberg's been doing it as some sort of publicity stunt for this bloody book of hers? No, think about it,' Pete insisted, as Matthew tried to talk him down. 'She turns up out of the blue, pumps everyone for information . . . And another thing.' He jabbed a finger at Matthew. 'Was your note addressed to home, or work?'

'Work,' Matthew said impatiently. 'What's that supposed to—'

'And Spike's?'

'Jane found it in his study. But I don't see—'

'Well, there you go!' Pete was triumphant. 'And she contacts Jane not at home, but at school.'

'So?'

'What goes into the Graduates' Association handbook? Work addresses, that's what. And thank God, otherwise she'd have sent the bloody thing here, and Linda might have found it.'

'You seriously believe anyone would go to those lengths? Even Sylvia Guttenberg?' Matthew was forced to admit that there was a certain persuasive logic in what Pete was saying. Why else would the woman have been digging round in Blackport Library, pestering Jane?

'You've met her.'

'All the more reason to go to the police and stop her then,' Matthew said angrily.

'And give her all the publicity she wants?

'For Christ's sake, Pete! If what you're saying is true, she's responsible for Spike's *death*.'

'You think you could prove that?'

'I don't know.' Matthew sat down on the garden wall, abruptly drained. He felt overwhelmed by sadness, suddenly. Had Spike really died because of some ridiculous publicity stunt? The thought was almost harder to bear than the idea of blackmail.

'Don't go to the police, Matthew. It's the worst thing you could do.'

Matthew put his head between his hands. 'I wonder if Toby and Ben have had them too.'

'I've no idea,' Pete said grimly. 'But one thing's for certain, they'd give you the same advice as me. Ignore the stupid cow. If no one reacts, she'll give up sooner or later.'

Matthew looked up with the ghost of a smile. 'You sound as if you're on fucking playground duty.'

'It's good advice, though.' Pete reached out, put a hand on Matthew's shoulder. 'Spike's dead, mate. Nothing we can do will bring him back. Why go out of your way to throw shit at the fan?'

Matthew was at the office before nine the following morning. He'd hurried Elizabeth away from the party straight after his conversation with Pete Preston the previous evening, claiming a headache, hating himself for the further deception. All night, he'd tossed and turned, trying to work out his seething emotions. In one way, it was appealing to hold Sylvia Guttenberg responsible for the notes; more appealing, anyway, than the possibility of blackmail. But it made Spike's death so futile – ridiculous, even. To have killed himself because of some tawdry scandal-mongering. Whatever could have possessed him?

What Pete Preston had said was right, of course: there was no way they could prove Sylvia had sent the notes, still less that she was responsible for Spike's death. But Matthew wasn't prepared to simply let things lie. If nothing else, he could let her know they were on to her game.

Now, sitting at his desk, he dialled Pete's number. He was dismayed when Linda answered.

'I was just ringing to thank you both for last night,' he extemporised.

'You're welcome. How's the head?'

'Sorry? Oh . . . fine.' Matthew forced a laugh. 'One too many Scotches, I expect. Can I speak to Pete?'

'Sorry, Matthew. He's in the bath.'

'Could he ring me back? I'll be at the office for the next half an hour or so.'

'It usually takes a bit longer than that, I'm afraid.' There was no trace of bitterness in Linda's voice. 'It's a hoist job. We only attempt it when the boys are around to help. He's heavier than he looks, you know.'

Matthew could only imagine how Pete must feel, being hauled about naked and helpless by his own children. 'Don't bother him,' he said quickly. 'Just tell him I think he's right about not informing the authorities.'

'Sorry?'

'Just something we were talking about last night. He'll understand.'

Matthew could feel the fury welling up inside him again as he replaced the receiver. Had Sylvia Guttenberg given any thought at all to the indignities that must make up Pete's life, before she'd sent him that sick card? Would she have cared? It wasn't a question he needed to ask. Keeping the thought in his head, he punched in the number from the card in front of him and listened impatiently to the ringing tone.

'Hello?' The voice was thick with sleep.

'What do you think you're playing at, you meddlesome bitch?' The sound of the phoney American accent only served to fuel Matthew's anger.

'Who is this?' Sylvia Guttenberg didn't sound particularly surprised; maybe she was accustomed to being so addressed.

'It's Matthew Cosgrave. Now I don't know what the bloody hell you're hoping to achieve by—'

'Matthew! You simply can't keep away from me, can you?' Sylvia sounded considerably more amused than rattled. 'Do you know what time it is over here?'

Matthew could make out the low murmur of a male voice.

'No, it's OK. It's nothing important,' Sylvia's voice was muffled. 'Go back to sleep.' She returned her attention to Matthew. 'You sound pretty pumped up, sweetheart. What's your problem?'

Matthew was gripping the receiver hard enough to strangle it. 'You know fucking well what the problem is. I saw Pete Preston last night, you scheming bitch.'

'Beg pardon?'

'Did you see it as a means of bumping up your book sales? Or is this research for the sequel?'

'Matthew, I haven't the faintest idea what you're talking about.' An edge of irritation had entered Sylvia's voice. 'Have you been drinking?'

'Don't you think you did enough fucking damage driving Spike to suicide without dragging Pete into it? Don't you think he's got enough misery in his life?'

There was a moment's silence on the other end of the phone. When Sylvia spoke again, she sounded wide awake. 'So Pete's caught up in this too?'

Too late, Matthew realised that if the woman hadn't been involved before, she was now.

'Forget it,' he snapped, and slammed down the phone.

It rang again within seconds.

'So what's the score, Matthew? Someone trying to black-mail you boys, is that it? Jane told me about Spike's note.'

'How the hell do you know my number?' Matthew demanded. He cursed his own stupidity. Why hadn't he just taken Pete's advice and let things be?

'How do you think? It came up on my phone.' Sylvia was dismissive. 'So now it's Spike, Pete . . . and you, of course, otherwise you wouldn't be talking to me. How about Ben and Toby? You been in touch with those two yet?'

'It's none of your damned business.'

'It is now. So are you going to tell me what's going on, or am I going to find out for myself?'

'I'm warning you, keep out of this, or I'll . . .' Matthew was blustering, and they both knew it.

'You'll what, Matthew?' The amusement was back in her voice. 'Gee, I hope you're not threatening me.'

'And stop pestering Jane Davenport.'

'*Me?*' A low chuckle. 'Pester the Virgin Queen? *Au contraire*, my friend.'

'There are laws against harassment in this country. Just leave her alone, or I'll go to the police.'

'Maybe you should do that very thing, Matthew.' The phone went dead.

Matthew breathed in hard, trying to calm himself. After a couple of minutes, he switched on the computer and tried to get on with some work, as if to justify the lie he'd given Elizabeth about needing to meet a deadline, but he found it impossible to concentrate. He wandered down the corridor to the cloakroom and swilled his face with cold water, then went through to the small kitchen to make himself a coffee.

The phone was ringing when Matthew got back to the office. He was tempted to ignore it; if it were not Sylvia again, it would be business. And at half-past nine in the morning on the Sunday before Christmas, when the place was officially closed for the next ten days, no one had the right to expect him to be there. Ten rings, twenty. Persistent, whoever it was. It occurred to him suddenly that it might be Elizabeth.

'Matthew?'

It took him a moment to recognise the voice.

'I tried your home. Elizabeth told me where you were.' Jane Davenport paused. 'I hope I'm not disturbing anything important.'

'Not at all. I was going to ring you later in any case.' Matthew had already decided that he should find out exactly what Sylvia had got out of her. 'I met up with Pete Preston last night, and—'

'Matthew, there's something I've got to tell you,' Jane cut across him. 'I've been trying to get in touch with Toby Gresham-Palmer. I wanted to find out—'

Matthew breathed in sharply. 'Look, Jane. I really don't think you should be getting involved in—'

'I made contact with his agent.' Jane wasn't listening to him. 'I've found out that—'

'Pete told me that Guttenberg woman's been snooping around. If you want my advice, you won't—'

'Matthew, listen to me.'

The urgency in Jane's voice silenced him.

'The agent said he isn't working any more. She said he had some kind of an accident. A couple of years ago.' Jane took a deep, shuddering breath. 'Spike, Pete Preston, Toby Gresham-Palmer . . .' Her voice was barely audible as she whispered, 'Matthew, what's going on?'

12

Christmas was torture. All Matthew could think about was tracking Toby down, finding out what had happened to him, discovering whether he too had received a note, but until the holiday season was out of the way, he couldn't even make contact with the theatrical agency; all he got was the ridiculous jingle of its answering machine. Instead, he was stranded in Shropshire with Elizabeth's sister and her family, trying to look as if he were enjoying the festivities.

He knew he should be grateful to see Elizabeth looking so happy; it was the first year since Daisy's death that she had been able to bear a family Christmas. But all he felt, as he watched her opening presents on Christmas morning surrounded by her sister's noisy tribe, was a desperate sense of loss, not just for Daisy, but for Elizabeth herself. She was cut off from him by the joyful, all-absorbing bubble of her pregnancy. He wanted to talk to her, hear her tell him that there was a logical explanation to what was happening. He'd always imagined he was the strong one in their relationship. But he was no longer sure of that, any more than he was sure of anything.

At last, Christmas and the New Year were behind them and the world went back to work.

'I don't want to be disturbed for the next couple of hours,' Matthew said as he hurried through his secretary's office on the first morning back, cutting short her 'happy New Year' greetings. He pushed aside the post marked 'Urgent' that was already arranged on his desk and dialled the number he'd got from Jane.

'Gold Star Theatrical agency,' a determinedly upbeat voice answered after the first ring. 'How may I help you?'

Matthew explained his need to contact Toby Gresham-Palmer and was asked to hold the line. Several verses of 'New York, New York' later, the voice confirmed that Toby was no longer on the agency's books.

'I realise that. It's a personal matter. I . . .' Matthew adopted his most authoritative tone, 'I need to speak to him as a matter of some urgency. Do you still have a contact number for him, please?'

'Just a moment.' The voice was less upbeat, more suspicious.

Matthew could hear a muffled discussion before a different voice said, 'Delia Gold speaking.' The voice was deep, grainy; its owner sounded as if she smoked too much. 'Can I ask what this is about?'

'As I've already explained to your colleague . . .' Matthew curbed the exasperation in his tone, started again. 'I understand Toby's had some sort of accident. Could you tell me exactly what happened, please?'

'I'm afraid I can't discuss my clients' personal details, Mr . . . ?'

'Cosgrave. Matthew Cosgrave. Toby and I were at university together.'

'Really.' Delia Gold sounded unconvinced.

'Yes, really,' Matthew snapped. 'And it's very important that I—'

'If you leave a phone number, I'll see if I can forward it to him,' the woman said coolly.

'I'm afraid that isn't good enough. I need to—'

'That's the best I can do, Mr Cosgrave. Do you wish to leave a number or not?'

It was clear to Matthew that the conversation had got as far as it was going. With as much good grace as he could muster, he gave her both his work and mobile numbers, stressed the importance of Toby contacting him as soon as possible, and rang off. He drummed his fingers and glared at the handset, unused to being spoken to in such a dismissive fashion. All he could do was to hope that the damned woman kept to her word and passed the message on. And that Toby would ring him back.

'Mr Cosgrave . . . ?' His secretary knocked, then ventured her head around the office door.

'I thought I told you I wasn't to be disturbed,' Matthew snapped, finding a wholly unworthy target for his pent-up frustration.

'Mr Masterton's been trying to get hold of you. He's got a meeting in London with the bank at three. He wants you down there by two with all the paperwork on the Italian sale.' She put a bulging folder down on the desk. 'I've got it all up to date for you.'

Matthew closed his eyes and ran a hand over his face. He knew how important the sale was to the company's long-term strategy. Various acquisitions to the core business were in the pipeline – hence Masterton's meeting with the bank – so non-profitable areas had to be identified and off-loaded as quickly as possible. Which was Matthew's remit. 'OK, Dorothy.' He forced a smile. 'Thanks. And sorry.'

'Coffee?'

'Please.' Matthew nodded, grateful that his secretary wasn't one to take offence. He opened the file, acutely aware that he hadn't given the problem anything like his full attention in the previous couple of weeks; equally aware that, Christmas or no Christmas, Masterton would be expecting to hear that he'd made some progress.

For the rest of the morning, Matthew managed to keep everything but work from his mind. He had a driver to take him down to the meeting, and spent the journey poring over the figures with a fine-tooth comb, coming to the conclusion that their only option was to take the marginally higher offer Montelli had just put in. He was still sure they could screw more out of the man if they had time, but they didn't. They needed the cash for the new projects. It was a question of short-term pain for long-term gain. He just wasn't sure Masterton would see it that way.

In the event, the meeting, which took place at Masterton's hotel, wasn't as difficult as Matthew had anticipated. Masterton, who had clearly spent his Christmas mulling the problem over, had come to much the same conclusion as Matthew himself.

'Never did think we'd screw the full asking price out of Montelli. Neither did Chambers.' Masterton swigged the coffee that was all he'd organised by way of lunch. 'The place needs millions spent on it to make it viable.'

It would have been helpful if either Masterton or Chambers had made their views clear from the outset, Matthew thought silently, remembering the protracted negotiations he'd endured in Italy.

'Got to keep you young upstarts on your toes.' It was as if Masterton had read his mind. 'Keep you earning your corn.'

Matthew, as always, found it impossible to know how far the older man was being serious. When he'd first gone to Langton Industrials, he'd found Frank Masterton's utter self-belief admirable; inspirational even. Lately, it had begun to irk him. Everything was so bloody black and white to him.

He wondered if the man might be secretly jealous of the fact that Matthew had found favour with Dan Chambers; the project had been Masterton's own until recently, after all. He found himself wondering how Chambers would react to the news that one of Langton's directors had stood trial for rape. It wasn't a pleasant prospect.

'Just make sure you stitch it up at no less than the price he's agreed. Montelli's bound to try to chuck in a few banana skins at the last minute. His sort always does.' Masterton checked his watch. The meeting had lasted barely half an hour.

Matthew, dragging his attention back to the matter in hand, nodded.

'Get it through smoothly and there could be a bit of a bonus in it for you.' Masterton got to his feet. 'Meet me back here for dinner at six thirty and I'll let you know how I've got on with those tight-arses at the bank.'

It wasn't so much an invitation as a command. Never mind that Matthew had another meeting scheduled back in Leamington at six, never mind that he might actually have preferred to eat at home instead of waiting on Masterton's convenience. But then, as the man said, if you wanted to get paid the salary, you earned it.

Once alone, Matthew ordered more coffee and a plate of sandwiches. Toby Gresham-Palmer had come flooding back into his thoughts now that work problems had temporarily receded. 'An accident' didn't tell him anything; for all he knew it could simply be Toby's way of getting out of show business; he'd hardly been a success, if Jonathan Freeman was anything to go by, and Toby had never been one to take failure lightly.

Matthew checked his mobile. He wasn't sure whether he was relieved or disappointed that there were no messages. He phoned the office, then Elizabeth, then the driver to break the news that the poor sod was likely to be hanging around until late.

He tried to estimate the size of any possible bonus. It shouldn't be hard to screw a better deal out of Montelli than Masterton was expecting. Maybe he and Elizabeth could fit in a decent holiday somewhere before the baby arrived . . .

Try as he might, his mind kept returning to Toby-Gresham Palmer.

On impulse, he took his personal organiser from his briefcase and looked up Jane Davenport's number. He hadn't spoken to her since she'd told him of Toby's accident; had cut the conversation abruptly short rather than risk letting slip something he might regret. He'd half expected her to ring again, but there had been no message from her on their return from Shropshire. He suspected his brusqueness might have offended her.

As he punched the number into the mobile, he wondered, somewhat guiltily, how she had spent her own Christmas. He realised how little he knew about her; how little he had asked her about herself. All Spike had mentioned was that she had a flat near his in Battersea. Matthew didn't even know if she had any family. He found himself hoping that she hadn't spent the holiday alone.

'Hello?'

Matthew could hear choral music playing faintly somewhere in the background. Closer to the phone, a cat mewed plaintively. Matthew tried to imagine Jane's flat, the solitary life she might be living there.

'It's me. Matthew,' he said. 'Matthew Cosgrave.'

'Yes?' She sounded wary.

'I'm in London.' The words were out of Matthew's mouth before he had time to think about them. 'Do you want to meet up for a drink?'

*   *   *

Matthew had a couple of hours to kill before he met Jane. He felt oddly nervous at the thought of seeing her again; wasn't sure why he had suggested the meeting at all, except that he owed it to Spike to make certain Jane was all right.

To pass the time until five rather than for any better reason, he decided to visit Spike's old college, which was no more than a brisk stroll from the smart Kensington hotel where Frank Masterton was staying. It was a bright, bitterly cold afternoon, the frost still unmelted on those stretches of pavement that the sun hadn't touched. Matthew relished the biting air after the overheated hotel. It was rare for him to have a couple of spare hours, and he made a conscious effort to clear his mind of all the other things he should have been doing and simply enjoy the exercise.

The college was oddly quiet when Matthew got there; the students were obviously still on holiday. Apart from a gathering of sober-suited men taking tea in the main reception hall – conference delegates, Matthew assumed – the place appeared largely deserted. He made his way past a series of darkened lecture theatres and along echoing corridors, shaking his head incredulously. The Blackport reunion seemed an age away, yet the academic system had slumbered through all that had happened in the intervening period. He'd always goaded Spike about the absurd length of university vacations. He felt a great wave of sadness that he'd never again be bombarded by his friend's outraged retorts to his teasing.

He and Elizabeth had often met Spike at the college before concerts; often enough for Matthew to be able to find his way without hesitation to Spike's study. He tried the heavy brass knob, unsurprised to find the door locked, more so to realise that the door-plate already bore a different name.

The study had been very much a part of Spike; much

more a reflection of his personality than the dingy flat in which he had spent so little of his time. Matthew wondered what had happened to the jumble of Spike's possessions that had cluttered every available surface, the shabby, eclectic mix of furniture that he had imported to crowd the small, comfortable room. He could understand Jane's need to be there so soon after Spike's death; the place had held the essence of the man.

'Can I help you?' An tall, elderly man, vaguely familiar with his stooping gait, eccentric hair and straggling beard, had emerged from a door further down the corridor.

'No, not really. I was just—'

'You're a friend of Spike Vardon's, aren't you?' The man's face crinkled into a smile. He joined Matthew and held out his hand. 'Oliver Leighton. We met at one of Spike's concerts.'

Matthew remembered. Spike had spoken highly of him, both as an academic and a colleague. 'Someone's taken his study already, I see,' he said, gesturing towards the new name label.

'Sad.' Oliver Leighton shook his head. 'Though inevitable, I suppose. Once you're gone, the waters close over your head without a—' He broke off, wincing. 'Sorry. Bad choice of metaphor.'

Matthew smiled despite himself. The unintentional pun had always appealed to Spike.

'Was there anything in particular, or did you just come to touch base?'

'Just that, I suppose.' Matthew shrugged, grateful that he didn't feel the need to fabricate a reason for the visit.

'Fancy a cup of tea?'

Matthew glanced at his watch. 'Sure. Why not?'

They walked together to the senior common room. Oliver Leighton talked about the impact Spike's death had had on

the college, the fondness of his students for him. It was
clear that the respect Spike had had for the older man was
reciprocated.

'He was a terrific teacher as well as a brilliant mind.'
Leighton dropped tea bags into a couple of mugs and
plugged in the kettle. 'It's a pretty rare combination, believe
me. How's his fiancée coping, by the way? He brought her
to one of the Faculty dinners. Smashing girl.' His expression
clouded. 'She must have been devastated.'

'Yes.'

The two men drank their tea in silence. After a while,
Matthew checked his watch again and got to his feet. 'I'm
meeting her shortly, as a matter of fact. I'd better make
tracks.'

'Do give her my very best regards.' Leighton unfurled his
gangly frame from his chair.

'I will.' Matthew shook the other man's hand as they
reached the door. 'Thanks for the tea.'

'Any time.' Leighton ducked his head, suddenly awkward.
'Spike rated you very highly, you know. He talked about you
and your wife with enormous fondness.'

He'd already turned to leave when Matthew said, 'Did
Spike seem happy?'

The abruptness of the question didn't seem to surprise
Leighton. 'Happier than I'd ever seen him,' he said, turning
back and scanning Matthew's face. As if to answer the
unspoken question he found there, he went on, 'There's
a lot of tittle-tattle in a community as close – some might
say as claustrophobic – as an academic department. There's
been a great deal of speculation about Spike Vardon's death,
as you can imagine. Well, let me tell you, I spoke to him just
the day before he went down to Cornwall that last time, and
he was like a dog with two tails. Why would someone so
completely, uncomplicatedly happy suddenly decide to kill

himself?' He pulled at his beard as if embarrassed by the vehemence of the question. 'It just wouldn't make sense.'

'No, it wouldn't.' Matthew shook his head sadly. 'No sense at all.'

13

It took Matthew longer to get back to the hotel than he had anticipated; the pavements were clogged with homeward-bound office workers, making the journey less a pleasant walk than an ill-tempered exercise in barging, weaving and stepping on and off kerbs to dodge swinging briefcases, shopping bags and the battalion of umbrellas raised against the needle-sharp sleet that had set in with the onset of darkness. Matthew hurried through reception to the dimly lit bar, pleased, after the scrum outside, to find the place all but deserted. Hot after his exertions, he was in the process of peeling off his overcoat and mopping his damp face with his handkerchief when a voice from a table in the corner spoke his name.

It was a second before Matthew realised that it was Jane Davenport. Her hair was brushed loose around her shoulders and, as she stood up to greet him, he noticed for the first time the shapeliness of her slim figure beneath her close-fitting trouser suit. There was nothing remotely provocative about her – her pale skin was still unadorned by any makeup, he saw as she came towards him – but, for the first time, Matthew was none the less very conscious of her as a woman, and an attractive one at that. It made him feel slightly uncomfortable.

'Thank you for coming,' he said rather formally when he had ordered drinks and they had returned to the table in the corner. 'I hope it wasn't too much of a trek for you to get here, but I've a meeting later, so there wasn't really time to—'

'I'm glad you called.'

The words might have increased Matthew's discomfort, but for the way they were spoken. For the first time, he noticed how tense Jane was. She was sitting on the very edge of her chair, the fingers of one thin hand working nervously at her engagement ring. Her nails, he noticed, were bitten to the quick.

'Sylvia Guttenberg rang me over Christmas. She said you'd been in touch with her.'

Matthew's hand tightened round his glass. He could guess what was coming next.

Jane looked at him hard. 'Why didn't you tell me you'd had a note too? And Pete Preston?'

'I didn't think . . .' Matthew swallowed. 'It didn't seem relevant.'

'Not *relevant*?' Jane's voice rose an octave. The barman glanced across, then discreetly away.

'I didn't want to upset you.' The man probably imagined they were having a lovers' tiff, Matthew thought inconsequentially.

'For God's sake, Matthew!' She glanced towards the bar and moderated her tone. 'I'm not a child.'

'You shouldn't listen to that woman. She's a trouble-maker.'

'As far as I can see, she's the only one telling me the truth.'

'And why do you think she's doing that?'

'Because she's concerned.'

Matthew snorted. 'I don't think altruism's that high on Sylvia Guttenberg's agenda.'

'Are you going to let me know what was in those notes?' Jane's voice was cold. 'Or am I going to have to find out for myself?'

Matthew looked into her taut face. Damn Sylvia Guttenberg

to hell. 'They were nonsense.' He repeated the rhyme, the carol, deliberately dismissive. 'Just stupid nonsense.'

Jane didn't need to speak; her expression did it for her.

Matthew sighed. 'And some silly references to the trial.'

'Tell me about her.'

'Who?' His eyes slid from Jane's searching gaze.

'You know who. Donna O'Mara.'

'I have done,' Matthew said, exasperated. 'She was a blackmailing little whore who got what was coming to her.'

'And is she still blackmailing you?'

'My God!' He gave a savage laugh. 'Sylvia Guttenberg has been busy!'

'As far as I knew, Spike had typed that note himself. And you were perfectly happy to let me go on believing that. So don't expect me to blame Sylvia Guttenberg for what's going on.'

Matthew closed his eyes. How the hell had he got himself involved in all this? 'I just didn't want you to—'

'Whoever wrote that note to Spike was responsible for his death.' Jane's voice was tight with fury. 'I think I have the right—'

'Don't you think I *know* that?' Matthew picked up his glass, his hand trembling.

Jane gave him a long look before she said, 'Maybe Donna O'Mara's still bearing a grudge against you all.'

'*She's* got a grudge? Have you the remotest idea what that bloody woman put us through?'

'But what if she's always seen things differently? You said yourself she was taken apart in court. What if she decided to get her own back by—'

'Christ! Here we go again!' Matthew attempted a bitter laugh. 'We're back to *The Curse of the* bloody *Virgin*, are we?'

'I'm serious,' Jane snapped. 'Sylvia's right. These things can fester in people's minds for years. What if—'

'Enough!' Matthew banged his glass down in frustration.

The barman, who had been checking the optics, coughed delicately.

'This was just what I was afraid of.' Matthew glanced across at the man, then lowered his voice. 'Can't you see what Sylvia bloody Guttenberg is trying to—' He broke off, struggled to control himself.

'She told me because she, at least, thought I ought to know. And because she's genuinely worried about you all.'

'Like hell she is!'

There was a long silence. Then Jane said quietly, 'Why are we arguing, Matthew? We're both on the same side, aren't we?'

'Yes.' Matthew picked up his drink, drained it. It was all so bloody complicated. For the briefest moment he felt an utter loss of control as all his problems seemed to join together, to surge towards him like a giant tidal wave: the Italian contract, the new baby, Daisy, Spike, all this stuff from the past coming up to haunt him . . . He breathed in deeply, forcing his emotions back under control as he replaced the glass more carefully on the table. 'Yes, of course we are.'

'Then will you hear me out?'

He sighed. 'If you think there's any point.'

'Something made Spike kill himself. Isn't that point enough?'

Another silence.

'Did he go in to the university the day you went down to Cornwall?' Matthew said, not really knowing what made him ask.

Jane frowned. 'I've no idea. Why?'

'Just that I was speaking to Oliver Leighton earlier, and he said how happy Spike seemed the day before. Which would suggest he hadn't seen the note at that point. I was just wondering when . . .'

'He could have done.' She gazed into space, concentrating. 'I've got a feeling he might have mentioned something about dropping off some books . . .' She bit her lip. 'That's the awful thing, isn't it? Not being able to ask.' Her voice wobbled. 'Not knowing.'

'It was just a thought.' Matthew was anxious not to upset her any more than he had already. 'We know he must have seen it sometime before you went down there. It's pretty academic when.'

'Tell me again what was written in the one you received,' Jane said after a moment. 'The exact words.'

Reluctantly, Matthew repeated them.

'One, two, three, four, five,' Jane repeated slowly. 'Spike, Pete, Toby . . .' She counted the names off on her fingers. 'Listen, I know it sounds far-fetched, but what if—'

Matthew knew what she was going to say without waiting for the end of the sentence. 'Far-fetched? It's total bloody rubbish!'

Dear God, it had to be rubbish. Didn't it? No rational person could seriously believe . . . With supreme effort, he said firmly, 'I think we've had enough "what ifs" for one evening. Let's try looking at this logically.' He counted off his own fingers. 'Pete was hurt in a hit-and-run on a dark night in poor visibility. It happens all the time. We've no idea yet what's happened to Toby, and there's no point in speculating until we do. I've left a message for him to get in touch with me. I'm sure there's some perfectly logical explanation. And as for Spike . . .' He looked down at his fingers.

Jane reached across the table, grasped his hand. 'Just promise me you'll be careful, Matthew. I couldn't bear it if anything happened—'

'I hope I'm not interrupting something.'

Matthew's head shot up to meet Frank Masterton's steely gaze. It was quite clear that the other man had entirely misinterpreted the situation.

Jane's reaction did nothing to put him straight; she dropped Matthew's hand, colouring deeply.

'Frank!' Matthew jumped to his feet, overhearty. 'Let me introduce you to Jane Davenport.'

Masterton gave her a curt nod.

'I must go.' Jane fumbled with her bag.

Matthew was suddenly angry. What right had Masterton to stand there like some kind of bloody avenging angel, whatever he imagined to be going on between them? He was Matthew's boss, for God's sake, not his spiritual bloody adviser. 'I'll be in touch,' he said, planting a very deliberate kiss on Jane's cheek. 'I'll call you as soon as I've heard from Toby.' He squeezed her arm. 'And don't worry. Everything's going to be fine.'

Jane nodded, cast a flustered glance in Frank Masterton's direction, and was gone.

'I'm not going to ask what that was about,' Masterton said as soon as she was out of earshot.

'Good.' Matthew could barely believe the nerve of the man. 'Now shall we get down to business? Because if it's all the same to you, I'd like to get home to my wife at some stage of the evening.'

Masterton blinked. For a moment, he appeared lost for words. Then he said, 'I value loyalty very highly in my staff. And my philosophy has always been that if a man can't be trusted at home, he can't be trusted at work either. And I can tell you that Dan Chambers, as a lay preacher, has much the same views. You'd do well to bear that in mind.'

The implicit threat was all too clear. 'For Christ's sake, Frank! She's a friend of the family. She was engaged to—'

'So you'd be quite happy if I told Elizabeth I'd seen you together this evening?' Masterton gave him a hard stare. 'No, I thought not. You're a fool, Matthew.'

Several different responses sprang to mind, at least one of which would have cost Matthew his job. He settled for, 'You've got entirely the wrong end of the stick. Jane and I are simply friends.' He was weary of all this subterfuge. It wasn't the way he operated; it never had been. But now it was as if every single area of his life were becoming infected by deception, pretence. It was only with difficulty that he controlled the utterly inappropriate urge to spill out the whole story. 'It's just . . . complicated,' he added lamely.

Masterton made a derisive noise in his throat. 'It always is.' He looked at Matthew as if expecting a response. Then pulling a sheaf of papers from his briefcase and spreading them over the table, he said briskly, 'However, as you're clearly in such a hurry to be off, let's get started, shall we?'

It was towards the end of an uncomfortable dinner that Matthew's mobile rang.

'Are you going to answer that damned thing or not?' Masterton snapped. His dislike of mobile phones was legendary.

'Whoever it is will leave a message,' Matthew said coolly. The call might be from Toby; he had no desire to conduct the conversation under Masterton's scrutiny.

A couple of moments later, the mobile signalled that he had a text message.

'Oh, for God's sake,' Masterton exhaled irritably.

'Excuse me.' Matthew took it from his pocket, perversely pleased to note the disapproval on the man's face.

The small triumph was short-lived. The illuminated dial told him he had one message received. He pressed the 'read' button. The sender's number was unfamiliar. He pressed the button again.

'take it u got 1 2,' the message read.

Matthew didn't need to re-examine the sender's details to realise the text had been sent by Toby Gresham-Palmer.

14

Matthew tried the number as soon as he left the hotel, but all he got was Toby's voice mail. He left a terse message telling Toby to ring, and sent a text for good measure.

For the first few miles of the journey out of London, the driver attempted conversation. He was an elderly man, a retired employee at Langton Industrials and a knowledgeable gardener. Matthew generally sat alongside him in the front, happy to talk, to pick up snippets of gossip about the company's past or compare notes on horticulture. On this occasion he took a seat in the back. He shut his eyes and feigned sleep, his mind racing as the driver eventually took the hint and petered off into silence. So Toby had also received a letter. When? What did it say? What had been Toby's reaction to it? Question after question sprang into Matthew's head. Surreptitiously, he tried the mobile again, and was again instructed to leave a message. The frustration of not being able to get through was almost unbearable.

It was after midnight when the driver dropped him off. Matthew was uneasy to see that the light was still on in the living room. For an absurd moment he wondered if Frank Masterton could have been in touch with Elizabeth; imagined her waiting to confront him in the way wronged wives did on the television. He felt himself tense as the door opened before he could find his key.

'Hi.' Elizabeth's face was weary, but her smile was warm as she stood aside to let him in.

'You're up late.' Matthew bent to kiss her, making a conscious effort to relax.

'Heartburn.' She placed a cradling hand across her stomach and grinned. 'I thought I might as well do something useful as I couldn't sleep, so I've been going through the credit card bill.'

It had always been a standing joke between the two of them; Matthew could quite cheerfully deal in millions every day at work, but it was Elizabeth who sorted out the household accounts with a scrupulous regard for every last penny entirely at odds with the size of their bank balance.

'Coffee?'

'Love one.' Matthew followed her back into the kitchen.

'There's an entry I can't sort out,' she said over her shoulder as she plugged in the kettle. Bills and receipts were spread out all over the kitchen table. 'It must be one of yours. Some place called . . .' she pushed her glasses onto her nose and ran a finger down the bill, 'Alla Moda Boutique, Blackport. Two hundred and ninety pounds.' She pulled a face. 'Seems an awful lot. What was it?'

Matthew sighed. He'd never told her about the scarf; the memory of the spectacle he'd made of himself with the shop-lifting incident wasn't one he'd been eager to share. 'It was something I'd bought you for Christmas. The weekend of the reunion. I . . . I lost it.'

'*Lost* it?'

'I put it down in a shop somewhere.'

'What, you mean someone stole it? Didn't you report it to the police?'

'No. I . . . The damned place was heaving. It would have been a complete waste of time.' He shrugged. 'You know how much I hate shopping. I'd have been stuck there for hours.'

'Matthew!' Elizabeth shook her head. 'What was it, anyway?'

'A scarf.'

'A *scarf*? For nearly three hundred *pounds*?' She couldn't have looked more shocked if he'd announced that he'd stolen it himself.

'We can afford it.' Matthew had always found her inability to comprehend their wealth endearing, when most of his colleagues' wives were only too happy to spend their salaries for them, by all accounts. He took her into his arms, more relieved to be back in the domesticity of his own kitchen than he could have begun to explain to her. 'You're worth it.'

'Shame I never got it, then,' Elizabeth grinned, pleased. 'Especially at that price.'

Toby Gresham-Palmer rang the following morning, his slightly strangled public school vowels instantly recognisable, even after so many years.

Matthew was in the middle of a budget meeting, so the conversation was by necessity tantalisingly brief, and Toby seemed reluctant in any event to discuss matters over the phone. His uncharacteristically evasive manner did nothing to alleviate Matthew's general unease, but it was clear that nothing further was to be gained until they could talk face to face.

Toby, it transpired, had gone back to live in Leicestershire, which made it feasible to meet. Matthew suggested the following evening, which was the only one he had free.

'We could meet halfway at a pub,' he suggested, hoping that Toby wasn't expecting an invitation to the house.

'No. You come here. Seven thirty. Do you know the way?'

'I'm not sure I can—'

'See you tomorrow.' The phone went dead.

Matthew stared at it in annoyance. Why the hell should he be the one to do all the travelling? And, he remembered belatedly, he and Elizabeth had arranged to go to the theatre, a production of *The Lion, the Witch and the Wardrobe* at the RSC that she'd been particularly looking forward to; a play that in previous years, she wouldn't have been able to face. The tickets had been booked for ages. He hesitated, on the point of ringing back. Toby always had been a patronising bastard. But if he didn't see the man tomorrow, it would have to be another week or so. He glanced around the board table at the half-dozen faces looking at him expectantly. Sod it. He'd just have to tell Elizabeth he was working late again, and get Dorothy to try to rebook.

'Sorry about that,' he said, attempting to drag his attention back to the matter in hand. 'Now where were we?'

It was a complete waste of time. Matthew struggled on with the meeting for a further half an hour then sent his mystified accountants back to their offices. After some deliberation, he rang Pete Preston to fill him in on the latest developments.

One of Pete's sons answered the phone.

'Dad's gone in to school,' he said, his cheerful voice competing with the blare of pop music. 'He always leaves everything till the last minute. Term starts Monday. Will Mum do?'

'No,' Matthew replied hastily. 'No, don't bother her.'

'Can I take a message?'

Matthew hesitated. 'Just tell him Toby's been in touch.'

'Hang on a sec.' The boy issued a muffled bellow to turn the music down. 'Tony's been in touch,' he repeated.

'Toby.'

'Oh, right. Got it.' The boy waited. 'D'you want him to call you back? He'll be in about—'

'No. Tell him I'll give him a ring in a couple of days.'

Matthew sat staring out of the boardroom window, wondering what Pete would make of the message, assuming his son got round to passing it on. He'd be bound to realise what it meant. Matthew wondered whether he should have mentioned Toby's accident.

He gazed at the mountain of paperwork awaiting his attention. He hadn't got time to waste like this, he told himself, drumming his fingers against the desk. He must focus, concentrate. He had a stack of things waiting for him in his office that needed his attention, not least the Italian deal. But they all seemed mundane, trivial compared to his impending reunion with Toby Gresham-Palmer. Matthew checked his watch. Another thirty-two and a half hours until they met. He hadn't experienced such a sense of fearful anticipation since he was a teenager on his first date. It was ridiculous. But, none the less, he knew he was going to find it utterly impossible to put his mind to anything else in the intervening period.

The following day, Matthew was proved wrong.

Pressure of work had dictated that he spend Saturday in the office. He was in the delicate process of rejigging the figures ahead of his planned visit to see Montelli, when his secretary, who had agreed to come in for the morning to type up reports, took the unprecedented step of bursting into the office without knocking.

'Your phone was switched through.' She flapped her hand inconsequentially towards her own adjoining office. 'I—'

'Well?' Matthew, who had been finding it almost impossible to concentrate without the added distraction of such interruptions, threw down his pen and glared up at her. It took him a moment to register the expression on the woman's face.

'It's your wife, Mr Cosgrave,' she said. 'There's been some kind of an accident.'

The drive from Langton Industrials to the Royal Warwick and Leamington Hospital took Matthew less than half an hour, but it seemed like an eternity. He wove and honked his way through the Leamington traffic and out onto the narrow country road that joined the two towns, his heart hammering, his brain sending unformed, frantic prayers to a God in whom he did not believe.

The entrance to the hospital was obstructed by building work; Matthew was forced to wait at temporary traffic lights while an ambulance flashed past the other way. His hands trembling, he slammed the car into gear as soon as the lights showed amber, and screeched his way around diversion signs that wound him past several car parks, all packed.

The forecourt of Accident and Emergency, when he finally reached it, was a jumble of ambulances. Cars were jammed bonnet to bumper on the kerbs, the grass, every available inch of space. Matthew swerved in past a 'No Entrance' sign and abandoned the Jaguar alongside one of the ambulances.

'Oi, you can't park there, mate.' A voice floated after him as he sprinted towards the automatic doors. Ignoring it, Matthew ran inside.

The place was heaving. Several dozen people sat slumped on ranks of grey plastic chairs. Some turned to look at him without interest, most simply sat staring ahead. There was a queue in front of the reception desk. An elderly man, his hand cupped to his ear, was being asked his address. Behind him, a harassed-looking woman was jiggling a bawling toddler on her hip. A young man in overalls stood impassively behind her, his hand raised above his head and wrapped in a bloodied teatowel.

Matthew shoved his way to the front of the queue. 'I'm looking for my—'

The receptionist glanced up, her face closed and hostile. 'There's a queue.' She went back at deafening volume to her request for the old man's address.

'No, you don't understand.' Matthew shouldered the man out of the way. 'My wife . . .'

'Oi, you.' He felt a tug on his arm and wheeled round to find himself face to face with an irate porter. 'Move your bloody car. You're blocking in the ambulances.'

'Move it yourself.' Matthew fumbled in his pocket, thrust the keys at him.

'It'll get clamped.'

'Whatever.' He took a handful of notes from his wallet, threw them at the porter and turned back to the receptionist.

'You'll have to wait your turn,' she said, without shifting her eyes from the form she was filling in. 'Number twenty-six, did you say, dear?'

Matthew grabbed the pen from her hand and hurled it down onto the counter. 'For God's sake, you stupid woman . . .'

This time, the woman did look up. She raised an eyebrow at the porter and said in a bored voice, 'Call Security.'

'Will someone, for Christ's sake, just tell me what has happened to my wife?' Matthew yelled the words with such desperate force that for a moment the crowded room fell silent.

A young Asian woman in a white coat appeared from one of the curtained cubicles that led off the main waiting area. 'You are Mr Cosgrave?' she asked quietly.

Wordlessly, Matthew nodded.

'Come this way, please.'

Matthew felt his legs go to jelly. The adrenalin that had got him from the factory to the hospital in record time deserted him. He followed the young doctor slowly through the door she held open for him.

He didn't want to know, he realised.

They went into in a small waiting room. Matthew took the seat the doctor indicated and wiped his sweating palms across his knees as he scanned her grave face for a clue of what was to come.

'Your wife has had a fall,' she said, sitting herself down opposite him.

'Fall?' Matthew echoed stupidly.

'It seems she lost her balance while waiting to cross the Parade in Leamington Spa. Unfortunately, she fell into the path of a motorcyclist.'

Oh God, he'd asked her to pick up that refill for his fountain pen. Why hadn't he just used a bloody Biro? Why had he let her . . . ?

'Mr Cosgrave?' The doctor leant forward and touched his hand.

Matthew shook his head as if to clear it. He looked down at the slim brown hand resting on his own, then, swallowing hard, looked up into the woman's face. 'Is she dead?' he whispered.

'No, no. Your wife sustained only relatively minor injuries. A sprained ankle, a few abrasions . . .'

'A sprained ankle?' Matthew felt faint with relief. He laughed out loud. 'Christ, I wondered what on earth you were going to tell me! I thought for a moment there—' He broke off.

The doctor was gazing at him, her eyes still displaying that same, terrifying compassion.

'What?' His voice rose in panic. *'What?'*

'There's a strong possibility that she's going to lose the baby, Mr Cosgrave. There's been some bleeding . . .' The doctor shook her head. 'The gynaecologist is with her now. I think it would be wise for you to prepare yourself for the worst.'

'Oh, is that—' Matthew checked himself. *Is that all,* was what he'd been about to say. The extent of his relief shocked him. But there could be other pregnancies, other babies. Elizabeth was all that mattered.

The doctor's eyes flicked across his face, her expression impenetrable. 'Your wife will need a great deal of support, Mr Cosgrave.'

'Of course.' Matthew nodded. 'Yes, of course. When can I see her?'

'She's been transferred to the pre-natal ward. You can go over there now, if you wish.' The doctor got to her feet. She flexed her neck in a gesture that spoke of infinite weariness.

Matthew made his way over to the maternity block. As he entered, a young couple came out, the woman cradling a swaddled new-born baby, the man laden with flowers, bags, a shiny pink balloon. Matthew stood aside to let them through and found his eyes were stinging with unwelcome tears.

Once on the pre-labour ward, he was shown into another shabby waiting room. After a while, the porter came in with Matthew's car keys and money. It was against all the regulations, but he'd parked the Jaguar in front of the doctors' residences, he said quietly. Matthew could pick it up any time he liked. Matthew nodded, barely registering the man's words. After another few minutes, the obstetrician appeared and confirmed the worst; the scan had shown no heartbeat. If Elizabeth didn't go into labour spontaneously within the following twenty-four hours, she would be induced.

'I'd like her to be transferred to a private room.' It was all Matthew could think to say.

'As you wish.' The obstetrician raised his shoulders slightly. 'It will make no difference to the outcome, I'm afraid.'

Elizabeth was in a side ward. The door was closed, but the glass panel in it allowed Matthew to observe her for a moment before he went in. She was lying on her back, staring at the ceiling, her left ankle bandaged, her cheeks marble-white but for the angry graze above her jaw. Matthew felt his heart contract. He pushed the door open, trying to formulate some word of comfort, anything that might take away the blank despair in Elizabeth's face.

'Oh, sweetheart,' he whispered, his hand closing around her limp fingers. 'I'm so sorry.' He lifted her hand to his lips. 'So very, very sorry.'

Elizabeth continued to stare at the ceiling. It was as if he hadn't spoken.

It wasn't until late the following night that Matthew left the hospital. He rang his mother-in-law to tell her it was finally over, then stood outside the maternity unit and stared up at the stars.

The foetus had been perfect: another little girl.

Matthew put back his head and shouted at the top of his voice, 'Fuck you, if you're up there.' Tears poured down his cheeks unchecked. 'Fuck you.'

15

It was almost midnight by the time Matthew got back to the house. The phone in the hall was flashing that he had seven messages, but he had neither the energy nor the inclination to listen to them. Instead, he went straight to bed and fell into a deep, mercifully dreamless sleep born of sheer exhaustion, from which he was reluctantly dragged at well after eleven the following morning by the arrival of an apologetic police constable. An accident report had to be completed, the young man explained, when Matthew had let him in. Just the formalities. Nothing to worry about.

'So what happened, exactly?' Matthew asked when he had made them both a strong coffee. He cleared his throat. With wakefulness had returned the heart-breaking memories of the previous night. He wished he could have slept for longer.

The constable was unable to add a great deal to the information Matthew had received in A&E. Elizabeth had apparently been standing at a pelican crossing when she had slipped off the kerb and into the path of the motorcyclist, who, fortunately, had slowed down as he'd approached the lights. The pavements had been crowded with shoppers taking advantage of the January sales. The most probable explanation was that someone had jostled her and made her lose her balance.

Suddenly, Matthew was wide awake. 'You're saying she was pushed?'

'Oh no, nothing deliberate, sir.' The constable looked startled.

'Were there any witnesses?'

'Several people saw the accident itself. And of course the motorcyclist—'

'But no one saw what made her slip?'

'Not as far as I'm aware, sir.' The younger man's tone was more guarded. He paused for a moment as if weighing his words then asked, 'Do you have any reason to suspect that Mrs Cosgrave might have been pushed?'

It was on the tip of Matthew's tongue to blurt out the whole thing: Spike's suicide, Pete's accident, Toby's . . . Was it possible that something terrible had happened to them all; was still happening? The words of the rhyme came back to him, unbidden, making the skin prickle on the back of his neck. *One, two, three* . . . Spike, Pete, Toby . . .

'Mr Cosgrave?' The policeman's gaze was fixed on him.

Matthew shivered. He looked back into the earnest young face. How could he hope to make him understand? Even as he sought the right words, he realised how ridiculous it would sound. A curse put upon them for a twenty-five-year-old crime they hadn't even committed? The man would think he was mad.

'No.' He rubbed his hand over his stubbled cheek and shook his head wearily. 'Just trying to find an explanation, I guess.'

'People often do.' The constable looked relieved. Conspiracy theories, his expression suggested, were not in a uniformed constable's remit. He fiddled for a moment with his notebook, his face creasing into a frown of genuine concern. 'I understand from the hospital that your baby—'

'Yes.' Matthew drank down his scalding coffee. 'Now, unless there's anything else . . . ?'

'I don't think so, sir.' The constable put away the notebook and stood up. To Matthew's surprise, he offered his hand and said quickly, 'I'm so sorry. The loss of a child . . . Well, there's nothing quite so bad, is there?' With an embarrassed duck of the head, the constable made for the door. 'Don't bother to get up. I'll see myself out.'

Alone again, Matthew put his head between his hands and took a few deep breaths, then went to the phone. The handset flashed that he had seven messages. Matthew ignored them, and rang the hospital. Mrs Cosgrave was as well as could be expected, was the unhelpful reply to his enquiry. He asked if he could speak to her, was told to hold the line, and after some muffled conversation, was informed that Mrs Cosgrave was asleep. Matthew suspected from the nurse's tone that it was more likely that Elizabeth had refused to speak to him.

'Tell her I'll be in this afternoon,' he said wearily. He put the phone down, wondering if he should have added a more personal message – that he loved her, perhaps.

With some reluctance, he played back the messages that had accumulated while he had been at the hospital. The first was from his secretary, asking after Elizabeth and warning him that Masterton had been in touch with some queries on the budget figures. Predictably, Masterton's voice boomed down the line next, audibly irritable that Matthew wasn't available. It wasn't until the end of his lengthy message, and after he had issued an injunction that Matthew call him back over the weekend and a reminder of Dan Chambers' presence at the board meeting in London on Monday afternoon that he added a brief and somewhat tetchy hope that Elizabeth was feeling better. It was Monday today, Matthew realised. He glanced at the hall clock, which showed it was already nearly twelve.

Tough.

There were two messages from Elizabeth's mother, who was due to arrive from Hampshire the following day, and one from her sister, asking where she should send flowers. The sixth was from Mothercare to inform them that the pram Elizabeth had ordered was in stock. Matthew, swallowing hard, quickly pressed the delete button. He didn't even know she'd been looking at prams. Why hadn't he tried harder to share her happiness? Why, as always, had he been too busy, too preoccupied to cherish what he had until it was too bloody late?

Toby Gresham-Palmer's voice was like a slap in the face as the final message played. Matthew closed his eyes. Christ, he'd forgotten all about their meeting. He wondered briefly how Toby had acquired his home number. But then Toby had always been able to talk the birds down from the trees; Matthew's secretary would have been no match for his charm.

'Where the hell were you last night?' Toby's voice sounded slightly slurred, as if he had been drinking. 'I'll expect you tomorrow. Same time. Unless you've chickened out, of course.'

Matthew was chilled by the bitterness of the laugh that accompanied Toby's parting shot.

He dropped in at work on his way to the hospital. He called in one of his accountants, an able if somewhat pushy and over-ambitious woman in her early thirties and, with the sketchiest of briefings, informed her that she'd have to hold the fort at the board meeting. The woman assured him she'd manage. Matthew found himself harbouring the unworthy hope that she wouldn't manage too well.

He stopped at a florist near the factory and bought a huge bunch of roses. A young man, taking the stairs down from the maternity unit two at a time as Matthew trudged up them, grinned at the flowers and offered his congratulations.

Elizabeth had been transferred to a room at the very end of the small private wing adjacent to the main maternity ward.

The door to her room was closed. She was lying in exactly the same position as when Matthew had left her the previous evening. She didn't turn her head as he entered, she didn't acknowledge the flowers, she didn't answer when Matthew, with mounting desperation, asked her how she was feeling. She just continued to stare at the ceiling. Her face, when he bent down to kiss her, was as cold and unyielding as if she were carved in stone. For some minutes, Matthew stood beside the bed, just holding her hand. He had absolutely no idea what to do or say. He had the unnerving feeling that he was in the presence of a total stranger.

'Give her time, Mr Cosgrave,' the sister on duty in the nurses' station said in her soft Scottish voice, when he expressed his concern. 'It's very early days.'

Matthew found her sympathetic smile intensely irritating. She knew nothing about Elizabeth, about either of them.

'I'd like to speak to her consultant,' he said briskly.

'I'm afraid Mr Rhodes is in theatre all afternoon.'

'When he's finished, then.'

'I'm not sure—'

'My wife is a private patient.'

A little of the sympathy went from the sister's smile. 'Mr Rhodes treats his patients on the basis of their clinical need, Mr Cosgrave, not their financial status.'

'Of course.' Matthew ran a hand through his hair. It had been an ill-judged comment, and he knew it. 'I'm sorry. It's just that Elizabeth . . . my wife . . .' He attempted to search for the right words, horrified to realise that he was on the verge of tears 'She's normally so . . .'

'But things aren't normal just now, are they?' The sister's voice was gentle.

'No.' Matthew swallowed hard. Christ, he'd almost forgotten what normal was.

The sister patted his hand in a gesture that, to his surprise,

Matthew found not patronising, but oddly comforting. 'I'll let Mr Rhodes know you're here. Now why don't you go back and sit with your wife?'

Matthew struggled to think of things to say to fill the silence of the room; he talked about work. He talked about the ideas he had for a new rockery in the front garden. He talked about holidays and how they would organise something really special once Elizabeth was feeling stronger. He talked about anything he could think of that didn't involve babies.

Elizabeth continued to stare at the ceiling.

A nurse knocked and came in with a tray of tea. Through the open doorway came the distant sound of a baby's cry. Elizabeth's jaw tightened. The expression that flickered across her face was unbearable.

The afternoon dragged on. By the time Rhodes arrived, just before six, Matthew had begun to glance uneasily at his watch. It was going to take him at least an hour to get to the village where Toby lived. He didn't want to miss the meeting for a second time; something in Toby's laugh had warned him that there might not be a third.

The obstetrician examined Elizabeth briefly, asked her a couple of questions that went unanswered and murmured reassuringly that she was doing well. He turned to Matthew.

'I think your wife would be much better at home, Mr Cosgrave.'

Matthew was horrified. How could the idiot think of discharging her when she was so patently in need of treatment?

'She's recovering well. She really doesn't need to be here.'

'But . . .' Matthew glanced at Elizabeth and lowered his voice. 'Maybe we could have a word outside.'

Rhodes smiled his professional smile. 'Certainly. Will you excuse us for a moment, Mrs Cosgrave?'

'Recovering well?' Matthew exploded as soon as they were

out in the corridor. 'You've seen what she's like. How can you possibly make out—'

'Physically, she's doing fine. Emotionally, she's responding as very many women respond.' Rhodes consulted the notes he had in his hands. 'This isn't your wife's first pregnancy, I see.' He looked up over the top of his glasses.

'No.' Matthew cleared his throat. 'We . . . we had a little girl. She died five years ago.'

'I see.' The man nodded gravely. In the main ward at the other end of the corridor, a baby screamed vigorously. Rhodes put his hand on Matthew's shoulder. 'Take your wife home, Mr Cosgrave. This isn't the right place for either of you. Don't worry, we'll keep a close eye on her via your GP. If she doesn't improve, she can be treated as an outpatient.' He smiled reassuringly. 'But I'm sure that won't be necessary.'

'OK.' Matthew rubbed a weary hand across his eyes. The man was probably right. 'Elizabeth's mother's coming up tomorrow, so . . .'

'Good. It's best that Mrs Cosgrave isn't on her own too much for the time being.' Rhodes scribbled something in the notes and headed back into Elizabeth's room. 'Your husband's going to take you home now, Mrs Cosgrave. I'll just write you out a prescription for—'

'Tomorrow.' Matthew's voice came out far louder than he had intended. 'I . . . I can't take you home tonight, darling.' He glanced from Elizabeth to Rhodes. 'I've got an important meeting.'

'A meeting?' Rhodes' expression gave nothing away.

'Frank Masterton.' Matthew turned back to Elizabeth. 'You know what he's like . . .'

How easily the lies came, once he'd started.

Slowly, Elizabeth moved her head so that for the first time she was looking at him. Or through him. It was impossible to tell which.

'Tomorrow will do,' she said tonelessly.

Matthew drove at break-neck speed through the Leicestershire countryside.

'A *meeting*,' he repeated savagely. What kind of a heartless bastard must Rhodes have thought him? More to the point, what must Elizabeth have thought? He slammed his foot on the brakes as yet another set of traffic lights turned to red as he approached them. 'Fuck Toby Gresham-Palmer,' he shouted. 'Fuck Donna O'Mara. Fuck the whole miserable fucking business.'

The village of Sileby-on-the-Wreake was easier to find than Matthew had anticipated. He stopped briefly at the local pub to ask directions to the address Toby had given him, and was told it was the gatehouse to Sileby Manor, a quarter of a mile further down the road. Matthew turned in through the vast ivy-clad gateposts at exactly seven thirty.

He turned off the engine. Some several hundred yards down the wide driveway, he could make out the gabled silhouette of the manor house. Matthew found himself wondering briefly what Toby made of living in the shadow of such an impressive-looking place; the gatehouse itself was a much more modest affair.

Matthew knocked. The faint babble of a television from somewhere inside was silenced, but no one came to the door. He knocked again.

'It's open.' Toby's voice floated out to him.

Matthew pushed the door open and stepped inside. The hallway was unlit. It took his eyes a moment to become accustomed to the gloom. Stepping cautiously round a cluttered coat-stand, he called Toby's name.

'In here.'

A feeble chink of reddish light showed under the door at the far end of the hall. Matthew made his way towards it, tripping over the edge of a rug as he did so. He could feel his anger rising as he grabbed at the banister and regained his balance. It was like being on the set of some silly bloody horror film. He suspected Toby had stage-managed the entire charade in order to take the piss.

He swung the door open with considerable force. The room was stiflingly hot after the chill of the hallway. A fire, the only source of light, blazed in the hearth, its flames casting weird, flickering shadows across the cluttered furniture. Heavy red velvet curtains swathed the windows. Again, Matthew had the impression of walking on to a film set.

'Come in.'

A big wing chair stood in front of the fire, placed in such a way that its back was to the door. Matthew could make out the top of Toby's sleek blond head. He breathed in sharply. He'd left Elizabeth in that bloody hospital, he'd broken his neck to get here, and the prat was trying to make a theatrical production out of it.

'Let's just get on with this,' he snapped. 'I haven't come here to play your stupid games.'

'Games?' Toby didn't move. 'Are there going to be games?' His voice was mocking. 'Oh goody.'

Matthew's anger boiled over. 'Christ, you haven't changed, have you? You always were—'

'Oh, I don't think anyone could accuse me of not changing.' Toby got to his feet. Slowly, he turned round.

If he'd been hoping to make an impact, he succeeded. Matthew took an involuntary step backwards, his hand flying to his mouth. He could feel acrid bile rising in his throat.

'Oh Jesus,' he whispered. 'Sweet Jesus. Whatever happened to you?'

16

Matthew was unable to drag his eyes from Toby Gresham-Palmer's face. Or what was left of it. Seams of scarring crisscrossed the cheeks and forehead. There was a nightmarish lack of symmetry: one eye higher than the other, the nose truncated and off-centre. More than anything, the once-handsome face resembled something that had been left out for too long in the sun, the features melted, running in to each other. One corner of Toby's mouth was eaten away, leaving the teeth bared, as if in a permanent snarl.

The startling blue of the now-lashless eyes was the only reminder of how he had once looked. That, and the hint of sardonic laughter in them as Toby drawled, 'You take my point. I have, in fact, changed quite considerably.' He gestured to a second winged chair. 'Sit down. You look as if you need a drink, my friend.'

Shakily, Matthew crossed the room and did as he was bidden. He took the glass that Toby offered, not caring what it held, and drank the burning liquid down in one. Toby drank his own, slopping it awkwardly into the good side of his mouth in an action that didn't quite stop some of it dribbling down his cheek. He refilled both glasses then bent down to throw another log on the already raging fire. Although Matthew was already sweating profusely it was a relief. At least the movement turned the hideous face away from him for a moment. He took a more measured sip of the brandy and attempted to compose himself.

'So . . .' Toby resumed his seat and stretched his legs out to the fire. 'You asked what happened.' The snarl widened into what Matthew could only assume was a grin. 'One could say I was hoist on my own petard.'

Matthew's heart lurched. 'Donna O'Mara,' he said in a low voice.

To his amazement, Toby threw back his head and roared with laughter. 'Donna O'Mara? Dear God, what a very provincial notion!'

When Toby Gresham-Palmer stopped laughing, he started talking. And once he started talking, he didn't stop. It was almost as if he were taking a perverse pleasure in reliving the event two years earlier that had ruined both his face and his life.

He'd been working in the West End, he said, describing a glittering acting career entirely at odds with Jonathan Freeman's assessment. He'd been using drugs recreationally for years – everyone did, he added, glancing at Matthew as if expecting a response – and had ended up doing a bit of supplying. Just for friends. Then he'd met up with a guy who travelled around a lot. The guy had access to a cheap source of cocaine, Toby had access to any number of enthusiastic punters. It had seemed a marriage made in heaven.

'Do you fancy a quick snort now, by the way?' Toby broke off his narrative to enquire.

'No.' Matthew had the distinct impression the other man was enjoying shocking him.

'There's a surprise. You always were a boring bastard.' Toby reached for the brandy bottle and put it on the table between them before resuming his monologue.

'Naturally, it couldn't last, any more than any other marriage.' He poured himself a generous measure and gestured towards Matthew's glass. 'You hitched up, by the way?'

Matthew nodded, but didn't speak.

'Yes, of course you are. You would be.' The snarl widened horribly again. 'So.' Toby emptied his glass. 'Where was I?' The brandy was beginning to take its toll; his words slurred slightly as he went on, 'There are some seriously big players out there, Matthew, my friend. Seriously big. I guess I got on someone's tits.' He sneered. 'Trod on someone's toes, if the phrase offends you less. I was coming out of a club one night when, guess what? Whoosh!'

Matthew recoiled as the dregs of Toby's brandy spattered his cheek.

'A faceful of battery acid, that's what.' Toby gave a bitter laugh. 'What you might call the ultimate make-over.'

Matthew didn't know what to say. 'Couldn't plastic surgery . . . ?'

'Have made it all better? I don't think so, do you?' Toby sounded bored. 'I couldn't see the point of spending months in hospital to end up looking like a poorly made patch-work quilt.'

Anything would have been an improvement, Matthew thought but didn't say. 'Did they catch whoever did it?' he asked instead.

'Oh, sure. I trotted along to the police station and said, "Please, Mr Plod, a nasty drugs baron threw acid at me, just because I relieved him of a few of his customers."' Toby dropped the little-boy whine. 'Christ, Matthew, what planet have you been on for the last twenty-five years?'

'You didn't *tell* them?' Matthew asked, astounded. 'No one asked what had happened?'

'Well, of course they wanted to *know*,' Toby snapped. 'And I wanted to stay alive. Whoever threw that acid cut off a piece of my hair. Now I don't know whether I'd just been watching too many films, but that suggested to me that they wanted my DNA. It was a neat way of letting me know that they'd be able to find me, even if I changed my identity,' he gave a hollow laugh, 'which in the circumstances would have been difficult enough, you have to agree.' He shrugged, his indifference not entirely convincing. 'I told the boys in blue that it had probably been a wronged husband. There'd been plenty to choose from, over the years, believe it or not.' Another bitter laugh. 'Needless to say, the police didn't pin it on anyone. I'm not sure they tried all that hard.'

It was understandable, Matthew thought. Toby would hardly have engendered much sympathy.

'So I came back here to Mummy and Daddy with my tail between my legs. If you'll pardon the pun. My tail being more usually between someone else's legs, in those halcyon days.'

Matthew ignored the remark. 'Your parents live in the manor house?'

'Aren't you impressed?'

There was malice in Toby's tone. The bastard had always looked down on him, even when they were at university.

'They've disowned me, naturally,' Toby went on. 'A disgrace to the family name and all that. Still,' he shrugged, 'I get this hovel rent free and an allowance just big enough to keep me pissed most of the time, so one mustn't complain.' He stared into the fire for a long moment. 'But enough of me. What about these voices from the past, then? You've had something, too? Yes, of course you have.' He prodded Matthew's arm and giggled campishly. 'Why else would you be here? I have to say I find the whole thing quite exciting, compared to my normal dull grey life. It's not often I get two visitors in one week.'

'Two?' Matthew was instantly alert.

Toby nodded. 'An old flame, no less. Although I fear my appearance dampened her ardour somewhat. Still, it was pleasant to talk about old times.' He glanced at Matthew. 'And more recent developments, of course. I didn't make the reunion, for fear of putting folks off their dinner, so I rather enjoyed—'

'Sylvia Guttenberg,' Matthew said flatly.

'Just so. Sylvia Johnson as was. She said you'd met.'

'You used to go out with her?'

Toby laughed. 'Hardly that. I fucked her once after a swimming club party. She was rather tiresome about it for a while afterwards, as I recall. It's usually the plain ones who expect undying love, in my experience.'

'What did she want?' Matthew attempted to disguise his disgust.

'Not another fuck, unfortunately. I have to say, she's aged remarkably well. I didn't recognise her.' Toby pulled himself unsteadily to his feet and reached over to the mantelpiece. 'No, she wanted much the same as you do, I imagine.' He dangled a postcard between thumb and finger, pulling back coquettishly as Matthew reached for it. 'I tell you what. I'll show you mine, if you show me yours.'

He scanned the note Matthew withdrew from his wallet. 'When did you get it?'

'A couple of days after Spike drowned.'

'Yes, Sylvia told me about him. Poor sod.' For a moment, Toby appeared genuinely moved. Then recovering himself, he handed over the postcard. 'It's clearly a serial mailshot, then. This arrived just after Christmas.'

Michelangelo's *David*. The face bore a poignantly strong resemblance to how Toby had once looked, Matthew realised, remembering him as he'd preened on the top diving board the first time they'd met. He turned the card over, knowing what would be written there before he looked. There were no additional words, this time. Maybe the statue had been deemed comment enough. The postmark showed it had been posted in Blackport on Christmas Eve.

'You let Sylvia Guttenberg see this, I take it?'

'I did. I found the interest of an attractive woman rather
gratifying, I have to say. It's all too rare these days.'

'Pete thinks she sent them.'

'Does he now?' It was difficult to read the expression on a
face so hideously marred. 'And why would he think that?'

'Publicity?' It sounded ludicrously feeble, even to Matthew's
own ears.

There was no mistaking the derision in Toby's snort of
laughter. 'I'd have thought it was absolutely bloody obvious
from whence these charming little missives have emanated,
wouldn't you?'

'But why, after all these years? For what motive?'

Toby lifted his shoulders in an elegant shrug at odds with
the face above them. 'Money, I imagine. Is there another
motive for blackmail? She clearly barked up the wrong tree
with poor old Spike.' Toby shook his head. 'I certainly
haven't got any money, and it doesn't sound as if Pete's
especially loaded. So unless Ben's done more with his life
than I'd expect—'

'He's a priest,' Matthew said impatiently. 'But I don't know
what you're—'

'A priest!' Toby gave a cackle of laughter. 'Well, bugger me!
If you'll excuse the phrase. Must have set a few bats flying in
his belfry, if she's been after him, then.' He seemed to find
the notion vastly amusing, in much the same way as he'd
appeared to regard the trial itself as amusing; his supercilious
smirk hadn't earned them any friends on the jury. Try as he
might, Matthew could summon no sympathy for the wreck
the man had become.

'Looks like you're it then, if our little Donna's decided it's
pay-back time. Rolex watch,' Toby nodded at Matthew's
wrist, 'that rather classy motor you rolled up in. The boy
done good, as the saying goes.'

'Are you insane? Play into the hands of that blackmailing

bitch?' Matthew jumped to his feet. Why was he wasting time trying to get sense out of this drunken lunatic? 'I'm going to the police. It's what I should have done in the first place.'

'*Me* insane?' Toby had dropped the glib façade instantly. He reached over and grabbed Matthew's arm, his grip surprisingly strong. 'What the hell good will going to the police do any of us?'

'So what do you suggest? Wait for Donna O'Mara to state her price and pay up?'

'Sounds good to me.'

Matthew looked at him coldly. 'Let go of me, please.'

'You fancy a spell inside, do you?' Toby's fingers dug deeper into his arm. 'Because don't kid yourself, chum, that's what will happen if she sets her mind to it. Hubert Vardon might have thought we were off the hook with that double indemnity crap, but there's the small matter of perjury. And even after twenty-five years—'

'Hubert Vardon? Double indemnity? What the hell are you—' Matthew broke off. Toby's grip had relaxed. He was laughing again. Laughing until the tears rolled down his ruined face.

'Dear God, Matthew,' he spluttered at last, wiping his eyes with the sleeve of his shirt. 'You don't know, do you? All that too-drunk-to-remember crap wasn't just a smart get-out after all. You really don't know!'

17

Matthew had no idea where he was driving and he didn't care. He watched the needle on the speedometer touch ninety and he didn't care. He'd been living a lie. His whole life, all their lives, had been a lie for the past twenty-five years. And all of them had known it but him.

Toby had seemed to think it was a huge joke; couldn't believe that Matthew *really* had no recollection of what had happened that night. They'd all assumed that Matthew had simply come up with a good cover story and was sticking to it, Toby said.

Matthew caught his own reflection in the driver's mirror. Did he look different? Would everyone be able to tell? How could he ever share Elizabeth's bed again, knowing what he'd done?

'Rapist,' he shouted at the top of his voice.

He was aware of headlights, the blare of a horn, the screech of brakes. He didn't care.

'Rapist.'

Matthew was never sure how far he drove that night. Eventually, he somehow found his way onto the M69 and towards home. It was late, the middle of the night, so he must have been in the car for hours. How he had avoided an accident, he'd never know.

As he began to calm down, think more rationally, he began to feel more than a little foolish to have taken Toby's bombshell at face value. The man was unhinged; years of overindulgence in alcohol and drugs had clearly addled his brain. The dramatic revelation he'd contrived had been no more than a malicious wind-up; part of the whole, stage-managed evening. He'd always made it clear that he considered Matthew a prig; would no doubt have taken delight in trying to shock him. And how magnificently he had succeeded! Matthew winced as he relived the moment. He couldn't have reacted more hysterically if Toby had written the bloody script for him. Under normal circumstances, he'd have seen through the man for what he was; the shock of Elizabeth's accident must have unsettled him, blunted his judgement, that was all.

He turned on the radio, allowing himself an incredulous laugh as he settled himself more comfortably in his seat and steered the car off the motorway and towards home. Christ, he'd nearly driven straight to the nearest police station and handed himself in!

It was as if his thoughts had summoned them. Suddenly, Matthew became aware of flashing blue lights. He felt a moment of utter panic as the patrol car drew alongside him and signalled for him to stop. What if it wasn't a wind-up at all? He gripped the steering wheel, sweat suddenly pouring from his palms. How could the police have known who he was? Where to find him? Maybe if he put his foot down, swerved off down the next sideroad . . .

He pulled over onto the verge.

The patrol car pulled in behind him. One of the officers got out and strode towards him. Wiping his palms on his trousers, Matthew wound down the window and said in a voice that amazed him by its steadiness, 'What seems to be the problem, officer?'

'Would you get out of the car, please, sir?'

Matthew complied, his heart pounding so much that he had to steady himself against the car door.

'Have you drunk any alcohol this evening, sir?'

'Well, I . . .' Trepidation followed swiftly on the heels of Matthew's relief as he remembered the amount of brandy that he and Toby had consumed between them.

'Would you mind blowing in here, sir?' the policeman said.

Matthew poured himself a further brandy when he got back to the house; after the evening he'd had, he felt he deserved it. He'd come within an inch of losing his licence; the policeman had left him in no doubt about that. Only one more bar on the intoximeter and the light would have gone from amber to red. Matthew had accepted the man's lecture without argument, promised to be more careful in future, cravenly grateful to have escaped arrest. The incident only served to make his earlier notion of turning himself in as a rapist the more ludicrous.

He dozed fitfully on the sofa for what was left of the night, unwilling to go up to the empty bedroom. The thud of the morning paper on the mat woke him at around seven. He was cold, stiff and had a thunderous headache. He dragged himself into the shower rather than risk going into a deeper sleep. His mother-in-law's train was due in at eleven, and her presence was likely to be difficult enough without him being late to pick her up.

The relationship between the two of them had never been close, and after Daisy's death had become increasingly strained. Nothing had been said in so many words – Elizabeth would never have tolerated it – but Olive Millon had none the less made it clear over the years that she blamed Matthew for what had happened to Daisy, as he knew she would find a way of blaming him for the miscarriage. For Elizabeth's sake, he was anxious to do nothing further to antagonise the woman.

Somewhat revived, he made himself some breakfast, although food was the last thing his body craved, and turned on the television to drown out the silence. The news headline was depressing: a coach full of children returning from a skiing holiday had crashed in France. Anguished parents were shown arriving at the scene. Matthew turned the television off again and wandered out into the garden.

It was just getting light, and the air was damp and chilly. A solitary blackbird was singing in the leafless magnolia tree at the far end of the lawn. A clump of snowdrops had started to flower beneath the weeping larch, Matthew noticed. Around the patio, the winter pansies were a mass of purple and white. It seemed an eternity since he had planted them. Absently, he pulled off some dead heads.

Suddenly, he was desperate for the sound of another voice. He decided to ring Pete Preston, tell him about Elizabeth's accident, fill him in on Toby's daft claims and his own even dafter reaction to them. He smiled as he imagined Pete's bellow of disbelieving laughter. Yes, some laughter, that was what he needed. He started back towards the house, then changed his mind, pulled out his mobile. At least out here in the garden he had the blackbird for company.

For once, Pete answered the phone himself. As soon as he realised who was calling, the babble of background noise was extinguished by the slam of a door and he demanded in a hushed, urgent voice, 'What did he say?'

Matthew wondered fleetingly how Pete knew why he was ringing. So much had happened in the intervening days that it took him a moment to remember the message he'd left with the other man's son.

'Matthew?' Pete was clearly rattled by his hesitation. 'Are you still there?'

'Of course I'm still here. He's had a postcard, although he's not any more sure than I am that Sylvia Guttenberg's behind them. He thinks . . .' Matthew found himself reluctant to mention the name, 'he thinks the other option's more likely.'

He could hear Pete breathing on the other end of the phone.

'He's in a terrible mess. Got mixed up in the drugs scene in London, apparently. Someone threw acid at his face.'

'No more than the bastard deserves.'

The bitterness in Pete's voice threw Matthew off balance. 'That's a bit harsh.'

'Did he have anything else to say?'

There was something in the way the question was asked that made Matthew uneasy. 'There was, as a matter of fact. He tried to make out the . . . the Blackport business actually happened.'

On the other end of the phone, there was absolute silence.

'Just winding me up, of course,' Matthew added. 'Got me going for a while, though.' He laughed mirthlessly. 'My God! I almost went to the police and confessed.'

'We need to talk.'

'About what, exactly?' Matthew asked carefully, hoping against hope he was reading too much into Pete's reaction.

'Listen, just what the fuck happened last night?'

The rising panic in the other man's voice told Matthew all he needed to know. 'I could ask you the same question.' He was suddenly furious. 'Like what the fuck happened twenty-five years ago? You're damned right we need to talk. I'm coming over right now.'

'You can't! I'm teaching. I've got to be at school in—'

'Get out of it.'

'How can I? Linda doesn't know anything about it. She'll want to know why—'

'I can always come to the school if it's more convenient.'

He heard the sharp intake of Pete's breath. 'No! I'll think of something . . . I'll say I'm feeling—'

'Sick? At least you won't be lying this time.' Matthew clicked the other man into silence. He stood stock-still in the middle of the garden he'd worked so hard to bring into order. How could he share Elizabeth's home, her bed, her life, knowing what he'd done?

'Rapist,' he shouted into the stillness, and watched the blackbird flap off in panic.

When had everything got so fucking complicated? When had it all gone so hideously wrong? It was a question he didn't need to ask himself. When they'd picked up Donna O'Mara in that club, that was when. What had happened that night had been festering silently ever since. And now it had come back to haunt them all.

Pete must have been looking out for him; the door clicked open as Matthew walked up the front path. Without a word, he gestured Matthew into the living room and wheeled himself through.

For a moment, neither man spoke. Then Matthew said in a low voice, 'No wonder you were so keen to pin all this on Sylvia Guttenberg, you bastard.'

'It could be her.' Pete didn't meet his eye.

'It could be the Queen of fucking Sheba, but chances are it's not. Chances are, it's someone with a pretty bloody good reason for blackmail, wouldn't you say? For Christ's sake, Pete! Why didn't you—'

'I wasn't certain that you . . .' Pete rubbed at his bloodshot eyes. He looked terrible. 'Look, sit down, will you? I can't think with you looming over me like that.'

Don't play the disabled card, Matthew thought, but he took the chair Pete indicated. If the man wanted eye-to-eye, he could have it.

'I wasn't sure how much you knew.' They might be on a level, but Pete still wasn't meeting his eye. '*Really knew,*

I mean. That story about being so blind drunk you'd no recollection . . .'

'You seriously think I'd make something like that up?'

Pete shrugged. 'It was as good a story as any.'

Dear God, had they *all* thought he'd been lying? Even Spike? That he hadn't been honest enough even to admit his guilt to his co-accused? Somehow, the cowardice it implied seemed almost as despicable to Matthew as the crime itself.

'It wasn't until the other night that I realised you really didn't know what had happened. I was frightened you might do something stupid.'

'Like go to the police, you mean?' Matthew was on his feet again. 'Damned right I'm going to do something stupid. I'm not going to spend the rest of my life—'

'No, wait!' Pete pushed himself backwards, so that the doorway was physically blocked by his wheelchair. 'At least let's talk about it first.'

'About what? About how we gang-raped an innocent woman? Or maybe how we allowed her to be torn to shreds in court? Or how about the perjury charge? Where do you want to start, Pete?' Matthew sank back into his seat as the full horror of the situation swept over him. 'Christ, I can't believe any of this. Toby, maybe. But you? Ben? *Spike?*' His voice cracked. 'No wonder he killed himself. I don't know how he lived with it so long.'

For the first time, Pete looked straight into his face. 'You think there's ever a day goes by that I don't think about it? Hate myself for what happened?'

'But what . . . ?' Matthew shook his head. His anger had drained away, leaving only appalled disbelief. 'How in God's name did it happen? Any of it? I mean, just on the physical level, we were all so blind drunk . . .'

'Not all of us.' Pete's voice was bitter. 'Toby was sober enough to think it would be a laugh to slip us all some speed.

Alcohol to loosen the inhibitions, amphetamines to increase the libido. "Lighten the boring wankers up a bit" – I think those were his exact words to Spike's father.'

'Hubert Vardon was aware of what had happened?' Matthew said, astounded. 'He let you plead not guilty when he knew . . . ?'

'It was on his advice. Listen. We were out of it – off our heads. None of us would have acted that way if Toby Gresham-bastard-Palmer hadn't tampered with the drinks. Would we? It was a sort of . . . temporary insanity. Christ, when I came to, I honestly believed I'd been watching a blue movie. It wasn't . . . real.'

'So why didn't you just tell the *truth*?'

'You were in court, Matthew. Do you think for one moment that jury would have believed us?'

It was a rhetorical question, and they both knew it.

'And as for this innocent girl stuff . . .' Pete hesitated. 'Well, she wasn't, was she? I mean, I know what we did was wrong . . .' his gaze slipped away again, 'unforgivably wrong. But she wasn't exactly a vestal virgin.'

'Oh well, that's all right then.' Matthew could hardly believe what he was hearing. 'Jesus Christ, Pete! What's the hell's the matter with you?'

'I'd just got my first teaching job, Spike was about to start on his Ph.D., you your accountancy training . . . We'd got our whole lives ahead of us. And as Hubert Vardon said at the time, if Donna O'Mara was such a bloody innocent, why did she come back to the flat and demand money, instead of reporting us?'

'I don't know.' Matthew closed his eyes, then opened them quickly as a vivid image of the girl, standing in the witness box, tearful and defeated, flashed into his head. 'I don't know what to think any more.'

'Well, try this for size. If you go to the police now, it won't just be your own life you'll be ruining. Think how many *really* innocent people you'd be hurting. And for what?'

'Conscience? Morality?' But even as Matthew said the words, they rang hollow to him. They'd go to prison, for sure. Elizabeth would be left to cope alone. Could he do that to her? After everything else she'd been through? Even if by some miracle they escaped jail, their lives would be in tatters. Careers, reputations, families . . . He thought of Linda, Pete's sons, Jane . . . Maybe it could be seen as self-indulgence to salve his conscience at the price of so many lives.

'Christ knows, we've paid the price in other ways for what we've done,' Pete muttered. He glanced at Matthew, his mouth curling into the hint of a sneer. 'Or some of us have, at least.'

'Perhaps Sylvia Guttenberg's "curse of the virgin" crap wasn't so far off the mark after all,' Matthew said savagely. 'Let's face it, it's no more than any of us deserves.'

'That isn't funny.'

'It wasn't fucking meant to be funny.'

For a moment, neither of them spoke.

'So what are we going to do?' Pete said finally.

'Toby thinks she's after money.'

'Well, if she is, let's just shell out and be done with it. I haven't got much, but I could probably raise a couple of thousand.' Pete leant forward in his wheelchair. 'If we want to settle our debt to her, it makes a bloody sight more sense to give her some cash, if that's what she's after, than to throw away our lives. Think about it, Matthew. Think about it honestly. Do you really want your baby to be brought up knowing his father was a . . . ?'

The end of the sentence hung in the air between them.

'It's not our decision, is it? We'll just have to wait and see whether it's money Donna O'Mara's after, or vengeance.'

Matthew shivered involuntarily, as if someone had walked over his grave. 'And hope to God it will be money.'

'So you won't do anything . . . rash?'

'No.' Matthew got to his feet. 'If you mean am I going to do the decent thing, then no, I won't do anything rash. I've got to go.'

He waited as Pete manoeuvred himself clumsily from in front of the door.

'And by the way, there is no baby,' he added quietly, as he left the room.

18

Matthew had missed his mother-in-law by the time he got to the station. He arrived at the hospital to find her interrogating a harassed-looking nurse. Olive's reception was frosty. She quite understood that Matthew had been far too busy to think about her, she said with a well-worn air of martyrdom. Matthew insisted on paying for her taxi. Olive refused, brushing aside his apologies. He offered again. Eventually, and with ill grace, she accepted the twenty-pound note he knew was far in excess of the fare, her mouth and her purse snapping shut in resolute disapproval. After the horrors of the previous forty-eight hours, Matthew found the familiar ritual oddly soothing.

Elizabeth herself seemed much improved. She was sitting in a chair at the side of her bed. Her face lit up as Matthew entered, and she held out her hand to him as her mother bustled around the room, finding fault.

'I'm sorry I'm late,' Matthew said, bending to kiss the top of her head. How could he defile that trusting hand by taking it in his?

'Never mind.' She rested her head against him. 'I just want to go home.'

'Of course.' Matthew edged away, picked up the case that Olive had already packed. 'I'll bring the car round to reception.'

Matthew suggested he sleep in one of the guest bedrooms that night; he'd have to make an early start the following morning, be in the office first thing to prepare for the trip to Italy the week after next. For once, his mother-in-law agreed with him. Elizabeth needed her sleep, she said, drawing on her store of platitudes to add that time was a great healer. Matthew tried not to read the expression in Elizabeth's eyes.

For the rest of the week, Matthew attempted to immerse himself in work. It wasn't easy. Each ring of the telephone, each new batch of post, set his heart racing. Toby's card had been posted more than a fortnight ago; it could only be a matter of time before Donna O'Mara made contact again.

Had Ben Fellows also been a recipient? Matthew found his thoughts returning often to the fifth of the flatmates. Ben must have contrived somehow to square his past with his conscience, although Matthew couldn't imagine how many Hail Marys it might take to cleanse a priest of both rape and perjury. But squaring it with the Catholic hierarchy would presumably prove even trickier. Matthew tried and failed to imagine what the other man's reaction might be if he, too, had heard from Donna O'Mara.

Remembering his copy of the Blackport Graduates' hand-book, he searched it for Ben's name, but it wasn't included; maybe priests weren't encouraged to join such organisations. He made a note of Sonia Beesley's number instead and rang her to ask if she and Ben were still in touch. She'd heard nothing of him in years, she said. If she found Matthew's sudden interest odd, she didn't say so.

At home, Matthew continued to sleep in the spare room, although sleep was hardly an accurate description of how his nights were spent. Violent, disturbing dreams punctuated what little rest he managed. There were occasions, deep in the middle of the night, when he even began to wonder if he'd been lying to himself all along. Several times he woke up,

sweating, the image of Donna O'Mara's frail body beneath
his so vivid that on one occasion, to his profound disgust, he'd
actually been ejaculating as he woke. How could he ever sleep
beside Elizabeth again? He knew she wanted him to, realised
her desperate need for the comfort of physical contact. He
saw the hurt in her eyes every time he moved away from
her, made an excuse to keep his distance. It tore him apart.
But there was nothing he could do.

It was a relief when, on the Saturday of the following week,
Olive announced that she needed to get home to the dog,
and suggested that Elizabeth went back with her. Elizabeth
said she'd prefer to stay at home. She was perfectly capable
of managing on her own, she insisted. The doctor had said
her ankle was healing well; she could even drive again when
she felt ready to do so. Both she and Matthew knew it was
not her ankle that was in question. It took all his powers of
persuasion to get her to agree to accompany her mother. The
sea air would do her good, he said. A change of scenery was
just what she needed. And anyway, he'd be in Italy for much
of the next week. He'd worry himself silly at the thought of
her being in the house on her own.

Finally, reluctantly, she agreed. Matthew picked up the
phone straight away and booked two first-class tickets on the
following Monday morning's train to Southampton.

Pleased, Olive went out to the kitchen and clattered around
preparing dinner.

'Maybe we could go out for lunch somewhere tomorrow,
if you feel up to it,' Matthew said, by way of recompense.
'Just the two of us.'

'Maybe.' Elizabeth stared into the fire.

'The break will do you good, you know,' he said gently.

She nodded. Suddenly she looked up, her eyes brimming
with tears. 'I'm sorry, Matthew. I'm so sorry.'

'Sorry?' The anguish in her face brought Matthew over to

her side, despite himself. Tentatively, he put his arm around her shoulder. 'For what?'

Her whole body was trembling. 'You blame me, don't you? For the baby?'

'No! God, no. You must never—'

'Then why are you being so . . . cold?' The word came out in a big, sobbing gulp. 'It's . . . it's as if you can't even bear to be in the same room with me.'

'Oh, sweetheart.' He took her face between his hands. 'I don't blame you.' His own voice was shaking with emotion. 'Nothing could be further from the truth. Nothing.'

'Then what is it?'

He searched her face, the almost overwhelming urge to spill out the whole hideous story, throw himself on her mercy, warring with his need to protect her from the truth. 'It's just . . .' He broke off, looked away, knowing that once the words were out, he could never take them back.

'Tell me.'

'Matthew, you'll have to come and open this tin.' Olive came bustling through from the kitchen. 'Why you have to have all these fancy gadgets instead of a simple, common-sense—' She broke off, looking from one of them to the other.

'Could you give us a couple of minutes, Mum?' Elizabeth's eyes didn't leave Matthew's face.

'I don't want to intrude, I'm sure.' Olive waited to be contradicted. 'Well, I'd better get back to cooking your dinner, then,' she muttered, shutting the door ostentatiously behind her.

'Tell me,' Elizabeth repeated, as if the interruption hadn't happened. But the moment had passed.

Matthew brushed her cheek briefly with his lips and got to his feet. 'I better go and give your mother a hand.'

'Matthew . . . ?'

He shook his head. 'Another time, maybe,' he said softly, and turned away from her.

It was late, after ten o'clock, when Matthew's mobile rang. Olive, who had been engrossed in a film on the television, glanced up and tutted in annoyance. Elizabeth's eyes didn't leave the screen; she'd hardly said a word since dinner.

'I'll take it in the other room,' Matthew said quickly. The number displayed wasn't one he immediately recognised. His heart hammering, he hurried through to the study before he answered it.

His initial relief at hearing Jane's voice on the other end of the phone was short-lived.

'Matthew, I've got to see you,' she cut across him as he asked her how she was doing. 'There's been another letter.'

Matthew attempted to gather his thoughts. 'Where are you?'

'In Coventry. The choir's been singing in a concert at the cathedral. It's the first chance I've had to ring. Can we meet?'

'Yes. I . . .' His mind was racing. 'Are you telling me *you've* had a letter?'

Her shaky intake of breath answered the question.

'What did it say?'

'I can't talk now. Can you get over here?'

'What, *now*?'

'I know it's late. But we've got another concert in the morning and then we're straight back to London.' Jane sounded close to tears. 'Matthew, I'm frightened.'

'OK. Where are you?' Matthew prayed he sounded more in control than he felt as he took down the name of her hotel and promised to meet her there in half an hour. 'Just try to keep calm. I'll be there as soon as I—' He broke off, aware suddenly that someone else had entered the room. He turned to find Olive standing in the doorway. 'I'll see you shortly,' he said in as businesslike a tone as he could muster, and switched off the phone.

She gave him a long look. 'Elizabeth's off to bed.'

'Right.' Matthew could feel himself colouring. He glanced down at the mobile. 'Problem at work. I'm going to have to go back in for a while.'

'At this time of night?'

'These things happen.'

'Maybe it's for the best that Elizabeth's coming back with me, as you're so . . . busy.' Olive pursed her lips.

For an instant, Matthew was tempted to rise to her bait. But only for an instant. 'I'll go and tell Elizabeth what's going on,' he said evenly.

Olive stood aside to let him pass. Her look spoke volumes.

The journey took Matthew longer than he had anticipated. It had started to snow heavily, the first snow of the year. The gritting lorries had been caught on the hop and the roads were treacherous. The fat, swirling flakes were as dense as fog; even with his wipers on full, Matthew struggled to keep the windscreen clear enough to peer through it. It was like driving through a white, silent tunnel.

The hotel, when at last he had negotiated Coventry's ring road and located it, was small and rather shabby. Jane was waiting in the lobby, her face pale and anxious. She gripped his hand. 'I thought you weren't coming.'

Matthew shook the snow from his coat. 'Is there anywhere we can go?' he asked in a low voice. He glanced towards the elderly woman who was sitting behind the small reception desk, pretending to read a magazine. 'Your room?'

Jane shook her head. 'I'm sharing.'

'The car's parked outside.' Matthew caught the receptionist's inquisitive gaze. 'We'll at least be private there.'

Matthew put the key in the ignition, turned up the heating. Jane was shivering; whether with cold or nerves, he didn't know. Snowflakes slapped wetly against the windscreen, obliterating the light from the streetlamp outside within seconds. Suddenly claustrophobic, Matthew flicked on the wipers again to clear them.

'I found this in my pigeonhole at school.' Jane pulled a folded sheet of paper from her bag, and handed it to him. Her teeth were chattering. 'How would anyone know where I worked?'

Despite the warm air that was blowing out from the heater and fluttering the edge of the paper as he opened it up, Matthew felt an icy trickle of sweat between his shoulder blades. If Donna O'Mara had decided to widen her net beyond the flatmates themselves, why not Linda, next time? Or Elizabeth?

It didn't bear thinking about.

'This has gone on long enough, Matthew.' Jane's voice was urgent. 'You've got to report it to the police.'

He forced himself to focus. Panicking would get them nowhere. He read the message, then read it again. He'd been expecting the demand to come sooner or later; but still it hit him with the force of a rabbit punch.

> Six, seven, eight, nine, ten . . .
> Wait to find out where and when.
> IT'S PAY-BACK TIME.
> £500,000.

For a moment, the only sound was the steady thud, thud of the windscreen wipers. Then Matthew said slowly, 'Well, at least we know what we're up against.'

Once it had sunk in, the message was almost a relief. He

had no idea how they were going to raise the money, but somehow, they'd do it. And then it would be over; their debt would be paid.

'"Then I let him go again,"' he murmured

'What?'

'The rest of the rhyme. "Six, seven, eight, nine, ten . . ." She's telling us that if we pay up, that'll be an end to it.'

Jane stared at him. 'Are you mad?'

'It's the only way.'

'Of course it isn't! For God's sake, Matthew, whoever wrote this has been walking around my school. This isn't just a matter of malicious letters any more. You've got to tell the police.'

'I can't.'

'What do you mean, you can't?' She snatched the sheet of paper off him, her eyes blazing. 'For God's sake, Matthew, how can you even think of—'

'I can't, because I'm guilty. Don't you understand? We were all guilty. As guilty as sin.' The shouted words reverberated around the car, hung in the fuggy air. Then suddenly, he was crying; crying as he hadn't since the day of Daisy's death, and then not in front of another living soul. Great wrenching sobs that seemed as if they would never end. And before he could stop himself, gain control, the whole story was out in a messy deluge of tears, mucus and words; a flood of words, until at last he was spent.

It seemed an age before Jane spoke. Matthew stared at the windscreen, frightened to see her expression, the silence between them punctuated only by the heartbeat thud of the wipers. He heard her swallow hard, clear her throat. Then she said shakily, 'Spike never spoke to you about it? Not ever, in all those years?'

Matthew shook his head, afraid that speech might start him weeping again.

'And you're saying that all that time his father knew the truth?'

He heard her ragged intake of breath as he dipped his head in assent. 'It went beyond Vardon simply knowing the truth,' he mumbled. 'Spike would never have lied in court if he hadn't been pressurised into it. I doubt any of them would.' He glanced at her, then away again. 'You knew him.'

'I thought I did.'

'He didn't know what he was doing that night, Jane. None of us did.'

'He knew when he stood up in court.'

'Can you imagine what would have happened to Vardon's career if it had come out that his only son was in jail for rape?' Matthew was desperate to convince her, salvage what he could of Spike's memory for her. 'You think he'd still have been made a judge? Oh, he tried to make out he was acting in our best interests, but you can bet your life it was his own skin he was most concerned with.'

'You really think he could have put that much pressure on Spike?'

'Yes, I do. We were all very young, remember. And Spike was tremendously fond of him. Vardon's a clever man,' Matthew ploughed on, sensing he might be winning her round. 'He'd have known all the right buttons to push to make Spike feel guilty enough to go along with him.'

Jane shook her head. 'You honestly believe any father would put his career before his own child like that?'

'Yes,' Matthew said in a low voice. Hadn't he, in his own way, done much the same thing?

For a long moment, she was silent.

'Hubert Vardon's as guilty as any of us,' Matthew pressed home what he hoped was his advantage.

'Then he must be made to pay,' she said simply.

19

Matthew hadn't known how Jane would react. When he'd arranged to meet her, he had planned to tell her nothing, and had ended up telling her everything – what Toby had said, what Pete had said, the drinking, the drugs that had rendered him capable of rape but unable to remember it . . . even, God help him, his own nauseating reaction to the flashbacks he'd been having.

Even as the words poured from him, with the relief of a dam bursting, a tiny voice had been warning him of the devastation that would inevitably follow. But there had been no hysterics, no recriminations. In the face of Jane's calmness, he had managed to regain some composure of his own. Insulated in the warmth of the car, they had talked and talked until the early hours.

By the time Matthew drove home, his head felt clearer than it had done in months. They were not to blame. It was the drugs that had made them act as they had; drugs that had been taken without their knowledge. Toby had acted irresponsibly, but even he could have had no idea of the outcome of what must have seemed no more than a stupid prank. And now, at last, they could recompense Donna O'Mara, who had been less than blameless herself, and put the whole sordid business to rest.

Part of him knew that in her desire to keep her memory of Spike intact, Jane's viewpoint was no less biased than his own. They were both clutching at straws, rather than face the enormity of what had happened that night in Blackport. But still, Matthew felt more optimistic than he had in weeks.

The snow had stopped. A hard, glittering crust of white covered the landscape as he drove back to Leamington. He looked up at the moon hanging high in the still, starry sky and thanked God that soon he and Elizabeth would be able to rebuild their lives together.

The house was in darkness. Matthew recognised the small act of spite that had made Olive turn off the porch light that Elizabeth always left on when he was late. But if she'd been hoping to inconvenience him, the moon was against her; Matthew's path was clearly lit as he made his way across the crunching snow.

He was far too wide awake to sleep. He padded through to the kitchen, realising how hungry he was, and made himself coffee and toast, which he took through to the study. He reread the note that Jane had been only too happy to hand over to him for safe-keeping.

Donna O'Mara was clever; he had to give her that. She'd set up a perfect no-lose situation. If they paid up, she walked off with half a million, and if they went to the police, she could watch safely from the sidelines while they were charged with perjury. Either way, she got her revenge. Matthew could almost find it in his heart to admire her.

He switched on the computer and called up the files that contained his personal finances and investments. A half a million – even his share of it – was a hell of a lot of money to put together, especially as the woman had given no indication of her time frame. Pete and Toby between them were unlikely to be good for more than a few thousand and, as a priest, Ben Fellows was unlikely to have much in the way of spare cash, even if they were able to track him down in time. It was going to be down to Matthew. Matthew and the Vardons.

Jane had been right about Hubert Vardon, as she had been

right about so many things. If Spike's father had encouraged them to tell the truth from the start, who was to say that a jury wouldn't have viewed the evidence in the same way as Jane herself had done? Whatever the rights and wrongs of the case, when all was said and done the fact remained that Donna O'Mara had chosen to try blackmail rather than going straight to the police as any truly innocent victim would have done. Surely any jury would have been able to see that. But Vardon had encouraged them all to lie rather than risk his own reputation.

Yes, Matthew nodded to himself as he jotted down some figures from the computer screen and started to make his calculations, Vardon owed as great a debt to Donna O'Mara as any of them.

He was grateful that Jane had suggested they meet up again first thing in the morning so that she could accompany him on the trip down to Cornwall. He doubted Hubert Vardon would so much as let him over the threshold without her presence. He rubbed his eyes, glanced at the clock on the computer screen. Ten past three. The prospect of the drive that awaited him in less than five hours, let alone the confrontation that was to follow, was not an appealing one. But with no indication of when Donna O'Mara might strike again, and with the Italy trip coming up so soon – and God alone knew how long it might take to stitch the deal up with Montelli – time was of the essence.

'What are you doing?'

Elizabeth's voice, thick with sleep, brought Matthew back with a start. Quickly, he flicked back to the main menu and turned around, already arranging his face into an apologetic smile. 'Sorry, darling. I didn't mean to disturb you.'

'It's the middle of the night.'

'I'm finished now.' He stretched and turned off the computer.

'What did Frank Masterton want?'

'What?' For a moment, Matthew didn't know what she meant. He shrugged, attempting to sound casual as he recalled his lie. 'Oh, just some nonsense about the Italian contract. I . . .' He cleared his throat, thinking fast. 'The first meeting's been brought forward to Monday, so I'm going to have to get off first thing in the morning, I'm afraid.' He could feel the blood rising in his face, was certain that she would see through the deceit, hated himself for doing it to her. But what point was there in dragging her into it all now, when soon it would be behind them for ever? He got up, took a step towards her. 'Why don't you get some travel brochures together while you're down with your mother? Decide where you'd like to go.'

She looked so sad, standing there in the doorway, her hair ruffled, her small feet bare against the thick pile of the carpet. Matthew felt an overwhelming surge of love and protectiveness towards her. She'd been through so much, and he'd barely been there for her at all.

He held his hands out to her. 'Listen, I know I've been a bit . . . distracted lately. But once this trip's over . . .'

She nodded. Pulled her dressing gown more tightly round her. 'It's cold,' she said. 'I'm going back to bed.'

Matthew was up and off before Elizabeth was awake the following morning. He left a note on the kitchen table saying that he loved her and that he would be back as soon as possible. He was relieved that she was still asleep. It was easier than saying goodbye to her face to face.

As was usually the way in the Midlands, the snow had not lasted long; some time overnight a thaw had set in. Only the vestiges remained, huddled into the gutters and the folds of the fields. The air was mild, with a hint of spring about it. Had the circumstances been different, it was the kind of morning to lift Matthew's spirits.

He picked Jane up from her hotel at eight thirty. The other members of the choir were piling on to the coach parked outside. An couple of elderly women waved to her as she got into the Jaguar, their eyes keen with curiosity.

'We're singing matins at a church in Warwick. I said I had a sore throat,' she muttered, head down. It wasn't until they reached the end of the street that she added, 'I rang Hubert to say I was coming. I didn't say you'd be with me.'

'And that was OK?' It had occurred to Matthew that something as banal as the Vardons being away for the weekend, and all the subterfuge would have been wasted.

She gave a tight smile. 'He sounded pleased.'

They spoke little during the journey; each locked in thought. Matthew glanced over a couple of times and wondered what Jane's might be. He could sense the tension behind her calm exterior.

It was lunchtime by the time they arrived in Boslowan Major. The sky was a flawless blue, the hedgerows already yellow with random daffodils, the first lambs gambolling in the fields. Matthew was reminded sharply of the contrast with the last time he had driven the narrow lanes, on the way to Spike's funeral. The year had been dying, then; life had seemed as bleak as it could get. But Elizabeth had sat beside him, and inside her, their child. The lack of her, the strangeness of having another woman sitting where she should be, hit him like a physical blow. He would gladly have had that autumn day back again.

'Could we stop at the church?' Jane said suddenly, as they drove past it.

Matthew nodded silently and pulled the car in to the car park.

He followed her through the churchyard to Spike's grave.

There was no headstone, just a small wooden cross with Spike's name printed on it. A bunch of fresh daffodils, inexpertly arranged in a dusty cut-glass vase, stood on top of the mounded earth.

'They have to wait,' Jane swallowed, 'the undertakers. For the earth to settle. Before they can fix the headstone.' She looked at the daffodils, her lips trembling. 'I should have brought some flowers. I didn't think . . .' She glanced at Matthew. 'It's the first time I've come. Does that seem awful?'

Matthew shook his head.

'Do you go to Daisy's grave?' she asked.

'No.' Matthew cleared his throat. 'She . . . she was cremated. We scattered her ashes in the garden in Leamington.'

Elizabeth's mother had never forgiven him for that; had said it was barbaric not to have the child in consecrated ground. But he hadn't been able to bear the thought of Daisy alone, under the cold earth.

'She was frightened of the dark,' he murmured.

Jane nodded, as if she understood. 'Spike's not here, anyway. Not the bit of him that matters. He's everywhere I go. He always will be.'

Yes.' Matthew took her hand and squeezed it. 'Yes, of course he is.'

Hubert Vardon's smile of welcome froze on his face as he opened the front door to Jane and saw Matthew standing beside her. For a moment, Matthew thought that he might be refused entry, but etiquette won the day and with the barest murmur of greeting, Vardon stood back to let them in. The drawing room into which he showed them was chilly; any warmth from the sun blocked by heavy, half-drawn curtains. The grate was filled with grey, dead ash. A thick patina of dust overlaid the heavy mahogany furniture. Half-drunk cups of tea and unwashed plates cluttered the side tables. The faint air of neglect that Matthew had sensed on his last visit had accelerated towards decay. Alice Vardon was nowhere in evidence.

'My wife is unwell.' Vardon followed his gaze. He turned to Jane, his expression softening somewhat. 'If you want any refreshments, you'll have to find your own way around the kitchen, I'm afraid.'

Jane shook her head. 'We're fine.'

Vardon looked from one of them to the other, then lowered himself into a chair and gestured to his guests to do the same.

'So, Matthew.' His voice was icy. 'To what do I owe this unexpected pleasure?'

Jane perched on the edge of the sofa, her hands working nervously at the strap of her bag, her face taut. Matthew remained standing. Never mind the pleasantries, he told himself. Cut straight to the chase. He reached for his wallet and took out the notes, seeing Jane's mouth tighten as he did so.

'This isn't a social call,' he said harshly.

It was a very long time before Hubert Vardon spoke. The silence was disturbed only by the sonorous ticking of the grandfather clock that stood in the corner of the room, and the slight rattle of the old man's breathing as he scanned one note, then the other, then went back again to the first. Jane stared straight ahead of her, her mouth clamped into a thin line of anxiety.

'I should tell you that I'm now fully aware of what really happened that night. And your involvement in the subsequent cover-up,' Matthew said by way of provoking a response.

Finally, Vardon's head came up. He regarded Matthew over the top of his horn-rimmed spectacles, his lips twisting into a brief, sardonic smile. 'I never presumed anything else.'

Any residual compassion Matthew might have felt for the older man evaporated utterly. 'Hard as you might find it to believe, I told the truth, both to the police and in court. I had absolutely no recollection of what happened.'

Vardon's only response was a slight raising of his eyebrow. He glanced down again at the notes. 'And where exactly does the American woman fit into this unsavoury scenario?'

Matthew stared at him, nonplussed.

'I assume it must be more than coincidence that brings you here only a day after her visit.'

'Sylvia Guttenberg? She's been *here*?' Matthew glanced towards Jane. 'What did she want?'

'To talk about the trial.'

'What did you tell her?'

'I told her I found her questions both vexing and intrusive, and asked her to leave my house.' Vardon appeared to be enjoying Matthew's discomfiture. 'She said she was a friend of yours.'

'Well she isn't,' Matthew snapped. 'What else did she say? Did she tell you about the other notes?'

'As I say, I didn't engage in lengthy conversation with her.' Vardon observed him pensively. 'So am I to take it that these are not the only communications?'

Matthew glanced again towards Jane, wondering if he should mention Spike, but her eyes were fixed on her bag. 'Toby Gresham-Palmer and Peter Preston have had them too,' he said carefully.

'Ah.' A small pause. 'I trust I can safely presume that none of you has seen fit to show them to the authorities?'

The tone was patronising; one Matthew could imagine him employing when dealing with a junior barrister.

'It would hardly be more in any of our interests to do so than it would be in yours,' he replied coldly.

Vardon placed the notes on the table, took off his glasses,

folded them and replaced them carefully in their case before asking, 'Might I ask why you have shown them to me?'

'I should have thought that was self-evident.'

'You're going to have to enlighten me, I'm afraid.' Vardon made a steeple of his fingers.

'Obviously, we shall have to pay the woman off,' Matthew said impatiently, 'if only as a matter of conscience.'

'Conscience?'

Matthew could feel his temper rising; he had the very distinct impression that the other man was mocking him. As evenly as he was able, he went on, 'And as it would appear you are at least as personally involved as—'

'I see,' Vardon nodded sagely. 'You've come here for money. I should have realised.' He held out his hands in a gesture that encompassed the shabby room. 'In which case, you've wasted your no doubt valuable time, I'm afraid.'

'I've never met a penniless lawyer yet.' The words sounded vulgar, even to Matthew's own ears. But this was no time for finesse. 'You don't want publicity any more than I do. And if raising half a million is the only way—'

Vardon laughed, a sound as dry and rusty as dead leaves. 'I'm old and I'm ill, Matthew. With any degree of luck, I don't have long to live. Do you imagine my reputation is of any interest to me whatsoever?'

Matthew was momentarily thrown off guard; Vardon didn't sound as if he were bluffing. 'If only for your wife's sake . . .'

An expression that could have been real pain flickered across Vardon's face. 'Regrettably, my wife's grasp on reality has been waning for some time, the more so since Spike's death. I very much doubt my reputation, or lack of it, would concern her greatly. Such modest investments as I have will provide care for her once I'm gone.' Vardon picked up the notes, glanced at them, and handed them back. 'So you see, I'm unable to help you.'

'Not even to keep Spike's memory intact?'

Jane's intervention seemed to catch Vardon by surprise, as if he had forgotten her presence. His gaze flicked from Matthew's face to hers and he said quietly, 'I don't believe you have any place in this discussion, my dear. It might be better if you were to wait elsewhere. Maybe some tea—'

Jane ignored him. 'Don't you think you have some obligation towards him?'

'I loved my son more than life itself. If I could bring him back . . .' Vardon looked away from her. 'But I can't. He's dead. No action on my part can help him now.'

'You never gave a damn about him!' Matthew heard the tremor in Jane's voice. 'Do you think I believe for one moment that Spike would have perjured himself, then or ever, if you hadn't pushed him into it? All you were interested in was avoiding a scandal.'

'Quite the contrary. Can you imagine what would have happened to my career, had it come to light that I had advised my own son to lie in court? But I risked it gladly, to protect him.' Vardon reached forward as if to take her hand, but Jane snatched it away from him. 'I can't make you believe that, my dear, but my only motivation was Spike's welfare.'

'You were a *lawyer*!' Matthew could contain himself no longer. 'Didn't the truth matter to you at all?'

'The truth?' Vardon turned a wintry smile on him. 'The *truth*? Forgive me if I've misunderstood, but isn't it the truth that you're now proposing to pay half a million pounds to conceal?'

'But if we'd been honest at the time . . . If you'd advised us to, as any decent lawyer, let alone a father—'

Vardon gave a contemptuous snort. 'Oh, it may suit you to take the moral high ground now, Matthew. But if I hadn't acted quickly, you'd all have gone to jail. Your lives would have been utterly ruined. And for what, when all is said and done? For giving some simple-minded Irish peasant no more than she'd asked for by going back with you in the first place. Oh, please. Don't look so shocked. I'm simply telling you what you want to hear. Am I not correct?'

Matthew clenched his fists. 'You're a disgrace to your profession.'

'That is as may be. But let us be quite clear on one point, as you are so intent on apportioning blame. You only ever heard what you wanted to hear.' He gazed at Matthew coldly. 'Might I remind you that guilt may be established as much by omission as commission.'

'What the hell is that supposed to mean?'

'I don't remember anyone making any great effort to question Spike's version of events. You were all eager enough to believe that Donna O'Mara had attempted blackmail.'

'*What?*' Matthew stared at him.

There was a moment's utter silence. Vardon registered Jane's intake of breath; his eyes darted to her face, then away again, as if he realised he had said more than he'd intended. He reached for one of the half-empty cups beside him, and sipped at the congealing contents, his hand shaking slightly.

'Are you telling me that the entire case against Donna O'Mara was set up?' Matthew said slowly, as the full implication of the other man's words began to sink in.

'You'd rather have had a criminal record?' Vardon placed the cup carefully on its saucer before leaning forward and looking Matthew full in the face. 'Somehow, I doubt that very much.'

'And the boy from her village?' Matthew had a sudden, vivid picture of Donna O'Mara in the witness box, her cheeks burning with shame and humiliation.

Vardon shrugged. 'Everyone has his price. There's no doubt it helped to sway the jury in our favour.'

'Dear God,' Matthew breathed as the last vestiges of self-justification slipped away from him. Between them, they'd wrecked an entirely innocent woman. 'What happened to her?' he demanded. 'After the trial?'

'I saw to it that the charges against her were dropped. She suffered no long-term damage.'

'You know that for a fact, do you?' Matthew could barely believe what he was hearing.

'Strangely enough, I do.' Vardon's voice was heavy with sarcasm. 'Ben Fellows, Father Benedict, I should say, contacted me some time ago. He'd come across the wretched woman, purely by chance, at some hospice he was working in at the time. Near Dublin, if I remember correctly.'

'When was this?' It was Jane who asked the question.

'Some seven or eight years ago.'

'You said a hospice.' Matthew's brain was working fast. 'So she was ill?' Some final act of vengeance? Was that why Donna O'Mara had decide to bring things to a head after so many years? The notion had a certain logic to it, at least.

Vardon shook his head. 'She was working there, I believe. She and Ben recognised each other at once. One can only imagine what must have been going through the man's head; he must have been terrified that she would go to his superiors. But she was married by then, apparently, and had a young family. They talked about the case at some length, as I understand it. She seems to have been quite content to let bygones by bygones.'

Matthew snorted and gestured to the notes. 'It doesn't look that way from where I'm standing.'

'Maybe she was seeking to heap coals of fire upon him with her apparent forgiveness. It would be an appropriate punishment for a priest, one would suppose,' Vardon said coolly.

'So Ben knew all the evidence against her had been falsi-
fied?'

'He did once the wretched woman told him. Regrettably,
his view was rather less pragmatic than her own. He seemed
to feel that he owed it to her to make the rest of you aware of
the exact circumstances of the trial. Needless to say, I advised
against it.'

'And why would he listen to any advice you had to give?'

'A valid point.' Vardon inclined his head. 'It was Spike who
persuaded him, not I. He went over to Dublin to see him.'

'I don't believe you,' Jane whispered.

'And neither do I,' Matthew said hotly. 'Spike wouldn't
have put pressure on Ben to go against his conscience unless
you'd found some way of—'

'I believe you had a child to whom Spike was particularly
attached.'

'You used my daughter to . . . ?'

'Maybe it was her welfare that swayed Spike.' Vardon
gazed at him unblinkingly. 'Where would have been the
justice in causing a small girl to grow up with her father in
jail, after all?'

Matthew was on his feet. He grabbed Vardon by his lapels,
dragged him bodily from his chair. If Jane hadn't intervened,
he'd have gone on shaking the bastard until his scrawny neck
had snapped in two.

'Leave him!'

Her voice scythed through Matthew's rage. He threw the
older man back into the chair.

A thin trail of saliva dribbled from Vardon's bluish lips. For
a moment, Matthew thought he'd killed him and was glad.
But as Jane pulled him away, Vardon let out a rasping gurgle
and tried to struggle to his feet, then sank back into the chair,
fighting for breath. Matthew stood over him, fists clenched,
shaken by the depth of his own fury.

'Leave him,' Jane repeated. She knelt down beside Vardon, scanned his face.

'Thank you, my dear,' he mumbled, still white and trembling. He fumbled in his pocket and pulled out a grubby, crumpled handkerchief, with which he dabbed ineffectually at his mouth.

Jane bent over the chair. For a horrified moment, Matthew thought she was actually going to kiss the wizened cheek.

She spoke so softly that Vardon had to strain forward, eager to catch her words.

'Spike had a letter as well. You didn't know that, did you?'

Matthew watched the old man's expression turn gradually from gratitude through bewilderment to shock as she went on, '"This is the first of punishments, that no guilty man is acquitted if judged by himself." I wasn't sure what it meant, at the time. But Spike knew, didn't he? That's what drove him to kill himself.'

Vardon slumped back in his chair, shook his head. 'Spike's death was an accident.'

'He walked out into the sea rather than live with the guilt any more.'

'No!' Vardon's hands had flown up to his ears, as if to block out her words.

'You did that to him.'

Matthew watched, mesmerised, as Jane pushed her face even closer. He wouldn't have believed her capable of such venom. 'You killed your only son, Hubert. As surely as if you'd held him under the water.'

'Come on. Let's get out of here.' Suddenly, Matthew had had enough. What was to be gained by tormenting this sick, useless old man? He put his hand under Jane's elbow and guided her to her feet. Even through her heavy coat, he could feel that her whole body was shaking.

She turned as they reached the door. Vardon was still slumped in the chair, his head in his hands. 'You killed him,' she shouted.

20

Matthew drove hard and fast for almost an hour, anxious to put as much distance between himself and Boslowan Major as he could. He forced himself to concentrate on the road ahead of him, to keep his jumble of disordered thoughts at bay. They were on Bodmin Moor before his need for a drink overcame him and, swerving the car from the main road, he followed the signs to a village inn.

Jane had not spoken since they had set off. She'd fallen asleep almost instantly, her head lolling, her face turned away from him towards the window, clearly exhausted by her outburst of emotion. Taking his eyes from the road to look across at her, Matthew felt a wave of sympathy. He'd been as shocked by the viciousness of her attack on Vardon as he had been by the physical violence of his own, but the fact was that she'd lost more than any of them. Once all this was over, he had Elizabeth to go back to, the threads of a life to pick up. What did Jane have?

It was late afternoon, and almost dark. A low mist hung over the moor, diminishing the visibility even further. Once off the main road, Matthew had to strain to keep to the narrow, winding lane. He just hoped that the inn would be open when they arrived.

It was. The mullion windows of the squat stone building were lit up, and a spiral of smoke drifted from the chimney and into the thickening mist. Matthew pulled up outside. Leaving Jane asleep, he stuck his head round the door. The place was empty, but welcoming, gleaming with horse brasses and polished wood, the low ceiling beams decorated with thousands of colourful beer mats. A blazing log fire burnt in the fireplace. The landlord, who had been sitting on one of the bar stools reading the paper, jumped to his feet.

'Still thick out there, is it?' he said. 'Come on in and get yourself warm.'

After the events of the day, Matthew felt cravenly grateful for the man's friendliness. He went back to the car and gently shook Jane's shoulder. She woke instantly, flinching slightly as she blinked, disorientated, then relaxing as she realised who had woken her.

'Where are we?' She pushed her hair from her face.

'I needed a break from driving. I thought we ought to get something to eat.'

They took the small table in the inglenook. It meant sitting cramped next to each other on an uncomfortably narrow wooden bench, but the temperature outside had plummeted as the mist set in, and Jane's teeth were chattering. Matthew insisted that she had a Scotch to warm her up.

The landlord brought over drinks and a menu, then resumed his stool by the bar. He seemed pleased to have company.

'You down this way on holiday, then?' It was clear he thought they were a couple.

Matthew glanced at Jane, but she was leaning forward to warm her hands over the fire.

'Just visiting for the day.'

'Got far to go?'

'The Midlands.'

The landlord blew out his cheeks. 'That's ambitious in the day. Wouldn't want to be doing that sort of a journey. Not in this weather. Mist can be a real bugger at this time of the year.'

'I can imagine.' Matthew picked up the menu, hoping to cut the conversation short, but the man wasn't so easily deflected.

'We do B and B, if you decided to stay over.'

'Thank you.' Matthew didn't raise his eyes.

'Just in case you didn't fancy that long drive.'

Matthew didn't reply.

The landlord appeared finally to take the hint. 'Just go and get some more logs in, then,' he said, getting to his feet. 'Do you want a refill, before I go?'

'Thanks.' Matthew emptied his glass. He turned to Jane 'Can I get you anything?' She was still staring into the flames. He touched her arm. 'Jane?'

'Sorry?' She started, as though lost in thought. She hadn't so much as put her lips to the Scotch, he noticed. 'Oh . . . orange juice, please.'

The landlord's conversation might have been irritating, but it was preferable, Matthew realised as soon as the man had picked up the log basket beside the fire and disappeared, to the silence left by his absence.

'Warmer now?' he asked.

'Yes.' Jane took a small sip of the orange. 'Thank you.'

He returned to his examination of the menu. 'Nothing very exotic, I'm afraid.' He felt uncomfortable, stilted. There was so much to say, and yet so little.

'That's OK. I'm not all that hungry anyway.' She didn't even bother to look. 'I'll have whatever you're having.'

'I wonder what it's doing out there?' Matthew got to his feet and peered out of the window. He could see nothing; even the car had been swallowed up in the blotted whiteness. With a muttered, 'Shit,' he came back to the table.

'Is it getting worse?'

He nodded. 'What time do you have to be back?'

'The last train from Coventry's at half-past ten.' She

glanced at him. 'If you wouldn't mind dropping me off at the station.'

'No. Of course not.' Matthew picked up his glass, swirled the whisky round in it. 'It's going to be late by the time you get home.'

'It doesn't matter.' She was staring into the fire again. A single tear rolled slowly down her cheek. 'I shouldn't have said it, should I?'

Matthew paused. 'You did what you thought was right.'

'He's an old man.'

'An old man with as much on his conscience as any of us.'

A small silence.

'He's not going to help you find the money, is he?'

'No.' Matthew sighed. 'No, he's not.'

'So what are you going to do?'

'I've no idea,' Matthew said heavily.

The landlord staggered back in with a stack of logs, letting a blast of icy air in with him. 'Can't see your hand out there,' he commented cheerfully. 'You chosen what you want to eat, yet?'

'Just give us a minute or to.' Matthew waited until the man had gone back to the bar, then said in a low voice, 'Listen, it really is bad out there. Why don't we stop over and make an early start in the morning? You could ring in sick, couldn't you? You're not going to be up to much anyway, by the time you get back,' he went on quickly, as Jane started to speak.

Matthew didn't know why he was so anxious to push the idea, other than that the prospect seemed infinitely preferable to the arduous journey that lay ahead of them. The warmth of the fire had made him realise how tired he was. A headache was building behind his eyes. He longed to get to bed, have some time on his own to think. He wondered fleetingly whether he should make it clear that he was talking of separate rooms, but even to mention it seemed crass.

'What about Elizabeth? Won't she be worried?'

'She's not at home. She's gone to stay with her mother.' It was almost true. Tomorrow it would be true.

'Oh.' Jane glanced towards the window. 'Well, if you think it's wiser.'

'It's not going to be an easy drive, that's for sure.'

'OK, then. I've got my head's number. I'll give her a ring and explain what's happened.' She rummaged through her bag as if grateful to have something else to think about. 'I must ring the cattery, too. Ask them to hold on to Petrushka for me. My cat.' She gave a small shrug. 'I was supposed to pick her up before work.'

'Right.' Once again, Matthew was struck by the loneliness of the life she must be leading. Most women of her age would be contacting family, flatmates, a lover; Jane's only concern was her cat. He smiled at her encouragingly. 'I think I heard her, when I spoke to you on the phone.'

Jane nodded. 'Spike gave her to me. As an engagement present.' She looked down at her hands, then said briskly, 'I'll pick her up tomorrow afternoon instead. There shouldn't be a problem.'

Matthew went back to the bar while she went to make her phone calls.

'Do you have two single rooms?' he asked.

'Singles?' The man scratched his head, evidently thrown by the request. 'Only doubles, I'm afraid. Twenty-five pounds apiece. I could do you a twin-bedded. 'Twould be cheaper than having the two.'

Matthew felt tempted to negotiate, if only as a matter of principle; any guest must be a windfall at that time of the year. But he said merely, 'Two doubles will be fine.'

The man looked pleased. He disappeared into a back room

and came back with two keys. 'Well, you just make yourselves comfortable, now.'

'I think I might go and freshen up.' Jane joined them at the bar.

'You go ahead, my lovely.' The landlord pushed a key across. 'Up the stairs and turn right. Bathroom's at the end of the corridor. There's clean towels and all. Just help yourself to anything you need.'

'See you in a minute.' She picked up one of the keys and headed for the stairs.

'So what can I get you both to eat?' the landlord asked.

Matthew returned his attention to the menu. He didn't even know whether Jane ate meat, he realised. He ordered vegetable lasagne, to play safe.

'Very good choice. Home-made, of course. None of that frozen rubbish. Fancy a bottle of wine with it, as you're not driving? Might as well make an evening of it. I could do you a nice Rioja.' The man, obviously thinking he was on to a good thing, produced a bottle from behind the bar. 'It's a bit pricey, mind. Set you back fifteen quid.'

'Fine. Whatever.'

'Right then.' The landlord looked more pleased with himself than ever as he uncorked the bottle. 'OK if I leave you to it for a bit? The wife's got some do on at the church, so I'm head cook and bottle-washer tonight. If anyone else comes in, just tell them to ring the bell,' he added as he ambled off to the kitchen.

Matthew took the bottle back to the table and poured himself a large glass. Trivialities dealt with, his mind strayed back to Hubert Vardon, and what the man had told them. Why had Donna O'Mara pretended to Ben that she'd come to terms with what had happened, when she so clearly had not? And why had she waited a further seven or eight years before making her move? It seemed to Matthew that the more he discovered, the less sense any of it made. He downed his glass in one, trying to get his head round it all, the combination of warmth and tiredness making it difficult to think straight. What the hell had Sylvia Guttenberg been doing at Vardon's house? Was it possible that she'd somehow discovered the truth? Talked to Ben Fellows, maybe? Matthew shook his head. She'd never have kept quiet with a scandal like that at her fingertips. But she'd know soon enough, along with the rest of the world, if he couldn't get the five hundred thousand pounds together.

One thing was for sure – they needed to track Ben down, and quickly. Correction – Matthew smiled sourly and poured himself more wine – *he* needed to track Ben down. He wouldn't trust Toby any further than he could throw him, and Pete was scarcely more likely to be any use – he'd been in such a panic the last time Matthew had seen him that he'd have been running around like a headless chicken, had he the legs to do so. He grimaced at his own sick joke, aware that the alcohol was beginning to take its toll. He emptied the glass anyway.

So, as always, it came down to him. But how the hell was he supposed to find time to play private detective? He'd be in Italy for at least a week, for one thing . . . Another set of worries leapt out to assault him. He hadn't given Montelli so much as a thought in days, yet later this week he'd be sitting across the table from the man, hammering out one of the trickiest deals of his career. Distractedly, Matthew ran his hand through his hair. He was just so damned tired. He had to think. But every turn his brain took, another problem loomed in front of him. He'd never been a quitter, but suddenly he thought how tempting it would be to let go, lose control, simply let it all wash over him . . .

He could almost understand what had made Spike walk out to sea.

'Are you all right, Matthew?'

His head shot up at the sound of Jane's voice.

'Fine.' He rubbed briskly at his cheeks. 'Fine. Sit down. Let me pour you a drink.'

'Christ, what a mess,' she said softly as she sat down next to him. 'What a horrible, bloody mess.' Abruptly, she began to cry.

Awkwardly, Matthew put his arm around her shoulder. 'It'll be all right,' he murmured, not knowing what else to say. He kissed the top of her head, as he might have comforted a child. 'Everything will be all right.'

She leant against him, her hair fanning across his shirt. They sat for a long moment, not moving. From the kitchen came the clatter of pans, a snatch of whistled music. A log crackled and flared, then collapsed into the embers. Matthew could smell the faint lemony scent of her shampoo. He was never to know whether it was the wine, the heat or the simple need for human contact that made him tilt her face up to his and kiss her, a gentle kiss that slowly deepened into passion as, with a deep, shuddering sigh, she opened her mouth to his.

Matthew felt himself harden. He wanted her. He ran his palm across the small slope of her breast and reached for the opening of her blouse. He felt her pull back, but he wanted her as he he'd never wanted anyone. Urgently. Desperately. Not to make love to her. To fuck her. Rip the clothes off her and . . .

Suddenly, the enormity of what he was doing hit him.

'I'm sorry.' He leapt to his feet, sending table and glasses crashing to the floor. 'I don't know what—'

'You all right out there?' the landlord called. Jane knelt to pick up the shards of broken glass, the curtain of her hair covering her face as he came bustling out from the kitchen, tea towel in hand. 'Bugger me.' He surveyed the wreckage. 'What happened here, then?'

'I must have caught it as I sat down.' Jane looked up, her face scarlet with embarrassment.

'We've decided we should be getting back, after all,' Matthew said quickly.

Jane nodded, not catching his eye, as she pulled on her coat.

The landlord looked dismayed. 'But what about the lasagne? I've just—'

Matthew took out his wallet and peeled off a couple of twenty-pound notes. 'That should cover it.' He added a third. 'And that's for the damage.'

They walked the short distance back through the blanketing mist to the car without speaking. Matthew fumbled in his pocket for the keys, his hands shaking. What on earth had come over him? As they reached the kerb, Jane lost her footing, and he reached out automatically to steady her. They each flinched from the contact, as if they had received an electric shock.

'About what happened in there . . .'

She shook her head quickly. 'You should let me drive.'

Matthew held open the passenger door. 'I'll be fine.'

'No, really.' She held out her hand for the keys. For a moment, their eyes met. 'You've had too much to drink.'

He nodded, wondering whether to say more, then handed over the keys and got into the passenger side.

Every sinew of Matthew's body was tensed as Jane eased the car back onto the road and edged forward into the darkness. Visibility was appalling. The headlights did little more than accentuate the solid wall of whiteness ahead of them; it was like driving blindfolded. Matthew's hands were sweating as he peered through the windscreen. Every time Jane braked, his foot hit the floor. It was madness for him to have let her drive. It was madness for them to have left the inn at all.

Almost as great a madness as to have stayed.

They were almost back to the A30 before he risked speaking, distracting her. But it had to be said. He cleared his throat. 'I'm so sorry about—'

'Don't.'

He sensed, rather than saw, the violent shake of her head. 'Jane . . .'

'You're a happily married man, Matthew. If you'd been sober, nothing would have happened. Would it?'

He turned to look at her. She was biting her lip, staring straight ahead, her hands clenched round the steering wheel. He forced his own eyes back to the road. He didn't know what was happening to him. He summoned Elizabeth, the dear, sweet face that was as familiar to him as his own. How could he even have thought of betraying her?

'I've never been unfaithful to Elizabeth. Never.' He turned again towards Jane. He wanted desperately to make her understand. 'I don't want you to think . . .'

But she was no longer listening to him. Her eyes widened in a split second of horror. Then screaming, 'Look out!' she swung the steering wheel and swerved the car violently towards the verge.

It happened in an instant. An instant that seemed to last for eternity. Matthew was aware of the endless screech of tyres, the slow, protracted shriek of ripping metal, the jarring, socket-wrenching thud of contact. A bright kaleidoscope of bursting colours.

Then only darkness.

21

White ceiling. Blocks of light. A man's voice, calling his name.

'Mr Cosgrave? Mr Cosgrave, can you hear me?

The flap of doors, opening and closing. The whoosh of air upon his face.

'Yes,' he wanted to say. 'That's me.'

Tried to move his lips. But was too tired. They'd have to wait. He was too tired.

Matthew regained consciousness to find himself in a narrow, white bed. The smell of antiseptic pervaded everything. He stared down at the plaster cast encasing his left arm. Gradually, he realised where he was, what had happened. He went to sit up, but the sudden motion brought a wave of nausea. Cautiously, he reached out and pushed the call bell on the wall.

'Ah, good morning. You're back with us, I see.' The door swung open and a nurse bustled in. She checked Matthew's blood pressure, his temperature, asked how he was feeling. 'Just lie back and rest,' she commanded, not waiting for an answer. 'Doctor will be round to see you soon.'

Matthew shut his eyes as the nurse swept out of the room. Scraps of memory were coming back; the car careering towards the hedgerow, the giant white balloon of the airbag pinning him to his seat, the flashing blue lights piercing the all-pervading mist. Jane, shaking him, calling his name . . .

'Jane,' he mumbled, his eyes jerking open as he struggled to pull himself up in the bed.

And there she was.

'You're OK.' Her face floated into his line of vision. 'Everything's OK. You've got a broken wrist, concussion. That's all.'

'What happened?' The movement had set his head throbbing. Gingerly, he raised his hand to the source of the pain, felt a bandage. 'Are you all right?'

'Fine.' Her smile was reassuring. 'A few cuts and bruises.'

'What happened?' he repeated. Recollection was flooding back, now. 'You swerved . . . Did we have a crash?'

'There was a woman. Standing right in front of us, in the middle of the road.' Jane's smile had slipped from her face. 'Didn't you see her?'

But Matthew hadn't been looking at the road. He'd been looking at Jane. 'A woman?' he echoed. 'Did you hit her?'

'The police think it must have been a trick of the mist. They didn't find anyone. She seemed so real . . .' Jane flushed. 'They thought I'd been drinking. Or maybe they always breathalyse people when there's been an accident. They say the car's write-off.' She looked away, biting her lip. 'I'm so sorry, Matthew. If I hadn't insisted on driving—'

'Thank God you did.' Matthew tried hard not to think of the damage. It was only a car, for God's sake. 'If it had been me behind the wheel, they'd have had a field day.'

Jane frowned. 'But even so . . .'

'It was an accident.' Matthew reached out his good hand. Risked touching her. 'You weren't hurt. That's all that matters.' They both looked down at his fingers encasing hers. 'Listen, Jane,' he started. 'About last night . . .'

'The police rang Elizabeth when you were first brought in. She's driving down.' Jane withdrew her hand. 'She should be here soon.'

Matthew nodded. He looked down at his fingers, empty where hers had been. For a moment, neither of them spoke.

'I must go.' She got to her feet. 'I've booked a taxi to take me to the station.' She looked down at him. 'I just wanted to make sure for myself that you were OK before I left.'

'Will you be all right?' Matthew realised that he was desperate for her to stay.

She shrugged, her face averted. 'Why wouldn't I be?'

'Can I see you again?'

Her gaze met his. 'I think that's for you to decide.'

'I'll ring you.' Matthew grabbed her hand, pressed her fingers to his lips, barely knowing what he was doing. 'As soon as I'm out of here, I'll—'

The door swung open and the nurse said cheerily, 'A visitor for you, Mr Cosgrave.'

Elizabeth was standing in the doorway.

It wasn't until Jane had gone, both her greeting and her hesitant attempt at explanation ignored, that Elizabeth said icily, 'So are you going to tell me just what exactly is going on, Matthew, or am I to work it out for myself?'

Matthew forced himself not to glance beyond her to catch a last glimpse of Jane before she disappeared. He listened as her quick footsteps faded in the corridor outside; the click of a door shutting.

He looked up at Elizabeth, this woman whom he knew better than anyone in the world, with whom he had laughed and cried; shared more than half his adult life.

'Things aren't as they seem,' he said. But how was he to explain to her what was happening, when he couldn't explain it to himself?

'Really.'

'Please, sit down,' he said wearily.

She shook her head.

'Please.'

With a slight shrug, she took the seat so recently vacated by Jane.

'I don't know where to start,' he said.

'Well, let's try something really novel,' Elizabeth snapped. 'How about the truth?'

Matthew breathed in hard. Why should he expect her to try to understand? He'd forfeited the right to that. 'A lot of things have happened in the last few months that I haven't told you about,' he said carefully.

Elizabeth snorted. 'So I gather.'

'Please—'

'Do you suppose I didn't realise there was something wrong? But I was naïve enough to think you were just grieving for Spike.' She gave a bitter laugh. 'Christ! What a fool! No wonder you were so keen to pack me off to Mum's.'

'No! That had nothing to do with—'

'With what, Matthew? I understand now why you didn't want to talk about Blackport, why you'd checked out of the hotel that night. And that Christmas present you so conveniently "lost" and couldn't be bothered to report. The three-hundred-pound scarf.' Elizabeth's face was stiff with fury. 'No prizes for guessing who that was for! Although I don't suppose it was a scarf at all, was it? Sexy underwear, more like. That's more the sort of thing a man buys his mistress, isn't it?'

'What are you talking about?' Matthew stared at her, appalled, his head spinning.

'For Christ's sake! You could at least have had the decency not to put it on the credit card. Did you *want* me to find out? Or was it just that you thought I was so bloody gullible . . .' Tears welled up in her eyes. 'And the pathetic thing is that I was, wasn't I? I believed every bloody word of it!'

'No! You've got it all wrong—'

'What, like I got it wrong about the meeting with Frank Masterton on Saturday? You might be interested to know he rang. About an hour after you'd supposedly gone to meet him. Even then, I tried to tell myself there had to be some sort of a mistake. Even on the way down here today . . .' Tears were pouring down her face. She rubbed them angrily away. 'None so blind as those who don't want to see, are there?'

'You don't understand—'

'I'm beginning to.'

Matthew's head was pounding. How was he ever going to get through to her, if she wouldn't let him get a word in? 'At least let me try to explain—'

'It's a bit late for explanations, isn't it?' She jumped to her feet. 'God, Matthew, I'd got used to playing second fiddle to your bloody job over the years, but I never thought—'

'No, that's not fair.' The sheer injustice of the accusation made him hit back. 'If I've put in too many hours at work, it's only ever been to provide the best for you. There may be many things you can reproach me for, but—'

'Fair?' Elizabeth's voice was rising towards hysteria. 'What's *fair* got to do with anything? How long, Matthew? Is Jane Davenport the first, or have you been fooling me all along? Maybe it wasn't the job I was playing second fiddle to after all! Is that it? All those late nights at the office, those so-called "business" trips. And I was stupid enough to believe you! Had your bloody dinner waiting for you when you did finally turn up. Even made sure your shirts were all clean and ironed ready for your next little fling. Talk about having your bread buttered both sides! Christ, you must have thought you had it made!'

'You know that's not true! I've never so much as looked at another woman.'

Elizabeth snorted. 'Give me some credit, Matthew. I'm not a complete moron.'

'Just *listen* to me, for God's sake—'

'Listen to you? Fifteen years of trying to second-guess what was going on inside your head apart from bloody balance sheets, of trying to get you to tell me *anything*, and suddenly you're asking for me to *listen* to you?'

'Well maybe if you hadn't been in such an exclusive bloody relationship with your uterus lately . . .' Matthew regretted the words even as they left his lips. He might have well have struck her. She even rocked backwards slightly, as if he had.

'You never wanted that baby, did you?' she said in a low voice.

'That isn't true! Look, I'm sorry. I shouldn't have said—'

'But you *did* say, didn't you?' Elizabeth's eyes were blazing. 'Had you already decided you were going to trade me in for a newer model? Is that why you were so completely disinterested in the pregnancy?'

Matthew thought of the tiny, perfect foetus that should have been his daughter. How had they come to this? Tearing so viciously at each other's scars when they needed each other so much? 'You know that isn't true,' he said quietly. 'About you or about the baby.'

'I know what I saw when I walked through that door just now.'

'Please, Elizabeth. If only you'd let me try to—'

But she wasn't listening. 'Well, she can have you. You've never really been there for me anyway. You were never there for any of us, when we needed you.'

Matthew didn't have to ask her what she meant. For a

moment their eyes met, then Elizabeth looked away, as if realising she'd gone too far.

Had it always been there between them? Simply awaiting this moment?

Of course it had.

Daisy had died because he hadn't been there for her. He'd murdered their daughter by neglect. How could he ever have expected Elizabeth to forgive him that?

'I'm sorry,' he whispered. 'I'm so, so sorry.'

She stood looking down at him for a moment, as if wondering if he might say more.

'So am I.' She took off her wedding ring and put it down on the table beside him. The anger had seeped away from her. The sadness was worse; there was good reason for the sadness.

Still Matthew didn't speak.

'I'll be at Mum's, if you need to contact me,' she said quietly, and walked out of the room.

Matthew was discharged from hospital later that day. He stood outside the building, clutching the letter he'd been given for his GP, and wondered what to do, where to go. A bit like a convict released from jail, he thought as he flagged down a taxi.

Except that his sentence would never be served.

'Pull yourself together,' he told himself savagely as he opened the door and got inside. He'd always detested self-pity in others; he wasn't about to start wallowing in his own. He'd concentrate on the practicalities, as he always had. Focus on the present. It had got him by before. It would now. It would have to.

'Where to then, mate?' the driver enquired patiently.

Matthew described the crash scene, and asked the man to take him there. He'd already contacted work and sketched in briefly what had happened. Frank Masterton had come to the phone, less than delighted to hear that not only might the trip to Italy have to be postponed, but that one of the company's most expensive cars was a write-off. It had been abundantly clear that there was a lot more the other man wanted to say. Matthew guessed he'd get it between the eyes when next they met. He'd thought better than to broach the subject of whether Jane had been insured to drive the Jaguar; he'd cross that particular bridge when he came to it. In the meantime, he could at least see the extent of the damage for himself.

'Nasty,' the taxi driver commented laconically when they reached the site.

The car was in the ditch where it had landed, the front near-side wing folded around a half-uprooted sapling. Matthew made his way clumsily down to examine it more closely, running his good hand along the jagged, dented metal of the front wing.

'You got off pretty light, by the looks of things,' the driver added, nodding at Matthew's plaster. 'Wonder no one killed theirselves, if you ask me. You was lucky.'

'Very lucky,' Matthew muttered.

'Looks like you've got a parking ticket, mind,' the man chortled.

Matthew followed his gaze to the sheet of paper fluttering beneath the windscreen wiper.

'Only kidding, mate,' the man called down as Matthew scrambled towards it. 'It'll be one of they notices to say the police know it's here. Always slap those on, they do. No need to go doing yourself a damage.'

But Matthew wasn't listening. His heart was racing as he pulled the paper free and read what was printed there.

YOU HAVE UNTIL THE END OF THE MONTH
TO FIND THE MONEY.

He breathed in sharply as he read the second sentence of the message. This time the threat was there in black and white.

NEXT TIME YOU WON'T BE SO LUCKY.

22

Matthew caught the train back to Leamington. The journey was a long one, and it was late by the time the taxi dropped him off from the station.

The house was empty, as he had known it would be, but still Elizabeth's absence hit him full force as he let himself into the silent hallway. She'd left the light on for him he noticed. He was moved by the small, unwarranted act of kindness.

He tried her mobile, but it was switched off. Quickly, he dialled his mother-in-law's number before he had time to lose his courage.

It was Olive who answered. 'She doesn't want to speak to you,' she said, the instant Matthew spoke.

'I just wanted to make sure she'd got back safely.' Matthew tried to keep the urgency from his voice.

'No thanks to you. Driving all the way down to Cornwall in her state of health. How you could have—'

'Will you at least ask her if she'll come to the phone?' Matthew cut her short. He didn't need Olive's recriminations.

'She's asleep.' The answer came back at him too quickly to be true. There was no way she was going to let Elizabeth know he'd rung.

'Just tell her that I—' he called out as the phone went dead.

He went into the kitchen, put on the kettle, tried to keep things normal. He glanced at the calendar on the wall, noting the circle around the twelfth of May; the date the baby had been due.

Don't think about it. Don't think about anything.

Focus.

Today was what . . . ? The twentieth of January. Which left him precisely eleven days. Matthew fought to control his rising panic. This wasn't about saving reputations any more. This was about keeping safe. His car had been forced off the road by that shadowy woman's figure. They could both have been killed . . . And if that hadn't been an accident, how about Pete's broken spine? Toby's disfigured face? Elizabeth's fall?

Concentrate.

He had two choices. Find the money, or find Donna O'Mara. Which was the more impossible, in just eleven days?

Maybe he should employ a private investigator. There must be ways to track someone down – electoral rolls, national insurance numbers . . . But it wasn't simply a case of finding her. He also had to find some way of stopping her.

He went through to the living room, turned on the television to drown out his thoughts. An American thriller. A man wielding a gun. A woman screaming.

What if he were to hire a hit man?

For God's sake, get a grip. He flicked the remote, and the screen went dead. This was real life, not make-believe.

Getting in touch with Ben Fellows would be a start. He was the last of them to have had any contact with Donna O'Mara. Could he be in touch with her still?

Sylvia Guttenberg. Whatever the woman's motivation, she seemed to have made it her business to track down everyone else involved in the trial. Might she have contrived to track down Ben too?

Matthew hurried through to the study, rifled through his

desk, cursing the heavy plaster cast that impeded every task. At last, he found Sylvia's card, punched her number into the phone. Waited. It was her recorded message that finally broke the monotonous ring.

'Hi! I'm busy right now, but if you leave your name and number, I'll get right back to you!'

The mockery was there, even in the message, but what choice did he have?

'It's Matthew Cosgrave,' he said grimly. 'Ring me.'

It was after midnight when Sylvia returned the call. 'What's the problem?' she asked without preamble.

Matthew kept things equally to the point. 'Have you contacted Ben Fellows?' he demanded tersely.

'Why?'

'Listen, Sylvia, I don't know what your game is, and for the moment I don't want to know. But if you've spoken to Ben—'

'Where are you?'

'I'm at home,' Matthew answered impatiently. 'Why?'

'I spoke to Jane earlier. What's this about a car crash?'

'Jane?' Matthew was momentarily side-tracked. 'Don't you ever give up?'

'She rang me.'

'And just why the hell would Jane ring you?'

'She wanted to know if I was still in Cornwall. She had some crazy notion about me jumping out in front of your car, or something.'

Matthew shut his eyes. Whatever had possessed her? Had she blurted out the whole story? Christ, no wonder Sylvia had rung back so promptly. 'What else did she say?' he demanded.

'Jesus, Matthew! How much more is there?'

Silently, Matthew blew out his cheeks.

'She sounded pretty screwed up,' Sylvia went on. 'Just what's going on here? I mean, someone running you off the road? This sounds like it's all getting seriously heavy. I really think you should take this stuff to the police, my friend. Let them deal with it.'

'Thanks for the advice.'

'Can we meet up?'

'No, we can't,' Matthew snapped, his relief turning to anger at the avid curiosity in the woman's voice. 'If you think I'm going to help you turn our lives into some sort of soap opera—'

'You rang me, pal.'

'To ask you a simple question, which I was foolish enough—'

Sylvia wasn't listening. 'Look,' she cut across him, 'let's get something straight. I started to follow up on you all because I was intrigued. I don't deny it. It seemed like a good story. And OK, maybe there was a teensy element of revenge in there too. Toby was a real shit to me when we were students, you know. But when I saw him . . . Jesus.' She gave a loud, melodramatic shudder. 'This just isn't funny any more.'

'It never was.' How had he ever expected to get any sense out of the bloody woman?

'No, but Spike, Pete, Toby, now your car crash . . . This has got to be more than coincidence, Matthew. You're being targeted here.'

What the hell had made him ring her, when all she was ever going to do was to fan the flames of his own panic? 'It was foggy.' He was irritated with himself for feeling the need to explain. 'Jane had never driven the car before . . .'

'You're happy to think it was just an accident? You really believe that?' She didn't wait for a reply. 'Listen, you rang me to ask if I knew where Ben Fellows is. Well, the answer is yes. He's living in a little place called Boswithiel. Which just happens to be not ten miles from Spike's father.'

'What?'

'Bit of a coincidence, huh? Right near where Spike drowned? Not a million miles from where your car went off the road?'

'Just what are you trying to make out?'

'Do you want to know what I've found out about him so far, or not?' Again, it was a rhetorical question. 'He's not a priest any longer, for one. He left under some sort of cloud about seven years ago. I took a trip over to Dublin to try to find out what, exactly, but—'

'Dublin?' Matthew echoed.

'He'd been resident over there at a hospice attached to a convent. I'm telling you, a couple of weeks with that sour-faced bunch of bible-bashers and you'd be grateful to have something terminal. I tried to find out what he'd been up to, but it was like trying to get blood out of a stone, even after I tried the nice-Catholic-girl bit.' She let out a sudden snort of laughter. 'Jesus Christ, I even went to confession!'

Matthew couldn't imagine that had helped her cause.

'Naturally, I lied,' she went on, as if reading his thoughts. 'But all I could get out of the dried-up old witch in charge of the place was that Father Benedict had gone to look after his sick mother in England. Which struck me as pretty damned unlikely. Had his hand up one of the altar boy's cassocks more like, was my guess. But I checked out where his parents had lived, which turned out to be a few miles up the road from the Vardons' place. And when I went down there, bingo!'

'You spoke to him?'

Sylvia gave a short laugh. 'No chance.'

'Give me the address.' Matthew scribbled it down.

'It's a real creepy place. A bit like the house in *Psycho*? I could hear someone moving around inside, but I couldn't get him to open up.'

It was clear she was relishing the memory. Matthew suspected she was embellishing the scene, ready for inclusion in one of her future novels.

'I asked around in the village. Seems Ben's been a complete recluse for years. He's on his own there, so the bit about him going back to look after his mother was a big fat lie. The woman in the post office, who, by the way, is the local equivalent of the CIA, reckoned he had a nervous breakdown when he was thrown out of the priesthood. I asked her if she knew what had happened. She didn't say it in so many words, but she implied it was some sort of scandal. With a woman. Which got me thinking. What if the powers that be had found out about the trial? I doubt Father Benedict would have put that on his CV when he applied for the job – what d'you reckon? Matthew? You still there?'

Matthew grunted noncommittally. Sylvia didn't know the half of it, and he intended to keep it that way.

'Now, hear this.' Sylvia's voice was excited. 'What if Ben starts to fester about how he's the only one to have suffered for what happened back there in Blackport? There are the rest of you, all getting on with your lives—'

'Ben?' It took Matthew a moment to catch up with her. He laughed incredulously. 'Are you trying to make out *Ben* sent the notes?'

'Think about it, Matthew. Barking mad, seems to be the official diagnosis around the village. What if he starts picking you off, one by one. Pete first – his accident was six years ago, right? Then Toby, then Spike . . .'

'Oh, for God's sake! This is the plot of your next book, is it?'

Sylvia ignored him. 'Now, from what your little girlfriend tells me—'

'She's not my bloody girlfriend.'

'Whatever. You're pretty certain Donna O'Mara's behind

these notes you've been getting. Right?' Sylvia didn't wait for a response. 'Well, the one Toby showed me said, "Remember Donna . . ."'

'I know what the fucking thing said,' Matthew snapped. 'I read it.'

'*Remember*. Just stop and think about that, before you shout me down. Would you put "*Remember* Matthew Cosgrave?" if you were addressing someone? No, you wouldn't. Now speaking as a writer—'

'This isn't la-la land. This is—'

'I think you could be in serious danger.' Sylvia's voice was sober. 'Will you ring me? Let me know how you get on if you go to see this guy?'

As if.

'What makes you think I'm intending to go and see him?' It was a senseless thing to say, given that Matthew had only rung to ask for Ben's address, and they both knew it.

'Just watch your step, is all I'm saying.' Sylvia paused. 'There's a hell of a lot more to this whole thing than meets the eye.'

Which was, Matthew thought as he replaced the receiver, probably the truest statement that had ever come from Sylvia Guttenberg's mouth.

23

Matthew slept more deeply than he would have believed possible. He awoke, to his profound relief, to the distant rumble of the morning rush hour. Light streamed through the bedroom curtains. He checked the alarm clock, saw that it was seven forty-five. Somehow, he had managed not to dream.

He got up, showered, made breakfast.

Keep things normal.

He rang the office, left a message on his secretary's answering machine instructing her to book him a seat on the evening flight to Milan.

'Get a driver here as soon as possible,' he added. 'There's some stuff I need to sort out before I go.'

Business as usual.

He went back up to the bedroom, packed for the trip, shovelling shirts one-handed into a case, cursing the plaster. It would be at least an hour, he knew, before a driver turned up. If he'd had his own car, he could have been there in fifteen minutes. He hated not being in control.

He went back to the kitchen, glanced at the morning paper, his brain taking in no more than the headlines. How the hell was he going to raise that much money in less than a fortnight? For tax reasons, most of his investments were in Elizabeth's name. He couldn't even use the house as collateral to raise a loan from the bank unless he had her consent. He had friends, colleagues who would probably lend him a few thousand without asking questions, but it was peanuts. No one, no institution, was going to loan him that sort of sum without a bloody good reason why they should, and what could he say? There was absolutely no one he could confide in. He'd never felt so lonely in his life.

He pushed the maudlin thought away.

It occurred to him that he should ring Jane, check that she was OK. He rang her number, refusing to acknowledge how much he wanted her to pick up the phone.

No one answered.

She'd have left for school, he told himself, attempting to quell the spasm of fear inside his brain as the phone rang on and on. Think how early Elizabeth used to get in to prepare the classroom, when she was teaching.

Elizabeth.

The house seemed dead without her; a beautiful, lovingly constructed shell containing . . . nothing. Somehow, he had to get through to her, try to make her understand. Nothing had happened with Jane. Nothing significant. A momentary loss of control that would never have happened but for the miss of Elizabeth. The utter hopelessness he'd felt after that terrible, lacerating row he could now see as an aftermath of the accident. He'd been in shock. They'd both said things they didn't mean. People did. But that was no reason to walk away from fifteen years of marriage.

He tried Olive's number again, bracing himself for another tirade.

'Hello?'

It wasn't until he heard Elizabeth's voice that he realised he had no idea what he wanted to say.

'Hello?' she repeated.

'Hi. I . . . it's Matthew. Sorry. I was expecting Olive.'

'She's out walking the dog.'

'Right. Yes, of course. I—'

'How's your wrist?'

'What?' He glanced down at the plaster cast. He was still wearing her wedding ring. It barely fitted over the first joint of his little finger, but he hadn't been able to bring himself to take it off. 'Oh, it's fine. Look, Elizabeth—'

'Mum should be back soon.' Her voice was cool. 'Can I take a message?'

What were they doing, talking to each other like strangers? 'No, of course not. It was you I wanted to speak to.'

Silence.

'Elizabeth, please.' Matthew was terrified that she might ring off. 'There's so much we need to talk about.'

'Is there?'

'You know there is! Please, darling. There's so much I have to explain. We can't just . . . Look, can we meet up somewhere? I could come down . . .'

'I don't know, Matthew. I'm not sure I'm ready to see you yet.' In the background, Matthew could hear Olive's voice, a dog barking. 'Mum's back. I'm going to have to go.' The phone went dead.

Slowly, Matthew replaced the receiver. 'Yet.' He grabbed at the word. It meant Elizabeth hadn't closed the door on him entirely.

He went through to the study, began to gather his papers. There was nothing more he could do, for now. Concentrate on one thing at a time. He made a mental list, as he always did in times of stress. Get the Italian deal sorted. At least that would get Masterton off his back. If he could earn a decent enough bonus . . .

A half a million? Who was he trying to kid?

Ben's scribbled address lay beside the telephone, where Matthew had left it. He picked it up, stared at it for a moment. Just where the hell did Ben fit into the equation? He wasn't going to find the answer unless he made contact with the man, that was for sure. He rang directory enquiries, finding that his heart was beating more quickly than normal as he repeated the address. What Sylvia Guttenberg had said was nonsense, of course. The notion of a mad priest skulking around the countryside, wreaking revenge . . .

The number was unlisted, Matthew was informed. He felt an odd mixture of anticlimax and relief.

The arrival of the driver forced Matthew's attention back to Langton Industrials. His secretary had sent his post so that he could read it on the way. A Post-it sticker attached to the front of the sheaf of papers informed him that Mr Masterton wished to see him as soon as he arrived. Matthew suspected that the meeting would not be a pleasant one, and he was right.

'Shut the door,' Masterton snapped as soon as Matthew entered the office. 'Sit down.' He slung down the pen he'd been using. 'If you decide to betray your wife, Matthew, I can't stop you. I've already made my views on that subject clear. What I will not tolerate—'

Matthew shook his head. 'You've got this all wrong, Frank. I've never—'

'Allow me to finish, if you please,' Masterton said coldly.

Matthew breathed in hard and studied his hands. He was in no position to argue.

'Do you have any idea how embarrassed I felt the other night?'

'I apologise. I shouldn't have told Elizabeth I was with you. But—'

'Damned right you shouldn't.' Masterton leant across the desk. 'What you do in your own time is your business. But I will not have you involving me. Is that clear?'

Matthew nodded.

'You're on thin ice, Matthew, very thin ice indeed. This firm expects total commitment from its senior management team.'

'Which I've always shown,' Matthew retorted.

Masterton gave him a withering look. 'By writing off a company car gallivanting around Cornwall with God knows who? By delaying a crucial deal? You were supposed to be meeting Montelli yesterday, according to your wife. Or is that something else I've got wrong?'

'The meeting's tomorrow, as well you know. I'm flying out this evening. For God's sake, Frank! I'm supposed to be off sick, you realise. I shouldn't even be here.'

'Are you expecting a round of applause?'

'I'm merely pointing out—'

'Just make sure you come back from Italy with a result.' Masterton got to his feet, signalling the end of the meeting. 'No one's indispensable, Matthew. Do I make myself clear?'

Matthew stood up. 'Crystal clear,' he said.

He was still seething as he got into the back of the car and set off for Heathrow. Just who did Masterton think he was? Matthew reran the scene over and over in his head, humiliated that he had so dismally failed to bite back. Why hadn't he told the pompous bastard to mind his own bloody business and shove his job? Not that making himself unemployed would do much to enhance his current situation, he acknowledged as he began to calm down. He'd worked too hard all these years to throw everything away in a fit of temper. Better to bide his time. With any luck, in a year or two Masterton would be pensioned off; a yesterday's man. It was the only thought that gave Matthew any satisfaction.

In the meantime, he'd better make bloody certain that the Italian deal went through without a hitch.

He picked up the file his secretary had prepared for him, his attention immediately caught by the fax she had stapled to the inside of the folder, and which she had marked 'Urgent'.

It had been sent from Italy just a couple of minutes before Matthew had set off. He read it, then read it again.

A couple of hours later, he was drinking champagne in the Executive Lounge at the airport. No matter that the fog had delayed his flight to Milan. If necessary, Montelli would just have to wait another twenty-four hours to agree the deal. And when he did, it would be to Matthew's tune he would be dancing. The fax had shown the results of the land valuation Matthew had requested. God alone knew how many palms had been greased to get it through so quickly. Matthew couldn't care less. The bottom line was that for all the nit-picking about profits, plant and equipment, the site itself hadn't been valued for more than twenty years. During which time the improved road network between the drab suburb in which the factory was situated and the centre of Milan had caused the price of land to rocket, much as it had rocketed around Leamington when the M40 had been built. A stunningly simple oversight that Montelli had spotted and Masterton hadn't. And that only Matthew had bothered to check. The site alone was worth more than Montelli had offered for the whole damned operation.

As the importance of his discovery began to sink in, Matthew began to wonder if the task of finding half a million was quite as impossible as it had seemed. The more he thought about it, the more obvious it became. Why should he settle for a paltry few thousand in bonus from a patronising bastard like Masterton? The man had made it abundantly clear that as far as he was concerned, Matthew was expendable to Langton Industrials, so company loyalty hardly came into the equation. If Masterton wanted dog eat dog, he could have it. Matthew finished his drink, and ordered another glass. He had the distinct feeling that his luck was about to change.

*   *   *

Another hour and a half, and the flight still hadn't been called.
As the immediate effects of the champagne wore off, Matthew
began to wish he had someone with whom he could share his
news. But who? No one at work, that was for sure. Elizabeth?
She was the one with whom he'd always celebrated good news
in the past. But this was something he'd never be able to share
with her, even if they managed to patch things up between
them. The thought depressed him momentarily. It made him
realise just how isolated he had become. He felt the miss of
Spike more keenly than he had ever done.

He called Jane.

This time, the phone was answered on the first ring.

'Matthew! How are you?'

'Fine.' It was good to hear some warmth in someone's voice
for a change. 'Well, the arm's a damned nuisance, but fine
apart from that.'

'And how are . . . things?' Jane asked more tentatively.

'I . . . I'm not sure. Elizabeth's gone to stay with her mother
for a few days.' What would she read into that, Matthew
wondered. What did he want her to read into it?

A small pause. Then Jane said, 'If there's anything I can
do . . .'

The response was as ambiguous as his own had been.

Would it be so wrong? How many men in their mid-forties
had never had a fling? Matthew could feel his body stirring,
even at the thought of that one passionate kiss. He still
loved Elizabeth, he always would, but it had been months
since they'd had sex, with her feeling so sick all through
the pregnancy . . .

He cleared his throat and said briskly, 'Listen, I think I've
found a way of getting the money together. I thought you'd
want to know.'

Another pause. 'That's good news. How did you manage
it?' Jane's tone was equally businesslike.

The moment had passed, Matthew realised with just the smallest tinge of regret. It was for the best, he told himself. Life was complicated enough, for God's sake.

He glanced around at the other businessmen in the lounge, most on their mobiles or working at laptops, and lowered his voice. 'I can't go into detail.'

'You're absolutely certain you should pay up?'

'I don't see I have many options.'

'Have there been any more notes?'

Matthew hesitated. 'Not that I know of.' Why panic her even further about the crash? 'I've found out Ben Fellows' address. I'll maybe contact him when I get back from Italy, see whether he's had anything. Although if I can find the funds myself, there doesn't seem a lot of point.' It swept over him suddenly, the glorious realisation that if he could just lay his hands on the cash, pay Donna O'Mara off, he'd never have to give another thought to Pete, Toby, Ben – anyone connected with Blackport – ever again.

'You've managed to locate him already?' Jane sounded surprised.

'Through Sylvia Guttenberg.' Matthew hesitated, wondering if she would respond. When she didn't, he asked, 'What made you think she had anything to do with the crash?'

'Sorry?'

'Well, you rang her, didn't you?'

'*I* rang her?'

'She said you accused her of causing the crash.'

'I haven't spoken to her for weeks.' Jane sounded perplexed.

'You mean you didn't tell her about the accident? You're absolutely certain?'

'Of course I'm certain! Why on earth would I want to . . . ?'

Matthew's brain was racing. If Jane hadn't told Sylvia Guttenberg about the crash, then who the hell had? Unless . . .

'This woman you thought you saw. What did she look like?'

'I . . . I couldn't really see. It all happened so quickly. Why?' Jane had picked up on the urgency in his voice. 'Matthew, what are you getting at?'

'Think, Jane.'

'She was wearing something long. Dark. That's why I didn't see her until—'

'Could it have been Sylvia Guttenberg?'

'*Sylvia?*' She gave a small, astonished laugh. 'Whatever makes you think . . . ?'

An announcement over the Tannoy drowned out the rest of her words. 'Would all passengers for British Airways flight number . . .'

'They're calling my flight,' Matthew pressed his hand to his ear and shouted over the babble. 'Look, I'm going to have to go. I should be back at the weekend. If Sylvia tries to contact you in the meantime, don't say anything to her, OK?'

'OK. But—'

'I'll speak to you soon.' He went to switch off the phone. 'Jane?'

'Yes?'

'Just . . . just be careful.'

24

Matthew met Montelli in a smart restaurant just around the corner from Teatro alla Scala. It was late, and the place was filled with after-show operagoers. The venue suited Matthew well; no one would overhear what he had to say over so much animated chatter and laughter. As soon as the *prosciutto con melone* had been placed in front of them, he took out the fax and laid it on the table between them.

Montelli gazed at it for a moment. He was an elegant man; one of the distinctive breed of Italian businessmen who had inherited old money but who were none the less intent on making new. His clothes, his manner, everything about him spoke of vast, understated wealth. Not a man to create a scene in a public place. With a gracious inclination of his head, he said, 'My compliments, Signor Cosgrave. I have long suspected that you might be a more formidable opponent than your *amministratore*, Signor Masterton. I trust he appreciates your . . .' he sought the appropriate word, '. . . diligence.'

Beneath the table, Matthew wiped his palms on the starched linen napkin and cleared his throat. 'This puts an entirely different perspective on the deal, of course.'

'Possibly.' A slight shrug. 'The sale would have benefited us both, I believe.' Montelli was watching him appraisingly. 'What is the opinion of your board?'

'As yet, I am the only member aware of the . . . change in circumstances.' Matthew could feel himself colouring.

'*Davvero.*' The smallest of smiles crossed Montelli's lips. 'And when do you intend to tell your colleagues?'

Matthew looked him in the eye. It was a huge gamble, but he had no option but to play it. 'That rather depends on you,' he said evenly.

By the following day, the deal was struck. Matthew would present it to the board that he had managed to secure the full asking price for the subsidiary by the cunning expedient of throwing in some additional equipment that Montelli needed and that was of no use elsewhere in the Langton organisation.

Everyone would be a winner. Montelli would pay thirty million euros for a site that was worth forty-five million. The board, and Dan Chambers in America, would be delighted that Matthew had struck a hard bargain on their behalf. And Milano Enterprises, an account set up by Montelli with an 'associate' at the local bank, would have an opening balance of seventy-five thousand euros, which by the end of the week would be exchanged into half a million in sterling and withdrawn in cash, with no questions asked. It seemed almost frighteningly simple. Montelli's only show of surprise was that Matthew's own cut was to be so modest.; Matthew had almost been tempted to ask for more. The only mild irritant was that he would never be able to point out Masterton's mistake.

There was little for Matthew to do while he waited for the money to come through except play the tourist. It was a rare experience to have time to spare; business trips normally involved no more than taxi journeys from airport to hotel to office and back again. But try as he might to concentrate on the sights, he took little in; the attractions of Milan were no match for the problems he'd left behind him in England. He visited the cathedral, saw da Vinci's *Last Supper*, newly restored in the church of Santa Maria delle Grazie, wandered around street after street of designer shops. He bought Elizabeth a Gucci scarf similar to the one he had lost in Blackport. He wondered if she would ever wear it.

He rang her every day from the hotel. Her mobile remained switched off. He left messages, sent texts. All went unanswered. On the land line, he failed to get beyond Olive and her recriminations. In desperation, he tried several times to compose a letter to Elizabeth, but each attempt ended up in the bin; he'd never been any good at expressing himself on paper, even when he knew what he wanted to say. In the end, he settled for a postcard, stating simply that he loved her and that he would be back in the country at the weekend.

Would he ever tell Elizabeth the real reason why he and Jane had been in Cornwall together? Would she forgive him more easily as a rapist than an adulterer?

At least he'd managed to find a way of paying off the blackmail demand, he told himself as he watched a couple stroll by hand in hand beneath the window of his hotel on his last evening in Milan. He'd faxed Masterton with the official details of the deal, and had been faxed back with the other man's congratulations. The ice on which Matthew was skating was evidently a little thicker, with an extra twenty million pounds in the company's accounts. By the end of the month, the last note had said. Another week. And then, please God, he could concentrate on putting his life back together again. And if that meant camping outside Olive's house until Elizabeth agreed to see him, so be it.

He wondered when the next instruction would come. Would it be waiting for him on his return? Would it come to him at all? It was one reason, at least, for him to be glad Elizabeth was with her mother. Again and again, he went over the last conversation he'd had with Jane, trying to make sense of what she'd said, but try as he might, he couldn't get the pieces of the jigsaw puzzle to fit. If Jane hadn't told Sylvia Guttenberg about the crash, where had she got the information? Was it really feasible that it had been she who had stepped out in front of the car? The notion was as outlandish as the plot of one of the damned woman's books. What on earth would she have been doing out on Bodmin Moor? What, for that matter, if Jane had hit her? What could possibly be so important to Sylvia Guttenberg that she'd be prepared to risk her own life for it? It made no sense at all, yet still the central problem remained; if she hadn't caused the crash, who had?

For the last night of Matthew's stay, Montelli had somehow organised a box at La Scala to celebrate the deal – Pavarotti, singing Cavaradossi in *Tosca*. Tickets were like gold dust. Under normal circumstances, it would have been an experience Matthew would have relished, but he was barely aware of the magnificent surroundings, the strutting crowds, the soaring music. The same time the following day, he would be back in England, with a briefcase stuffed with illegally obtained cash. He wondered what awaited him there.

'Your mind was not entirely with poor Tosca's fate, I think,' Montelli observed, as the curtain calls finally came to an end and the lights in the theatre went up.

Matthew hadn't the remotest idea of the plot. 'Not at all. It was marvellous. Extremely moving.'

'But you have much to occupy your thoughts, I think.' Montelli smiled his urbane smile. 'It is perhaps fortunate that your . . . luggage is in my safe-keeping until tomorrow.'

Matthew forced an answering smile. Montelli had arranged for the briefcase to be delivered to the airport.

'Don't look so worried, my friend!' Montelli clicked his tongue reprovingly, his eyes glinting with humour. 'Signor Masterton will be expecting to see smiles, not furrowed brows.' He gestured to the plaster cast, his smile broadening.

'It is maybe a good thing your accident occurred before you arrived. He might have suspected you had . . . what is your English phrase? Been caught with your hand in the till.'

Matthew laughed uncomfortably. He had never thought of himself as an embezzler.

But then until a few weeks earlier, he had never thought of himself as a rapist, either.

He arrived back at Heathrow on Friday night, the briefcase clutched to him as it had been throughout the journey. This time, it had been a dispute concerning Italian air traffic control that had caused the delay; he'd spent an agonising eleven hours at Milan airport, hardly daring even to visit the lavatory for fear of putting the briefcase down. His heart had been hammering so hard as he'd taken it through check-in that he'd been sure he would be stopped; he couldn't have felt more nervous had he been planning an act of international terrorism. Surely, he'd thought, his guilt must be imprinted on his face. The official in charge had barely glanced at him; he'd been just another businessman in a hurry to get away.

Because of the hold-up to his flight, his secretary had booked him into a Heathrow hotel overnight and arranged for the driver to pick him up first thing in the morning. Matthew was not sorry for the delay in getting back to Leamington; he was more reluctant than he cared to admit to himself to face the house that no longer felt like home, and whatever might be waiting for him there.

Once at the hotel, he ate a solitary meal in his room, fearful of taking the briefcase down to the dining room. The hushed, impersonal surroundings served only to exacerbate the tension that had been steadily rising inside him all day. Barely four months ago, he'd been a well-respected, law-abiding member of the community; utterly trustworthy, maybe even a little staid. He'd had nearly everything: a successful career, a happy marriage, a child on the way whom one day he might have come to love almost as much as he'd loved Daisy. A friend he could trust . . .

And now it was an utter stranger who stared back at him from the bathroom mirror. A man who had broken the law not once, but twice.

Matthew had hoped that after the meal, he'd be able to get some sleep; God knew, he'd had little enough in Italy. He got ready for bed, lay down and closed his eyes, but he couldn't settle. He got up again, made himself some coffee. The silence of the room was oppressive. Despite the rain that hammered against the glass, he attempted to open the window, if only to hear the outside world, but it was firmly sealed against the noise from the runways.

He became more and more restless. He flicked from channel to channel on the television, attempted the crossword puzzle in the *Telegraph*, listened to a few minutes of a late concert on Radio Three. He considered ringing Elizabeth – even the prospect of a further haranguing from Olive seemed preferable to his own company – but it was past midnight, and he knew that both she and her mother would have been in bed for hours. He sent her a text instead, telling her he was back, begging her to get in touch.

He wondered whether to call Jane. He needed to find out if Sylvia Guttenberg had been in touch with her, for one thing. But something other than the fear of waking her held him back. If he spoke to her tonight, while he was within a few miles of her, he might suggest they meet. And if he saw her again, face to face . . . The prospect engendered an unwelcome *frisson* of excitement that warned him he'd be safer to wait until he had the ninety-mile journey from London and Leamington between them before speaking to her again.

At last, with some considerable help from the hotel's mini-bar, he nodded off, falling into a confusing tangle of vivid, erotic dreams. When he awoke, sweating, he could visualise every detail of the naked body that had been pressed against his own, the saltiness of her smooth skin, the softness of her breasts, the firmness of her thighs that had entwined themselves so urgently around him as he'd thrust into the warm, welcoming darkness of her. She was sweetly familiar, utterly unknown. The memory of her was both intensely exciting and horribly disturbing. Try as he might, Matthew could not recall the woman's face.

The flashing green light on the alarm clock told him it was one thirty; he'd been asleep for less than a hour. It was the only sleep he had that night.

The journey back to Leamington the following morning seemed to take an age, although the driver who had come to collect him kept the car at a steady seventy. Exhausted as he was, Matthew found it impossible to doze as he might normally have done. As they approached the house, he could feel his guts tightening. His hand was shaking as he fitted the key into the lock and pushed open the front door. The cleaning woman had put the post on the hall table, beside the telephone, so that Matthew would see it as soon as he let himself in. Carefully, deliberately, he walked over to it and put down the briefcase.

It took him no more than a moment to sort through the harmless collection of bills and circulars. Matthew sank down on the stairs and waited for his heartbeat to subside. What had he been expecting? A horse's head? He pulled himself to his feet, picked up the briefcase, and hurried up the stairs. What was he getting so worked up about? Carry on like this, and he'd end up with as many screws loose as Ben Fellows. He had the money. All he had to do was wait for the next set of instructions.

He had had a safe installed under the floor-space in one of

the spare bedrooms when he and Elizabeth had first moved into the house. He took the briefcase upstairs, pulled back the carpet to reveal the section of false floorboard and prised it up. He hadn't used the safe for a while; it was largely empty, apart from a few pieces of jewellery that Elizabeth seldom wore, and a bundle of legal documents. He punched in the code – Daisy's date of birth, so that he would never forget it – and stuffed the wads of fifty-pound notes inside. It was unbelievable, he thought, that the means of buying back his life could be fitted into so relatively small a space. Whistling under his breath, he went down to the kitchen and put the kettle on.

It was while he was making coffee that he found Elizabeth's mobile, lined up neatly by the cleaning woman beside the remote control for the portable television. Elizabeth hadn't taken the damned thing with her. Matthew felt his spirits rising as he checked the list of text messages and missed calls; all from him. No wonder she hadn't returned any of them. He made up his mind to drive down to Hampshire the following day. Somehow, he'd find a way to get past Olive and make Elizabeth listen to him.

Matthew spent the rest of the morning in the garden. It was a beautiful day, crisp and sunny. The first of the crocuses were opening up, and a battalion of sharp green shoots signalled that the daffodils wouldn't be far behind them. He worked hard, raking up dead leaves, cutting back a straggling jasmine bush, weeding out the neglected remains of last year's annuals, bringing back some order. It wasn't easy, hampered as he was by his plaster, but he managed, glad of the physical exertion after the mental strain of the previous days.

The work invigorated him. After a snatched sandwich and a coffee, he laboured on into the afternoon. As the light began to fade, he lit a bonfire in the spinney at the bottom of the garden and stood watching the slow spiral of smoke, his body already beginning to feel the effort of his labours, his mind blissfully empty. He felt more content than he had done in weeks. Something to eat, a good soak in the bath . . . He realised how hungry he was. Fish and chips, he thought suddenly; that's what he fancied. He hadn't had them in years. The problem was that the nearest chip shop was miles away, and he was stuck here, without transport. Sod it, he'd call a cab. He piled the last of the dead leaves onto the bonfire, stretched luxuriously, and made his way back to the house. Pulling off his boots, he went into the kitchen and called the local taxi firm. Whoever had heard of rolling up to a chippie in a taxi? Matthew shook his head, grinning. But why not? He'd got the money.

The kitchen was chilly. Elizabeth would have told him off for leaving the back door open while he was in the garden, he thought with a small smile. Rubbing his hands, he locked it and drew the kitchen curtains, then went through to the hall to turn up the thermostat on the central heating.

The note was propped up against the telephone.

Matthew could feel the blood draining from him. He clutched at the banister to steady himself. He took a deep breath, then slowly, reluctantly, he picked up the note and opened it.

'Down by the water where the little fishes play . . .'
TOMORROW
NOON
BRING THE MONEY

25

She must have been watching him.

The simple pleasure of the day's gardening had vanished utterly. She'd been here. Been in this house.

Might be here still.

Matthew held his breath, straining to hear anything over the pounding of his own heart.

All was silent.

Clutched with panic, he ran up to the spare bedroom, checked the safe, but the money was still intact.

As fear receded, anger came flooding in to fill its place.

'Are you there?' he called. 'If you're there, come and show yourself, you bitch.'

His voice reverberated along the empty landing.

He went from room to room, his fury swelling at the thought of her snooping around the house, touching his and Elizabeth's possessions. Nothing was disturbed. The house was utterly quiet, its very stillness an oppressive, alien presence.

The sound of the doorbell made him jump convulsively. He stood stock-still. The bell rang again. He hesitated, then ran down the stairs and threw open the door, almost laughing with relief as he saw the taxi parked outside.

'Ready, mate?' The taxi driver looked at him curiously. Matthew was still wearing his old gardening clothes. He stank of bonfires.

'Yes.' He grabbed his keys and his wallet and slammed

the front door behind him. No matter that he looked like a scarecrow. He just wanted to get out of the house.

'Where to?'

Matthew had no idea. His appetite had deserted him; the quiet night he'd planned in front of the television no longer held any appeal.

'Chelmsley Wood,' he said on impulse.

The taxi driver's eyebrows shot up. 'It'll cost you.'

'That doesn't matter.' Matthew thrust a handful of twenty-pound notes at the man. He suspected Pete would be less than delighted at the visit. Tough. It was he, Matthew, who had put his job on the line to get the money. He who had borne the brunt, right from the start. Why shouldn't the others share some of the pain?

'Can you pick me up later?' Matthew asked as, some three-quarters of an hour later, the taxi pulled up outside the Prestons' house.

The driver shrugged. 'Dunno, mate. What time'll you be finished?'

'I've no idea.' Matthew peeled off another couple of twenties. 'Does it matter?'

The driver grinned and handed him a card. 'Just give me a buzz whenever you're ready.'

Matthew strode up the front path and rang on the doorbell, not caring who answered. It was Pete who came to the door.

'Jesus!' He glanced at Matthew's filthy clothes, his face ashen. 'What the hell are you doing here? What's happened?'

'Can I come in?'

'No!'

From somewhere inside the house, Matthew could hear the babble of a television, a sudden burst of laughter.

Pete's head swivelled round anxiously. 'Look, there's a

pub.' He turned back to the front door, his voice was so quiet that Matthew had to strain to hear it. 'A couple of hundred yards down the road. It's called the Green Man. I'll meet you there in ten minutes.'

The pub was noisy, smoky, crowded and infinitely preferable to the elegant house Matthew had left behind him in Leamington. He looked around for a table, but they were all taken. He bought himself a whisky and found a vacant stool by the bar. The barman gave him a hard look, as if he were about to refuse to serve him, until he saw the colour of his money.

While he was waiting for Pete to turn up, Matthew took out the note and reread it.

'Down by the water . . .'

What the hell was it supposed to mean? He shook his head. It had to be a reference to Spike. What else could it be?

He looked up as a sudden scraping of chairs told him that Pete had arrived. A middle-aged couple sitting by the door glanced at the wheelchair and stood up, gesturing to Pete to take their table.

'One of the benefits of being in that thing, I suppose,' Matthew observed with a sour smile as he joined him.

Pete didn't react. 'So what's going on?' he demanded. His gaze travelled from Matthew's shabby clothes to the plaster cast. 'What happened to your arm?'

'It's a long story.' The thud of pop music competed with the general hum of conversation, the raucous laughter of a group of youngsters at the bar and the electronic babble of a rank of fruit machines. 'This is hardly an ideal place to talk.'

'It's a bloody sight more ideal than my front room,' Pete snapped. 'What the hell did you think you were doing, turning up like that?'

'Things have moved on a bit since last time we met,'

Matthew said grimly. 'I thought it was time I brought you up to date.'

Pete listened in silence, his face paling as Matthew recounted the conversation with Hubert Vardon.

'Oh fuck,' he muttered inadequately. 'You mean . . . ?'

Matthew nodded. 'The entire case. Lies from start to finish. You never suspected?'

'As God's my witness. It was bad enough knowing we were lying about the night itself, without—'

'Toby was right about the blackmail,' Matthew said quickly. He hadn't come here to get into a guilt-fest.

'Half a million?' Pete's voice rose an octave, when Matthew filled him in.

A woman at the next table turned round and looked him up and down inquisitively.

'Nice one, Pete,' Matthew hissed. 'Why don't you just tell the whole pub?'

'What are we going to do?' Beads of sweat had broken out on Pete's forehead.

'Pay up.'

'Are you kidding? How the hell are we going to lay our hands on—'

'The money's available. There's no need to discuss the whys and wherefores,' Matthew went on impatiently as Pete opened his mouth to speak. 'What I'd rather talk about is where Sylvia Guttenberg fits into all this.'

'She doesn't, does she?' Pete was still looking shell-shocked. 'I mean, I know I started off wondering if she might have—'

'No. This is different.'

Matthew told him about the accident, his subsequent conversation with Sylvia.

'How could she have known about the crash unless she was there?' he demanded. 'Now listen. I've been going over and over it. That night in Blackport, at the reunion, can

you remember anyone recognising her? Jonathan Freeman
certainly didn't and he'd worked with her on the student
newspaper for—'

'What are you talking about?'

'This woman that no one seems to remember turns up out
of the blue, knowing all about us, claiming to have written a
book based on us . . .'

'So?'

'Just think about it. What if . . . ?' Matthew hesitated. The
possibility had been nagging away at him for days. But now
that he was about to share it, it seemed too ridiculous to put
into words.

'What if *what*?'

Matthew shook his head. 'I'll get some drinks in first. You're
going to think I'm nuts.'

'I already think you're bloody nuts. I haven't got the first
fucking idea what you're on about.'

'What do you want?'

'Some sense?'

'To drink.'

'A lager.' Pete shook his head impatiently. 'Anything. Just
get on with it, for God's sake.'

Matthew fought his way to the bar and ordered a pint
of lager and a double whisky. Sylvia would be about the
right age, the right height and build. There was no other
resemblance that he could remember. But the plastic surgery
would have seen to that. And if Jonathan Freeman – and Toby
Gresham-Palmer for that matter – were to be believed, she
bore no resemblance to the Sylvia Johnson she claimed to
be either.

Pete was pulling nervously at his chin and rereading the
note when Matthew returned with a tray balanced precari-
ously in his good hand. Barely waiting for his drink to be put
in front of him, he said, 'Go on, then.'

Matthew downed the whisky in one swig. 'What if Sylvia Guttenberg and Donna O'Mara are the same person?'

'You what?' Pete stared at him in open-mouthed astonishment.

'It's not as daft as it sounds. Why else would one of the notes go to Jane Davenport, for one thing? How would Donna O'Mara know anything about her?'

'The engagement announcements?' Pete said doubtfully.

'Sylvia's been on to Jane right from the start, pestering her, pumping her for information about us all. What better link in to the rest of us than Spike's fiancée?'

Pete shook his head. 'I can't get my head round all of this. I thought you said Ben Fellows had met Donna O'Mara? That she'd got a husband and family?'

It was a question Matthew had been asking himself. 'But that was seven years ago, remember. Anything could have happened since then.'

'Must have been something pretty major to make her want to change her whole identity.'

'It must have been something pretty fucking major to make her suddenly decide to blackmail us after all these years,' Matthew snapped.

Pete took a long swig of his lager, then stared into his glass 'So you're just going to pay up?' he said eventually.

'Unless you've got a better suggestion.' Matthew grimaced. 'And yes, I have considered a hit man.'

Pete inhaled slowly. 'Look, maybe we should just go to the police after all. Or at least get a private detective to check her out. Why don't we talk it over with Toby and Ben—'

'There isn't time. She's made sure there isn't.' Matthew handed over the latest note. 'This came this afternoon.'

Pete scanned it. '"Down by the water . . . "?' He looked up questioningly.

'It's got to be where Spike drowned himself, hasn't it?

Polperron Cove. I'm going down there first thing in the morning.'

'Shit.' Pete swallowed the rest of his drink.

There didn't seem much else to say.

'Well, that's got you up to date with the news.' Matthew got to his feet, gathered the glasses and smiled down grimly at the other man. 'Now how about we both get pissed?'

Pete didn't seem in any more of a hurry to get home than was Matthew. A giant television above the bar had been switched on; a football match. They both turned their chairs to watch it, drinking steadily and saying little until the match was over and the barman called last orders.

'Well, that was a load of crap,' Pete said heavily. The game had ended in a goalless draw. Not that either of them had been concentrating on it.

'D'you want another one?' Matthew asked.

Pete shook his head. They sat in silence, surveying the pile of empty crisp packets in front of them. After a moment, he nodded towards Matthew's plaster and asked, 'Can you still drive then, with that thing?'

'No. Not that I've got anything to drive. The Jag was a write-off.'

'So how are you going to get down to Cornwall?'

It was a good question. 'Taxi, I suppose. Same as I got here.'

'Taxi?' Pete sounded genuinely shocked. 'It'll cost a fortune!'

It was the first time Matthew had laughed out loud in a very long time. 'I'm giving the fucking woman half a million pounds tomorrow morning, you silly bastard! And you're fretting about a taxi fare?'

The hefty tip Matthew had given the driver on the way over

ensured that the man arrived in record time to pick him up again. He appeared in the doorway at eleven on the dot, scanned the still-crowded bar, stuck his thumb up when he spotted Matthew, and went back to wait in the cab.

'Well, wish me luck.' Matthew stood up.

'You'll let me know how you get on?' Pete said.

'I think you can safely take it that in this case, no news is good news,' Matthew replied drily. He held out his hand. 'Goodbye, Pete. Don't take this the wrong way, mate, but I fervently hope that we never set eyes on each other again.'

The taxi driver, clearly feeling the tip obliged him to provide entertainment as well as transport, kept up a steady patter of conversation on the way back to Leamington. Matthew found he was grateful of the company. He established that the following day was the man's rest day. It didn't take too much persuasion to get him to negotiate a fee for the trip down to Cornwall.

'Looks like you've got a visitor,' the man commented, as they turned into the driveway. The house was in darkness. A blue Renault Clio was parked in front of the garage doors. It was not a car Matthew had seen before.

'Would you mind waiting here for a moment?' he asked, as casually as he was able. Stealthily, he walked across the lawn towards the car. In the light from the taxi's headlamps, he could make out a figure in the front seat. It appeared to be slumped over the steering wheel.

His heart in his mouth, Matthew quickened his pace. The figure remained motionless. Now that he was closer, he could see that it was shrouded in a blanket. Gingerly, he tried the handle. The door was locked.

'Everything OK, mate?'

The driver's voice behind him nearly made Matthew jump out of his skin. Before he could stop him, the man banged on the windscreen of the car. 'You all right in there?' he bellowed.

The figure jerked upright. A small, terrified face appeared from under the blanket. It was Jane. Her face and hands were streaked with blood. Wild-eyed, she looked at the man and began to scream. Scream and scream as if she would never stop.

26

It took Matthew some time to calm Jane to the point where she was able to tell him what had happened. The taxi driver, sensing a good story, had been reluctant to leave. Matthew had finally persuaded him everything was fine, and had arranged to ring him the following morning to confirm whether the trip to Cornwall was still on.

Once inside the house, he poured Jane a stiff brandy. Her hands, when he pressed the glass into it, were like ice. She must have been out there in the car for hours, he realised. He put a match to the fire that the cleaner had laid in the living room and sat her in front of it, forcing himself not to question her until she was ready.

It wasn't until the shaking gradually subsided that he asked quietly, 'What's happened?'

'It was horrible.' Jane's eyes were wide with remembered terror. 'I didn't know where else to go. I couldn't stay there. Not after . . .'

'Has someone tried to hurt you?'

She shook her head and gazed down at her bloodied hands. Shuddering violently, she began to cry.

'Start at the beginning.' Matthew was amazed to hear how successfully his voice belied his own mounting fear. 'Just take it slowly.'

His calmness seemed to steady her. She nodded, swallowed hard, clamped her hands between her knees to stop their trembling.

'I'd been away overnight. We had a concert. We'd joined forces with a choir in Canterbury to sing the Berlioz *Requiem*. It needs two choirs . . .'

Matthew nodded, trying not to rush her, however desperate he was to get her to the point.

'I'd never been there before. I decided to drive down, stay overnight. I thought I'd have a look at the cathedral. Anyway . . .' she took a deep breath, as if sensing his impatience, 'I got back to the flat about four. I don't really like driving in the dark. Especially after . . .' She glanced up, pushed the hair away from her eyes.

Matthew nodded again, not needing to ask her what she meant. 'Is this four o'clock this afternoon we're talking about?' he prompted.

Jane didn't reply. Her eyes had filled with tears again. 'I knew there was something wrong as soon as I got in and she wasn't there, but I thought maybe . . .' She shook her head. 'Then I went into the kitchen . . . and that was when I found her.' She pressed her hands to her eyes, as if to rid herself of the sight. 'There was so much blood,' she whispered.

'Found who?' Matthew gripped her hand in his, trying to bring her back from whatever horror she was locked into. He had given up all pretence of controlling his own panic. 'Tell me, Jane,' he shouted. 'You've got to tell me.'

'Petrushka.' She met Matthew's uncomprehending gaze. 'My cat.'

'Your *cat*?' Matthew had to stop himself laughing out loud. He took one look at Jane's face and hastily rearranged his features. 'I'm so sorry.' Spike had brought her the animal, he remembered; it must seem to her as if the last link with that part of her life had been severed. He strove to say something that didn't sound as if he were making light of her loss. 'That's the awful thing with cats, isn't it? They need their freedom, but with the busy roads somewhere like London . . .'

Jane's head jerked up. 'She hadn't been run over.' The expression on her face was the closest Matthew had seen to contempt. 'You really think I'd have driven all the way up here because my cat had been run over?'

Matthew flushed. 'Well, I can imagine how much she must have meant—'

'Her body was laid out on my kitchen table.'

Matthew was unsure what to say. 'Maybe she'd managed to—'

'She'd been beheaded, Matthew.'

'What?' He tried to steady his voice. 'Are you sure she hadn't just been . . . ?'

Jane stared at him, wild eyes. 'Her blood had been used to daub "WHO NEXT?" on the kitchen wall.'

'Oh, sweet Jesus,' Matthew breathed.

'I left her there.' Jane's teeth were chattering. 'I just ran out of the flat, got in the car and drove. I'm so frightened, Matthew.'

'How long do you think she'd been there?' Matthew's brain was working fast. The note had been left sometime between when he went back into the garden after lunch – two-ish at the earliest – and when he'd come back in again at dusk. Jane had found the cat at four . . . Sylvia Guttenberg might be smart, but even she couldn't be in two places at the same time.

'I don't know.' She glanced up at him fearfully. 'Why?'

'It doesn't matter.' Matthew shook his head. He'd tell her about the note when she'd calmed down a bit. He glanced at his watch; it was after midnight. 'Look, you can stay here for tonight. The spare bed's made up,' he added quickly. 'Why don't you go up and have a bath? You'll feel better when you're cleaned up a bit. You sit here and keep warm, and I'll go and put a few things out for you.'

Jane nodded, biting her lip. Matthew could see that she was still back in the kitchen of her flat. He put a tentative hand on her shoulder. 'You're safe here,' he said. 'I'll look after you.'

Briefly, she touched his fingers. 'I'm sorry, Matthew. I didn't know where else to go.'

Matthew cleared his throat. 'I'll go and run that bath.'

He prepared coffee and a plate of sandwiches, more to occupy himself than because he thought either of them was hungry. He could hear Jane moving around in the guest bathroom above the kitchen, the faint splash of water as she got into the bath. His mind was in turmoil. He should never have suggested that she stay. What would Elizabeth think, if she were to walk in now? What would anyone think? But he could hardly have thrown her out onto the street in the middle of the night, after what she'd been through.

The anger that he'd felt earlier swept over him again. He'd never considered himself a violent man, but if Donna O'Mara, Sylvia Guttenberg, whatever the bitch wanted to call herself, had been standing there at the moment . . . He gripped the knife he'd been using to slice bread. Why the cat, for Christ's sake? What had Jane Davenport ever done, apart from fall in love with Spike? The poor kid probably hadn't even been born when they were all at Blackport.

It was a sobering thought.

'I found this dressing gown . . .' Jane was standing in the doorway, her hair wrapped in a towel. She was wearing Elizabeth's bathrobe. She broke off, gazing at the knife still clutched in Matthew's hand.

'I thought you might be hungry.' Quickly, he put it down and busied himself with the tray, trying not to visualise her nakedness beneath the robe. He glanced at her and away again. 'Better now?'

'Much.' She hesitated. 'You don't mind me being here, do you? I wasn't sure whether Elizabeth—'

'Why don't you go back through to the lounge?'

She looked down, colouring. Matthew could see that he'd snubbed her with the brusqueness of his tone. 'I'll just finish getting the coffee, then I'll be through,' he added.

She was perched on the edge of the sofa. He put the tray in front of her and took a chair on the other side of the fire. She scanned his face, as if hoping he might speak, then said, 'Why did you want to know how long Petrushka had been dead?'

Matthew showed her the note. He said merely that it had been delivered by hand that afternoon; he didn't want to spook her by telling her that Donna O'Mara had been inside this house as well.

'I don't think she'd been dead long. The blood . . .' Jane faltered, drawing the robe closer around her. 'It was still wet.'

'You're sure?'

'You saw my hands.' She chewed nervously at her bottom lip. 'Could someone else be in on it, do you think?'

Matthew frowned. 'According to Ben, Donna O'Mara was married. I suppose it's feasible she could have told her husband.' God knew, the poor bastard would have grounds enough for a grudge, he added silently, imagining how he would feel if it had been Elizabeth.

'You don't think Ben could have had anything to do with it?'

The question took Matthew off guard. He looked at Jane sharply. 'Has Sylvia Guttenberg been talking to you again?'

'No.' She looked as surprised by his question as he had by hers. 'It's just that I've been thinking. From what Hubert Vardon said, Ben seemed to want some sort of vindication for Donna O'Mara. I know I've never met the man, but I can't help wondering—' She broke off. 'Do you really believe Sylvia Guttenberg and Donna O'Mara are the same person?'

'I can't see how else Sylvia would have known about the crash, do you?'

'Unless Ben told her.'

'Oh, come on!'

'No, listen. I only thought it was a woman who stepped out in front of us because of what she was wearing,' Jane had evidently been mulling it over for some time. 'A long dark dress?' She looked at Matthew expectantly.

'So?'

'Well, Ben's a priest. It could just have easily have been a cassock, couldn't it?'

Matthew stared at her in amazement. 'This is madness! Just what are you saying? That you think they're in it together? That Sylvia's an innocent bystander and Ben's master-minded the whole thing himself? What?'

'I'm not pretending to understand what's going on, Matthew.' There was anger in Jane's voice. 'It's just that you seem so completely hellbent on—'

'Sylvia Guttenberg's trying to throw suspicion on Ben to take it away from herself. It's obvious.' Matthew's own voice was rising in anger. 'I can't understand why you keep defending the bloody woman.'

'I'm not!' Jane shouted. She stopped, breathed in hard. In a more controlled voice she went on, 'It just seems odd to me that he's been within a few miles of the Vardons' house all these years, and yet he's never made contact, not even to come to Spike's funeral.'

'I don't suppose he and Hubert Vardon parted on the best of terms, last time they spoke, do you?'

'But why hasn't he got in touch with the rest of you? If he's had a note as well—'

'I doubt he has had a note,' Matthew said impatiently. 'If this is about vengeance, Ben had his comeuppance seven years ago. Sylvia told me that herself.'

'But that's just the point, isn't it?' Jane ran her hands through her damp hair in frustration. 'You're saying we can't believe anything Sylvia's told you.' She leant forward, her face earnest. 'Think about it, Matthew. Most of what you know about Ben has come from Sylvia, and everything you know about Donna O'Mara has come from Ben.' She frowned. 'There's something just too . . . pat about it. Do you see what I'm saying?'

'I don't know.' Matthew shook his head. 'This is all too bloody complicated for me. I just want to pay the money and get it over with.'

'But there are just too many loose ends. Don't you want to find out—'

'Not really.' Matthew looked up. 'To be brutally honest, I don't care any more who's involved, or why. I just want to have my life back.'

For a moment, the only sound in the room was the crackle of the fire. Then Jane said decisively, 'I'm coming with you.'

'No.'

'You can't drive yourself.'

'I've organised a taxi.'

'A taxi! Don't be ridiculous. My car's outside.'

'I don't want you there.' Matthew's gaze slipped away from hers. 'We don't know. It might be dangerous.'

'For God's sake, Matthew.' Jane's voice was gentle. 'Isn't it time you stopped trying to carry the entire weight of the world on your shoulders? I want to be there.' She paused. 'And I think I have the right, don't you?'

Suddenly, Matthew was too tired to argue. 'OK,' he nodded wearily. 'If it's what you want. But only if you promise to wait somewhere for me when we get down there. I'm not having you going back to Polperron Cove. Not with all the memories it must have for you.'

'All right.' She got up, came and sat on the arm of his chair. Matthew wondered fleetingly if she might be about to kiss him. But she just brushed her finger across his cheek.

'You're a nice man, Matthew,' she said softly. 'Elizabeth's a very lucky woman.'

They sat for a moment, utterly still, as if each were waiting for the other to make the next move. Then she stood up. 'We've got an early start in the morning. If you don't mind, I think I'm going to get some sleep.'

Matthew didn't follow Jane upstairs, although he was desperate to shower and change out of his old clothes. He was far too keyed up to sleep, but that wasn't the only reason he remained in the living room when Jane had gone up. He was acutely aware of her proximity, even though they were on different floors. The silent house seemed to crackle with unspoken sexual tension. He knew that she wanted him as much as he wanted her. If he were to climb the stairs, get undressed . . . He stayed in the living room because he was afraid that he might end up doing something he knew he would regret for the rest of his life.

He must have dozed, because he came to with a start to find Jane standing in the doorway, fully dressed. Disorientated, he pulled himself up in the chair and looked around him. The fire had died, and the room was very cold. The mantel clock showed that it was just after five.

'I couldn't sleep.' Jane was shivering. 'I didn't mean to disturb you. I just thought, if you were awake too we might as well set off. In case there were road works or anything.'

Matthew was wide awake now. 'You're sure you want to do this?' he said.

Jane's face was drawn, but determined. 'I'm sure.'

Matthew nodded. 'I'll get the money.'

It took him a matter of minutes to get everything ready. He found an old rucksack that he used sometimes on holiday, and packed the bundles of fifty-pound notes into it. It would look less noticeable, he thought, than the briefcase; and at least it meant that, even with the plaster, he had a free hand for the scramble down to Polperron Cove.

He showered as quickly as he was able, and pulled on some clean clothes. Jane was waiting for him in the hall when he came back downstairs.

'Right, then.' He took a deep breath and glanced around, fighting the nonsensical presentiment that he was seeing the place for the last time. He picked up his keys and wallet and looked around for his mobile.

'What's the matter?' Jane asked.

'I'm trying to remember what I've done with the damned phone.' He patted at his empty coat pockets.

'When did you have it last?'

'I don't know.' He hadn't had it the previous evening. He'd had to ring the taxi driver from the pay phone at the pub. He shook his head impatiently. 'I don't need it, anyway.'

'But what if we need to talk to each other?' Jane's voice was edgy. 'You don't want to be stranded on that beach without any means of getting in touch with me.'

'I'll be OK.' Matthew unlocked the front door, anxious to be on the way.

'At least let's look for it.' Jane was rummaging through the drawers of the desk.

Matthew fought to stifle his impatience. 'If it's that important to you I'll take Elizabeth's.' He fetched it from the kitchen and held it up to her before slipping it into his pocket. 'OK?'

'Sorry.' Jane gave him a tight smile. 'I guess now it's actually happening, I'm more nervous than I thought.'

Matthew knew how she felt. 'Come on,' he said determinedly as he threw the front door open on to the freezing darkness. 'The sooner we get started, the sooner this will be over.'

* * *

They spoke little on the journey. The roads were deserted, and they made good time; too good. By the time dawn was breaking, they were already near Bodmin.

They stopped at a transport café off the A30 to kill some time; it would take them less than another hour to reach Boslowan Major, and the prospect of hanging around once they got there was not an appealing one.

Attached to a filling station, the café had pretensions at odds with its prefabricated exterior; inside, it was all mock beams and willow-pattern. Souvenirs and knick-knacks cluttered the Formica counter, tea towels with garish depictions of the Cornish coastline hung from the walls. It reminded Matthew of the sorts of places his parents had stopped at when he was a child.

In contrast to the prissy décor, the food on offer was standard lorry drivers' fare. Matthew, hungry despite the nerves that were churning his stomach, ordered a full English breakfast and attacked it with gusto.

'We're far too early,' he said as he swallowed the last of his fried bread, and consulted his watch; it was still well before nine.

Jane, who had done little more than toy with the single slice of toast that she'd ordered, looked up from her plate. 'You could always call in and see Ben Fellows,' she said tentatively. 'It's not far out of our way.'

Matthew sighed. It was clear from the expression on her face that it was more than simply a random suggestion. 'To what purpose?'

'I don't see what you've got to lose.' She shook her head as Matthew started to speak. 'Aren't you even remotely curious to find out what happened to him?'

'I haven't got his address with me.'

'How many unhinged ex-priests do you think there are in Boswithiel?'

'You said yourself we only have Sylvia's word that he's unhinged.' Matthew drew his fork across the congealing remains of his breakfast.

'Even more reason to find out, surely? I don't understand why you seem so anxious not to see him.'

Matthew didn't understand either. He was utterly certain that the other man wasn't responsible for what was happening; the notion was too nonsensical even to consider. So why? Was it because Ben had known Donna O'Mara before she'd reinvented herself as Sylvia Guttenberg? Might a meeting with the other man resurrect memories of the vulnerable, innocent girl they'd ruined – the girl who was so much harder to hate than the slick, manipulative bitch she'd become? Or was it simply that he, Matthew, didn't want to face the fact that of all of them, Ben had been the only one who had wanted to do the decent thing? In his heart of hearts, Matthew knew that before he could rule a line under the whole sordid mess and pick up the pieces of his life, he needed to find out.

Reluctantly, he pushed back his chair and got slowly to his feet.

'What makes you think Ben Fellows will even let me through the door?' he said.

27

Sylvia Guttenberg's story had been true in one respect, at least: the old girl behind the counter of Boswithiel Post Office and Village Store was a fund of information and gossip. A wiry little woman with bright, inquisitive eyes and a shock of frizzy white hair, she was only too happy to pass the time of day between dispensing Sunday newspapers to the half-dozen or so customers who called in on their way to morning service at the parish church across the lane. Potted biographies of each were inserted into her detailed directions to Ben Fellow's house a couple of miles out of the village. Matthew was also the unwilling recipient of her recollections of Ben as a young boy, together with a lengthy catalogue of the man's more recent and apparently increasingly bizarre behaviour.

'A friend of yours, is he?' she enquired.

Matthew nodded. Realising that an explanation was expected, he added, 'We were at university together. I was in the area and decided to look him up.'

'Ooh, you'll see a big change.' The woman shook her head with relish. ''Tis a proper shame. He was such a lovely little lad, with that mop of red hair.' She sighed in reminiscence as she rang up the copy of the *News of the World* that a stout, elderly man in a tweed suit had handed across the counter. 'You remember him, don't you, Walter? Young Ben Fellows?'

The man grunted, clearly anxious not to be drawn in.

The post mistress dropped her voice as he went out. 'On

the parish council, he is. Has the *Sunday Telegraph* delivered, then pops in on the sly to pick up that rag. You watch, he'll fold it up now and stick it inside his jacket.'

Matthew glanced round to see the man acting exactly as she had predicted.

Her eyes danced with mischief. 'The tales I could tell you!'

Matthew could imagine.

'I had heard that Ben's become rather . . .' he sought the right word, not wishing to add fuel to the woman's fire, '. . . reclusive in recent years.'

'Downright odd, more like. He won't let anybody in, you know. Not even to clean. I don't know what state that house of his must be in. His mother must be turning in her grave.' Elbows on the counter, she leant forward confidentially and went on, 'Strange to tell, we had an American woman in here a couple of weeks back, asking after him. Bit of a madam, she struck me, all done up like a dog's dinner. Wouldn't have been poor Ben's cup of tea, even before he went funny. Not that he was supposed to be interested in women, of course, him being a priest and all.' She pursed her lips in a manner that suggested she could tell much more if pressed. When Matthew didn't oblige, she put her head on one side and asked, 'Would you know who she'd have been, then? This American?'

Matthew shook his head, hoping his expression didn't give him away. 'Well, thanks for your help.' He glanced towards Jane, who was sitting outside in the car.

'Oh, yes. You don't want to keep your wife waiting.' The woman craned her neck to get a better look, and gave Jane a cheery wave. 'You could always try taking his groceries, if you can manage them with that arm of yours. You might at least get him to open the door to you. He does sometimes, depending on his mood.' She winked. 'And you'd be saving me a trip on my bike. My old knees aren't what they used to be.' She bobbed down beneath the counter and reappeared with a cardboard box, frowning at it as she handed it across. 'He can't be taking proper care of himself. 'Tis a wonder a full-grown man survives on so little.'

Matthew could see what she meant; he picked the box up one-handed with ease. He glanced at the contents: a few tins of soup, a loaf, a packet of tea bags. The Ben of old had been as legendary for the size of his appetite as Matthew himself.

'You could put them in your rucksack if it would be easier.' She came round from behind the counter. 'Take it off, and I'll help you pack it.'

'No!' Matthew clutched the strap. 'I can manage, thanks. It's not heavy.'

'Oh. Well, as long as you're sure . . .' The woman regarded him curiously, clearly taken aback by the sharpness of the refusal.

'Might squash the sandwiches,' Matthew extemporised. 'We thought we might stop for a picnic somewhere.'

The explanation seemed to satisfy her. 'You've got a nice day for it, my bird, long as you're wrapped up warm. Oh, by the way,' she added as Matthew reached the door. 'I'd leave your car a little way down the lane, if I were you. If he catches sight of it, you won't stand a chance.'

Sylvia Guttenberg had also been accurate in her description of the place as spooky, Matthew was forced to agree, as, several minutes later, he approached the house on foot, the box of groceries clamped under one arm. Even the lane that they'd driven up to get there had seemed menacing, the overarching trees making it so dark that Jane had had to switch on the headlights, despite the wintry sun. Matthew had wondered whether she might object to being left in the car, had already formulated his argument: from what the woman in the post office had said, he'd be lucky to get over Ben's threshold, without having a complete stranger in tow. But the eeriness of the place appeared to have got to Jane even before they caught a glimpse of the house through the tall, straggling conifers that partially screened it from view. She hadn't argued when Matthew had asked her to reverse the car back down the lane and wait for him there.

'Don't be too long,' was all she'd said, in a small voice, as she'd glanced up at the shadowy vault of trees and pulled her coat closer around her.

'I'll probably be back in a couple of minutes,' Matthew had replied, trusting he sounded more sanguine than he felt.

Now, pushing open the heavy, rusted iron gate, he felt his unease increasing. The house was bigger than he had envisaged it; a solid Edwardian villa built on three storeys, maybe once the holiday retreat of some businessman from Bristol or Exeter, now fallen badly into disrepair. Had he not known Ben lived there, he would have thought the place was unoccupied. It looked dark and forbidding; utterly deserted. The windows, several of them broken, seemed to stare back at him with blank hostility.

Just reaching the front door was a struggle; brambles tore at Matthew's coat, twigs tugged at the rucksack. A couple of times he stumbled on the uneven slabs of the path that was itself half-concealed by grass and weeds, before tripping over the roots of a huge gnarled apple tree close to the house. He grabbed at a branch to steady himself, dropping the cardboard box as he did so. Cursing, he bent clumsily and, one-handed, gathered the meagre groceries back together.

A carpet of rotting fruit lay beneath the tree, smelling of decay and death. A single magpie circled the conifers, its ugly clattering the only sound to break the silence. Matthew tried to shake off the foolish impression that the bird was watching him. Despite the chill air, he was sweating inside his heavy coat by the time he put the box down on the step and, not allowing himself time to change his mind, banged the tarnished brass knocker.

Nothing.

He banged it again, taking a step backwards to check for any hint of any sign of life behind the curtained windows. Nothing moved. If Ben were concealed somewhere behind one of them, he clearly intended to stay there. More anxious to get back to the car than he cared to admit, Matthew turned away.

It wasn't until he was nearly at the gate that he heard the click of the latch, the creak of a hinge as the door was opened. Matthew tensed. For a ridiculous moment, he considered making a run for the car. Then arranging his features into an amiable smile, he turned back towards the house.

In some ways, Matthew was more shocked by Ben Fellows' appearance than he had been by either Pete Preston's or Toby Gresham-Palmer's. There was no obvious sign of disability or disfigurement, but the contrast between the stooped figure who stood in the doorway and Matthew's remembered image of the man was nothing short of staggering. Ben's unshaven cheeks were sunken and haggard, his once-stocky frame thin and wasted beneath the dusty cassock. His head had been shaved of its fiery curls to reveal the fragile skull below. He looked an old, old man.

The surprise did not appear to be mutual. Ben gazed at Matthew for a moment, then slowly nodded his head. 'I've been expecting you,' he said as he stood aside. The slight lilt of his Irish accent was the only thing about him that hadn't changed. 'Please, come in.'

Matthew followed him into the hall. Neither bothered to bring in the box of groceries. His sweat turned cold and clammy as the iciness of the gloomy interior hit him. The place smelt dank, musty, as if the chilly air had been breathed in too often. The heavy curtain that hung over the front door blocked out any ray of sun that might have found its way through the dense shrubbery outside. The only source of light was the small devotional candle that flickered beneath the crucifix on the wall. The place felt almost subterranean. Matthew was reminded of the strange, twelfth-century church built into a rock face near Aubeterre that he and Elizabeth had visited once while on holiday in Bordeaux.

Ben led the way past closed doors to a room at the back of the house; apparently the only one he occupied. Thick with dust, every surface was cluttered with a jumble of papers and books, empty tins and dirty crockery. In one corner, a mattress lay on the floor, a single thin blanket thrown back to reveal dirty, faded ticking. Another, larger crucifix hung from the wall above it.

'Sit down.' Ben swept a pile of unwashed clothes from a wooden stool and gestured to it.

Wordlessly, Matthew complied. He could barely remember what he had hoped to achieve by the visit; he had absolutely no idea what he was going to say.

Ben pulled up another stool. He placed it in front of Matthew, too close for comfort, and sat down, studying Matthew's face with disconcerting intensity. Then leaning forward, he took Matthew's good hand in both his own and said, 'You've come to seek redemption, my son. I knew you would. We shall pray together.'

Matthew had never felt so acutely embarrassed in his life. The man really was barking mad. Hastily withdrawing his hand, he said in as conversational a tone as he could muster, 'I heard you were in the area, so I thought I'd take a chance and call in.' He glanced around at the squalor and cleared his throat. 'Have you been living here long?'

Ben ignored the question. 'God sees into our souls, Matthew.' His eyes were burning with fervour. '"Be not deceived; God is not mocked: for whatsoever a man soweth, that shall he also reap."' He nodded emphatically. 'Galatians, chapter six: verse seven.'

'Right.'

'"Be sure your sin will find you out."'

Matthew moistened his lips with his tongue. It was a risk to take the direct approach with someone so clearly unstable, but he had no intention of sitting around all morning to have the Bible quoted at him. 'We're talking about Donna O'Mara, I take it?'

'Repentance is not enough.' Ben pointed a grubby finger at him. 'We have to pay the price of our sin before we can be truly redeemed.'

Pay the price? Involuntarily, Matthew's hand went to the strap of the rucksack still slung across his back. Christ, could Jane have been right after all? Was Ben sufficiently unhinged to have dreamt up the whole thing himself? He glanced towards the door. What would the man's reaction be, he wondered nervously, if he were to simply get up and walk out? Did he bite, as well as bark? He looked pretty frail, but if he turned nasty, would Matthew be a match for him, one-handed?

As if reading his thoughts, Ben jumped to his feet with an agility that Matthew found both surprising and alarming. But he seemed more interested in rummaging through the papers heaped on the mantelpiece than in preventing Matthew's escape.

'God's words!' He appeared to have found what he was looking for. Whirling round, he thrust a crumpled sheet of paper in Matthew's face. On it was printed the quotation from Galatians. And beneath them, the words that told Matthew Ben was not the perpetrator, but as much a victim as the rest of them.

Matthew snatched it from him. 'Not God's words, Ben.

Her words.' He scanned the demented face, unsure whether any sort of rational conversation was an option. 'We've all had them. Even Spike.' Would anything he said go in, or was Ben too far gone for that? 'Spike's dead,' he said slowly and deliberately, as if he were addressing a child. 'Did you know that?'

The face collapsed abruptly. Clutching his hands to his thin elbows. Ben began to rock. 'He paid the price,' he keened. 'We have all paid the price. Paid with what was most dear to us, but none so high as his.'

Matthew grabbed him by the shoulder. Through the coarse fabric of the cassock, he could feel the bone, fragile as a bird's. 'What do you mean? What do you know about Spike's death?'

The roughness of his grip at least served to silence the keening. Ben stared at him, wild-eyed. 'All except you, my son. What do *you* hold most dear? For with that you can be sure you will have to part, before you can hope to find salvation.'

'I don't know what you're talking about.' Matthew strove to ignore the chill Ben's words struck in him. They were just the ranting of a madman, for God's sake.

Sinking back down onto the stool, Ben muttered, 'Peter has lost his strength, Toby his beauty. And I . . . I have lost my vocation. All that is left to us is to crave death and God's ultimate mercy.' He raised red-rimmed eyes. 'From which Spike has cut himself for eternity by the taking of his own life.'

Matthew grasped at the only strand of the man's rambling to make any sense at all. 'For a recluse, you seem to know a hell of a lot about what's happened to everyone,' he said brutally.

'The news came to me through an instrument of the Lord.' Ben produced a second letter, this time from the pocket of his cassock. 'The scales have fallen from my eyes and now I can see God's plan. That is why I knew that sooner or later you would come.'

Matthew took the letter from Ben's trembling hand and read it. It documented the circumstances of Spike's death, Pete's accident and the acid attack on Toby Gresham-Palmer. It spoke of curses. It warned that the writer suspected Ben of complicity in each of those events, and intended to investigate matters further. It was signed 'Sylvia Guttenberg'. The scheming bitch was trying to persuade this pathetic lunatic that he was to blame for everything that had happened. What better way to muddy the waters, if anyone decided to check her out?

'It wasn't an instrument of the Lord.' Matthew crumpled the letter in his fist. 'It was Donna bloody O'Mara. Listen to me, Ben.' He grabbed at the sleeve of the other man's cassock, trying to keep his attention. 'She didn't stop at getting you thrown out of the Church. She's reinvented herself as this Sylvia Guttenberg character. It was *she* who sent the notes we've all been getting.' He looked at Ben with a mixture of exasperation and compassion. 'Are you taking in any of this at all? It's got nothing to do with God's judgement. It's about blackmail – half a million pounds worth of blackmail.' He pulled the rucksack from his back, held a bundle of fifty-pound notes up to the priest's bewildered face.

'Donna?' Ben gazed unseeingly at the money. 'Donna O'Mara?' He looked up suddenly, an alertness in his expression Matthew hadn't seen until that moment. 'But Donna's dead.'

'*What?*'

'She was killed in a car accident.'

'She can't have been.'

'She was run down outside the hospice, as she was leaving work.'

'No . . .' Seconds earlier, Matthew might have thought it

just another of Ben's delusions, but the calm certainty of the other man's voice unnerved him more than any amount of raving. 'No, that's not possible. It must have been part of the plan to change her identity.' He was thinking as he spoke. 'She must have faked the accident somehow as a way of—'

'I administered the last rites.' Ben spoke with absolute clarity. 'She died in my arms.' His fingers moved across his thin chest to make the sign of the cross. 'Donna O'Mara, God rest her blessed soul, has been dead for more than seven years.'

28

Matthew sat on the rickety stool in Ben's cluttered room and watched the carefully constructed theory of Sylvia Guttenberg's dual identity crumble before his eyes.

Ben talked rapidly and with surprising lucidity. It was as though he had been waiting all of those seven long years for the opportunity.

He and Donna had met when he had first taken up his post at the hospice some months before her death, he said. They had recognised each other at once.

'And that's when you contacted Hubert Vardon?' Matthew prompted, trying to fit the pieces together in his head.

Ben nodded. 'For eighteen years, I had prayed each day for a way of making amends for the terrible wrong we had done that poor girl. To have been sent to that place, to see her again . . .' He gazed into the distance. 'It was a sign from God. I knew at once what I must do.'

'But Vardon managed to talk Spike into making you see things differently.' Matthew couldn't keep a trace of irony from his voice.

'Not Spike.' Ben gazed at him. 'Donna. I told her that I intended to make public confession, and would urge the rest of you to do the same. She asked what good would be achieved by revisiting the past? She'd been blessed with a happy marriage and healthy children. I was doing God's ministry . . .' Ben's eyes blurred with tears. 'She said that working with the dying had taught her not to squander the present by dwelling in the past. She said that she herself had offended God, and how could she ask His mercy, if she were not willing show mercy in her turn?'

'Offended God?' Matthew asked sharply. 'What did she mean by that?' Could whatever Donna had had on her conscience be in any way relevant to the matter in hand? But how could it be? She'd been dead for seven years.

'A black stain on her soul, she said. She would utter nothing more, not even at Confession. But her trespasses will be forgiven, as she forgave those who trespassed against her.' Ben's smile was beatific. 'She forgave us, Matthew. That dear woman forgave us all.'

'It's a shame you didn't tell Spike that,' Matthew said roughly. Ben's religious fervour was becoming more than he could tolerate. 'It might have stopped him walking into the sea at Polperron Cove.'

'Donna told him herself.' Ben's face was still lit by the same luminous smile. 'As soon as I contacted his father, Spike came across to Ireland. The woman was a saint, Matthew. She gave him her blessing, said she hoped he would find happiness as she had done.'

'I don't believe you. Spike would have told me. I was his closest friend, for God's sake!'

Which was precisely why Spike *hadn't* told him, Matthew realised. How could he have explained Donna O'Mara's forgiveness for a crime they were not supposed to have committed? All those years, Spike had been protecting him from the truth.

'If she was so bloody saintly, how come she still got you thrown out of the priesthood?' he said savagely.

'"Vengeance is mine; I will repay, saith the Lord."' The manic glitter had returned to Ben's eyes. 'God sent my accuser to extract retribution.'

Matthew glanced down at his watch. It was already almost

eleven. 'Ben, I don't have much time,' he said evenly. 'Can you for Christ's sake stop talking in tongues and just tell me what the fuck happened?'

It was really quite simple. Too simple. Just weeks after Donna O'Mara's death, one of the volunteers at the hospice had gone to the bishop and accused Ben of indecent assault. Ben had chosen not to deny the allegation. The scandal had been hushed up, but he had been sent back to Cornwall, disgraced. That the accusation bore no link to what had happened to Donna O'Mara was too much of a coincidence to be considered.

'I had not paid for the sin I had committed.' Ben stared up at the crucifix above his bed. 'So God saw fit in His wisdom to punish me for one that I had not.'

Matthew followed his gaze. The Sunday school he'd attended as a child had peddled the idea of a gentler Jesus, but he wasn't inclined to discuss theology; his mind was already working along different lines.

'This other woman, the one who accused you . . .' Donna must have confided in someone before her death. But who? Someone so hellbent on revenge that she had set about disgracing the priest Donna herself had forgiven? A sudden chill shiver of apprehension ran down Matthew's spine. Someone who might then have sought revenge on Pete and Toby too? On Spike?

'She was merely God's instrument.' Ben's eyes were still fixed on the crucifix.

For the moment, Matthew had almost forgotten the other man was there. 'What was her name?' he demanded.

'I have little recollection of her.' Ben was utterly dismissive. 'Her identity was unimportant to me.'

'For God's sake, the woman got you thrown out of the priesthood! You must remember *something* about her.'

Briefly, Ben looked at him. 'Volunteers came and went at the hospice. Few stayed for long. I barely knew the woman.'

'Well, was she young? Old?' Matthew was thinking fast. Sylvia Guttenberg had to fit into the equation somewhere, of that he was certain. 'She didn't have an American accent, did she?'

But he had once again lost Ben's attention. The other man had dropped to his knees, his hands clasped in front of him. 'We should pray together, my son.'

'Your so-called instrument of God is about to screw me for half a million pounds, you realise that?' Matthew shouted in frustration.

Ben's lips were moving in prayer.

Matthew jumped to his feet, grabbed the rucksack. 'Have you any idea what I've had to go through to get hold of this money? I've risked my entire bloody career!'

Ben's fingers worked feverishly at his rosary.

'It isn't just your life this woman's ruined. If you know anything about her, for Christ's sake tell me!' Matthew only just managed to control the urge to pick the other man up and shake the information out of him.

'Is wealth so important to you, Matthew?' At last, Ben swivelled his eyes from the crucifix. 'Have you nothing more precious that God can take from you? For if that is the case, my son, you are the most pitiable of us all.'

'How did you get on?' Jane demanded as soon as Matthew got back to the car.

'The man's crazy.' He threw the rucksack onto the back seat, still stung by Ben's parting words.

'You were in there an awfully long time just to discover he was crazy.' Jane was looking at him closely. 'What happened?'

Briefly, and with some reluctance, Matthew told her.

Jane listened, her face tense with concentration. Her eyes widened in surprise when Matthew revealed that Donna O'Mara was dead, but she made no attempt at interruption. It wasn't until he finished speaking that she said soberly, 'So she had nothing to do with any of it.'

'Evidently not.'

She shuddered. 'What he said about each of you losing what was most precious to you . . .'

Matthew had known he was doing the wrong thing in repeating that part of Ben's rant even as the words had left his mouth. 'Like I say, the man's certifiable,' he snapped. 'Forget the hocus-pocus. Let's concentrate on the facts. Sylvia Guttenberg's involved. Somehow. She's got to be.' He stared out of the windscreen, his fingers drumming on the dashboard. He shook his head. 'What I still don't understand is why the notes only started in the last few months. Even if what happened to Pete and Toby *is* connected to Donna O'Mara in some way – which seems extremely unlikely,' he added hastily before Jane could interrupt – 'why wait until now to start up again? Unless . . .' his fingers stopped drumming.

'Unless what?'

'What if Sylvia met up with this woman, somehow?' Matthew said slowly. 'The one who made the allegation against Ben, I mean. Got the whole story out of her?'

It made sense. A whole lot more sense than his original notion of Donna O'Mara changing her identity. Sylvia Guttenberg was exactly who she said she was. For whatever reason, she'd decided to follow up on them all, maybe with the hope of a sequel to her ridiculous novel, maybe simply to open up old wounds . . .

Jane frowned. 'I don't see what you're getting at.'

'What if once she'd got herself involved, she spotted an easy way of supplementing her royalties?'

Jane looked at him blankly.

'Maybe she sent the first notes with the intention of simply stirring up trouble – she admitted herself she'd got a score to settle with Toby, didn't she?'

'Did she?'

Matthew nodded impatiently. 'She was one of his conquests. So let's say it all started as a bit of malicious muckraking . . .'

'If it did, surely she'd have backed off as soon as Spike killed himself.'

'No. Not necessarily. It might have made her realise just how much leverage she really had. Don't you see?' The more Matthew thought about it, the more plausible it became. 'That's when she must have come up with the idea of blackmail.'

'But Pete's accident. Toby's—'

'Just that. Just a random accident and an assault entirely in keeping with Toby's lifestyle. Sylvia's had us spooked with this "curse of the virgin" crap right from the start. It was all part of her plan, and we fell for it hook, line and sinker. Her only weak link was Ben, because he knew Donna was dead. Christ, no wonder she was so desperate to warn me off going to see him!' He blew out his cheeks. 'Fair play to the woman, she's bloody smart. All that telling me we should go to the police!' He snorted derisively. 'She knew damned well we'd never actually call her bluff and do it.'

'And the car crash? Petrushka? You honestly believe Sylvia would stage-manage those just to spook us too?'

'Half a million's a hell of a lot of money to be playing for.'

Jane looked unconvinced.

'Well, can you think of any better explanation?'

For a moment, neither of them spoke. Then Matthew looked down at his watch and said decisively, 'It's time we got going. I'm supposed to be at Polperron Cove in half an hour.'

Jane looked as if she would have liked to say more, but whatever her thoughts, she kept them to herself. It wasn't until they had driven back through Boswithiel that she asked, 'What were Ben's exact words? The bit about what Donna had done.'

'I don't know.' Matthew lifted his shoulders dismissively. 'Some clap-trap about offending God.'

'That's all?'

'Something about a "black stain" on her soul. It was pretty hard to keep track of him, when he got into all the mumbo jumbo.'

'A black stain,' Jane repeated quietly.

He glanced across, unable to read her expression, wondering briefly if she might be Catholic herself, and he had upset her. 'Why?'

'I just wondered.'

It was clear she had something on her mind.

'What are you thinking?'

'Nothing.' She shook her head, then flashed Matthew a small, sideways smile. 'Just curious.'

'Well, whatever it was, it's got nothing to do with any of this, has it? Not unless Donna was planning to come back from the grave and haunt us all.'

It was ten miles from Boswithiel to Polperron Cove. When at last the lane petered out into the narrow track that led steeply to the beach below, it was just after a quarter to twelve.

'You're sure you don't want me to come with you?' Jane asked.

'Quite sure.' Matthew opened the door. 'This shouldn't take very long.'

'Don't forget the money.' Jane pulled the rucksack from the back, as he went to close the door.

'You hang on to it, for now.'

She stared at him, perplexed. 'But the note told you to—'

'Yes. But the rules have changed a bit since then, haven't they?' he said grimly.

Matthew scrambled down the path to the deserted beach. He sat down on a rock to wait for his would-be blackmailer, his face turned towards the feeble winter sun, calculatedly relaxed. Let Sylvia Guttenberg see at once that he wasn't afraid.

What she had apparently failed to notice was that the strength of her plan was also its weakness. With Donna dead, the only people who would testify to the truth of what had really happened that night in Blackport were a mad priest and some woman who had already accused him falsely of indecent assault, and so had every motive for throwing in the allegation of an earlier rape for good measure. If the rest of them stuck to their original story – which they would – there was no credible witness to challenge the verdict the court had passed twenty-five years before. And Sylvia Guttenberg could whistle for her half a million pounds.

He had been there no more than a couple of minutes when he heard the distant crunch of tyres from the path above the cliffs. He looked up, his heartbeat subsiding as he saw a youngish man striding down the path towards him, a boisterous Labrador barking at his heels. The man gave him a friendly, incurious nod as he passed, then went down to the water's edge. He picked up a stone and threw it for the dog. The creature hurled itself into the sea in a frenzy of excitement, plunging its head under the surface and emerging, triumphant, the stone clamped between grinning jaws. It rushed out, dripping, deposited the stone at the man's feet and crouched expectantly until he threw it again. Matthew found himself envying the creature's uncomplicated happiness. The game went on unabated for several minutes, then man and dog retraced their footsteps and disappeared together back up the path, the man half-raising his hand in valediction.

Matthew continued to wait. The sky clouded over. A spatter of rain pock-marked the sand, disappearing as quickly as it had come. A stiff wind had sprung up, pushing in more cloud. Without the sun, it was bitterly cold. Matthew drew his coat more closely around him and checked his watch. Half-past twelve. He felt a sudden prickle of apprehension. What if Sylvia had seen the man, and gone away?

So what? He held all the cards now, he told himself.

But Sylvia didn't know that, a small voice inside his head responded. He remembered what she'd done to Jane's cat, his apprehension increasing.

This was no game Sylvia was playing.

Matthew waited for a further two hours.

No one came.

He had arranged to walk the mile or so back into Boslowan, meet Jane in the Smugglers' Rest. She'd be getting worried by now.

He was beginning to regret his earlier bravado. Maybe Sylvia had been watching from somewhere, had spotted that he'd come empty-handed. Thwarted, and not yet realising she'd been rumbled, there was no telling what she might do next. He glanced up to the deserted cliff. Soon, it would be dark. She wasn't going to come now.

Suddenly filled with anxiety, he pulled himself to his feet, stiff with cold, and began to scramble clumsily up the path. It was when he was nearly at the top that Elizabeth's mobile signalled that he had a text message.

He pulled it from his pocket, and pressed 'read'. The sender's number was his own.

It took Matthew a moment to work out what was going on.

Sylvia Guttenberg must have taken his mobile when she'd left the note at the house. She must have seen Elizabeth's, realised he'd use it when he couldn't find his own.

His heart hammering, Matthew pressed the button again and the message flashed up on the screen: 'WRONG FISH, MATTHEW. THINK ABOUT IT. SAME TIME TOMORROW. BE THERE.'

Wrong fish? What the hell was she talking about? Matthew gazed about him, his brain racing. 'Down by the water where the little fishes play . . .'

And then it hit him.

It wasn't Spike she'd been referring to.

It was Daisy.

Matthew stood stock-still, the phone still clutched in his hand. But how could Sylvia Guttenberg have known about Daisy?

'What do you hold most dear? For with that you can be sure you will have to part, before you can hope to find salvation.' Ben Fellows' words came flooding back to him, unbidden.

Filling him with nameless terror.

29

'Just tell me what's going on.' Jane glanced across, her hands clenched on the steering wheel. 'For God's sake, Matthew. Talk to me.'

Matthew had run all the way back to the pub. Gasping for breath, he'd told her only that they must go. Straight away.

Jane hadn't argued. She'd followed him to the car, driven back along the A30 and onto the M5 as he'd instructed. He'd merely shaken his head when she'd wanted to know where they were going and, infected by his urgency, she'd kept her foot down and her mouth closed. It was only as they approached Glastonbury, that she asked again.

'It was Daisy she was talking about. The little fish . . .' Just saying it made Matthew's throat close up so that he had to struggle to breathe. 'It wasn't Polperron Cove. It was the lake. At Swaddlington Hall.'

Jane pulled abruptly into the side of the road, and turned to Matthew. 'Are you saying that what happened to Daisy is a part of this?'

'I don't know.' He looked up, trying to force a smile through the tears that were suddenly pouring down his face. 'Ben thinks God's punishing us for what we did. Taking what's dearest from us. And the funny thing is . . .' He started to laugh; laugh and cry at the same time. 'The funny thing . . .' He swallowed, made a supreme effort to regain some measure of self-control. 'He thought that in my case, it was money.'

'He's a madman, Matthew. You said that yourself.'

'So why have I got to go back to where Daisy drowned?' he whispered.

'Listen to me, Matthew. If you really think this has got something to do with Daisy's death, you've got to bring the police in.'

Jane could have found no better way of pulling him together if she'd slapped his face. 'The police?' He stared at her in amazement. 'How can I? I've just embezzled half a million pounds!' He looked at the rucksack, sitting on the back seat of the car like a time bomb. 'I'd be ruined.'

'You're worried about that, when this woman might have murdered your *child*?'

'No.' He shook his head vehemently. 'It was an accident.'

'Like Pete? Like Toby? Like Spike? How much longer can you go on pretending that everything that's happened to you all is down to no more than random chance?'

'Look . . .' He raked his hand through his hair. 'Look, let's just try to be logical—'

'Logical?'

'She's trying to spook us again, that's all. She must have seen that I hadn't got the money with me. Maybe she was following us when we went to see Ben. She must have realised I'd seen through her.' He nodded his head. 'She could have found out about Daisy from anyone, of course she could. She's found out about everything else that's happened to us, hasn't she?'

'You really think that's all there is to it? You honestly believe that?' Jane stared at him with something approaching dislike. 'Or is it just that you want to believe it, rather than risk your precious reputation?'

'Do you suppose I could live with myself, even for one second, if I thought anything else?' Matthew smashed his fist down hard on the dashboard.

The violence of the action momentarily silenced them both.

He stared out of the windscreen. 'Look, why don't you just drop me off? It's only another couple of miles to the village. It won't take me long to—'

She wheeled back to face him. 'I'm not leaving you here on your own!'

'I'll be fine.' He reached into the back and grabbed the rucksack.

'But what are you going to do?'

'I'm going to give her the bloody money. She can have it. I just want her off my back.'

'At least let me be here with you.' Jane caught his sleeve as he opened the car door.

'No. I've got to do this on my own.'

'Please, Matthew! I don't have to come to the lake if you don't want me to. I can stay out of the way. But let me at least be here with you.'

He hesitated, turned back towards her.

'It's not as if I've got anywhere else to go.'

Again, they were both silent. Then slowly, Matthew shook his head. 'It could never work, Jane. You and me. I could never leave Elizabeth.'

'*She's* left *you.*'

'No. She's angry with me now. Hurt. But we'll get back together, when this is all over. We've got too much history together. Too much shared pain, if you like. You and I could only ever be lovers.' He took Jane's hand, held it briefly to his lips. 'You're worth more than that.' He shook his head as she began to speak. 'And so is Elizabeth. Go back to London, Jane. Put all of this behind you.'

'How can I?'

'You have to.' He made his tone deliberately crisp. 'Pick up the threads of your life, the same as I intend to pick up the threads of mine.'

'So that's all there is to it?'

He hadn't wanted it to end like this; he still wasn't completely sure he wanted it to end at all. He had to force himself to meet her eyes. 'That's all there is to it.'

'My God, you can be a heartless bastard, Matthew.'

He was shocked to register real anger in Jane's face. It was as if he were looking at a stranger. Maybe it was no more than he deserved.

'Sometimes it's the only way,' he said.

He got quickly out of the car and, shouldering the rucksack, strode off down the lane. He didn't turn back. After a moment or two, he heard the engine start up, heard the car reverse. Another moment, and the lane was silent.

It was dark, and the route unlit, but Matthew had no difficulty in finding his way to the village. He remembered every inch of the route: the bluebell wood where, as a family, they had picnicked in spring, the hill where Daisy had fallen off her toboggan the year it snowed, the stables where she had had her first ride on a pony. The infants' school she'd skipped into so confidently that first morning, her whole life ahead of her. And, as finally he reached the centre of Swaddlington itself, the little church where her funeral service had taken place. Each step he took held a memory. And each memory bound him more tightly to Elizabeth.

His heart contracting with the sharp pain of nostalgia, he came at last to the farmhouse. Smoke spiralled from the chimney. A Range Rover was parked in the drive. Somehow, ridiculously, Matthew had expected to find it empty, a sorrowful reminder of what had been. The presence of new occupants seemed an intrusion. He moved a little closer. There was a light in the living-room window. Through the undrawn curtains, Matthew could see a man sprawled in an armchair, reading a newspaper.

The room itself had barely changed: the same oak-beamed

ceiling that had taken the two of them almost a year to
restore, the same deep inglenook fireplace in front of which
they'd toasted crumpets on wintry Sundays like today. Daisy
had taken her first faltering steps across those same uneven
flagstones, he and Elizabeth holding their breath, arms out
ready to catch her in case she took a tumble. It was home,
as nowhere else before or since had been home. Maybe they
should have been in less of a hurry to run away from their
memories, Matthew thought as he ran his hand along the
weathered stone wall that kept him on the outside, looking
in. Maybe if they had stayed here, things would eventually
have been all right . . .

He had no time for pointless regrets, he told himself
impatiently. A house was just bricks and mortar, a thing.
And this house belonged to the man who might at any
moment look up from his paper and spot Matthew lurking
outside his gate, an intruder.

With a last glance, Matthew turned his back on the farmhouse, and carried on walking.

Although it was a matter of no more than a few hundred
yards to reach the grounds of Swaddlington Hall from the
back garden of the farmhouse, it was almost a mile around
the winding lane that skirted the estate's high brick boundary
wall. By the time Matthew reached the wrought-iron entrance
gates to the hotel, it was after six.

He was dismayed to find the gates not only closed, but
padlocked. He'd given little thought to how he would kill the
time until the following day, but it was clear that it wasn't
going to be by staying at Swaddlington Hall; a sign on the
gate informed him that the hotel was closed for refurbishment
until the first of March. He gave the wrought iron a final, futile
shake and set off wearily on the walk back to the village. He'd
have to put up at the pub.

But there might be people there who would remember him, who would want to talk . . .

He couldn't face the thought of company.

It was on impulse that Matthew tried the little side gate to the farmhouse as he retraced his steps. It was without any preformed idea of what he intended to do that he slipped into the darkness of the garden and moved stealthily round to the back of the house. In the light from an upstairs window, he could make out the heart-stoppingly familiar layout of shrubs and bushes, the willow overhanging the same bench where he and Daisy had sat that last afternoon, the same path leading down towards the blackness of the paddock beyond. It was as if he'd never been away.

The dark bulk of the summerhouse he and Spike had built together loomed at the far end of the lawn. Daisy had loved it; had laid out endless tea-parties there for her dolls. It had been the scene of a thousand imaginary games; her own private domain. Hardly knowing what he was doing, Matthew made his way across the grass towards it, his feet sodden in seconds. He felt for the latch. It gave readily to his touch, as if it had been expecting him. The door swung silently open, and he stepped inside. Cobwebs pressed against his face. In the far corner, he heard the faint scrabbling of a mouse. As his eyes became accustomed to the darkness, he could make out garden implements, a lawn-mower, a stack of folding garden chairs. The place was clearly used only for storage, now there was no Daisy to cherish it.

Matthew closed his eyes, summoned up the remembered image of her, crouched down on her haunches pouring orange squash from her plastic teapot as she held court over her assembled dolls and teddies. He felt that he might reach down his hand and feel her soft hair, so close, so real did she seem.

Carefully, lest anyone from the house should hear him, he

unfolded one of the garden chairs and, wrapping his coat around him, settled down for the night.

Dawn was just beginning to break when Matthew opened his eyes. He came to with a start, wincing as he tried to sit up. He couldn't believe that he'd managed to get any sleep at all; his limbs felt as though they'd never be straight again, and he was chilled to the bone. Yet despite the foul taste in his mouth and his desperate need to urinate, he felt curiously energised as he hauled himself to his feet.

He'd never have thought himself capable of revisiting the farmhouse; had never even been back to Somerset, except to drive through it on the motorway, and then only of necessity. As much as anything else, it had been the prospect of seeing the place again, of disturbing old ghosts, that had made him get into such a state of agitation the previous day, he realised. But he'd done it. Taken it head on. And found, to his surprise, that it was as much a place of happiness as sadness; the memories friends, not demons. If Sylvia Guttenberg had been hoping to unnerve him by the ploy of bringing him back here, she'd failed miserably.

Matthew rubbed a hand through his tousled hair and peered at his watch. Six fifteen. If the man inside the house worked anything like the same hours as he himself did, there was no time to lose; he needed to be on his way before someone spotted him and took him for the vagrant he must look. He wondered fleetingly what would be made of his absence at work. He was supposed to be making a presentation to the board at ten. In the present circumstances, it seemed utterly irrelevant.

Quickly, he folded the chair and replaced it. He picked up the rucksack, and glanced around to make sure that he had left everything undisturbed. As he did so, his eye was caught by something glinting between the rough timber boarding of the floor. He bent and prised it out, memory flooding over him as he looked at the small silver hair slide that lay in his palm. It was fashioned in the shape of a daisy, each petal decorated with a paste diamond. He'd picked it up at one of the retail outlets at Heathrow; not valuable, but Daisy had loved it. He'd turned the place upside down for her when she lost it, but he'd never found it. Until now.

Matthew placed it carefully in his pocket. Somehow, it seemed like a good omen. Cautiously, he pushed open the door of the summerhouse and glanced back across the lawn to the still-slumbering house. Then, the collar of his coat pulled up about his ears, he made his way quickly down to the bottom of the garden, across the paddock and towards the lake beyond.

30

It was amazing, Matthew thought, that the most mundane and basic of activities could bring so much pleasure, when everything else had been stripped away. Just emptying his bladder was an exquisite luxury; the absence of pain, as his cramped limbs began to loosen up, a joy. Never mind that he was unwashed, freezing, starving; that all the comforts of life that he took so much for granted were missing. As he strode across the frost-covered paddock, he heard a blackbird singing somewhere in the trees above him, and felt the blood warming in his veins.

As he reached the gate from the paddock, and stepped into the grounds of Swaddlington Hall, his spirits began to falter. The last time he had walked this path, it was to find Daisy. How would he be able to look into the lake and not see her there? But she wasn't there, any more than Spike was in the graveyard in Boslowan church. Daisy was everywhere he went. She always would be. Matthew clung on to the thought as he cut down the last stretch of overgrown footpath that led to the water.

The breeze from the day before had strengthened, scudding the clouds across the sky, rustling through the reeds, ruffling the surface of the lake. Bracing himself, Matthew went straight to the water's edge and walked purposefully out along the mooring slip from which Daisy had lost her balance and fallen. He forced himself to look down. All he saw was his own reflection, fragmented by the ripples.

He felt his body relax. He walked back to the lichen-encrusted bench that stood near the path and sat down. It was barely seven o'clock. He had ample time to walk back to the village, buy himself something to eat, a paper. But he was reluctant to lose the feeling of peace that had descended on him. To go back to the outside world, even the small world of the village, was to face reality and, for the moment at least, Matthew wanted none of it. A myriad of worries awaited him there.

What if he were unable to regain Elizabeth's trust? He knew she'd come back to him, eventually, but simply coming back was not enough.

What if Masterton found out what he had done? He could still end up in jail, lose everything as surely as if he'd thrown the first note in the bin and let Sylvia Guttenberg do her worst.

What if, God help him, the half a million was not enough, and she kept coming back for more?

So many worries. He'd face them all, deal with them, as he always had. Cope, because he was a coper. But not yet. For now, he'd rather just stay here, at the water's edge, and listen to the blackbird. He arranged the rucksack as a pillow, stretched himself out on the bench and shut his eyes. His hand closed around the hair slide in his pocket. Daisy was with him; she always would be. What had once seemed a curse now seemed a blessing.

He must have slept, because when he next looked at his watch, it was five to twelve. His earlier tranquillity had vanished. His guts tightened as he swung himself upright, clutching the rucksack to him. His heart began to pound. Something had woken him. This was reality, and he was going to have to face it. Any minute. He wheeled round, suddenly convinced of a presence behind him, but no one was there. Slowly letting out his breath, Matthew turned back towards the lake. A small figure was silhouetted against the pale sun, standing on the landing slip as he had stood, staring down into the water.

Matthew rubbed his eyes, wondering for a brief moment if he could still be dreaming.

Slowly, the figure turned towards him, her face breaking into a smile.

'Jane,' he said in bewilderment. 'What on earth are you doing here?' He ran his hand across his stubbled chin as she came towards him. 'I'm sorry, but I meant what I said last night.' His voice was firm. 'There's no future for us. I hoped I'd made that clear.'

Jane's smile was fixed, unwavering. It was as if he hadn't spoken.

'Look, now isn't the time.' Matthew glanced uneasily behind him. 'Sylvia's going to be here any minute, and I don't want to frighten her off again. Go back to the village. Wait for me at the pub. I'll meet you there in—'

'Oh, I think I've waited long enough,' she said softly. 'Don't you?'

'I . . .' Matthew took a step backwards. It was the sort of thing that happened in films; thwarted lovers, refusing to let go. Jane was lonely, not even her cat now to keep her company. With hindsight, he could see that she might be just the type to take rejection badly. He could almost see the black humour of the situation. Christ, as if he hadn't enough on his plate, without a stalker! Clearing his throat, he said coldly, 'I'm sorry, but this has to stop. I should never have allowed it to start.'

Jane didn't reply. She just stood there, smiling.

Matthew kept his tone deliberately formal. 'I apologise if I've hurt you. We were both at low points in our lives, but I hold myself entirely responsible for what—' He broke off. As the sun caught it, he registered for the first time the scarf that was draped around her shoulders. The scarf he'd bought for Elizabeth. 'What are you doing with that?' he asked, bewildered. 'How in God's name did you . . . ?'

'Don't you think I deserve a little present?' The words were spoken in a childish wheedle. 'To make up for all those birthdays and Christmases you missed?' Her expression altered, darkening like storm clouds scudding across the sun. 'What's one paltry scarf to a man who can lay his hands on half a million?'

Matthew was stunned by the naked contempt in her face. 'I . . . I don't know what you're talking about.'

'I can see that!' She looked him up and down, then sat on the bench and patted the space next to her. 'Come and join me.' The smile was back on her face. 'Sit down and I'll tell you all about it. Daddy.'

31

Matthew felt his knees buckle. It was only with supreme effort that he stayed on his feet. He gripped the arm of the bench to steady himself. 'Daddy?' he echoed.

Jane smiled, as if savouring the moment. It was some time before she spoke. Then she said, 'The black stain on Donna O'Mara's soul? Not a very nice way for a mother to describe her firstborn, was it?'

Matthew stared at her, aghast.

'I imagine it was only because she was Catholic that she didn't abort me.' Jane's tone was conversational. 'She dumped me with the nuns instead. Naturally, they'd got her down as a fallen woman. And me as the spawn of the devil who would follow in her fornicating ways unless I was chastised for my sins. What's the matter, Daddy? Cat got your tongue?'

His mind was reeling, grappling to make some sense of what she was saying. Could she be bluffing? Hitting blindly out at him because he'd ended the relationship?

'I can go on calling you Matthew, if it would make you more comfortable. I have to admit, I find "Daddy" a bit strange myself.' She looked up at him through her lashes. 'Especially since we became so . . . close.'

'You're making it up,' he blustered. 'I don't know what you're hoping to achieve, but—'

'You honestly didn't have a clue, did you? My God, Matthew! For such a *successful* man –' the word was laced with venom – 'you really can be amazingly obtuse.'

'You're lying.' Matthew was still trying to gather his scattered wits.

She laughed; a strident, frightening sound. 'These things can be proved, you know. Or have you never heard of DNA? I'm sure your GP would be willing to arrange a test. Although Elizabeth might not be too pleased. Particularly under the circumstances.'

Matthew realised that it was no bluff; the expression in Jane's eyes told him that. It was as if he had been punched in the stomach. He sank down onto the bench beside her, his head between his knees, winded. It had never crossed his mind, not once, that one of them could have made Donna O'Mara pregnant. How could he have been so stupid?

'Have you any idea what my childhood was like?' Suddenly, Jane's voice was filled with fury. 'While you were out there, making your way in the world, setting up home with that precious family of yours?'

Too dazed for speech, Matthew lifted his head, tried to focus on her.

'Let me tell you about *my* sixth birthday, shall I? One of the nuns gave me a box and told me to open it. This was in front of the whole school, just so you get the picture. I was still simple-minded enough at that age to think it might be a present.' Her face twisted. 'Can you guess what it was, Matthew?'

Dumbly, he shook his head.

'It was a collection of all the newspaper cuttings about my mother. Just so that I was in no doubt what a lying whore she'd been.'

'I'm so sorry,' he mumbled. 'So sorry.'

'It's a bit late for apologies, don't you think?' Jane's smile was infinitely more chilling than her rage.

'How did you . . . ?' Matthew cleared his throat, strove to pull himself together. 'How did you find me?'

'It's a long story.' Jane was still smiling. 'But then, we're not in a hurry, are we?' She drew the scarf around her shoulders. 'After all, it isn't as if you have got anywhere to go.'

'What is it you want?'

'Oh, don't let's rush things! I've waited such a long time for this moment. Don't you want to know what I've been up to all these years?'

Warily, Matthew nodded. She was dangerously unpredictable; that much was clear. Humouring her seemed the only way.

'Well, when I finally escaped the loving embrace of the convent, I set about tracking down the illustrious Donna. You know, thank her for at least choosing a bunch of undergraduates to fornicate with, so I'd inherited more brains than she had herself. A nursing auxiliary! I ask you! Cleaning up other people's shit and vomit. Still,' Jane stared at Matthew, her eyes cold, 'maybe that's all she thought she was worth.'

He reached out his hand. 'Jane, I—'

'Were you never taught it was bad manners to interrupt?' Her mouth hardened. 'I was. I had the strap-marks to prove it.'

Matthew tried to think of something, anything, to say, but the relentless monologue had started up again.

'Donna was married by then, of course. Good for her, I thought. One in the eye for the nuns.' That same bright, dangerous smile. 'Thing was, she'd never actually got round to telling her husband about that nasty black stain on her conscience. So the last thing she needed was to have it turning up in the flesh expecting a family reunion.'

'Here, take it.' Matthew thrust the rucksack at her. 'You deserve it, after what you've been through.' He fumbled with the strap of the rucksack, pulled out wads and wads of notes.

'You're *so* impatient, Matthew,' Jane pouted, feigning disappointment.

'Please, take it. All of it.' He pressed the money on her. 'What can I do to make amends? Anything . . .'

Anything except tell Elizabeth she had a stepdaughter. Anything but that. God help him, was that what this half-demented creature was expecting?

Jane opened one of the bundles, watched as the notes fluttered down onto the bench between them. 'You haven't even listened to the end of the story yet.' She lifted her gaze to meet Matthew's. 'And believe me, I've hardly started.' Her eyes were cold as steel; cold enough to silence him as she went on, 'I showed her the little box of goodies the nuns had given me. She cried, of course, said she was sorry. And then she told me what had really happened.'

'I swear to God if I'd had any inkling of what I'd done to your mother, to you—'

But Jane wasn't listening. She gave a small, incredulous laugh. 'She seemed to imagine that telling me it wasn't her fault somehow made everything all right. All those years, I'd been branded a harlot's bastard, and the silly bitch had never uttered a word! Even when Father Benedict Fellows, healer of souls and defiler of virgins, had turned up on her doorstep. She had her family to consider, she said.' Jane's face contorted suddenly with fury. 'What about me? *I* was her family.'

'Sweet Jesus.' Matthew felt a heavy, icy dread settle in the pit of his stomach. 'You killed her, didn't you?' he whispered. 'You ran down your own mother.'

'Mother is as mother does.' Jane sounded bored. The fury had vanished as swiftly as it had appeared.

Matthew shut his eyes, if only to shut out the blankness of her expression. 'And then you set about the rest of us,' he murmured, finally beginning to understand. 'It was you who accused Ben.'

'He'd been there, working alongside her all that time and she'd done *nothing*.' Jane gave a snort of laughter. 'You have to admit it, Matthew. The silly cow deserved everything she got.'

Matthew forced himself to look at her again. How could someone who looked so normal be so utterly, terrifyingly insane?

'Ben just rolled over and died,' she went on conversationally. 'It had been so simple to deal with him that I decided to see if I could find the rest of you. It helped that I'd chosen Blackport University, of course. Like a salmon swimming upstream, I returned to the place of my conception.' She grinned, pleased with the simile. 'I got myself a part-time job in the Graduates' Office, so it wasn't too difficult to find out where each of you worked. After that, it was simply a case of watching and waiting. Pete Preston was almost as easy as Ben Fellows. If messier. He jogged the same route every evening. Very dangerous road. I'm amazed no one had hit him before.' She frowned. 'Toby Gresham-Palmer took a bit more thinking about, but his lifestyle did rather lend itself to violence.'

'You cut off a piece of his hair.' Matthew's voice echoed to him, as if from a long way off.

'Well, naturally I wanted to be absolutely certain which one of you was my father,' she said mildly. 'Nail-clippings from Ben's waste basket.' Her nose wrinkled in distaste. 'I didn't need to bother with Pete, of course. There was enough of him stuck to my bumper.'

It was so immense that Matthew could do no more than mumble foolishly, 'You killed your own cat?'

'Petrushka?' Jane looked genuinely shocked. 'What's she ever done to me? No, I just invented that to spice things up a bit, get things moving.' She shook her head reprovingly. 'You have to look for the logical explanation all the time, don't you, Matthew? It can be very boring, you know.'

'But Spike?' Matthew was barely listening to her. 'It was you who killed Spike?'

'Oh, no. I didn't want him dead. Don't you understand? I didn't want any of you *dead*. Ben got that bit right, at least. The idea was to take what each of you most prized.' She grinned triumphantly. 'Much better than death, don't you think?'

Matthew glanced down at the rucksack. Even through the horror of what he was hearing, a tiny part of his brain was thanking God that Jane had so totally misread him.

'No, Spike killed himself.' She was looking pensive. 'He was the hardest to figure out of all of you. That's why I left him until last. I racked my brains! So little seemed important to him.' She smiled reminiscently. 'You know what he was like. I did wonder about brain damage, but then Spike wouldn't have known anything about it, and that would rather have defeated the point. Then it occurred to me that as an only child, he'd probably quite like a son and heir. And that Hubert would like a grandchild, which seemed a neat way of killing two birds with one stone, metaphorically speaking. So I joined the choir. Once I'd realised how lonely Spike was, it was almost tediously straightforward. He was desperate for a wife, you see. Desperate to be the same as you and Elizabeth. So I went along with it all, laughed at his silly jokes, endured his fumblings.' She shuddered. 'I waited until he announced our engagement to all and sundry, and then I told him the truth.' She lifted her shoulders in a small shrug of resignation. 'Which he was supposed to share with the rest of you, of course.'

'But he drowned himself instead,' Matthew said hoarsely.

Jane sighed. 'That was irritating. It meant I had to start all over again. Write all those wretched notes. I mean, there's not a great deal of point in revenge if no one recognises it as such, is there?'

Matthew ran his tongue over his dry lips. The words were in his throat, sticking there like shards of glass. He didn't want to say them, but he knew he must. 'You said Spike was the last,' he whispered.

She gazed at him, her head on one side. 'I fixed up some work experience at Daisy's school as part of my teacher training. She was quite happy to come with me, you know. I think she was grateful for the company.'

'No!' Matthew put up his hand as if to shield himself from a blow.

'I had to think up something really special for you, didn't I?' Jane frowned. 'Except it wasn't special enough. I realised that at Spike's funeral. You and Elizabeth together, a replacement child on the way . . . You'd made far too good a recovery.'

'The baby?' Matthew whispered fearfully, tears streaming down his face. 'The baby too?'

'I'd already decided by then to hit you where it would *really* hurt. In the wallet. Revenge is a dish best eaten cold – I'm sure you've heard the phrase. Well, I decided to eat mine with a silver spoon. After all, I was only claiming my birthright, when you come to think about it.' She smiled. 'Elizabeth's miscarriage was just a case of God helping those who help themselves, you might say. Although it was rather useful. As was coming across Sylvia Guttenberg, of course. Her meddling certainly speeded the whole process along. She's just discovered Donna had a bastard, by the way.' Jane reached into her bag and produced Matthew's mobile. 'She left a message for you on your voice mail. Sounded very pleased with herself.'

'I'll go to the police! I'll tell them—'

'And allow Elizabeth to find out the truth?' Jane sounded amused. 'No you won't.'

Matthew knew that she was right. 'Sylvia will work it out,' he murmured, his eyes still shielded from her. 'Sooner or later, she'll put the pieces together. And then you'll be finished.'

'I don't think so,' she said coolly. 'Sylvia has the attention span of a gnat. As soon as I stop pulling her strings, she'll lose interest. In any case, Jane Davenport has already ceased to exist, just as Jenny O'Mara ceased to exist seven years ago. It's not so difficult to reinvent yourself. Particularly with half a million pounds at your disposal.' She got to her feet, picked up the rucksack. 'Oh, before I go, there were a couple of messages from Elizabeth too.' She walked down to the water's edge and hurled the mobile into the middle of the lake. 'Nothing important.'

Matthew took his hand from his face at the sound of the splash. Mesmerised, he watched the ripples spread out across the surface of the water. Then he said slowly, as if in a trance, 'You murdered Daisy. You murdered my little girl.'

Jane opened her eyes very wide. 'But *I'm* your little girl, Matthew. A strand of Daisy's hair proved that five years ago.'

'You monster!' Matthew threw himself at her. The sheer bulk of him knocked her off her feet. Dragging himself astride her, he twisted the scarf around her throat. 'You bloody, insane . . .'

'You won't do it.' Jane stared up at him, unblinking. 'You won't kill your own daughter.'

For an instant, his grip slackened. But only for an instant. He didn't look at her. He concentrated on the myriad colours around her neck, focused on nothing but the shimmering amber and gold, blocked out all other sights and sounds, ignored the writhing, jack-knifing body between his thighs. His fury was all-absorbing; orgasmic. After what seemed an eternity, the struggling stopped, but still he gripped the scarf, twisting and twisting until at last he could be certain that his only remaining child was dead.

He rolled away from her, retching and gasping for breath. The rucksack had burst open. Notes flapped around his face, fluttered on the wind like a sudden snowstorm, some spiralling upwards on the wind, some flopping onto the edge of the lake like so many water lilies. He lay on his back, staring up into the sky, the fury spent, his mind mercifully empty.

He knew the respite couldn't last, of course.

As he regained his breath, he regained his sanity. His brain clicked remorselessly into gear. Pulling himself to his feet, he lumbered back across the fields, back through the gate to the garden of what had been his home, back to the shed, his hand closed all the time around the little hair slide in his pocket. He knew what he must do. Grabbing a heavy garden spade, he turned back towards the lake.

He chose a spot far from the water's edge in a tangled, neglected thicket. The grave took him over an hour to dig, one-handed. It had to be deep; deep enough that no fox would unearth her. Deep enough to seal in the poison. Deep and dark and cold. He made a pillow for her with the wads of notes. Then slowly, painfully, he dragged her over to her final resting place. He was close to exhaustion, but still he wasn't finished.

He tied the scarf around the face before he set about pulping the body with the mud-clogged spade.

Don't look.

Don't register the sickening sensation of splintering bone and splitting flesh.

His flesh. His blood.

Concentrate.

He forced himself to focus on the practicalities as, with the last vestiges of his strength, he heaved the bloodied remains into the grave. Jane Davenport had already ceased to exist – she'd set that up herself. No one was going mark her disappearance. And if her bones were ever discovered in this forlorn, unvisited place, he had made sure that they were shattered beyond any chance of identification.

He rested for a while before he filled in the grave, covered it with a shroud of leaves and branches until it was invisible. The sun was warm, now. He took off his jacket. By blanking his mind, he could almost imagine he was at work in his garden. He stood back at last, satisfied, to survey his handiwork.

It was over.

There was only one more thing he had to do.

The gentle, steady motion of Matthew's body through the icy water soothed him. He swam, awkwardly because of the plaster cast, for what seemed like hours, until his limbs were heavy, his hands and feet numb with cold, the blood all washed away. He turned for a while onto his back. The clear blue sky above him was vast, the water's edge a long way behind him, now. A few stray banknotes had become caught up in the branches of a tree, and fluttered there like a small flock of birds. It all seemed very peaceful. He'd left a text on Elizabeth's phone. Told her that he loved her, had only ever loved her. That he was sorry. She'd think him cowardly, a quitter, would ask herself for ever why he'd done it; why he hadn't fought harder to win her back. But this was the best he could do for her. How could he carry so terrible a burden of knowledge and never let it slip? Never tell Pete, or Ben, or Toby?

This was the only way.

Sylvia might speculate, but even her fertile imagination wouldn't come up with a scenario as terrible as the truth. Sooner or later, she'd lose interest and go back to fiction. Pete would wonder; maybe Toby and Hubert Vardon too. But they would be grateful to let their secrets die with him. Ben would simply imagine it was God's judgement. Maybe Ben was the only one of them who had got it right.

Matthew rolled over onto his front again and looked down into the calm depths of the water. Beneath him, he saw a pale, wavering oval that could be a stone, could be a child's small face. Undulating tendrils that could be seaweed, could be strands of soft blonde hair. He let the hair slide go, watched it spiral slowly downwards. Turning his head, he took a last look back at the neat pile of his clothes on the shoreline.

Then he sank willingly, hopefully, beneath the surface of the water to look for Daisy.

Georgie Hale
Without Consent

It's Danny Nolan's big chance – to show off his natural talent as an actor in front of two screen legends, to break himself out of a cycle of rejection, unhappiness and petty crime. But Danny has run away.

Detective Inspector Ray Whitelaw thinks Danny is just another young thug. But Danny's drama teacher escaped himself from a similar existence when he was a teenager. Kieran Henshall knows Danny would never abandon his dog, knows that someone had scared Danny badly. And soon, Whitelaw has traced a connection between Danny Nolan and two murder victims . . .

All the trails lead back to one family – the Denstones. The glamorous actress, the rich local businessman she married, are somehow involved in the story of the boy no one wants. And until Whitelaw untangles the lies and deceptions, a killer is walking free.

NEW ENGLISH LIBRARY
Hodder & Stoughton

George Hale
Tread Softly

As Blackport University starts a new academic year, two more girls fall victim to the killer they are calling the Beast of Blackport. Students, prostitutes . . . no attractive redhead is safe, and Detective Chief Inspector Dave Shenfield is at breaking point. He knows that Gavin O'Driscoll, once a student at Blackport, has returned to the town where he took his first victim seven years ago before disappearing into thin air. But can he prove it?

Meanwhile, a new student has arrived at the University from the Isles of Scilly, with a background more sheltered than most. Flora Castledine is pretty. Red-haired . . .

While Flora falls in love and Shenfield grapples with unsympathetic colleagues and uncooperative university authorities including his own long-estranged son, the murderer hits out once more with devastating consequences for each of them.

NEW ENGLISH LIBRARY
Hodder & Stoughton